ABOUT THE AUTHOR

A qualified parachutist, Harvey Black served with British Army Intelligence for over ten years. His experience ranges from covert surveillance in Northern Ireland to operating in Communist East Berlin during the cold war, where he feared for his life after being dragged from his car by KGB soldiers.

Since then he has lived a more sedate life in the private sector as a Director for an International Company, but now enjoys the pleasures of writing. Harvey is married with four children.

ALSO BY HARVEY BLACK:

Devils with Wings:
The Green Devils assault on Fort Eben Emael

DEVILS
WITH
WINGS
– SILK DROP –

HARVEY BLACK

Matador
9 Priory Business Park
Kibworth Beauchamp
Leicestershire LE8 0RX, UK
Tel: (+44) 116 279 2299
Fax: (+44) 116 279 2277
Email: books@troubador.co.uk
Web: www.troubador.co.uk/matador

ISBN 978 1780881 058

This Novel is a work of fiction. Names and Characters are the product of the
author's imagination and any resemblance to actual persons, living or dead, is
entirely coincidental.

Cover Picture: BArch, Bild 101I-562-1172-23A / Wahner

British Library Cataloguing in Publication Data.
A catalogue record for this book is available from the British Library.

Typeset in 11pt Bembo by Troubador Publishing Ltd, Leicester, UK
Printed and bound in the UK by TJ International, Padstow, Cornwall

Matador is an imprint of Troubador Publishing Ltd

To my Mum, Sylvia, and Harry

CHAPTER ONE

"Come on Paul, you can finish your letter later. You know we daren't keep the Raven waiting," called Helmut, one of Paul's fellow Company Commanders.

"Yeah, yeah," responded Paul, frustrated at trying to correctly word his latest letter to Christa. They had met in a Maastricht hospital where Paul had ended up as a result of the injuries he received during the assault on the Belgium fortress, Fort Eben Emael. Christa, had been one of the nurses who had helped treat him and care for him during his time there. He was trying to get the tone of his letter just right, not wanting it to sound too pressing, but equally not wanting to sound too uninterested. In fact, he was desperate to see her again.

He touched the scar above his left eye, the consequence of a piece of shrapnel gouging a thin furrow from just above his left ear to his eyebrow, missing his eye by a hair's breadth. They had stitched it well and although not invisible, the scar wasn't unsightly. The injury to his back, although still slightly sensitive, had also fully healed.

"Oberleutnant Brand, get your arse in gear, we need to get going."

Helmut's shout pulled Paul out of his reverie and he jumped up out of his seat.

"Come on then, let's get going," said Paul, grabbing Helmut's arm and dragging him to the exit door of the officer's canteen.

"Hang on," replied Helmut, "there are some cakes left over there, do you think they will be missed?"

Before Paul could answer, Helmut had grabbed two of the cakes and stuffed them into his tunic pocket.

"Food will be the death of you," scolded Paul. "Let's go, now."

They left the canteen, walking through the small hallway and stepping out of the door onto the road than ran in front of the brick built barracks. Opposite them sat a further building similar in design and build.

Turning left they headed for the parade ground, where a platoon of Fallschirmjager were being put through their paces, passing two further red bricked buildings either side of them. Keeping the parade ground on their left, they headed for the battalion headquarters opposite, a similar, three storey brick building, where the battalion briefing was to occur. As they walked, they heard the marching platoon being halted and dismissed; the young Leutnant in command was also destined to attend the briefing.

As they stepped through the door of the briefing room, they were met by a wave of heat, the room stuffy and baking in the hot July, summer weather. Its clinical, white walls were unadorned, apart from a portrait of The Fuhrer, which dominated the far left wall. To the right, three tall sashed windows overlooked the parade ground they had just passed.

The small room, that had been set aside for battalion briefings, although ten metres at its widest point, was cosy to say the least, but sufficient to accommodate the Officers and senior NCOs of the Fourth Battalion, the first Fallschirmjager Regiment. The windows had been kept closed, to deter inquisitive ears, which was indicative of the importance of the meeting.

The tall windows furnished shafts of light, and dust particles glinted as they floated in the fetid air, having been disturbed by Paul and Helmut's entrance, but slowly settling back down on the surfaces of the room. Paul surveyed the briefing area. How times had changed, he thought. A matter of months ago he would have attended a Company level briefing as a mere Platoon Commander, now he was a Company Commander in his own right.

To the left, below the portrait, was the ubiquitous six foot, wooden table, behind it, draped on the wall, a map of Great Britain, the focus of todays briefing. The initial war with England, the fight against the British Expeditionary Force in France was over. But the English were still courageously fighting a battle against the Luftwaffe. The Luftwaffe were currently bombing England, a pre requisite to a full German invasion of the solitary Island, that was now standing alone against the might of the Third Reich. Most thought the invasion would be a simple matter that could start as soon as the Luftwaffe had finished off the Royal Air Force, the RAF. German troops could then land and England would succumb quietly. Paul was not so sure, he thought they would be a tough nut to crack, and in their own country they would fight even more aggressively to maintain their independence. There were also rumours that the Luftwaffe pilots were not getting it all their own way and were sustaining high casualties.

In front of the table were a row of chairs, usually reserved for the Company Commanders and the Adjutant, Oberleutnant Kurt Bach. Two chairs were already occupied by two of their fellow officers, Oberleutnant Bauer, Two Company and Oberleutnant Hoch, Three Company. Behind the first row of hard, wooden seats, were two further tiers, currently occupied by the Platoon Commanders, sat there ahead of schedule, not wanting the be late for the Battalion Commander's briefing. Not wanting to incur the wrath of their Company Commanders, and definitely not of the Battalion Commander, the Raven.

On the left, sat Leutnant's Nadel, Krause and Roth, who started to stand in acknowledgment of their Company Commander's entrance, but a quick nod from Paul allowed them to sit back down. Further to their left, the rest of the Battalion's Platoon officers were also settling back down in their seats. On the far right of the room, ensconced on the sill of one of the two tall windows, Paul could see Feldwebel Max Grun, his Company Sergeant.

A nod in his direction was all that Paul needed for a connection to be made between them. Max's nod said it all. The Company was ready for whatever was required of them. The Platoon Commanders would have thoroughly checked their respective unit's readiness, on the subtle suggestion from Max. It was not only the imposing size of the stocky, ex-Hamburg Docker, that would have leant weight to his suggestions, but also his self assured presence, his knowledge and experience, honed by being involved in actions in Czechoslovakia, Poland and Belgium. Not to mention the Iron Cross Second Class ribbon and the Iron Cross First Class medal pinned to his tunic pocket. Sat either side of Max were the other company sergeants, and in front of them the platoon sergeants, it was a full house. To the right, the rest of the headquarters staff, from Clerks and Signals to Engineers and Medics.

Paul and Helmut made their way forward, taking their places on the reserved seats, acknowledging their fellow officers.

The Adjutant, who until then had been stood behind the table, walked round the front to join them, perching himself on the edge of the surface, in front of the four officers.

"The Hauptman will be along shortly, he's had a last minute communiqué from Regimental HQ," Bach informed them.

"Is this a follow up to the Op Sea lion briefing sir?" asked Paul.

Although they were of the same rank, Bach was the Adjutant, effectively the Battalion second in command. The day Hauptman Volkman was bumped up to Major, the slim, mousey haired officer, would follow suit and be appointed Hauptman.

"Yes, he wants to ensure we're ready."

"He's been riding us for weeks sir," interjected Paul.

"You know the Raven gentlemen, he'll not brook any mistakes." They all grinned.

"Will we get an update on the wider situation?"

"Yes Paul, I'm sure he will."

"Is my leave still on the cards?"

"As far as I know, he's not indicated otherwise."

"Where are you off to?" enquired Helmut.

"I was thinking of spending some time at home."

"Ah, going to see that nurse I bet," grinned Helmut on seeing Paul blush.

The others joined in laughing at Paul's embarrassment.

Max looked up from his conversation with Steffen Fink, the second company Feldwebel, Feld, and looked across towards the source of the laughter. He could see his young company commander blushing, and could hazard a guess he was being ribbed about Nurse Keller. He had invited Max back to Brandenburg, to stay with him and his parents on his next leave, but he had tactfully declined. He knew that Paul would be obliged to entertain him, and he didn't want anything to distract his commander from a reunion with Nurse Keller.

Max's thoughts were interrupted by the crashing of the briefing room door opening and the entrance of Hauptman Volkman, the Battalion Commander, preceded by Oberfeld Schmidt, the battalion senior sergeant.

"Shun," called Oberfeld Schmidt.

The entire room rose up and brought themselves to attention, watching their commander closely as he made his way to the end of the room where the table and map were situated. They were all trying to judge his mood. The tall, immaculately dressed officer, his dark hair and hooded, deep set eyes, his prominent, almost Roman like nose that had quickly given him the nickname, The Raven, stopped in front of the table, turned and surveyed his officers that were stood in front of him. He nodded to his Adjutant and acknowledged his four most senior officers, Oberleutnant's Brand, Bauer, Hoch and Janke, his Company Commanders. These were the officers that would lead his men into battle.

"Gentlemen." His was voice, quite soft, but penetrating, almost school master like. "Please be seated."

The assembled men shuffled back into their seats, or the positions they had found to perch on earlier and looked at their commander expectantly, knowing this was an important meeting. Paul and Helmut looked at each other sharing the close bond that had been formed during their Fallschirmjager training in Stendal and later in battle when their unit fought in Poland and later in Belgium.

The Raven perched on the edge of the table. He looked at each one of his Company Commanders, the intensity of his stare, making them want to look down, but resisting it, knowing he was testing their resolve. They held his gaze and he looked away from them satisfied.

"Feldwebel Grun," he called, "have our new recruits been allocated to their respective units?"

Max jumped down from the windowsill and brought his heels together in an ear splitting crack, arms rigid by his side.

"Jawohl, Herr Hauptman."

Max, his powerfully built frame almost bursting out of his Fallschirmjager tunic, had been tasked, in the absence of the battalion Feld, with settling in the twenty new recruits who had arrived straight from training.

"Excellent, you haven't corrupted their minds yet I hope, Feldwebel Grun?" The entire room laughed, one of the few times the Raven cracked a joke with his troops.

"Their first task was to write home to their Mothers, sir," responded Max, still stood ramrod straight.

Volkman smiled, even he struggled to get the better of this tough, fair haired sergeant. In the Raven's mind, he had already identified Max as a potential battalion Oberfeld. Max was not only respected by his men, but also by the officers and his fellow NCOs.

"Thank you Feldwebel, I'm sure their mothers would thank you, stand at ease."

Max relaxed and resumed his seat on the window sill, noticing Paul's raised eyebrows, a slight reprimand, as if saying, 'you'll say too much one day Feldwebel Grun'. The frown didn't last for long, and a smile soon slipped from his mouth.

The Raven got up from the table and made his way behind it, the map of Britain behind him and to his left. He took off his cap and placed it on the table, shortly followed by the swagger stick, a fall back to his Prussian, aristocratic roots. In less than a minute it was back in his hand, tapping the side of his leg.

"Oberleutnant Bach, the map if you please."

The Adjutant unrolled a map that had been held in his hand and proceeded to pin it up on the board alongside its smaller scaled partner. While he was doing this the Hauptman continued. He turned to the map behind him and tapped the southern part of the country.

"Operation Sea lion, gentlemen. We've had our warning order for this operation, the invasion of England. Well, it has now been confirmed, the invasion is to go ahead and we will play a full role in it."

Bach had finished pinning the second map to the board. It was a map of England, but a much larger scale than its cousin, showing just the Southeastern corner of the country.

"Continue with the briefing if you please Oberleutnant."

Bach faced the first battalion officers and NCOs and picked up from where Volkman had left off.

"The focus for the impending invasion is to be this stretch of the country along the southeast coast," he said turning to the map and pointing to a sixty kilometre stretch of the English coast.

"A force of one hundred and sixty thousand men will conduct the initial assault, and as inferred by the battalion commander, the Fallschirmjager Division has a key role to play."

Volkman interrupted. "Now we have a full Divisional

establishment, being assigned a Machine Gun, Flak and Sapper battalion, we'll be in a much better position to create even more mayhem behind enemy lines."

"The Luftlandesturmregiment will land here," continued Bach, pointing to Dover, "where they will secure and hold the Military Canal; and the heights of Paddlesworth." There was a chuckle around the room as the Adjutant struggled to get his tongue around the English words. "They are to hold those positions until the 17th Infantry Division hit the beeches at Folkestone and relieve them."

Volkman raised his hand to Bach and continued the brief.

"Our Regiment will parachute drop an hour later, here," he said pointing to an area called Postling. "It will be up to us to move towards the Luftlandesturmregiment, reinforcing them until we are all relieved. I'm afraid Brand, Janke, you won't have gliders as taxi's this time round, you'll have to put your trust back in old Tante June."

Everyone laughed. Both Paul and Helmut had been involved in the invasion of Belgium. Helmut helping to secure one of the bridges across the Albert Canal, Paul landing on top of the supposedly impregnable Fortress Eben Emael, by glider. Less than eighty men had taken on the Fort's defenders of over five hundred, defeating them and securing the fort.

"We understand sir," they both replied in unison, smiling.

"The Raven is in good humour today," whispered Helmut.

"Quiet," hissed Paul, "listen."

"Our battalion will be dropped in two waves," added Volkman.

The three Fallschirmjager Regiments, FFR1, FFR2 and FFR3, were made up of three battalions, but Volkman's battalion was an independent unit, supported and sponsored by the First Regiment, FFR1.

"Do we know which companies will be dropped first sir?" piped up Paul.

"We're still working through the details Oberleutnant Brand, but I will take that as you volunteering your company to be the first down?" He didn't give Paul an opportunity to answer. "I want the battalion, your companies, to be ready to do what is asked of them. That's why we're going to train for it gentlemen, and train hard. I want you to give your units a good shake up, get them ready, and work them hard. Start with platoon exercises, working up to company size actions, and then we'll test the entire battalion, moving towards a full battalion size jump. So, work your men hard. Believe me, I will work you hard." He remained silent, scanning the room, allowing the message time to sink in. They all knew that he wouldn't accept any mistakes; failure just wasn't in his vocabulary.

The Adjutant broke the silence. "There will be a full training schedule posted by tomorrow morning, make sure you read it and digest it. Make your units fully aware of what is planned and what is expected of them. Any questions?"

"Do we know how many aircraft will be allocated to us for the drop sir?" asked Helmut

"We are expecting at least thirty Junkers, so that gives us a drop size of a third of a battalion, so three drops will have us all down."

"How long will the battalion exercise be for sir?" questioned Paul

"It will be a full forty eight hours," intervened Volkman. "So we'll have an opportunity to insert, consolidate, conduct an attack and receive a resupply."

"Will we be working with any other units?" asked Hoch.

"The Regimental artillery battalion has assigned a battery to us, to suppress the enemy just before we make our attack. It will also provide us with an opportunity to test our coms and coordination with other assets, particularly artillery," responded the Adjutant.

"Can we have an update on the Luftwaffe's battle over England sir?" requested Paul.

Volkman took the question, indicating to Bach to stand aside. "Their current targets are shipping moving through the English Channel, along with attacking some of the RAF's airfields."

"How are they standing up to the RAF fighters sir?" asked Bauer, who up until now had been silent.

"They are finding it tougher than expected," mused the Raven, almost to himself. He walked around to the front of the table and started to pace up and down, slapping his stick against the side of his thigh.

"If it was just a numbers game," he continued, "we shouldn't have a problem. But on a one to one?" He paced back the other way, obviously thinking carefully about what he was going to say next.

"The Spitfire is proving to be an exceptional fighter aircraft, easily a match for our fighters, but it is the bombers that are taking the brunt of it. The Stuka's, in particular, are proving to be vulnerable and are being withdrawn from any further action over England."

The room was silent, and although their battalion commander hadn't said anything to worry them, the fact that the Luftwaffe weren't walking all over the RAF was a little disconcerting.

"We'll succeed in the end, Reichsmarschall Goring has assured the Fuhrer of success. So, let the air force worry about their task, let us worry about being able to fulfil our role once they have completed theirs. Dismissed."

The room stood to attention and Hauptman Volkman and the Adjutant left the room, slowly followed by the remaining officers, NCOs and support staff.

Paul called out to his platoon commanders and to Max, to remain behind.

"Feldwebel, I want the company assembled within the hour, I want to update the men and prepare them for the training ahead."

"Jawohl Herr Oberleutnant."

Max snapped a salute, turned left and marched out of the room. Paul turned to his three Leutnant's.

"Once the company briefing is over, I want to go over platoon training plans with the three of you. Once we have the battalion training schedule we'll look at a company training plan, understood?"

"Jawohl Herr Oberleutnant," they all responded in unison.

"Right, join your companies. Dismissed."

All three came to attention, saluted and left the briefing room, following the same route of the company sergeant, Max, to join their platoons and prepare for the company assembly that Max was pulling together. Helmut, who was still in the room, having also briefed his three platoon officers, sauntered over to Paul.

The stocky Leutnant was three inches shorter than Paul's six foot two, but what he didn't have in height, he made up for in strength and presence. Everyone knew when Helmut was around, whether it was his constant demands as to the location of food, or his general boisterous nature. He slapped Paul on his back, rocking him on his feet, his usual greeting for his fellow officer.

"Well, busy times ahead I guess."

"It looks like it. Are you briefing your men now?"

"Yes, I thought I would do it straight away, knowing you would be on the ball, and not wanting them to find out second hand," he said smiling, playfully punching Paul on the shoulder.

"Anyway, if I do it later it'll get in the way of lunch," he said laughing.

"We couldn't possibly do anything that would get in the way of that now could we," scoffed Paul

"Have you heard from Erich?" asked Helmut, suddenly serious.

"Yes. He's fine, but still pissed off at getting a Regimental appointment. He wanted to lead his own company, like us."

After being involved in Belgium, second in command of a unit securing one of the bridges crossing the Albert Canal, at the start of the Blitzkrieg attack on France and the Low Countries, Erich was subsequently posted to Regimental HQ, as aide to the Regimental Commander. A posting like that could go one of two ways. Advance an officer's career as a result of exposure at a senior level or through learning the intricacies of running a Regiment. Or, it could be detrimental. Seen as lacking the experience of command and missing out on leading men from the front.

"It does mean he'll get experience at a Regimental level," Helmut said.

"Admin is not his strong point though," responded Paul frowning, "and he won't be commanding a unit."

"I tell you what, let's go and see him."

"On what pretext?"

"Check over the records of the new recruits?"

"You're on, tomorrow then?"

"Right, tomorrow it is," agreed Helmut, "now let's sort our men out so we can get some lunch," he added, rubbing his stomach.

CHAPTER TWO

The men had been loaded onto the trucks that were to take them to Hildesheim, where they would join the rest of the battalion ahead of a full unit parachute drop as practice for Operation Seelöwe, Sea lion, the invasion of England. Although there was an airport at their Braunschweig camp, the aircraft they needed were at the Hildesheim airfield.

Paul had gathered his three platoon officers and Max together around the cab of the front vehicle. It would be a simple journey, via Salzgitter, taking them no more than two hours to get to the Luftwaffe base. It would bring back memories to some of the Fallschirmjager in Paul's unit, many of them had spent six months hard physical training at the camp in preparation for the glider assault on Eben Emael.

Max was leant against the mud guard of the three ton, Opel Blitz, one of the workhorses of the Luftwaffe, watching Paul brief his officers.

Leutnant Krause was the youngest, at nineteen, and the least experienced of the companies officers and the one with the least confidence. His head of cropped, brown hair, shaved on the back and the sides above the ears, the preferred military style, one Max didn't adhere to, was nodding vigorously at Paul's instructions, trying to absorb every word his company commander was imparting. Max had already sussed the new officer out and was concerned. He thought back to when Leutnant Brand first assumed command of a platoon, Max being the platoon sergeant. Although hesitant at times and occasionally questioning his own abilities as a leader, he took command of the platoon with confidence and quickly got the measure of his sergeant and control of the platoon.

Max smiled at the thought. On their very first meeting, he had tried to put the young officer in his place and ensure that the platoon was run by him, Paul following his lead. But Paul wasn't having it. A quick reference to a recent incident, where Max had been arrested for fighting whilst on leave, quickly turned it round. Since then a bond had slowly been formed between them, underpinned by the fighting in Poland and the attack on Fort Eben Emael.

On joining the company for the first time, some of the older hands had tried to humorously undermine their new, young company commander. When Max had asked if Paul wanted him to say something to the hard-core group of three that were making the waves, he was reprimanded and told absolutely not. After one week of relentless training, forced marches, physical exercise and weapons training, the three admitted defeat and their respect for their new company commander was assured. The other two Leutnant's, Nadel and Roth, needed some coaching, but other than that, they were fine. They all had good platoon sergeants, Unterfeldwebel's Eichel, Fischer and Kienitz, and Max would ensure that he tutored them well.

Out of the corner of his eye Paul caught sight of Max's smile. Paul's immediate thought was, 'what has that rogue been up to now'. He depended heavily on his company sergeant, on Max, who in Poland, had saved his life and looked after him when he had been injured in Belgium.

"Once we get to Hildesheim," he continued his briefing, "I want a full kit inspection, everything, understood?" Leutnant's Nadel and Roth both nodded and responded.

"Jawohl, Herr Oberleutnant."

But Leutnant Krause unintentionally groaned. Suddenly realising what he had just done, he snapped to attention, ensuring his company commander that he understood. Paul looked at him for a few moments, making the officer uncomfortable and fidgety.

Paul was worried about Krause and had asked Max to keep a subtle eye on him, although he suspected that Max was already doing that. Leutnant Nadel, tall, with a pinched, pale face, on the other hand was a strong solid leader. Thought through his actions, explained them to his men, elucidating what he expected of them, rather than forcing his orders through. Leutnant Roth, was completely the opposite. The short, cherubic faced officer, his blonde wiry hair, was impulsive and quick to make decisions. Not a bad thing, but he did need to be reigned in at times, preventing him from making rash decisions.

"Make sure Unterfeldwebel Eichel does the checks with you Leutnant Krause, I don't want any mistakes. Hauptman Volkman could call for a full battalion Inspection at any time," Paul added. "Right, let's go!" Paul indicated to Max that he was ready for the company to move out, rotating his right arm in the air.

"See you in Hildesheim sir," said Max as he walked by. "Fun and games await us."

Paul jumped up into the cab and Max continued to walk down the line of eight trucks, banging on the side of the cab doors, giving them a two minute warning. Paul looked in the truck's wing mirror and seeing Max climb aboard the last vehicle instructed the driver to pull off. The driver crashed the gears in his hurry to get moving, taking a sideways glance at his passenger, waiting for a bollocking. But the Oberleutnant either hadn't noticed, or had chosen not to.

Paul's mind was elsewhere, staring out of the window, contemplating the approaching exercise, ticking off the list of things he needed to have done in preparation, necessary for its success. He felt satisfied that he and his company were ready, and any way, Max would have ensured that nothing would have been missed.

The convoy drove through the camp gates and he returned the guard's salute. They were off and would be in Hildesheim camp before they knew it. This time the weather would be much improved. When he was last there it was extremely cold. Situated in the foothills of the Harz Mountains, the winter weather had been harsh.

They turned right out of the camp and right again onto the autobahn taking them west. Within minutes they were heading south on another autobahn, only possible as a result of The Fuhrer's road building programme. The driver interrupted his thoughts. "There's a flask of coffee over there sir, if you'd like a drink," he said pointing to a flask in a bin to the right of the gear stick. "I'm afraid there's milk and sugar already in it."

"I don't mind if I do," responded Paul, glad of the distraction from his racing thoughts. "Milk and sugar is fine." He poured himself and the driver a hot drink, placing the driver's in a holder, obviously home made, on the dashboard.

The driver was older than most Luftwaffe soldiers, probably in his early forties. He thanked Paul and they continued the journey in silence.

They skirted round the west of the city, Paul looking out of the window as he sipped his hot coffee, watching the built up area slowly diminish as they entered deeper into the rural part of their journey.

Travelling north of Wolfenbuttel and south of Salzgitter, the autobahn was bracketed by farms and cultivated fields, the last ten kilometres taking them through the rich green forest of Schellerton. The journey lasted exactly one hour and forty minutes and once they had passed the camp guardroom and were inside the camp, they were allocated accommodation, the top floor of one of the large, three-storey barrack blocks. The camp was relatively large, with a canteen, small airfield and even a cinema. Primarily the home of the German Air Force and the Long Range Recce school, it was now the home of the Fallschirmjager. Once settled, they were given some lunch, much to the pleasure of Helmut. Afterwards they were given a final brief on the next day's events by the battalion commander, and then left to their own devices. Some chose to take advantage of the film being shown in the Cinema, others flaked out on their bunks or joined a card school.

They were sat in the canteen, Paul, Helmut, Manfred and Meinhard, just chatting and relaxing before the next day's activities. Max and his fellow sergeants were sat round another table putting the world to rights. The ground floor of the two-storey building served as the eating area while the adjoining single level building, the clash of pans and shouted orders emanated from its interior, was the cookhouse.

"It's going to be a bloody long forty eight hours," grumbled Helmut

"Have you got a parachute for your donkey?" questioned Paul.

"What bloody donkey, what are you on about?" answered a bewildered Helmut.

"To carry your food supplies of course," replied Paul keeping a serious look on his face.

The other two burst into laughter. Helmut's reputation, his constant desire for food was already legendary throughout the battalion. Even the Raven had been known to make a comment.

"Bugger off all of you."

They continued to prattle about nothing for another hour before calling it a night. A rapport had formed between the four officers and they enjoyed each others company. Although Paul liked them all and was particularly close to Helmut, he missed his friend Erich. Helmut and Paul had gone to see Erich at the Regimental HQ the previous day to speak to him and catch up on events, but he had been away from the unit on some errand for the Regimental commander. He would see him again soon he hoped.

They pushed back their chairs, said their goodnights, checked with their sergeants that last minute preparations were complete and retired to their bunks. It was ten at night, on the twenty seventh July, 1940 they would be up at 3:30 the next day, parachuting onto the target at 5, twilight.

★★★

Paul's company were making final preparations in the large aircraft hangar, put aside specifically for the forthcoming exercise, which was close to the apron, and a stones throw from the runway. It was four fifteen am.

After a quick meal, the paratroopers had assembled in the cavernous hangar, checking their equipment one last time before embarking on their transport waiting on the runway. The company was grouped by platoon, the Leutnant's checking the readiness of their men, assisted by their platoon sergeants. The other three companies were also in the throes of preparations and the hangar was filled with an echoing drone of over four hundred men getting ready, the clinking of equipment and the low chatter of men preparing for battle, albeit a practice.

Paul walked over to second platoon to inspect their progress. Unterfeldwebel Fischer sprang to attention and saluted his company commander.

"All present and correct sir, we'll be ready in ten," he informed him. They were joined by Leutnant Nadel, who also saluted his senior officer.

"Unterfeldwebel Fischer informs me all is well Dietrich?"

"Yes sir, we're at full strength and raring to go, just giving everything a final once over."

"Good, carry on, and no more saluting, we're on a combat footing remember."

He approached the neighbouring platoon where he was joined by Max on route.

"Looking good so far Max."

"Yes sir, they're a good bunch."

"How are Fischer and Kienitz settling in to their new roles?"

"Doing well, their platoon commanders seem to welcome their experience and enthusiasm, Eichel too. Although I suspect Eichel is taking on more than he should."

Although all of the officers in the company were naturally senior to Max, as the company sergeant he reported directly to Paul. This gave him the right to raise potential issues regarding the company's officers and men. Both Fischer and Kienitz had been Unteroffizier's in Paul's unit when he was a platoon commander during their tours in Poland and Belgium. Like Paul, Kienitz had been wounded during the attack on Eben Emael, a minor wound to his right leg. He was now fully recovered.

"We need to keep a close eye on first platoon during the exercise then."

"Will do sir, but I have every faith in Eichel."

"Let's go and see how our Leutnant Krause is getting on then."

They approached the platoon they'd been discussing to see Leutnant Krause adjusting his own equipment, while Eichel was inspecting the platoon.

"All ready Heinrich?"

"Yes sir," he responded, fumbling a salute.

"No saluting Heinrich, remember? We're assuming combat conditions."

"Sorry sir."

"Have you reviewed your platoon and are they all set?"

"Unterfeldwebel Eichel is doing that now sir."

"But are they ready to your satisfaction Leutnant Krause?" demanded Paul, his usual patience being severely tested.

"I… I think so sir."

"Well I suggest Leutnant Krause, you check them now, and report to me when you are satisfied they are ready for battle, do I make myself clear?" Krause quickly came to attention.

"Jawohl Herr Oberleutnant."

"See that you do."

With that Paul turned on his heel and left, Max following behind.

'Let's check the last platoon Max, before I get really angry. Well, what are your thoughts?"

"Eichel has it under control sir. I think he's actually enjoying running the platoon."

"But that's not the point Max. It's not his job."

"I understand sir, I'll keep my eyes peeled."

"Good. Right, let's go and see how Roth is doing."

They approached the final platoon, in full swing, getting ready. They had a spot alongside one of the high walls of the hanger, their kit propped up against it.

"It looks like he's trying to be first to finish as usual," whispered Max.

"Well Viktor, your men seem to be ready?"

"Yes sir," replied Leutnant Roth, standing proud

Unterfeldwebel Kienitz has them well organised, isn't that so Unterfeld?"

"Ja, Herr Leutnant," the twenty three year old NCO replied. "We're ready, just showing the rest how it's done," he said grinning.

"How's that leg of yours?" asked Paul

"Don't even know it's there sir."

"Only a bloody scratch anyway," interrupted Max. "Just a way to get sympathy from the girls, sir."

"So your platoon is ready Viktor?"

"Yes sir."

"So you wouldn't mind if we do a check ourselves then?" tested Paul.

"Well, we plan on doing one last check, if you'll excuse us sir."

"You had best get on with it then, carry on."

Paul and Max walked away, grinning at each other. They both suspected that in his haste to be the first platoon ready, he might well

17

have missed something. Even the staunch Kienitz would have difficulty in restraining the impetuous officer.

Five minutes later, all three platoons indicated their readiness to move, just as the battalion commander joined them. He was accompanied by the three other company commanders, whose men were also in the hangar getting ready for their turn to load the aircraft.

"Oberleutnant Brand, you're men ready?"

"Yes, Herr Hauptman."

"Excellent, I want your men to move out in five minutes. The aircraft are warming up their engines now."

It was short and sweet, the Raven was quickly on the move again, no doubt checking all aspects of the exercise, wanting nothing to go wrong. He was probably liaising regularly with the regimental commander, who would undoubtedly be watching the exercise closely.

Paul was a little surprised when he felt the thump on his back from the exuberant Helmut, and his good luck wishes.

"Well Paul, first on the ground then. Make sure you get everything set up for us, right?"

"Sure. We'll suss out a bar and a cafe for you, ok?"

From his tunic he produced a cold bratwurst, wrapped in paper.

"Just in case you let me down, I've brought my own snack," he said smiling broadly.

Feldwebel Jung interrupted. "Excuse me sir, the platoon commanders are ready for you."

"I'll be right with you Jung."

The Feldwebel departed along with the other two Oberleutnant's, who had also wished Paul and his men luck.

"Well, work calls, so I'd better get going. Give them hell out there," he said clapping both Paul and Max on their shoulders.

"You too Max."

"The best are leading the way sir," responded Max.

"If I wasn't commanding the best company in the battalion Feldwebel Grun, I might agree with you," he said tapping Max's massive shoulder with his gauntlet.

He left them to go and organise his own unit.

Paul was already dressed in his first pattern jump smock and combat trousers and was in the process of pulling on his protective, external pads to cushion his knees on the hard landing he would encounter when he hit the ground. He ran his hand across the front of the almost cricket pad like guards, with their horizontal padded tubes, mentally checking they were fit for the job. He bent down and adjusted the elasticated straps at the back of his knees, settling them until they were comfortable. While he was crouched down he checked that his side-laced, jump boots were tightly secured, not wanting to be tripped up at the wrong moment. Standing back up, he checked that his Zeiss, binoculars, his two canvas magazine pouches, leather map case and water bottle, along with his P38, Walther pistol, were well secured under is jump smock. Once satisfied, he tucked his gauntlets into his belt. Looking around him, he could see that his company was moments away from being ready.

He turned to his Feldwebel, grabbing him by the shoulder. The latent force beneath Max's powerful shoulders never ceased to amaze him.

"Come on Max, let's get this show on the road."

"I'll round them up then sir," and off he went.

"Right one company," he bellowed. "Let's get this show on the road."

This kicked the platoon commanders and sergeants into action. Orders were shouted, the disparate paratroopers were formed in files of two, ready to march to the aircraft. The huge, heavy hangar doors were pushed back on their rails, squealing in protest as they slid back. A cool breeze wafted into the now stuffy aircraft hangar, and Paul and Max made their way to the front of the unit.

"Attention, forward march," shouted Paul, and in a file of two's, they marched towards their aircraft, now silent as the engines had been shut off for embarkation of the paratroopers.

The company split up into nine man groups, one group per aircraft, and made their way to their specific plane. The weapons canisters had been loaded earlier, carrying the soldier's weapons, extra ammunition and supplies. The groups of nine boarded the Junkers 52s at their disposal, climbing up the metal steps into the confines of the transport plane. Both Paul and Max indicated for their respective teams to go on ahead, and they met in between two Junkers.

"Well Max, this is it. Nothing more we can do now."

"There's nothing to do sir. We've done the prep, all we can do now is deliver the goods when we hit the deck."

"No gliders this time eh?"

"No bullets either sir. Let's just hope the artillery are on target."

They clasped hands.

"Right, let's get going, out taxi's are waiting," said Paul. They separated, returning to their exclusive aircraft.

Paul was the last on his allocated plane, and would be the first to jump. He sat, squatted on the narrow bench situated down the side of the aircraft, opposite the exit door. To his right, Unteroffizier, Uffz, Forster, commander of one troop, one platoon. Another paratrooper who was with Paul on Eben Emael. In fact, the entire troop, and the majority of one platoon had served with him in Poland and Belgium.

"They could have made these a bit more palatial for their elite soldiers sir."

"Just think back to those gliders Forster, this is luxury." The rest of the troop joined in with the ensuing laughter.

The plane was cramped. The men sat on the narrow benches down each side of the cabin, shoulder to shoulder, their knees touching. The space would be tight for anyone, but for the paratroopers, with their parachute packs and personal equipment, it was worse.

The Junkers vibrated as one of the engines turned over, probably the central one. The vibration and shaking got steadily worse as the engine revs were increased. Then, when reaching a steady rhythm the shaking settled down until the other two engines took their turn to go through the start up process. Now with all three engines running, it was almost impossible to continue any conversation, even shouting would be pointless. The Absetzer shut and secured the aircrafts rear door, which excluded some of the noise, but not enough.

Obergefrieter Herzog, diagonally opposite Paul, was checking the straps on his harness, his eyes rolling up into his head when he caught his company commander's eye, as if to say, 'here we go again'.

The engines suddenly screamed and the Absetzer's thumbs up, indicated to Paul that they would be taking off shortly. The engines continued to scream, their combined 2,175 bhp, pulling at the brakes that were still on, holding the throbbing beast back. The aircraft suddenly shot forward, Paul feeling the pressure of Forster against him as the 'G' force tried to push him and his comrades to the back of the plane.

The Junkers steadily gathered speed, rattling and juddering over the occasionally rutted, runway, jerking upwards as the pilot sensing the plane was ready, rotated the aircraft and it slowly left the runway behind. The engines were still at full throttle as it steadily gained height, banking in a circle to allow the rest of the flight to form up, so they would be over the target in formation.

CHAPTER THREE

The lumbering Junkers JU52, a low winged triplane, the major workhorse of the Luftwaffe transport fleet, rumbled through the dawn sky at six thousand metres, buffeted by slight easterly winds.

They flew north, skirting to the east of Hannover, to end up over the Munster training area, where they would complete their drop. The noise through the thin corrugated alloy skin of the battered well used aircraft sought to drown out the voices of the occupants nervously cracking jokes with each other. The nine paratroopers, 'Green Devils', commanded by Oberleutnant Paul Otto Brandt, were sat opposite each other on the benches of this ageing but dependable workhorse. The Junkers, affectionately known as 'Tante June', or 'Auntie June', transporting the bulk of number one troop, of One Platoon, commanded by Unteroffizier, Uffz, Forster, were to be the first to drop.

Paul was approached by the Absetzer, the dispatcher, the shaking Junkers making his movements unsteady. It was his job to get the men ready in their jump line up, making sure their 9 metre static lines were attached to the wire cable in the ceiling of the aircraft and open the door ready for the exit and give the final signal to jump. He proceeded to shout instructions into Paul's ear.

"We are about ten minutes away sir, better get the troops ready."

Paul nodded in agreement and looked round towards his men, indicating to them that they were near their objective. The message was passed along the line to each Fallschirmjager. He could feel the aircraft slowly dropping in height and gradually losing speed. Once they reached a height of about one hundred and fifty metres and a speed of approximately one hundred miles an hour, they would be in position to jump. Five minutes later the light at the door of the aircraft glowed red, indicating they were minutes away from the drop zone. All stood, static lines held between their teeth, leaving their hands free to steady themselves, should the plane be rocked by a gust of wind or indeed enemy flak had they been on operations.

A rush of wind suddenly whistled through the side door as it was opened in readiness to discharge its load out into the dawn sky. The platoon shuffled along the aircraft getting closer to the door, the noise now deafening not only from the engines of the aircraft, but also from the gale force wind that tore through the aircraft attempting to wrench the helmets from the war clad occupants.

"Get ready." The Absetzer shouted his orders.

All connected their static lines to the wire.

"Get ready to jump."

The aircraft door was wide open, waiting to receive them through its gaping hole. With the wind from the open doorway tearing at his clothing, Paul waited at the head of the line of expectant paratroopers. The green light came on and a shrill sound filled the air.

"Ab. Ab. Ab. Jump." The jump master gave the final order.

Paul launched himself from the aircraft in the spread eagled position, as he had been taught back in training. As he was leaving the plane, he recalled that this was only the seventh occasion he had leapt out of an aircraft. In Poland they had been transported by Boxer trucks and in Belgium they had used, the now famous, DFS 230 glider.

As he left the plane others were following close behind him. The rush of air in his face almost took his breath away. He was suddenly tugged back harshly at his shoulders as the chute was dragged from its casing by the static line still connected to the aircraft. Within seconds a string of parachutes blossomed out in the wake of the Junkers, disgorging its load as if in relief to get rid of its burden. Once the pressure on the link between the parachute and the static line reached the right tension point, it snapped, freeing the parachute, allowing it to billow, swinging him from side to side. He could almost sense the other paratrooper, who had exited immediately after him, above and behind.

He looked down. He could see the landmark of the church tower two kilometres north of his position, west of the hill in front, a railway line running west to east to his south. The fields they were to land in, bordered by low hedges, were getting closer by the second. Paul sensed, rather than saw the ground rushing towards him, at some five metres per second, striking the ground hard and rolling as taught deflecting the force of his landing throughout his body and not feet, backside and head as he had done countless times in training.

Once on the ground, he scrambled around as fast as he could. Although the wind was fairly mild, it was still enough to fill the canopy, which he needed to quickly get under control. He grabbed the risers, quickly picked himself up off the ground, and ran towards the chute, pulling in the risers as he went, quickly collapsing the canopy. He speedily released the buckles on his harness. They were trialling the new RZ20 parachute, similar to the RZ16, but with quick release buckles.

He rapidly looked about, at the same time instinctively checking that his pistol was accessible. In the distance he could see the hill the battalion was to assault, and to its left, the forest and road his company was to secure. He could see other paratroopers on the ground, but some were still landing. The drop from Paul's plane was spread across less than a two hundred metre stretch, meaning they must have left the plane at an acceptable rate of less than a second per soldier. The faster they exited the Junkers, the closer they would be when they hit the ground. To his south he could see second platoon, which had jumped from the plane that had been flying parallel to his aircraft, gathering up their chutes and releasing themselves from the restrictive harnesses.

He scanned the area for the weapons canister that would have been ejected after the last man had left the plane, spotting it over his shoulder, about a hundred paces away. He sprang up from the dew-covered grass and sprinted towards it, taking in the remaining Junkers above disgorging the last of their human cargo.

A few paces later he slid down by the canister, its inflated canopy still billowing and tugging at the weapons container. He released the straps and hit the clips to release the lid, exposing its contents. Hurriedly grabbing his MP40, he took a magazine and loaded the weapon, with his loaded pouches, he was fully armed.

Paul scanned the horizon again, searching for any enemy response to their landing, before pulling his smock off his shoulders and relocating his webbing and personal equipment on the outside. Herzog and Forster threw themselves down beside him, and before he knew it, the entire force of one troop was acquiring their weapons from the numerous canisters scattered about the field and sorting out their kit as Paul had done. Just as they had finished getting themselves organised, Nadel, the commander of first platoon, joined them.

"Dietrich, I want you to take your platoon," he said pointing to the north, "and secure that hedge line there. Look out for any enemy activity on the hill and send a runner if you see them making any moves, ok?"

"Jawohl, Herr Oberleutnant."

Nadel gathered his platoon together. The remaining two troops had landed, recovered their weapons from the containers and were ready to move out. The rest of the company was slowly converging on Paul's position. Where he was situated immediately became the temporary company command post. Max's huge form plonked itself down next to him.

"That was bloody good, not done that for a while," he said grinning like a Cheshire cat.

"You're not on holiday Max," admonished Paul.

"Sorry sir, what have you got for me?" he replied, the grin still firmly fixed.

"I'm going to join Nadel along the northern hedge line, I want you to wait here and group the remaining two platoons. I want first platoon to the west and third platoon to the east. But keep a troop from the third here with you, to watch our back and liaise with the battalion when they get here. They can also consolidate our weapons canisters"

"Will do sir, I'll get going."

Paul was also up and off, running swiftly to join first platoon, his mind racing as he ran through all the actions he needed to take, his breathing rapid, partly adrenaline driven.

Once there, hidden by the hedge line, he looked over the disposition of Nadel's men. His MG 34 section was on the left flank and the Leutnant was observing the hilltop through his binoculars. It was grass covered and fairly bare, the odd tree and shrub spoiling its relatively smooth outline. The odd dark smudge at the top, indicative of freshly dug positions.

He turned to face his company commander, "all quiet sir."

"I doubt we'll see anyone until after our artillery have had their go," suggested Paul. Two Army infantry platoons had been allocated to act as the enemy and defend the hill. A full company was believed to be billeted in the village, to provide immediate support to the troops on the hill if attacked.

"But keep watching, we need to keep our eyes peeled for any Landser tricks," he said smiling.

Paul's company had three tasks to perform. First it was necessary to secure the landing zone, enabling the rest of the battalion to land safely, he then needed to allocate a platoon to secure the road that meandered from the village to their northwest, cutting around behind the hill and continuing east. His final task was to put in place a blocking force west and south, where he was now, of the hill to prevent the enemy from edging down the hill and outflanking the battalion. The remaining companies when they arrived, would attack the hill from the north and east. He was sending Leutnant Krause's platoon to secure the road, it was an opportunity to see what he was made of. He and his platoon were already setting up along the northern hedge line, west of Nadel's position and south of the hill.

"Right Dietrich, I'll leave you to it."

He jumped up and crouching low as he ran, Paul sped along the hedgerow until he met up with Krause's platoon.

"Well Heinrich, ready then?" Krause jumped when Paul descended alongside him, not a good sign.

"We're ready sir."

"Well, you know what you've got to do, so move out."

"We move in two," he hissed to his men.

Feldwebel Eichel joined them. "Which is the lead troop sir?"

"Ugh, number one," he responded.

Paul's fear of his officer's inability to lead his platoon had just been compounded. If it hadn't been too late in the day, he would have switched the defence of the road to another platoon. But it was too late now he thought angrily, blaming himself for letting this happen. On reflection, he should have sent Max with him.

The platoon moved off, climbing through a gap in the hedgerow, they ran across the one hundred metre meadow, staying close to the hedge on their right hand side. Hitting the hedge line parallel to the road, they followed the road that ran alongside the wooded area they needed to secure, Krause hanging back, still studying the map. He should know the area like the back of his hand, even without the map, pondered Paul. He couldn't hang around any longer; he had a company to command, so he sped back to second platoon.

"Any movement?"

"Nothing sir," replied Nadel handing him the binoculars.

Paul quickly scanned the hilltop, he saw nothing moving. He looked at his watch, it was 5:30, and they had been on the ground for no longer than thirty minutes. Another thirty would see second company dropping onto the LZ. All they could do now was wait. The silence was only disturbed by the second wave of Junkers aircraft, carrying Two Company and part of Third Company. Hauptman Volkman would also be in this wave. The final wave would bring the rest of the battalion. The attack would then begin. If this was not an exercise, they would have had a larger allocation of aircraft and the full battalion would have been landed within the space of an hour.

He watched as line after line of paratroopers poured out from the three Junkers transports flying in arrow formation. The un-inflated chutes and paratroopers initially horizontal as they were whipped from the aircraft, eventually falling vertically as their chutes billowed open dangling their human cargo beneath. It was a spectacular sight to watch, and would instil shock and fear in an enemy. Second Company, and elements of the Third, consolidated and moved up to the hedge line, joined by the battalion commander.

"Sitrep Brand?" There was no small talk with the Raven, he thought as he responded.

"Perimeter of the LZ secured, hilltop quiet, first platoon dispatched to secure the road, Herr Hauptman."

"That's Leutnant Krause's platoon?"

"Yes sir."

Volkman looked at him, but said nothing. Paul knew exactly what he was thinking.

"He has to be given a chance sir."

"Be it on your head if things go wrong Brand."

"Sir."

"This is Oberleutnant Graf, he will be acting as an umpire, he'll be with you. We also have an umpire with the main body." The two men shook hands. "I'm going to move east with two company, leaving elements of three to maintain security. I want you to leave a platoon here as a blocking force and your remaining platoon on the west side as planned, ok?"

"Yes sir."

Volkman left and was immediately replaced by Max.

"All sorted back there sir, Hauptman Volkman released me. Update sir?"

"Leutnant Krause has moved out, I've sent a runner for third troop and once they arrive we'll move out to our positions."

"Leutnant Nadel remaining here sir?"

"Yes."

Third Platoon, causing a minor ruckus as they mingled with their comrades, suddenly joined them.

"Leutnant Roth, Feldwebel Grun and myself will be joining you. So you lead off and we'll slot in between your first two troops."

"I'll get them organised sir."

Within minutes third platoon was ready to move out. Max grabbed hold of Unterfeldwebel Kienitz as he walked passed.

"Keep a tight reign on your guys Karl, make sure you use those trees for cover. We don't want those clod hoppers catching us on the hop."

"Will do Feld." Many NCOs would be offended given such specific guidance by their senior. But they all respected Max for his experience and know how, and welcomed his advice, no matter how obvious.

"Let's get moving then!" said Max, slapping Kienitz on the back.

They moved out. Leutnant Roth leading first troop, Paul and Max in front of second troop and Kienitz in front of the tail end troop.

It was 6:15 and the grey sky was getting brighter by the minute, they needed to get to the trees quickly. Although they had clearly been seen parachuting down, the exercise didn't officially kick off until the third wave relinquished their passengers over the drop zone. But, the paratroopers didn't want to give anything away. They followed first platoon's route, but crossed the road and moved through the trees that surrounded the base of the hill, steadily making their way to its western slope, but staying within the trees, keeping out of sight. Paul and his men then formed up along the tree line, looking up at the shallow slope in front of them, hidden from any prying eyes, or so they hoped. He had sent a small section of four men deeper into the trees, just to cover their backs, in case Leutnant Krause was overrun. They didn't have long to wait before they heard the drone of the final wave of aircraft coming over.

"Standby, standby," hissed Paul. Before he could say another word, the whistle of artillery rounds flew from the west and started pounding the hilltop, only stopping when ordered so as not to interfere with the incoming planes. Behind him, Max could hear gunfire.

"That sounds close sir," exclaimed Max.

"It does, take a couple of men with you and investigate, quickly."

Grabbing hold of two paratroopers, informing Leutnant Roth of what was happening, he then headed into the trees. The umpire tagged on as well. They rapidly joined the section that was guarding their rear. From here Max could see the road. A section had ambushed an enemy unit that had disembarked from their trucks under the sound of the artillery fire and were attempting to attack Paul's force from the rear and reinforce the hilltop's defenders. The sudden additional firepower from Max and the two paratroopers forced the attackers to seek cover. But the attackers were too many and they would soon be over run or outflanked.

"Where the hell is Krause?" Max cursed to himself.

The umpire crouched down beside Max.

"You've got about two minutes Feldwebel, then I will be ordering you to withdraw, ok?"

"Understood sir."

They kept up a high rate of fire, the umpire moving forward to liaise with is fellow umpire attached to the enemy force. All of a sudden, all hell broke loose. A force of paratroopers was taking the infantry from the other side of the road and the enemy was forced to withdraw, no doubt to prepare for a second, bigger assault. Unterfeldwebel Eichel and the umpire joined Max again.

"Luck is on your side this morning Feldwebel. I've told them that due to high levels of wounded, they have to wait one hour to regroup before they can attack."

"Thank you sir."

Max turned to the recently arrived Eichel, "Where the fuck have you been?"

"Sorry Feldwebel," he responded startled by Max's anger.

"What happened?"

"We thought it best to position ourselves so we could bounce the enemy, Feldwebel Grun," interjected Leutnant Krause who had suddenly appeared standing above them.

"Is that right?" Max said turning to Eichel, who just lowered his eyes, obviously embarrassed, but unable to disagree with his platoon commander.

"I will set up the platoon here Feldwebel, you might want to let the company commander know that all is well and that we have his back covered, dismissed." Max responded in the only way he could, suppressing the deep anger he felt. He knew that the Leutnant had got lost.

"Jawohl, Herr Leutnant."

"I'll speak to you later, Eichel," hissed Max, and he jumped up to return to his company commander.

When he arrived there Roth's platoon was on it's feet and he could see his commander talking to Hauptman Volkman and one of the Umpires.

"Glad you could join us Feldwebel Grun." Max came to attention in front of his seniors.

"Is it over sir, have we taken the hill?"

"We have Feldwebel, thanks to your efforts I believe. Right Oberleutnant Brand, the exercise is finished, were forming up on the drop zone and a field kitchen will be joining us so the men can get some hot food down them." They came to attention again and Volkman left them to it.

"Did I hear the mention of food?" hailed Helmut, who suddenly appeared behind them.

"I knew something would get you up and about," responded Paul

"The food is only for the heroes sir," added Max.

"Well then Feldwebel, I'd better make my way to the DZ, fourth company practically captured the hill on its own."

"Max, send some runners out, pull the men in and we'll form up on the DZ," ordered Paul.

"On my way sir."

Helmut put his arm around Paul's shoulder and guided him away from the troops.

"The rumour is already spreading that Krause has fucked up, what happened?"

"That's one of my officers Helmut. It's for me to look into and take action if necessary."

"I know, I know," he said backing off, "but he's becoming a liability and is going to get your guys into trouble or even killed."

"I know you mean well, but keep out of it."

Helmut raised his hands, palms out, in front of him, "I'm backing, I'm backing, let's go and get some grub."

"You go ahead, I'll catch you up. I need to go and speak to someone."

CHAPTER FOUR

Paul yawned and stretched his arms, pushing the blanket and eiderdown aside. His mother always put far too much bedding on for him; thankfully the window had been open throughout the night. Paul had been home now for five days, tomorrow was his last day. But, today he was meeting Christa.

He glanced towards the window; the late August was sun just starting to rise and its rays were filtering through, promising a good day for them both. He rolled over in bed, hugging his two down pillows, suppressing the inner excitement that was threatening to well up and swamp him in its overwhelming force. They had not met since May, but had written several letters to each other, the passion growing stronger in each missive they had read. Today they would discover if the passion was still there, and if it was real. He pushed those thoughts aside, as he did his bedding and threw his legs over the edge of the bed. It was 6:30, time to get up.

He glanced around the familiar room, his bedroom since he could remember. The large, chunky chest of draws, the two substantial wardrobes, the blanket box at the end of his bed, so familiar to him. He had spent all of his life in this house. He stood up, the view in the distance, the Havel. He never ceased to enjoy its allure and felt privileged at having been brought up in such a beautiful part of Germany. Padding across the wooden floorboards, he grabbed some clothes from his wardrobe, the one that specifically held his military uniform. Although he would have rather worn civilian clothes, his unit was classed as being on active duty, so uniform must be worn at all times. He threw his flieger blouse on the bed, grabbed a white shirt and black tie, and made his way to the bathroom to shave and bathe.

Crossing the landing he could hear his mother below, clattering about the kitchen, no doubt preparing even more food that she would insist he eat. He washed and shaved, and then spent a few moments soaking in the bath. He heard his mother calling, so stepped out of the bath, dried off, went to his room and dressed, afterwards heading down the stairs.

He walked into the large kitchen. The cream, two plated Aga, the long farmhouse kitchen table laden with ham, cheese and numerous types of bread was laid out in front of him.

"Morning son," said his father looking up from his morning paper.

"Morning Papa, Mama," he said in return.

Paul sat down at the table, grabbing a serviette.

"Did you sleep well?" said his mother coming over to him patting his hand.

"I certainly did, now I'm ready for one of your breakfasts Mama."

Her face beamed. She headed back to the Aga, picking up the boiling kettle to make coffee and checking on the boiled eggs. She knew Paul liked them soft. His father looked up at him and they smiled at each other. His father knew that she fussed too much and tried to over feed their son. But he wasn't home that often, so Paul could cope with the extra attention for short periods of time.

"How's the factory going Papa?" he asked as he gathered a piece of dark bread, spread it liberally with butter and added a slice of Westphalian ham, his favourite, only equalled by peppered salami. He added some cheese and took a deep bite.

"Busy, busy son. We're working full time manufacturing aircraft parts for the Luftwaffe, orders have doubled."

"They'll be needed to help them fight the British," responded Paul.

"Why can't we just leave them alone," he said scowling. "We've kicked them out of France, surely that's enough."

"Enough you two," scolded his mother, "get on with your breakfasts." They again smiled at each other.

His mother joined them at the table, spooning two boiled eggs onto her son's plate.

"So, you're going to see your young lady today?"

"She's not my young lady Mama, she's just a friend."

"All the same, we'd like to meet her one day, wouldn't we Papa?"

"Leave the boy alone woman." This time they both laughed. She looked from one to the other. He so looked like his father she thought.

"You two and your private jokes."

His father put the paper down and stood up. Tall like his son, a touch over six feet, not looking twice the age of his son. The only signs of ageing being a few flecks of grey by his temples.

"I must get to the factory, we have new schedules coming in today. Do you still want a lift to the station?"

"Please Papa, I'll be with you in a few minutes."

"You shouldn't make him rush his breakfast."

"It's ok Mama, I've nearly finished and I've had enough now."

His father kissed his wife on the cheek, clasped his son's shoulder on the way out of the kitchen and went to get himself ready for work.

The train journey from Brandenburg to the centre of Berlin was short and he was in the city by eight thirty, a full hour before he was meeting Christa. He left the railway station and made his way south, heading for the Tiergarten, enjoying even more of the freedom from the restrictions of barracks and military life as he walked through the green park. They were to meet on the southwest side of the park, at the beginning of the Kurfurstendamm. He got to the outskirts of the park and headed south passed the Zoologischer gartens, hitting the Kurfurstendamm at its most eastern point.

He caught sight of her first, or at least his heart did as it started thumping like an express train. She was as he remembered her, slender, petite, wrapped in a cream, flowery, summer dress, her skin looking soft and lightly tanned. He heard the rhythmic tattoo of her heeled shoes on the pavement, above all the other sounds around him. People passing by, wondering why this tall German soldier, in his splendid paratrooper's uniform, his medals proudly displayed, was standing there as if mesmerised. She looked up, her auburn hair bouncing on her shoulders; it had grown since he had last seen her. Their eyes met, her eyes dark and mysterious, his hazel and sparkling with delight at seeing her. He came out of his trance and strode powerfully towards her. They met, pedestrians swirling around them, but they were oblivious to their presence. Paul threw his arms around her waist, crushing her slender body to him, the scent of her hair in his face. She looked up at him longingly.

"Oh Paul, I hoped you would come."

"I'm here now darling, I just had to see you, be with you again. Your letters were not enough."

She reached up with her right hand, gently touching the scar above his left eye.

"You're letters were the only thing that kept me going. Oh Paul, I've missed you so much."

Paul bent his head down, and holding her chin gently in his hand he kissed her softly on the lips. The taste of her moist lips, the scent of her skin, made his head swirl with intoxication. They were interrupted abruptly.

"I'm sure you two lovers have a lot of catching up to do," said a short, stout man in a brown apron, "but you're blocking the entrance to my shop and customers can neither get in or out."

They both looked about them, realising they were obstructing the shop doorway and were completely unaware of all that was going on around them. They quickly parted.

"I'm sorry sir," apologised Paul.

"That's ok officer, take her somewhere nice eh?"

"I will," said Paul smiling, gently guiding Christa away from the shop.

She linked her arm into his and within seconds they burst into laughter and joked together as they wandered further down the Kurfurstendamm, no destination in mind. The shopkeeper watched them go, shaking his head. Any nervousness or unfamiliarity had been broken; it was as if they had always been together. They continued to meander down the street, talking about Christa's work, Paul's comrades and Max, his parents and pointing in shop windows that caught their eye. They briefly touched on the war. They turned off the main street, exploring one of the smaller side streets. They found themselves outside a bijou cafe situated next to a small, relatively private square; Christa tugged him to a seat next to a small bistro table.

They had ended up in a small square, their cast iron bistro table and chairs situated alongside a dozen others on a raised, fenced wooden platform with huge parasols strategically placed protecting them from the now bright sunlight.

"I need to sit down she said, my legs are shaking."

"Mine too," admitted Paul, "they feel worse than when I completed my first parachute jump."

"You must tell me about that," she said, touching his face with her fingers. "I want to know all about you and what you've done. I've never been compared to a parachute jump before," she added pouting.

A voice coughed close to them, a waitress in a black dress with a white apron was stood next to their table.

"Good morning Oberleutnant, what can I get you?"

Paul looked at Christa. She turned to face the waitress. "One Viennese chocolate please, with extra cream."

"And I'll have a white coffee please," added Paul. The waitress left to get their order.

"So, what plans have you got for us today then Oberleutnant Brand?" she said smiling.

"I have to confess I didn't think beyond meeting you Christa," he said embarrassed. She reached across and fingered the medal on his tunic pocket.

"You have had much on your mind my poor man."

"Well, I shall come up with something then," he said, determined to make her day enjoyable.

She slipped her slim handbag off her shoulder and after rummaging around for a few moments produced two tickets, which she proceeded to flutter in front of him.

"What about the Staats-theater? Flucht vor der Liebe?" she said with a twinkle in her eye.

"Christa, you never cease to amaze me, that sounds great."

The waitress returned with their drinks, placed them on the table and then left.

"Where did you go after Maastricht?" asked Paul

"I was asked to go to France, they had converted some of the French hospitals to military hospitals. It was horrible Paul. So many wounded and they were just boys. What about Belgium, tell me what happened."

He talked about the attack on Fort Eben Emael, occasionally touching his scar reminding him of how close he came to being killed. He mentioned also the exercise they had just completed. She listened attentively, intermittently asking questions, particularly about Max and the junior NCOs who came to the hospital to visit him. Before they knew it they had been there for two hours, their drinks remaining untouched. Realising this brought about another outburst of laughter. And after calling over the waitress they ordered the same drinks again along with some lunch. Paul had smoked ham and cheese on sonnenblumenkenbrot, sunflower seeds in a dark rye bread, his favourite, followed by a slice of black forest gateaux. Christa had a more gentile meal of a German tomato salad.

The tickets were for the 2:30 show, so they finished their meal, paid the waitress and walked the three kilometres to the theatre on the other side of the Tiergarten. The three hour show was enjoyed by both of them and when they left they were buzzing with excitement. Not just because they had enjoyed the performance, but the sharing of it together. They were stood outside the theatre, debating what to do next, when Christa reached up placing her hand round the back of his neck, pulling him down and kissing him full on the lips.

"You go back to your unit tomorrow?" she asked, her voice dropping to a whisper.

"I'm afraid so," he replied.

"Then tonight you must stay in Berlin, with me."

Their eyes met.

"Stay overnight?" he said.

"Yes," she said almost breathlessly.

"I know where."

He grabbed her hand and they headed off to the hotel Paul often stayed over in with his parents.

He was floating on air. He couldn't remember ever being this happy. It was almost worth being wounded in order to have met this wonderful woman. Christa was equally happy.

★★★

Paul's time with Christa now seemed like a dream. The affection, the intimacy between them was indescribable and their evening of passion during their overnight stay in Berlin was exhausting. They parted the next day, committing their undying love to each other and promising to meet up again as soon as he could get away on leave. When he returned home the next day to collect his gear, ready for the journey back to his unit, he'd had to explain to his mother where he had been overnight, although she had suspected. Although initially worried about him not returning home the previous night, she could see the elation in her sons face and clucked around him like a mother hen. His father was at work, so he didn't get to say goodbye to him, but left him a short note. He would understand.

On Paul's return from his leave in Brandenburg he was called immediately to Hauptman Volkman's office where he had been met with some shocking news that Leutnant Krause had requested a transfer to another unit, which had been immediately accepted by Volkman, who was pleased to get rid of him. Paul was initially displeased.

"He just needed time sir, he lacked confidence."

"He's a liability Brand, and we're best rid of him."

"But he was my responsibility sir," anger clearly showing on his face.

Volkman stood up, slapping his stick down on his desk.

"If it was peacetime Brand I would agree with you, but we're at war, we haven't got time for complacency."

"But sir."

"Drop it Brand, dismissed."

Paul came to attention, saluted, turned on his heel and left the Raven's office. One piece of compensatory news though, was Krause's replacement, newly promoted Leutnant Leeb. One of Paul's Unteroffizier's, one of his troop commanders during their time in Poland and Belgium, he had been flagged as potential officer material and he had been accepted for accelerated officer training.

Paul had gathered his men together outside of the canteen. It was too nice to be stuck inside on this warm autumn day. They had dragged the chairs and a couple of tables out of the canteen and placed them on one of the few stretches of grass on the Luftwaffe base. An area often used for BBQs when the base's occupants put pressure on the mess staff. The Luftwaffe Feldwebel responsible for the day to day running of the canteen had protested vehemently at having the canteen disrupted in this way. But a little persuasion from Max had calmed him down. That's not to say that Max's impressive size and sheer presence didn't help influence the outcome.

The newly appointed Leutnant Leeb stood out with his pristine eagles on his tunic denoting his new rank. Sat either side were his fellow platoon commanders. To his left the Impetuous Roth and to his right the steady Nadel. Max was stood behind them, like a rock, his hands resting on the backs of their chairs, as if watching over his charges. The role reversal between Max and Leutnant Leeb would be interesting, thought Paul, Leeb now being senior to Max, in rank at least. Paul was also coming to terms with the authority he held, not only due to his rank of Oberleutnant, but also the fact that he was one of the now famous 'Green Devils'. As Max often muttered to himself, "he's coming out of his shell." Even so, he was still very protective of his young commander.

"Come on people, sort yourselves out," shouted Max.

"Grab yourselves a drink on your way to your seats," added Paul.

Max had suggested to the Luftwaffe cookhouse that the provision of an urn of orange juice would be most agreeable. They were eager to comply. The company had finally settled down in their seats, the occasional roar of an aircraft engine being tested and the odd plane landing or taking off in the background. It was far from the front lines of the French Coast and England, but it was still an operational airfield.

"Right," Paul coughed, clearing his throat. "I have just come from a briefing with the Battalion Commander." He hesitated before he continued speaking, allowing the assembled soldiers to finish their speculation of what the briefing may have been about. He rarely held formal briefings, preferring to sit with his platoons and talk with them over a coffee or a beer, or while they were partaking in some scheduled training, and get individual feedback on his suggestions, ideas. Today though, required a more formal setting. "I'm afraid I have some bad news and some good news gentlemen."

All of a sudden the low hum from the soldiers died down and they looked pensive, clearly concerned that something disastrous may have happened.

"Our Luftwaffe have been unable to completely destroy the RAF." There was a groan from the hundred men gathered around their company commander. "It was imperative that the air force destroyed the RAF before launching Operation Sea lion. To that end, the operation has been cancelled."

The groan deepened. Not so much the disappointment of the failure of the Luftwaffe, or even the invasion of England. It was more a disappointment of not being able to utilise their paratrooper skills in helping to lead the German Army to victory.

"I know it's not what you, what we, expected or wanted to hear, but that's the way it is gentlemen."

"Is the decision likely to be rescinded sir?" piped up Max.

"No Feldwebel Grun, it has been well and truly axed."

"And the good news sir?" said Max, suspecting there wasn't any good news.

The rest of the company looked from one to the other, the expression on Max's face giving out a message of doubt. Then a smile slowly spread across the tough sergeant's face, softening some of the hard lines. Equally Paul's face split into a grin, then they all knew what was coming.

"We get to do extra training Feldwebel Grun, of course." They both burst into laughter, steadily followed by the rest of the company.

"Dismissed."

The cook looked out of the window, shaking his head. Even the Battalion Commander picked up the sound of laughter carried towards his office on the gentle breeze. He stood up from his desk and moved to one of two windows that looked out onto the camp. His dark, hooded eyes peered through the glass. Brand, he thought. Why am I not surprised? The world could be falling apart and it still wouldn't dampen his spirits or that of his men and his sidekick of a sergeant.

He smiled for the first time that day. He was as disappointed as the rest of the Fallschirmjager that Operation Sea lion had been cancelled.

CHAPTER FIVE

Paul hailed Max as he saw him striding across the parade ground," Feldwebel Grun."

Moments later the burly sergeant was stood to attention in front of him, saluting.

"We've a job at last Max."

"About bloody time too sir, I was thinking of transferring to the cookhouse, they get more action than we do."

"You a chef Max?"

"Well maybe not sir, don't want to lower my sights do I? Anyway it sounds like you've come to my rescue. Where are we going?"

"Greece Max, Greece."

"What's happened out there for them to need us?"

"Well since we came to Mussolini's rescue the battle has been progressing well Max. 9th Panzer Division have reached Kozani and are looking to force a river crossing. They'll be across the Aliakmon River before we know it."

"Where the bloody hell is that sir?"

"West of Thessaloniki and they're heading south to Corinth, Geography not your strong subject at school then Max?"

"School of life me sir. So, let me get this right, the Greeks kick the Italians out after they fail to invade them and we have to come to their bloody rescue, can't they sort themselves out?"

"They're our allies Max and they obviously need our special talents."

"Of course they do sir. I could have told them that."

"Are the troops still on the ranges?"

"Yes sir, I was about to join them."

"Let's go together then, I can brief the men. Have you got any transport?"

"I've got a Steiner and driver sir, follow me."

They made their way through the barracks to the waiting Steiner jeep, and sped off for the short journey to the camp's firing range. The regular cracks from the Kar 98s, indicated that range firing was in full swing.

The jeep pulled up, dropping the two paratroopers off before returning to the barracks HQ. Paul and Max headed for the range firing points, having stuffed cotton wool in their ears. The company was on a range training day. It was imperative, as an elite unit, that they maintained a high level of competency in handling and firing their personal weapons. He pulled the cotton wool from his ears as the men had ceased firing at the sight of the officers approaching.

"How will the guys react Max?"

"They'll be relieved to get away from the camp sir."

"You'll be able to top up your tan Max and flaunt those muscles of yours."

"One of the lads has been to Greece, I'll have to get his feedback on the Grecian women."

"We'll no doubt be far too busy to allow you time for philandering Feldwebel Grun."

Max came to attention smiling. "Jawohl Herr Oberleutnant." They both laughed.

Max relaxed leaning against one of the firing posts. In the distance they could see that Leeb had got his men together and along with Unterfeldwebel Eichel, was taking them through some refresher weapons training. Although a number of his platoon had seen action, as had Leeb, his specialism was small arms and he had quickly earned the respect of his men and his NCOs.

"Is the full battalion going sir?"

"No, just our company to start with."

"Hauptman Volkman has either got it in for us or he favours us. Not quite sure which yet."

"He's making sure you get first options on the Greek beauties Max, didn't you know."

"I didn't think of it like that sir."

"How was Hamburg?"

"Not as bad as I expected, the RAF have missed most of the residential areas, but the docks are a bit of a mess."

"You might want to get your father to move Max, it will always be a target. It's got shipyards, U-boat pens, oil refineries; the RAF will hit it regularly. Is your father ok?"

"He's fine thanks sir, it would take more than the RAF to do for him, and he won't budge. How's Berlin sir?"

"I've just had a letter from my Mother, she says that the first bombing was fairly light, but the more recent one was quite bad. They're just retaliating, I hear the Luftwaffe hit Buckingham Palace not so long ago."

"Did you see anything when you went home at Christmas?"

"I didn't go into Berlin, so didn't get to see the damage."

"Ah," said Max smiling. "Nurse Keller came to yours for Christmas didn't she?"

Paul quickly changed the subject. "Will you give Leutnant Leeb a shout? Where are the other platoons?"

"Second are cleaning weapons and the third are in the hut getting a brew," said Max pushing himself off the firing post, recognising it was back to work.

"Tell the Platoon Commanders I'll see them in the hut will you Max?" He looked at his watch. "Say in about ten minutes? I want to go and talk to some of the men."

"Will do sir."

Max saluted and strode off to seek out and gather the other two officers and Paul wandered over to Leeb's platoon. He approached the platoon and sat on the ground as their commander gave them some advanced instruction in the use of the Kar 98. The Karabiner 98K was a control fed, bolt action rifle, with an effective range of up to five hundred metres. Leeb was showing them a quicker method of loading the internal magazine, which could hold five 8 x 57mm rounds, with a stripper clip. On noticing his Company Commander, he leapt up from his crouching position, immediately calling his platoon to attention.

"Shun."

They quickly clambered up of the ground straightening their uniforms as they did so. Paul quickly flagged them down with a wave of his hand.

"Relax men, at ease."

Paul crouched back down and the paratroopers resumed their previous positions on the sandy ground by the firing points. The wooden posts at regular intervals apart, like sentinels. The posts were used to mark the three hundred metre line from the targets and butts. The firing posts were adjacent to a slit trench, fronted by sand bags. On Paul's direction, Leeb left the platoon, crossing over the open space between the firing positions and the administration area, to go and join Max and the other two commanders in the range hut.

"Something in the air sir?" Uffz Fischer was the first to ask the question that was now on all of their minds. They could sense something was afoot.

"Extra duties for your troop no doubt," called Konrad, the other troop commander. The assembled men laughed.

"We're going to Greece gentlemen."

There was a stunned silence which must have lasted nearly a full minute. Paul looked at their faces, mouths agape, waiting to be put out of their misery by their company commander. The only sound was the men shifting position to get more comfortable on the sandy ground.

"Yes Unteroffizier Jordan, Greece."

"Wow", said Fessman, "that's somewhere I've never been."

"There'll be no poaching there," shouted a few members of the platoon. It was well known that in a past life Walter Fessman had been a poacher, a skill that had proven useful when taking out a sentry, silently, during their first action in Poland.

"Do we know what our mission is sir?" asked Oberjager Kempf.

"Not yet, but I would expect to know before we fly out, or at least as soon as we get there."

"The full Battalion?" questioned Straube.

"Initially no, but I'm sure they'll not be far behind us."

"They're sending the best first then sir," suggested Roon. This brought a bout of agreement from the men and triggered a melee of questions, comments and suggestions. Paul stood up ordering the platoon to remain seated.

"I also need to go and tell your platoon commanders what's happening."

He left them buzzing. The main topic of conversation being their observation that the Company Commander had informed them about Greece even before the platoon commanders. It gave them a sense of importance and their already high respect for this young officer was enhanced further.

He walked away from the now silent range, the targets down at the butts looked like silent sentries, but peppered with holes from the recent target practice. He arrived at the cabin and pushed his way through the stiff, wooden door of the small range hut. It had a damp and stuffy feel about it, the wood burner in the centre was off and cold. Max was stood next to it, his coffee cup on top, his left hand tapping against the cold chimney disappearing up out through the roof. It was a small hut, only designed as a shelter for troops on the range, or a place to prepare hot soups and drinks and a store for the ammunition they would need for the day's shoot.

Paul walked across the wooden floorboards, now dirty and badly scarred from the many hob-nailed, booted soldiers who had crossed it over the years. The three Leutnant's had stood up and Paul motioned for them to sit back down. He grabbed a vacant chair and dragged it up to the table the others were sat around. Moments later a coffee appeared in front of him, customary for Max, feeding his commanders addiction.

"You have something for us sir?" asked Leeb.

"All in good time Leutnant Leeb."

"Sorry sir, just keen to do something, anything other than loitering around the barracks."

Paul understood their frustration. These were men of action, and although they understood the need for training and honing theirs and their men's military skills, you could spend too much time in a barracks. A chair scraped across the floor and Max squeezed his bulk between Roth and Leeb, both moving aside to make room for him, and joined them at the table.

"Well you shall get your wish Leutnant Leeb, were moving to Greece tomorrow."

Their eyes lit up, without exception. Even Max couldn't suppress the gleam in his eyes.

"We'll be going ahead of the battalion," he continued, "and it's possible that we'll be acting as an independent unit."

"Is that the battalion as an independent unit sir, or just our company?"

"Just our company. Hauptman Volkman clearly places great trust in us and I intend to ensure that we don't let him down." Paul looked at each of the officers and Max in turn, making it clear that it was a joint commitment.

"Have we any details yet sir?" asked Leeb. Always the one to ask questions, even as a troop commander in Paul's old platoon. Now he was having to build his confidence up all over again, as a newly appointed officer.

"Not yet Ernst, but I will no doubt know more by tonight and will share it with you the minute I know."

"Where are we shipping out to sir?" questioned Nadel.

"Initially we'll be flying to Plovdiv in Bulgaria."

"Bloody hell, that's some journey sir," exclaimed Max

"A mere two thousand kilometres Feldwebel Grun."

"Happy times stuck in a Tante June then sir," added Roth laughing.

"We'll be flying out at dawn," Paul pressed on.

"Will the weapons containers be flying across with us sir?"

"Yes Feldwebel, we need to be prepared for a full operation immediately on arrival."

"Are events moving swiftly then sir?"

"Yes Viktor, it appears that 9th Panzer Division has already crossed the Aliakmon River."

"They obviously need some real soldiers to help ease their way," Roth said smiling.

"They've called for the best eh?" interjected Nadel.

"That makes it even tougher for us Heinrich. They naturally have high expectations of us, so the pressure is on. Do we have a full company Max?"

"Yes sir, no sickies and no injuries."

"Excellent. Right then gentlemen. We shall wrap it up for now and I'll leave you to get your men ready. I've already spoken to your men Ernst, so be ready to be bombarded with questions before you even begin to brief them."

"Thank you for that sir," he replied grinning.

"Inspection tonight?"

"Of course Max, but only after you have done yours."

"Jawohl, Herr Oberleutnant," he replied with a mischievous smile.

Leeb was already aware of the tight bond between the company commander and the company sergeant, the other platoon commanders were also slowly becoming aware. Although they were all senior to Feldwebel Grun by rank, they didn't relish the prospect of any faults being found by this war decorated hero. More importantly, it would reflect badly on their professionalism. But, any mistakes found were never passed on to the company commander, Max always gave them a discrete nod giving them the opportunity to put things right before Paul's final scrutiny.

"Right, snap to it," ordered Paul as he stood up.

They all jumped up from their seats, stood to attention, saluted and called out, "Jawohl, Herr Oberleutnant."

They then left the hut to go and prepare their men for the forthcoming operation. Max, as usual, hung back knowing that his company commander may have some concerns that he would want to run by him.

"Anything you want me to pick up on sir?" asked Max as he leant up against the back of his chair.

Paul drifted over to one of the hut's small windows, watching his platoon commanders gathering their men together to give them the same briefing just given by him. Then they would be marched back to the barracks. No Steiner jeep for them, thought Paul smiling to himself. He turned to face Max.

"Leeb is the most junior officer I have, yet the most combat experienced," he mused.

"We didn't have that experience either sir, until Poland and Belgium, it's something we all have to go through. You got us through it and you'll lead Leutnant's Nadel and Roth through next one in the same way."

Paul brushed his hand over his short cropped, fair hair, then touched the scar above his left eye, something he did unknowingly when myriads of thoughts rattled through his mind.

"I know Max, but you had, and will have, a big role to play as well."

He reflected back briefly to the moment when the Polish soldier

47

had risen up in front of him, weapon aimed directly at his chest and the muffled retort of a machine pistol and the artilleryman's silent scream as he was struck by the bullets spat out from Max's machine pistol. He shuddered at the thought at how close he had come to death.

"We still need to keep an eye on all of the men Max."

"Will do sir, anything else?"

"No. Wait, yes, extra water bottles. It was bad enough running out of water at Eben Emael, Greece will be altogether different."

"Battle certainly gives you a thirst sir, I'll see to it."

It was already on Max's list, but the NCO knew that his commander needed to offload these thoughts. His company commander may only be twenty two years old and less experienced than Max, but was rapidly overtaking his senior NCO in the area of combative skills and had proven to be a shrewd tactician. Paul headed for the door.

"Come on Max, let's walk back."

"Agreed sir. Stretch our legs before they get cramped up in a Tante June."

They made their way back to the barracks, a good three kilometre walk, but nothing to these tough veterans. Once back at the camp, they eat and then involved themselves in the rigorous preparations necessary to go to war. Checks were made and made again and again. Both Paul and Max were relentless in their pursuit of perfection. It wasn't resented by the men. Many had seen combat and many had seen combat with Paul and Max and knew the consequences of being ill prepared. Equipment lists were made, remade and finalised. Extra supplies were drawn from the Quartermaster's store, Max having to overcome the usual reluctance of the stores to release any of their precious stock. The soldiers often wondered who actually owned the stock; the German Army or the Quartermaster himself. It was the same the world over. They would take a small amount of ammunition with them, just in case they were in action immediately on landing, but would draw the remainder when they arrived in theatre. The weapons canisters were loaded and checked, all sixty of them. Enough to give the company its minimum requirements to sustain combat for at least twenty four hours.

They had spent the evening in one of the aircraft hangars, specifically put aside for the paratroopers. The parachutes were decked out on the long, six metre tables, and pairs of paratroopers working together to pack their chutes. They were packing the new RZ20 chute, a vast improvement on the previous models, the RZ1 and the RZ16. The canopy was camouflaged green and brown, rather than white, and had four quick release buckles enabling the paratrooper to release it swiftly on landing.

Once Paul, Max and the three platoon commanders were satisfied, and only then, the men were released to get some food and rest. It had been an exhausting day. The leggy officer, his thickset, fair haired sidekick stayed behind, going over a few minor details. Scanning their eyes over the packed parachutes, the readied canisters and the other paraphernalia of war.

"Job done sir."

"Yes Max, job done."

He patted Max's solid shoulder. "we just wait now and see what tomorrow has in store for us."

"Hauptman Volkman not more forthcoming then sir?"

"No, he's not giving anything away at the moment. I'm not so sure he knows anything himself yet."

"Well, we'll find out soon enough no doubt. With your permission sir, I'll join the NCOs for a few minutes before I knock it on the head for the night?"

"Of course Max. I'll see you at the crack of dawn."

Max came to attention, saluted his company commander and left the hangar.

It was late in the evening now and the large hangar was empty and in the dim, even eerie, light, Paul looked about him. To his right were the parachute tables with the meticulously packed chutes. In front, in the distant cavernous space were three Luftwaffe fighters, three Messerschmitt bf 109s, in for repairs. Although not a forward airbase, it still fulfilled a minor role in the servicing and repair of damaged aircraft. To his left, two DFS 230 Gliders, used for training glider pilots. He gave an involuntary shiver as he had a flashback of the glider landing on top of the Eben Emael Fort, the flak speeding towards them and the thud as the glider hit the hard, grassy surface.

What would be expected of them over the next few days, he reflected. This time he was responsible for a full company, not just a single platoon. Would he be up to the task? He had to be. His men were dependent on him. Not just thirty this time, but nearly one hundred men. He turned around to face the tall hangar doors as the flashlight of a Luftwaffe airman disturbed him.

"Have you finished in here sir, so I can shut the doors?"

"Yes, I have, carry on."

Paul took one last look around, and then strode out through the doors to his billet.

CHAPTER SIX

In the twilight they boarded the twelve Junkers transport aircraft that would fly them to Plovdiv in in Bulgaria. The take-off was without incident. The first leg of the flight took them five hours and after a brief stopover in Austria to refuel, they continued the rest of their journey for a further five hours.

Paul bent his head down between his knees, feeling slightly nauseous, the fumes from the engines, the cramped conditions and the constant buffeting for the last hour of this second leg were having their effect.

"You ok sir?" asked Max, gripping Paul's shoulder

"I'm fine Max, I shouldn't have eaten during the stop over."

"Just keep your head down sir and breath nice and shallow."

All were relieved when the journey was over. The paratroopers were exhausted. Although they had been sat down through the entire journey, apart from a sixty minute stretch during the stopover in Austria, ten hours crammed together on a droning transport was far from pleasurable.

The next day they were off again, transferring from Plovdiv to a former British airfield in Larisa, Greece. The co-pilot came back and warned Paul that they were on the final approach to the airfield and would be on the ground in the next ten minutes. Paul thanked him and leant towards Max, sat opposite him, who was shouting something.

"We'll know what it's all about soon sir."

"It all comes to those that wait Max," he responded.

Then to himself, "Whatever it is, it will be coming our way soon."

They landed and the plane taxied to the end of the runway, along one of the taxiways and onto a concrete apron where they were able to disembark. The planes came to a halt and the relieved paratroopers clambered down through the now open door at the rear of the plane, sucking in the fresh as they did so. Max stretched his arms above his head, rolling his burly shoulders, easing the tension in his rock like form. His five feet ten frame ached just about everywhere you could imagine. Paul, with his extra ten centimetres had fared equally badly.

"Thank God we didn't have to jump straight after that lot."

"That's why they made Tante June so small Max, to encourage us to leave when we get over the target," said Paul smiling.

"What now then sir?"

"One of the ground crew informed me we have that row of tents over there," said Paul pointing to a string of eight man tents.

"Nice and cosy, eh sir? Looks like there are a couple of battalions here already," said Max looking at the one hundred or more tents in lines close to theirs.

"Get the men allocated to their billets Max, and see if you can suss out the messing facilities while I go and find Regimental HQ."

"Meet up with you in the canteen afterwards sir?"

"Sounds good Max."

"I'd like to do a final equipment check afterwards sir."

"Don't you trust our Luftwaffe ground crew?"

"They don't know their arse from their elbow that lot sir."

"Very succinctly put Max. We'll get on to it as soon as we've eaten."

"You never know what's coming sir."

"What would I do without you, Feldwebel Grun?" said Paul patting him on his arm.

"You need never find out sir," he replied smiling.

Paul was about to walk away but stop and turned. "Oh and make sure the platoon commanders and Unterfeldwebel's join us as well."

"Will do sir."

Max headed over to the row of pitched tents allocated to their company and could see the men were already making themselves comfortable.

Paul headed along a different row of tents, all neatly laid out in typical military fashion. He looked about him as he walked in between the rows and could see that all the soldiers in and around the tented compound were Fallschirmjager. It had all the makings of a large airborne operation in the offing.

The sentry, in full combat gear, his Kar 98K at the ready, stood to attention in front of the large tent as Paul approached the Regimental Command Post. He returned the paratroopers salute and bent down to enter what was more of a marquee than a tent. As he pushed his body through the flaps of the entrance, a fog of smoke and fetid air met him. A smoky layer hovered in the upper parts of the tent, swirling around the three suspended lights providing a limited, but warm glow.

He pulled the tent flaps back together. Although fairly mild outside, it was warmer still inside the HQ. He looked about him attempting to identify the occupants. To his left was a six foot, wooden, fold up table supporting various pieces of radio communications equipment manned by two Fallschirmjager signallers. To his right a second table covered in various maps, some fostering military markings, showing positions of friendly and enemy troops. At the far end a smaller table, with three compact, plain wooden chairs around it. Two were occupied. In one sat, Volkman, his battalion commander. The hooded eyes and slightly bent nose making him look very much like his nickname, The Raven.

He made his way to the table and was met halfway by his commander, who had seen him enter.

"Oberleutnant Brand, glad you could join us," he said returning Paul's salute.

"How did you get here so quickly sir?"

"Compliments of our fly boys Brand, and a two seat fighter. But, to business." The Raven was well known for his lack of small talk, but his approach to his job could not be faulted.

The Raven turned to his left and spoke to one of the officers, who looking at the maps fanned out across the table, turned to face them.

"Ah, the famous Oberleutnant Brand. Herr Oberst, we are in first rate company this evening."

The Regimental Adjutant, Major Fuchs, tapped his commander on the shoulder and the Oberst also turned to face the group. In his early forties and barely five foot six, with thinning fair hair, Paul towered above him. Paul again went to salute, but Egger grabbed his hand and just shook it.

"Good to meet you at last Brand."

"And welcome to the fold," added Fuchs. "Hauptman Volkman has volunteered your company to assist us with a small problem."

"What do you require of us sir?"

Egger turned back to the map table, pulling Paul with him, joined by Fuchs and Volkman. He pointed to the map uppermost on the table.

"The Isthmus of Corinth Brand, we have to secure it, so our panzer troops can quickly cross."

Fuchs continued the brief. "The Corinth Canal runs from north to south and divides the Peloponnese from the Greek mainland. There is only one road bridge crossing this obstacle. And believe me, it is a formidable obstacle with a sheer cliff on both sides."

"You want my company in support sir?"

"Yes," interrupted the Raven. "Do you mind sir?" He said looking at Egger.

"Please Gunther, continue."

"The Oberst wants your company to cover their backs. The main assault will be by glider on the approaches to the bridge on both sides of the gorge. A parachute drop will to do the mopping up afterwards. What we want your men to do Brand, is two fold. First secure the southern flank and secondly command the high ground."

"Where will we be dropping sir, and will it be gliders or chutes?"

"It will be a silk drop Brand and it will be here on this high ground west of Kavos. It's about two to three kilometres west from the coast. You'll be dropped about five minutes after the main glider assault goes in, we don't want to give the enemy early warning of our intentions."

"My full company sir?"

"Yes. We don't anticipate the high ground being occupied, but there are some one thousand plus troops in the area, so they may quickly move to secure it, to bring fire down on the assault."

"But no heroics Brand," added Fuchs. "Just attack and secure your target. Make a few probes towards the canal to keep the enemy occupied and on their toes, but don't follow through with a full assault. Back off and dig in."

"We don't want you getting mixed up with the follow up forces and we end up shooting at each other," interjected Egger.

"Is there an exit route sir, should the main attack be unsuccessful?"

"It won't fail Brand," interjected Fuchs, "but if it should, then we will attempt an extraction by sea."

"Do you have a problem with any of this Brand?" asked Egger.

Volkman jumped in. "He's part of my battalion sir."

"Is there anything you need?" checked Fuchs.

"Nothing sir," responded Paul, still reeling from the enormity of the mission being thrust upon him and his men. "Just access to maps, ammunition and supplies. Oh, and somewhere for my men to prepare."

"Have you brought your own chutes with you?" asked Fuchs.

"Yes sir, parachutes, weapons and weapons canisters."

"Excellent. There is a building west of the airfield you can use as your base. I shall have someone show you. Make sure you give them a list of your ammunition and supply requirements."

There was a sudden drone of aircraft overhead.

"More aircraft arriving by the sound of it," observed Volkman.

"How many so far?" Egger asked Fuchs.

"We have two thirds here already sir, another one hundred and thirty will be arriving the rest of this evening and tomorrow."

"When is the jump off sir?" questioned Paul, keen to glean as much information as possible and then get his unit ready.

"The main drop is at oh seven hundred the day after tomorrow."

Paul did a quick calculation in his head. That meant the morning of the twenty seventh of April, which gave him and his men a full day to prepare.

"Your men will drop five minutes later."

"You will be allocated fifteen Ju 52s for your men and equipment. Once you've been informed of which ones, it will be up to you to liaise with the flight commander, understood?" continued Fuchs.

"Yes sir."

Paul turned to his battalion commander, "is the rest of the battalion taking part sir?"

"They will be joining us in a few days, but you are on your own for this one."

"Right," interrupted the Regimental Commander. "If you've no more questions gentlemen, I need to focus on other elements of the operation."

It was a gentle dismissal and Volkman and Paul saluted and the

Raven escorted him to the entrance of the HQ.

"Sorry to drop this one on you Brand, but you have the most experienced company and you will be the representatives of the battalion so I can't afford any cock ups."

"My men will welcome some action sir. They were getting pretty bored back at the barracks.

"They may think differently when they hit the ground," suggested the Raven. "Go and get your men ready."

Paul saluted and left the HQ, his mind already swirling with the myriad of tasks he had ahead of him to prepare for the drop in less than two days.

CHAPTER SEVEN

The men were lined up, the engines of the Junker 52's throbbing behind them. Paul didn't give a speech; he had spent the previous day with his men as they were all preparing for today's assault. He had probably spoken to most of them individually at some point. He had gone through the plans in detail with his three platoon commanders. After numerous troop, platoon and a full company exercise, Paul, Max, Roth, Nadel and Leeb were satisfied that they were ready. The men were grouped into their flights, which equated to one troop per aircraft, the rest of the transports carrying their weapon canisters. Paul approached each troop, wishing them luck, finishing with a final confab with his officers and Max.

"Well this is it gentlemen, we embark in five minutes, time check."

They all looked at their watches and synchronised the time with their commander, it was five minutes past five, and they were due to parachute drop in just over two hours.

"Leeb, your men must get their weapons from the canisters quickly and run like hell to secure the slope to the north east. We won't have the cloak of darkness when we land, so speed is of the essence."

"Yes Herr Oberleutnant."

They had been over and over it the previous day, but Paul had learnt that you could never be too well prepared and they hadn't exactly had a great deal of time to absorb their mission requirements.

"Nadel, your platoon will have to gather the weapons containers sharpish and group them on Leeb's position, we may well need that ammunition."

"Jawohl Herr Oberleutnant."

"Roth, your three troops will be responsible for our immediate security and they must recce west, south and east. But, keep your men within two hundred and fifty metres of our landing spot. I don't want us spread to the four winds if we get bounced."

"Understood sir."

"Max, I want you with Leeb's platoon and I'll stay with Nadel until I know what our next steps will be."

"Sir."

Paul noticed one of the Luftwaffe ground crew nervously trying to attract his attention, the engines now shut down ready for embarkation.

"They're ready for us sir."

"Right, let's go."

The paratroopers made their way towards their respective aircraft and Paul gripped Max's arm.

"See you on the ground Feldwebel Grun."

"I've no other plans sir," he said grinning from ear to ear.

Paul smiled back at Max's infectious grin.

Paul made his way towards his assigned aircraft and joined Leeb's first troop. Max would be on a different plane. The rest of the officers would also be dispersed around the fleet, ensuring that command was spread throughout the flotilla should they encounter heavy fire and lose some of the planes. In the distance, Paul could see some fighter planes lifting off, rapidly climbing and disappearing into the blackness of the still early morning, the roar of their engines quickly drowned out by the huge flotilla of the first wave of Ju 52s following behind them.

Paul stood at the side of the access door to the belly of the aircraft, loaning them the use of his arm for support as they clambered up the metal ladder.

"Thanks for organising this little jaunt just for us sir." Stumme was heard to say as he heaved himself up into the guts of the plane.

"Don't thank me just yet Oberjager Stumme, you haven't seen the scenery yet," responded Paul. He sensed a presence behind him.

"Anyway Stumme, you're responsible for refreshments on this trip," shouted Max after the paratrooper.

"Jawohl Herr Feldwebel."

Stumme was then the target of ribaldry from the rest of the troop.

Paul twisted his head around, Max had come by to give his final report.

"All well Max?"

"Yes sir, my troop will be loading shortly, they'll be the last ones to board."

The last trooper to board Paul's plane was Fessman, a close friend of Stumme.

Paul turned to Max and gripped his hand.

"I'll see you on the ground Max. You keep that unsightly head of yours down, I don't want to have to run the company on my own."

"At least I don't stand out above the crowd sir," he said laughing referring to his commander's lanky height. Max turned around and walked away and Paul took his turn to heave his body into the aircraft, aided by Fessman. He looked around the darkened interior and took his seat opposite the doorway.

"All in sir?" asked the Absetzer, the Dispatcher.

"Yes, seal her up Unterfeldwebel."

The Dispatcher closed the door immediately, shutting out some of the din from the three throbbing BMW engines and the noise of the other fourteen Junkers that had restarted and were warming up their engines for the departure.

"Make yourself comfortable sir, it's going to be a bumpy two hour ride."

"No entertainment Absetzer?" asked Fessman, who was sat on Paul's right.

"You men will have all the entertainment you want when you hit the deck, we don't want to overload you now, do we?" he said smiling. The Unterfeldwebel was obviously an experienced Dispatcher and knew how to handle the boisterous Fallschirmjager.

"You're the men from the Eben Emael escapade aren't you?" he shouted over the excessive noise as the engines revved to full throttle. Paul blushed slightly, at being recognised for their past exploit.

"I thought we'd travel in style this time," he shouted back.

The comms handset buzzed and he turned to pick it up. He spoke into the hand set. "Yes, yes." He then turned to Paul. "We're off now sir, we'll do one circuit of the airfield then head straight for the target."

The message was passed down the line and the troopers made last minute adjustments before they set off.

Looking through the window, diagonally opposite, Paul could see they were manoeuvring from the apron onto the runway. They were passing a JU 52 on their left and looking over his right shoulder he could see one on their right.

Once in the air, the three aircraft would fly in an arrow formation, with five further kettes behind them.

"Where is the donnerbalken, thunder-beam, on this taxi Unterfeld?" hollered one of the paratroopers from the front.

"When we're at three thousand metres, I'll open the door and the entire landscape will be your latrine," he responded. The aircraft occupants burst in to laughter, easing some of the tension.

Paul felt his stomach drop as on reaching take off speed the pilot wrenched the stick back and the lumbering plane lifted off leaving the runway behind. After a few moments the pilot banked the plane to the left to complete a circuit of the airfield allowing the remaining aircraft to take off and form the chain that would fly to the target. Once completed, the fifteen aircraft settled down to a steady drone at three thousand metres at a speed of one hundred and eighty kilometres an hour.

A trooper at the front burst into song and after a couple of seconds the entire troop was singing a traditional unit song.

"Trup zwei! drei! vier!

Hinter den Bergen Strahlet die Sonne

Glühen die Gipfel so rot...."

They sang it through to the end. Then it was just silence, just the steady rumble of the engines and the wind rush through the thin metal skin, leaving each individual to his own thoughts.

Paul also drifted into his own world. Fighting to keep the rising doubts that often fought their way to the surface just before going in to battle. Had he done enough preparation? Would his tactics prove to be right? Would he lead his men bravely and successfully?

He was brought back to reality with a shake from the Absetzer.

"We're ten minutes out sir."

The flight time had passed relatively quickly. Next they were given a five minute warning. The two hour flight was nearly over.

They had flown over the Pindus Mountains and were now dropping down to only fifty metres above the Gulf of Corinth making a beeline towards their objective. There was a haze covering the gulf which would help to cover their approach, although they could be heard and the glider assault ten minutes earlier would be warning enough that all was not well.

"Ready," shouted the Absetzer.

The paratroopers stood up as one and turned to face the doorway.

"Hook up."

They took the static line from between their teeth, held there so their hands were free to hang on should the plane be buffeted by a strong gust of wind or anti-aircraft fire, and hooked it onto the central cable.

"This is it sir," called Fessman from behind him.

The dispatcher yanked open the door and a blast of wind tore through the aircraft causing those near the hatch to squint. The Unterfeld held up two fingers indicating two minutes. Then one minute. On the other two aircraft, part of Paul's Kette, the same thing would be happening. Almost all of first platoon would land on the ground at the same time, along with up to ten weapons canisters.

Paul was called forward; he would be the first to leave the plane. He shuffled closer to the doorway, the wind taking his breath away, grabbing the two handles ready to launch himself forwards.

"Geh. Geh. Geh. Go. Go. Go."

Paul launched himself from the security of the metal box, his safety net for the last two hours, followed seconds later by one of his men. He was whipped sideways as he exited the plane and plummeted downwards. The static line snatched the chute out of its bag, successfully deploying his parachute, yanking him backwards as the chute filled out gripping the air. The drag on the shoulders was vastly reduced, thought Paul, since they had replaced the older model.

His thoughts quickly ran through a checklist. Looking up to confirm his chute had fully deployed, noting they weren't receiving any incoming anti-aircraft fire and as yet no small arms fire from the ground. He looked about him as best he could and was able to see that other parachutes were above him and paratroopers were now tumbling out of the second Kette. Terra firme was rapidly approaching, the scrub covered ground looking dark brown in the early morning light.

Thump.

He was down, sprawled on his hands and knees, his gloves and knee pads providing some protection. He jumped up and quickly ran round his chute, collapsing it, releasing his harness and at the same time looking about him. He saw a weapons canister land close by and sprinted towards it. He would feel much happier with an MP40 in his hand, rather than just his pistol. He was lucky, the markings showing it to be the canister containing his personal weapon and ammunition. Other troopers were also approaching to collect their weapons.

He ripped open the top, grabbed the MP40 that was secured inside, along with a second MP40 and two Kar 98s. Fessman slid down beside him and quickly acquired a rifle, speed was of the essence. Paul grabbed ammunition and magazines and placed them in his pouches, which he had transferred from the inside to the outside of his tunic. He looked about him again. He could hear the crack of rifles in the distance, coming from the north east close to the bridge over the canal. The chain saw like buzz of an MG 34, indicating that the paratroopers at the bridge were laying down some heavy firepower.

Paul's men were on what could be deemed as a shallow hillock, the ground typical to the area. Hard, dry, dusty, interspersed with dry looking shrubs and the occasional olive or lemon tree. To the south the ground tapered away to an orchard of olive trees, while to the west it was fairly open. To the north, where they were headed, it dropped away more steeply to a tree line of more olive trees, separating the hillock from the outskirts of a small town or village.

Leeb joined them and knelt down, quickly followed by Max.

"One troop is already on their way sir, it's about five hundred metres," informed Leeb.

"Good, and the rest of the Company?"

"The full company is on the ground sir, Feldwebel Grun and I will join my platoon."

"Ok Leeb, I'll join you both shortly."

The officer and NCO shot off towards their objective. Two troopers from second platoon attached wheels to the weapons canister ready to transport it to the tree line, which Leeb's platoon was securing, consolidating their ammunition and supplies in one defendable location.

"Finished sir?"

"Yes, yes."

They too left the area, leaving Paul alone with his Signaller.

"I have comms with Regimental HQ sir," indicated the radio operator, part of his Company HQ. He grabbed the handset from him and spoke into the mouthpiece.

"All successfully down sir, over."

The tinny response could be barely heard. "Any enemy activity, over?"

"None sir, and we're moving into position now, over."

"Good, carry on Brand, out."

The conversation was short and sweet. Oberst Egger would be focussing on the taking of the bridge over the canal, not Paul's small sideshow. He handed the handset back to Bergmann.

"Let's go."

He leapt up and sprinted towards Leeb's position, Bergmann close on his heels, the canister with the radio in it rattling behind him. They both arrived at Leeb's position, breathing heavily, in part due to the exertion of running and part due to the adrenaline pumping blood through their veins. Leeb had two troops facing north above the tree line and one troop covering their rear in a semi-circular arc. This could be the company base, Paul thought.

He looked about him, feeling the coolness of the morning on his skin, but the sun was close to rising. It was all quiet apart from the shots in the distance, the cicada's symphony in the undergrowth and the occasional dog barking. To his front the ground gradually sloped away from them, the other side of the tree line showing the first of the dwellings they would have to patrol through later.

The light was brightening by the minute and he could see a number of square, white buildings, typical to this country, through the trees — whitewashed three times a year to keep their homes cool, the blue domes on top of some representing the sun and the sky. Further to the right, he could see what looked like a church, a small dome supported by four slim pillars on top of the main building. A good place to locate a spotter, thought Paul. The increasing light was definitely starting to give shape and definition to objects and he had an uneasy feeling that they would be badly exposed in the full light of day. He made the decision that he would move the unit down into the tree line, leaving a small force on top.

Ten minutes later he was joined by his remaining two platoon commanders, he gathered them and Max around him. With a stick he had found close by, he scraped a square into the gravelly surface, representing the hillock they were now on, placing a row of twigs to represent the tree line below them.

"Report."

"All of the weapons canisters have been secured sir, only one was damaged but the contents are ok," responded Nadel, his pale, but blackened face, looking even more pinched than normal.

"Leutnant Roth?"

"We've done a complete sweep sir and nothing. It's pretty desolate, except for a derelict building to the east." He placed a stone on the eastern part of Paul's ground plan.

"It is pretty exposed here sir."

"I concur Roth, hence we're going to move." He pointed at his layout. "North of the tree line, at the bottom of the slope we have the start of the outskirts of a small town," he said placing a number of small pebbles. "There is what looks like a church with a small tower, here about fifty metres into the town." He placed a larger, darker stone to represent it. "The south here, on the opposite slope, there looks to be an orchard of some sort."

"Probably an olive grove sir," suggested Max

"That is likely Feldwebel Grun. And to our west there seems to be some scattered habitation. So, this is what we're going to do gentlemen. Roth, you'll need to split your platoon. I want one troop dug in here."

"We'll be badly exposed sir," interrupted Roth, concern clearly etched on his face.

"I know Viktor, but we can't afford to let the enemy get the high ground and come in behind us."

"Understood sir."

"But you'll need a little more than shell scrapes Leutnant Roth," suggested Max.

"Agreed," Roth nodded. "The other two troops sir?"

"Send a troop to occupy the derelict building to the east," he pointed to the single stone placed there earlier. "That will be our fall-back position and where we'll exfil through. That's the route we'll take to join our forces in the main town, or down to the beach should we need to be extracted by sea."

"The final troop sir?"

"You'll need to split that troop into two sections, one patrol to the west and one to the east, understood?"

"Jawohl."

"Nadel, your platoon is to space itself out along the tree line, below. If there are any enemy forces based in the town, then it is likely they'll come from that direction to move us off the hillock, so be ready. Keep a three sixty watch though, in case they slip through Roth's patrols."

"Will we pull back through Leutnant Roth's position sir?"

"Yes Feldwebel, we'll collapse in on the tree line, before moving east along it then up to Roth's troop situated in the derelict building."

"The trigger sir?"

"A green flare," Paul said tapping the flare gun in the holster strapped to his side.

"Right, your platoon Leeb. I'll take a section forward to the church we can see in the town. We can man the tower and use it to keep a watch on our area of operations. You are to take the rest of the platoon on a fighting patrol through the town."

"How far in sir?"

Paul pulled a map from his pocket and spread it out in front of him and pointed to the town.

"Through to the far side, but don't go beyond that. There's a further drop this afternoon with the specific purpose of mopping up and we don't want to get entangled in that. I don't want casualties from friendly fire. But, we do need to make contact with the enemy, draw some of them away from the canal area."

"Will you stay with the tower team sir?"

"No, once I've had a chance I will join Leeb's platoon. That's also where I want you Feldwebel."

Max nodded.

"Right. Let's get to it," Paul ordered as he stood up. He

immediately crouched back down. "Listen." The men remained crouched, straining to pick up the sound that their commander could obviously hear.

"There," hissed Max, "I can just make out the drone, it's a Junker's flight coming in."

"It sounds like the next wave coming in to support the glider attack," added Leeb.

Paul stood up. "We need to go now, we need to start distracting the enemy."

The rest got up and headed for their respective platoons to carry out their orders.

CHAPTER EIGHT

The parched, brown hillock dropped down towards a tree line on the edge of what appeared to be an olive grove, interspersed with the odd lemon tree. Paul led the small section forward ahead of the main force, dropping down the side of the hillock eventually passing through the first of the olive trees. The section was made up of Uffz Forster, Obergerjager Herzog, followed by Petzel, Stumme and Fessman. All had fought with Paul before in Poland and Belgium.

They patrolled carefully through the olive grove, the trees bare, the olives having been picked clean during November and December, the narrow, wide spaced trunks offering little cover. Within minutes they were through to the other side and hit a stoned road running west to east, alongside, at irregular intervals, were a number of white washed houses. Opposite and slightly right another road ran north.

They looked left and right, it was clear. Paul indicated for two men to cross the road and secure the junction. Once they were in position, the rest stepped out of the cover of the grove and in a staggered formation, three on each side, they made their way down this new road. They moved further into the town, different shaped dwellings either side of them, their small, high windows making it difficult to see in.

"Keep back from the doorways," Paul hissed reminding them of their trade craft, that some appeared to have forgotten.

Fessman, the trooper on point, suddenly jumped, startled by a woman leaving her home through the front door of her house. His finger was a hair's breadth away from squeezing the trigger of his Kar 98K. The old woman, dressed in black with a shawl wrapped round her head and shoulders, saw the weapon pointing in her direction, screamed and ran back into the house slamming the door behind her, the sound of bolts being slid across could clearly be heard. Fessman looked back at the men behind him, shrugged his shoulders and grinned.

"I don't know who was more bloody scared, her or me."

"You're enough to scare anyone," muttered Stumme.

"Move out," called Forster, impatient to get his men moving again, conscious that his company commander was in attendance.

The section continued on, hearing an increase of gunfire in the distance, the recently landed Fallschirmjager clearly in action. The buzz saw resonation of an MG 34 adding to the cacophony of sound. They must have passed a dozen houses and as the road started to bend round to the right the church came into view on the right side of the stony road.

"Down, down," hissed Fessman.

The unit stopped and hunkered down, Paul ran forward in a crouch to see what the problem was. Fessman pointed to the soldier leaning against the front of the Church, facing away from them, smoking a cigarette, his Lee Enfield propped up against the wall. His Slouch hat indicating he was Australian Infantry, part of the British Commonwealth Forces. He was dressed in British tropical uniform, shorts with knee high socks. The church was situated on the corner of a junction, the soldier positioned a couple of metres from the corner.

"Can you handle him Fessman?"

"Of course sir," replied a disgruntled Fessman amused at the question as his commander had seen him in action taking out a sentry in Poland. "There's a road back there on the left sir," he said pointing back down the road they had patrolled down. "It will take me on a circuit and bring me to the corner without being seen."

"Ok, we'll cover you from here, do your stuff."

Fessman made his way backward slowly, not wanting his boots to scrape on the ground. Although the fire fight in the distance covered some noise, the scraping of a boot on the gravelled road would be quite distinctive. He left the bulk of his equipment with Stumme, all he needed was his knife and pistol.

"Found something for you to do at last?"

"Best man for the job Friedrich mate."

Stumme patted his shoulder as Fessman ran softly down the road, turning left, heading east. After he passed half a dozen houses there was a narrow passageway on his left, he darted down it until it brought him out on the road that dissected with the corner of the church. He turned left, moving more slowly now as he could see the T-junction at the end. He passed the last house and was now up against the Church's southern wall. He crept forward, running his right hand across the cool, flaking white washed side of the building, all was quiet.

Two metres from the corner, he sidled further forward, desperately trying to bring his breathing under control, sounding like a wind tunnel in his head, listening for any activity coming from the vicinity of the enemy soldier. There was the crump of an explosion in the distance, thank God for the firefight. He crossed himself. Although not a religious man, he thought it better not to take any chances.

He got to the corner and could see the Oberleutnant covering him and keeping his eye on the sentry. He was given the thumbs up; the soldier was still looking the other way. He crouched down and anxiously peered round the corner of the church wall. The soldier was still leaning against the wall, lighting up yet another cigarette, almost nonchalantly, oblivious to the German paratroopers close by. He placed his Luger P08 in its holster.

He peered around the corner once more; the soldier was at least two metres away. He wouldn't be able to creep right up to him; the crunch of grit beneath his boots was bound to give him away. He would be able to take a couple of steps and then would be reliant on speed and surprise. He didn't dwell on it any longer, slipping round the corner, gripping the knife he would use, tightly in his right hand.

He eased forwards, then froze as the soldier shuffled slightly, relighting his cigarette. He used this opportunity to move closer to the unsuspecting Australian and when within one metre he made his strike. Stepping forward onto his left foot, reaching round with his left hand, clamping the surprised Australian's mouth in one swift movement before the soldier could take a second drag on his cigarette, crushing his jaw preventing even the slightest sound from escaping. Sliding the blade between the base of his jaw and neck, pushing it through the soft flesh, blood running down the knife onto his hand, at the same time yanking him backwards and down onto the ground on top of him wrapping his legs round the soldiers thrashing limbs, gripping them like a vice, restricting his movements.

The thrashing accelerated as the soldier's panic escalated, his hands tearing at Fessman's in a last desperate attempt to pull them away, knowing that death was moments away. But it was too late, Fessman's kill was assured as the knife went deeper, severing the Carotid Artery, and slicing into the gristled oesophagus, extinguishing life.

The body went limp, a warm trickle of urine released by the dead body wetting Fessman's combat trousers, the smell as the bowels also evacuated making him gag. He pushed the now limp, but heavy corpse off him, extracting the knife that may be required at a later date, wiping it on the Allied soldiers tunic top.

He was joined by the rest of the section.

"Well done Fessman," whispered Paul grasping his shoulder. "You're getting to good at this."

"Glad to be of service sir, but I think it unlikely he is on his own."

The rest of the section covered the entrance to the church and the surrounding area as a couple of paratroopers dragged the body away from the doorway.

"Stumme," he hissed.

"Yes sir?" he responded joining his commander.

"Your turn. He probably has some friends in the tower. I want you to check it out. I'll be right behind you."

"What's the AI, Immediate Action, sir?"

"If there's just one of them, then take him out silently. If more than one then it will be both of us and it'll be pistols."

"Understood sir."

Stumme led the way, his Model 38, Sauer, drawn and in his right hand, his knife tucked into his belt ready. Paul had also drawn his Walther and was ready to support him. They made their way through the doorway beyond the pushed back, wooden double doors and entered the dim, cool interior of the church. Stumme waited, allowing his sight to adjust to the sudden dark interior, four metres above him the flat roof supported by decorative dark wooden arches.

They inched their way down the central aisle, ornate, wooden pews in neat rows either side of them, heading for the alter and the door that was located to its right, where they felt sure they would find the steps that would lead them to the tower. They reached the alter, beyond it the paraphernalia of objects associated with the locals religious beliefs, probably Christian Orthodox. An ornate wooden framework stood behind it, some three metres high, taking it close to the ceiling, religious paintings either side, a large two metre high cross stood in the centre. To the right, the door.

Paul nodded to Stumme, indicating that he should proceed through the door. The heavy wooden door was ajar and he carefully eased it open, praying that the hinges were well oiled, peering round it to the left. He indicated that all was clear and stepped silently through the doorway.

Paul followed finding himself in a narrow corridor, leading round to the left going behind the wall containing the religious idols. They both waited, allowing their eyes to adjust to the gloom inside. After less than a minute, but seeming longer, they were both able to see a faint light coming from the centre of this second wall, and what looked like concrete or stone steps leading upwards.

Paul tapped Stumme on his shoulder and they made their way up the steps, taking them one at a time and being careful how they placed their booted feet. Stumme leant back against the dusty wall edging round to the right as he slowly ascended, peering upwards as he went, his Luger gripped in his right hand, his left hand cupping the butt. After three full circuits of the upward winding steps the light had improved significantly and Stumme held up his hand and hissed to Paul.

"I can hear voices sir, sounds like two of them."

He acknowledged and they continued upwards, both gripping their pistols tighter as they went, their breathing laboured as the adrenaline kicked in, knowing now that it would be pistols and not a knife that would deal with the spotters above them. Stumme hesitated and called his commander forward pointing to the brightly lit exit right in front of them and the two soldiers leaning, chatting, on the parapet wall that encircled the tower.

There were four sides to the tower, the entrance where they stood and three sides, with a one and a half metre parapet wall closing them in, overlooking the town below. A supporting leg on each corner, holding up the dome above them. The two soldiers were directly opposite the entrance, one of them using binoculars, probably attempting to ascertain what was going on at the Canal.

"I don't know what's bloody keeping Davy, said the taller one, "he was only going for a piss."

"We'll give him five minutes, then you can go and look for him," said the other who was wearing a Lance Corporal Chevron on his sleeve.

"Probably chatting up some local bird," the other responded.

"Yeah, but with these Krauts about we'd better be sure."

Paul was about to indicate that he would take out the soldier on the left, the one closest to him, and Stumme the other, when the taller soldier turned to face them.

"I'm going to find the lazy... " He didn't finish his sentence. His mouth dropped open, his eyes widened as he saw the two helmeted, dusty German Paratroopers, pistols held out in front of them, looking back at him.

He grabbed for his rifle that was resting by his side up against the parapet, but Paul's pistol barked twice as he double tapped and two nine millimetre rounds stopped him in his tracks. One round hit him in the chest, the second his shoulder. The enemy was pushed back against the wall and then slumped to his knees, his hand clutching his chest as his heart failed him, pink froth forming at his mouth as he coughed, trying to clear his lungs and catch his breath as his lungs started to fail, falling forward on top of the Lee Enfield rifle he was so desperate to reach for.

The second Australian had even less time to react as Stumme's two, 7.6mm rounds, both hit him in the side of his chest as he turned, finished the soldier's life in seconds as he too collapsed to the ground.

The two paratroopers reacted quickly not allowing the killings to cloud their thoughts; there would be time for that later. They rushed forwards, moving any weapons out of reach and checking the two men for life. There was none. It was war, thought Paul, but somehow it didn't make the killing any easier.

"Let's drag them out of the way," he instructed Stumme. Paul grabbed the one he had shot, pulling his body into a corner of the tower, Stumme following suit.

"Someone was bound to have heard that sir."

72

"Possibly, there is so much going on out there that they may not suss where it came from," he replied placing the Walther back in its holster. Suddenly Forster crashed through the entrance, down on one knee, his MP 40 sweeping the area seeking out potential targets.

"A bit dramatic Uffz," he joked, grinning.

"That's how they do it in the movies sir," he said standing back up. "But it looks like we weren't needed. What now sir?"

"I'll take Fessman with me and we'll re-join the Platoon while you take command here. I suggest you leave two men at the door downstairs, or else," he said as he mimicked a knife blade across the throat.

"Yes sir, lesson learnt there I think," he replied as he looked about him at the two dead Australian soldiers.

Paul moved across the concrete floor of the tower to the parapet and looked out over at the flat roofed houses, some with orange, terracotta tiles, the relatively straight streets crisscrossing below.

The tower gave them a two hundred and seventy degree view, fortunately where they needed it, from the northwest to the southwest. He looked right and could just see the hillock. He pulled out his Zeiss binoculars from their dark brown, leather case and scanned the area. Paul could just make out Roth's troop digging in on the top, realising how exposed they were. Should they evacuate the church tower, they would have to move from the top of the hillock, an enemy spotter up here could bring down accurate artillery or mortar fire right on top of them. Their shallow trenches wouldn't be sufficient protection, he thought. Looking down he could make out the olive grove and the tree line where Nadel's men were set up, although he couldn't see them. When they pulled back through this position, moving east along the edge of the grove would provide them with good cover.

Sweeping the binoculars slightly left he could see the derelict buildings where the rest of Roth's platoon would be ensconced, giving them cover while they pulled back from the hill top. They too were well hidden.

He switched to the east, shielding the lenses from the sun that could clearly be seen on the horizon, preventing any glint from the lenses giving away their position. He could make out the coast, but wasn't high enough to get a good view of the canal where the battle was still in progress. He stuffed his binoculars back in their case and turned just as they were joined by two troopers who would take the first stint with their troop commander, Uffz Forster.

"We'll leave you to it. Any enemy movement, send a runner to look for us."

"Jawohl, Herr Oberleutnant."

"Let's go."

He made his way through the exit at the top of the stone steps, descending much quicker than when he came up, taking two steps at a time, a supporting hand on the right hand wall. He was followed by Fessman. They made their way back through the centre of the pews, Herzog alert at the entrance to the Church, Petzel obviously outside.

"All quiet?" asked Paul

"Yes sir, not a peep."

"Stay alert, it's only a matter of time before we get paid a visit."

They left the church, passing the crouched Petzel as they went. Turning right, they continued down the street, moving deeper into the town, seeking out Leeb and his men.

It didn't take long before they came across Leeb, Max and some of his men. They were at a T-junction. Straight ahead, the street lined with more block shaped dwellings took them to the far edge of the town, turning right would suck them deep into the centre.

"Sitrep Leeb."

"I've positioned a troop along the edge of town sir, just more bloody trees at the far end. I was leaving a half section here to cover any withdrawal and moving further into the town with Uffz Konrad's troop, see if we can't stir something up."

"Sounds good Ernst."

He briefed Max and Leeb on the situation back at the church, they then moved out.

CHAPTER NINE

They split the troop into two half sections and patrolled east along two parallel streets.

Paul led one along with Max and Leeb led the other supported by Konrad. They had been making their way slowly east, the occasional civilian venturing their head out of the door, but withdrawing it rapidly when they saw the soldiers. They must have made a pretty ferocious sight, thought Paul. Weapons on display, bandoliers of MG 34 ammunition around their necks, stick grenades stuck in their belts, their uniforms and faces covered in a film of dust and their hob nailed boots crunching on the gravelly surface. Paul was sweating, as were the rest of his men, from the exertion and the steadily increasing temperature.

He stopped his men, giving them the opportunity to quench their thirst.

Max came up to Paul and whispered, "as soon as we see a water source, we need to top these up sir."

"Agreed Max, it must be pushing twenty already."

"And will get warmer sir."

They continued their patrol. All was quiet until suddenly, from an alley, some fifty metres to their front right, half a dozen soldiers charged out, sliding to a halt when they found themselves confronted by the German paratroopers. Paul's men were quick to react. Paul and Max both dropped to one knee spraying the area in front of them with a hail of fire, aiming high to compensate for their low position. Two, 9mm parabellum rounds from Paul's machine pistol smashed into the Corporal leading, one ripping through his throat, immediately stifling the scream that was welling up, the second shattering his upper jaw, splintering teeth and bone, giving him an almost manic grin.

Max had been more successful, downing two soldiers, his thirty two round magazine quickly emptied. Muller, who had been on point, ran back under the covering fire of his Officer and NCO, throwing himself down beside them, his Kar 98 quickly brought into action. Kempf and Straube had been equally quick to react and were prone in seconds, the MG 34 up into Kempf's shoulder was soon inflicting death.

The Australian soldiers had not been idle and two, initially hidden behind their comrades' bodies in front, had also reacted quickly. A short, squat Sergeant had also dropped to his knee and his Sten gun vibrated in his hands as rounds hurtled towards the Fallschirmjager. Oberjager Halm took the full force of the bullets, three of them punching their way into his body as he was attempting to bring his Kar 98 into play. The second Australian, heavy jowled and angry, drew the pin from a Mills 36 grenade throwing the pineapple directly at the German soldiers. It was a mistake. Instead of either tossing it just behind the group of enemy soldiers, or holding on to the grenade for a couple of seconds before releasing it, he threw it immediately to their front, the seven second fuse giving Max ample time to scoop it up and throw it back, the subsequent explosion added to the rest of the cacophony of sound. The shrapnel from the grenade, small arms fire and the heavy calibre rounds from the MG, round after round ripping through the tightly packed soldiers broke their spirit as well as their bodies. It was over in what seemed like minutes to the paratroopers, but was in fact just seconds.

"Cease fire, cease fire," shouted Paul.

The firing stopped. The silence was almost eerie, even the firefight at the bridge failed to intrude. A cloud of gun smoke hung in the air and Paul could taste the tang of cordite on his tongue as he licked his dry lips. He looked up at the sun, shielding his eyes. He suddenly had an overwhelming thirst. Max moved first, his movements jarring Paul into action.

"Muller, Lanz, cover that alleyway. Kempf, keep the MG facing down the road. Renisch watch our backs."

Paul joined Max at the side of the badly wounded Halm. "I'll check the enemy, you look after him."

Leaving Max with Halm, he made is way over to the six soldiers, their bodies in disarray around the entrance to the alleyway they had shot out from.

"All clear?" Paul asked the two troopers standing watch.

"Yes sir, shall we scout further down?"

"Ok, but not too far. The company is pretty well dispersed as it is and this fire fight may well bring some of their friends our way."

Paul had kept a close eye on the allied soldiers as he was talking, now he checked them individually, kicking their weapons aside ensuring they were out of reach. The Corporal with the smashed face was dead, along with his comrade killed by Max's machine pistol, his vacant eyes staring up at him. The third had taken the full blast of the grenade, his uniform shredded, his bare arms, legs and face lacerated, he too was no longer alive. The remaining three, one slumped against a house, the whitewashed wall now stained with splashes of blood, already drying in the steadily rising heat of the day. The second was sprawled face down on the ground not moving while the remaining soldier was sat up gripping his shattered legs, groaning and rocking backwards and forwards. Paul doubted there was much he could do for him, but he would try.

He called Fessman over. "See what you can do for this one, I'll take the one by the wall."

Approaching the soldier slumped against the wall he could see that he was probably the least wounded of the lot. It looked as if he had been the Bren Gun handler and two rounds speeding their way towards him had ricocheted off the light machine gun, one smashing the stock, the heavy calibre rounds narrowly missing him. But he was not so lucky with the 9mm round which had clipped his shoulder.

Paul loosened off the soldier's webbing, using his gravity knife to cut some of it away along with parts of his kaki shirt, exposing a small, bluish, ring shaped hole welling up with dark blood. The soldier winced as Paul felt round the back of the wound, although the injury was still numb, the worst of the pain was yet to come, retrieving his hand sticky with blood.

"You're lucky," he said to the pale faced soldier, the makings of an eleven o'clock shadow starting to show. "The bullet has gone straight through, it'll mend in no time."

He clearly didn't speak German, so Paul held his right thumb and the soldier nodded. He found a first aid bandage amongst the soldier's things, an item carried by all professional soldiers. He tore at the brown hessian like packaging, revealing a large, layered wad of absorbent material, placing it against the wound, grabbing the soldier's left hand pressing it against the bandage to hold it in place while he wrapped the attached strapping around his body.

A piece of brick and white plaster was chipped from the wall above Paul's head as a .303 bullet smacked into it, followed by the thudding boots of Muller and Lanz heading back down the alley way towards them. They flung their bodies down beside Paul and the injured Australian, immediately returning fire down the alleyway at the advancing soldiers.

"How many?" called Paul.

"At least half a dozen sir, but definitely more following behind them," responded Muller in between shots he was still putting down.

Max rushed over to Paul. "I think it's time we got out of here sir."

"Yes, yes," he replied, his mind racing. "How's Halm?"

"Fucked sir. I doubt he'll make it through the day."

At that same moment, the rest of Leeb's troop, that had been patrolling parallel to Paul's position, joined them.

"Leeb." shouted Paul above the din.

Leeb loped over to join them.

"Sir?"

"I want a half section to cover our withdrawal, we'll be like a magnet for every unit in the immediate vicinity."

As he spoke, further up the road, two hundred metres to their east the advanced guard of a platoon came into view, quickly setting up a Bren Gun. They were now under attack from two sides.

"Shit, that decides it sir," Leeb exclaimed and called out to the paratroopers close by.

"Fessman, Renisch, grab Halm and take him back to the tree line, we'll cover you."

"Jawohl Leutnant," responded Fessman, grabbing his comrade and running towards the unconscious Halm.

"But keep your eyes peeled, they may well have infiltrated behind us," Max yelled after them.

Renisch heaved Halm up onto his shoulder in a fireman's lift while Fessman kept watch. They would have to take it in turns to carry him if they were to get back to the tree line in double quick time.

Leeb had set up a blocking force across the street, rounds ricocheting off the ground around him, kicking up flying chips of stone, one searing his cheek bare. He instinctively put his hand up to the gash, withdrawing it, seeing the blood, but not having the time to contemplate its severity.

Although the enemy had now set up a firing position down the far end of the street and were putting down some light fire, it was proving difficult for them as they identified that their own men were mixed in with the German soldiers.

"Let's go," he shouted to his men, "move now."

They ran down the street, Leeb's half section covering them, Leeb remaining with his men. They hit the T-junction where they had originally met up with Leeb and his troop and could see Halm being carried away in the distance.

"Max, set up an all-round defence here, I'll fire off the flare."

Max quickly organised the men. Eichel and Straube covering the street they had just come down with the MG 34, Lanz and Muller covering the northern approach, warned by Max to keep their eyes open for the rest of Leeb's platoon that would also be bugging out and heading in their direction once they saw the flare. Kuhn was covering the south, their next route of withdrawal.

With a Crack and whoosh, the green flare shot up into the sky climbing high above the town's flat, white and orange tiled roofs.

Within minutes of Max's men settling into position, Leeb's half section came pounding down the street, having completed their task of delaying the enemy. They tore passed Kempf calling, "They're right behind us."

Paul called Leeb over. "Continue south, meet up with the men at the Church if they're still in situ. We'll collapse back on you, make sure the junction beyond is covered."

"Jawohl."

He called his men together and they set off at a pace, south.

The MG 34, the butt pulled tight into Kempf's shoulder, kicked off, rounds hurtling towards the enemy, the sound deafening in the narrow street, the ammunition belt running through Lanz's fingers as he guided the belt into the receiver and top cover. The Allied soldiers went down, some to avoid the hail of steel coming towards them, some because they had been too slow and the heavy slugs had smashed into them. One, although dead, was still convulsing on the floor, his confused nervous system smashed by the bullet that had torn through them, was still sending signals to his limbs.

"They'll be on top of us in a minute," yelled Kempf, intermittently spraying the area to his front with bullets. Max joined them to add his support, immediately joined by Paul.

"As soon as Jordan's lot get here we bug out," shouted Paul above the ever increasing noise of gunfire. "How long can you hold them off?"

"We're ok for ammunition," Kempf responded. "But they only have to chuck a couple of grenades and rush us and it'll all be over." As if to make the point, half a dozen rounds ripped into the plastered wall Max was crouched against, leaving a row of jagged holes where his head had been moments ago.

"Shit, that was close. That sounded like an LMG," he said brushing bits of white encrusted plaster off his arms. "They'll start to outflank us. We need to move again soon sir."

"We'll wait a while longer Max, I want Jordan and his men back in the fold first."

No sooner had he finished saying it, than they heard the booted feet of Jordan's troop even before they could see them. The men had run flat out from the northern edge of the town as soon as they had seen the flare, heading back to the T-junction where they had separated from the platoon.

"Not a moment too soon sir," hollered Max as the rate of fire steadily increased from the enemies lines.

"Kempf get ready to move. Lanz, get two grenades ready. Max, tell Jordan to take his men direct to the tree line and join Nadel."

Max was up and off as Paul produced two stick grenades, that were tucked into his belt.

"Ready?" called Paul to Lanz, not waiting for an answer as he unscrewed the base cap allowing the cord, and the porcelain ball attached to it, to fall out, doing the same to a second stick grenade. Just as Paul was about to give the command to throw, two grenades bounced down the street some forty metres away from them and he and Lanz threw themselves to the ground. The grenades exploded issuing forth a cloud of dense smoke, obviously a prelude to an attack.

"Now," screamed Paul, recognising that timing was now critical if they were to extract themselves from this alive. Pulling the cord that ran down the centre of the hollow, wooden handle and igniting the five second fuse, he got ready to throw it. Counting two seconds, he heaved the grenade as far as he could, quickly followed by Lanz. They hit the deck, immediately pulling the cord of their second grenade. Thirty metres down the street, the two grenades detonated and both were instantly back up on their feet throwing the second pair, the steel cans blasting the air apart seconds later.

A full section of ten allied soldiers had been storming down the street under cover of the dense smoke, the discharge from the first two grenades blowing them aside smashing them into the walls of the houses either side of the narrow street. The second pair adding to their injuries and disorientation, the wounded groaning as they lay stunned on the ground, their comrades too dazed to advance directly.

"Go, go, go," screamed Paul at his men.

"Come on, fucking move," added Max helping Kempf up off the floor with his MG. "Their back up will be following through any second now."

They sped down the street, picking up the men at the church on their way, skirmishing back in good order, always ready to put down a swathe of fire if the enemy got too close, not stopping until they joined their comrades situated in the tree line at the base of the hillock.

Paul grabbed Nadel's shoulder. "They'll be preoccupied for a while, but if they're platoon strength or above they'll be on our tail soon. Cover us while we withdraw to our extraction point, then pull back to join us. Make sure you move the men off the top quickly, they're bound to have spotters in the church by now."

Max interrupted them. "Halm's had it sir."

"Damn, well we're still taking him back with us."

"I've had them rig a stretcher with branches and a poncho."

"Right Nadel, we'll leave you to it."

They hurried along the tree line after Leeb had checked that his full platoon was in attendance. After about four hundred metres they found themselves directly opposite the derelict buildings, that would now be the company HQ and their extraction point. They climbed slowly upwards, challenged by one of Roth's men who had been put in position to watch out for their arrival. Within seconds he was in conference with his Platoon Commander.

"Show me your defence positions."

Roth led him on a tour of the building they had occupied. It could probably be classed as an abandoned building as opposed to a derelict one. The roof and the doors were secure and it was relatively dry. Although there was no glass in the windows they had been secured by shutters. It consisted of four rooms in an L shape, three at the front, the fourth on the north end at the rear, all the size of an average family room. Three rooms faced the west and Roth had stationed a paratrooper at each un-shuttered window, the window facing east in the wing room was also manned.

"Where is the 34?" demanded Paul.

"On the roof sir, with two other troopers covering them. I also have two men patrolling the perimeter."

"Excellent, once we've been in touch with HQ we'll know what to do next."

He moved across to one of the windows and the paratrooper stationed there acknowledged him and moved aside. He looked out across the top of the hillock and could see the troop that had earlier been dug in, moving north and down the hillside to join their Platoon Commander.

"Bergmann, contact HQ and get a sitrep."

"Jawohl, sir."

Paul felt a nudge, it was Max offering him his water bottle. He accepted it and gulped down mouthfuls of the tepid water, reminding him that he had a raging thirst.

Crump, crump, crump. Three explosions outside alerted the soldiers, each man flinching involuntarily as the explosions hit.

"What the hell was that?" exclaimed Roth and Max simultaneously. Paul turned round and joined by Roth, looked out of the window.

Three more rounds straddled the hilltop, throwing up debris and other fragments into the air.

"That's got to be a mortar sir, probably a British 3 inch," suggested Max.

The first rounds had bracketed the dug in positions, the second batch were practically on top of where the paratroopers had been positioned only minutes ago.

"They must have spotters in that church again sir," noted Roth.

"It's to be expected, but we couldn't leave any men there, they would only have been isolated and picked off. Max, I need to get in touch with HQ. I want Leeb's men in the tree line to the north opposite here and Nadel's platoon to the south. Once they suss out our position they may try and outflank us."

"Should we send a sortie towards the coast sir, just in case we have to evacuate by sea?"

"Good idea Max, send one of Nadel's troops, give Leeb's men a breather."

Max shot off to carry out his instructions. Paul turned to his radio operator.

"What do you have Bergmann?"

"The attack is progressing well sir. There will be another drop in about an hour for a further mop up. We have orders to hold until the drop and then exfiltrate through to Corinth and join up with the rest of the Regiment."

"Ok, follow me."

Paul exited through the only door of the building, facing the olive grove and the town beyond it, Bergmann close on his heels, bumping into the returning Feldwebel.

"All done sir."

"Come with me, I want to look over the positions myself."

They ran north down the shallow slope leading to the trees of the extended olive grove, some two hundred metres away, that ran the entire length of the side of the hillock from west to east. They found Leeb's platoon ensconced there, the Lieutenant leaning against the thin trunk of an olive tree, surveying the area in front. There wasn't much to see, but row upon row of staggered trees, in the otherwise seemingly well maintained grove.

The platoon commander, now with a bandage taped to the side of his face, informed them, "We're ready for them sir."

"How's the wound?"

"It's ok sir, looks worse than it is."

"Where are your men positioned?"

"I have all three troops along the edge of the grove sir," he indicated with the sweeping of his hand. "But with an MG on each flank, particularly back towards our starting position."

"Good, they'll probably take the same route we did so they don't expose themselves skirting the hill to get behind us."

"What's happening over there?" he said pointing towards the bridge and Corinth.

"It's going well, Ernst. We have the bridge and there will be another drop in an hour's time to mop up what's left."

"What are our orders sir?"

"We hold here until the battalion has landed then all being well we can exfiltrate back to Corinth."

"Do you think they will hit us here sir?" asked Max

"I think it likely. Although they need to concentrate on the main force, they won't like the idea of us being at their backs."

"A Battalion drop will focus their minds a little," added Leeb with a grin.

"Too true," said Paul pushing himself off the tree he had been leaning against. "I'll leave you to it Ernst, I want to look at the rest of our positions."

Paul, Max and Bergmann weaved in and out of the trees as they tracked their way along the edge of the grove heading east. Exiting at the end of it they were confronted by a shallow rise in front of them, paratroopers could be made out digging shell scrapes on the top of it. Max waved his hand and they acknowledged that they had seen them, the last thing they needed was getting shot at by their own side. They ran across the open terrain, skirting the southern point of the higher ground and after one hundred metres they turned south into another olive grove that ran from north to south along the eastern edge of the Company Headquarters. This time it was well interspersed with orange and lemon trees. They were immediately challenged by the paratroopers who were guarding the edge of the grove.

"Where's Lieutenant Nadel," called Max. The two paratroopers pointed back along the grove towards a group of men in obvious conversation. Nadel was talking to one of his troop commanders. They moved to join them.

"What's the situation?" asked Paul.

I've got one troop covering the far edge," he said pointing back to the high ground they had just passed. "I've put a half section on the top of the rise to give us early warning of an approaching enemy. Second Troop is interspersed along the edge of the tree line and Third Troop have just got back from patrolling towards the coast."

Paul turned to the Uffz he assumed had been in command of the patrol. "What did you see?"

The grove goes right up to a main road running right to left," he said pointing back towards the coast, "beyond that more trees, but as you come out of them there is a track running down to the sea."

"Excellent, well done Uffz, that's the route we'll take should we need to, or we could follow the road in," he said turning back to Max and Nadel.

"What's the bigger picture sir?"

"A Battalion drop in an hour sir." Max informed him.

"We should be able to hold them here for a while then," suggested Nadel."

"Not if they pinpoint us with artillery," corrected Paul.

"Have we any casualties so far?"

"Just Halm, unfortunately he didn't make it. I need to get back to HQ, send a runner if there's any change."

They left Nadel to it and headed up the slope back to their isolated, whitewashed HQ, one of Roth's men on the flat roof acknowledging their return, warning the rest of the platoon of their company commander's approach. They made their way round to the side of the building and in through the door of the first room, where Roth had set up a makeshift HQ. Bergmann immediately set up his radio, knowing Paul would be wanting an update. Paul waited until it appeared that Bergmann's conversation was over.

"Any change?"

"Nothing since the last transmission sir."

"Can I smell coffee?"

"Yes Feldwebel, over there."

Max could see a small stove propped on a pile of bricks, alongside it a steaming jug of coffee. He grabbed a mug from Paul's kit bag, sorted out his own and poured them both a hot, black cup of coffee.

"If you aren't hot now sir, you will be after drinking this, but you'll find it refreshing," he said handing Paul a mug of the steaming dark liquid.

Paul slung his MP 40 over his shoulder and cupped the mug in both hands, savouring the smell, taking a sip of the bitter tasting drink, making him shiver.

Max took a sip of his. "All we can do is wait now sir."

Paul looked at his watch. "Thirty minutes and they should be over their target," he mused.

"We've done our bit sir, time to let some of the others do some fighting," added Max wiping sweat off his brow with his tunic sleeve.

He put his half empty mug down on the floor and removed his helmet, in the vain attempt at trying to cool himself down in the stifling heat of the confined space. The heat had been steadily increasing throughout the day. It was now twelve thirty and the sun was close to its high point, they had been fighting and manoeuvring for five and half hours and Max was starting to feel it.

"Think they'll give us a breather after this jaunt sir?"

"It was only a few days ago Feldwebel Grun, that you were thinking about becoming a cook."

"Got to be flexible sir." They both laughed.

Roth looked over at the two Fallschirmjager. You wouldn't think they were in the middle of a battle listening to the two of them, he thought. He slightly envied the close camaraderie they obviously had. He had a good rapport with his platoon sergeant, Unterfeldwebel Kienitz. But then there was a bond between all Fallschirmjager, they were all of one family. But the bond between those two went beyond that, he thought. He had talked to Kienitz about it once, he had fought with them both. He too held them in high esteem. There was almost a hero worship amongst the company for the two men. Roth also aspired to be respected by his NCOs and his men and silently admitted to himself that he also looked up to these two soldiers. His thoughts were interrupted by the approaching Kienitz.

"All well out there Unterfeld?"

"At the moment sir, but I don't doubt they'll be seeking us out."

"They won't have far to look, there aren't many places we can hide."

There was a burst of laughter from across the room.

"They seem happy enough sir, so things can't be too bad."

"It seems that little perturbs our company commander Unterfeld, but we're also dependant on others, so let's go and check the lines again. The enemy could strike at any moment."

Five minutes after Roth and Kienitz had left to check the lines, a runner came charging in, coming to an abrupt halt in front of his company commander.

"There's movement to the south sir, Leutnant Roth sent me to tell you."

"Can you see how many?"

"Not when I left sir, but the Leutnant thought you should be told immediately."

"Lead on then, we'll follow. Feldwebel Grun, Bergmann with me."

The paratrooper scooted back outside, turned right heading down the gentle slope to the trees below, with Paul, Max and Bergmann close on his heels. Once at the bottom they turned south running along the edge towards the positions covering the southern defence line. Passing Nadel's platoon as they went, warning them of potential enemy movement on their right flank. They were met by Roth.

"What can you see?" asked Paul.

"There are some farm buildings on the other side of the tract of land in front of us sir, the enemy seem to be clearing the buildings."

They moved forward and crouched down beside some bushes, Roth's men prone either side of them.

"Probably making sure they have nothing behind them before they make an assault sir," suggested Max.

"How many?"

"At least a platoon sir," continued Roth, "maybe more. Kienitz felt sure he saw some tubes."

"If that bloody drop doesn't happen soon sir, we're going to be in a right pickle," interjected Max.

Paul scanned with his own binoculars across the buildings some three hundred metres to their front. A full platoon assault they could handle. Even with a full company assault they would struggle to dislodge them, especially if he brought more men to the line. But with mortars, that was a different ball game. They could pound them into submission along with smoke to cover their attack from the front and on the sides.

"How many men have you got here?"

"One troop sir, but eleven men won't be enough; I need another troop brought from HQ."

"Max, head back to HQ, get Leutnant Nadel to move one of his sections to HQ defence, then bring one of Leutnant Roth's troops here, pronto."

"Consider it done sir," replied Max shooting off back to HQ.

Within five minutes Max was back with Roth's number two troop, providing much needed reinforcements should the enemy press forward an attack.

Paul looked at his watch, it was five past one, the drop was late.

"Where the bloody hell are they," hissed Paul to himself, conscious that they could be facing a major assault soon, and possibly on more than one front.

"They'll be along any minute now sir," Max responded.

No sooner had the words left his mouth when Roth hissed, "listen."

They became silent, Max's hand cupped to his ear.

"There, listen, you can just hear them."

"Not a bloody moment too soon," uttered Max.

Within minutes the distant rumble grew into a steady drone and looking up they could see waves of aircraft approaching across the bay towards the dropping point.

"Where is the drop sir?"

"To the west of Corinth, then they'll sweep back to the bridge mopping up as they go."

"There," called Roth pointing upwards.

They looked up as plane after plane disgorged its load of paratroopers and weapons containers, covering the sky in a shower of floating canopies. The Allied soldiers would be in no doubt what was in store for them next. Rounds were being fired into the air in an effort to forestall the inevitable. Although the odd, unlucky paratrooper was hit, the majority made it to the ground safely. The bridge assault force and reinforcements to their east, this new battalion sized force to the west and Paul's company a thorn in their side to the south was slowly boxing the Allied troops in. The level of gunfire in the area of the landing zone escalated as this new force came to grips with the enemy pushing them back towards the canal they had earlier been retreating from. Paul again scanned the farm below, the buildings jumping into the lens as he centred on them. He could see the odd soldier darting from building to building, but could not see any preparations for an attack.

He turned to Bergmann, his constant shadow.

"Ask HQ for an update on the battle round Corinth, how it's progressing."

Bergmann contacted the radio operator at the other end, the metallic response barely audible.

"Well?" asked Paul.

Bergmann passed him the handset. "Hauptman Volkman wants to speak with you sir."

"Yes Herr Hauptman, over," Paul shouted down the mouthpiece.

"It's going well at our end Brand, what's your position, over?" A crackled response came over the airwaves.

"We're back at our original position sir, on the hillock. We've withdrawn from the town, over."

"We've taken quite a few prisoners Brand, you've been giving them quite a headache it seems, over."

"What's our next move sir, over?"

"I want you to do a sweep into the adjacent town, over."

"Any particular area sir, over?"

"The small town to your north, Isthmia. Come at it from the west, move straight through, then head for the canal. Watch out for friendly forces, over."

"Jawohl, Herr Hauptman, over."

"See you in Corinth Brand, out."

Paul gave the handset back to Bergmann and scanned the farm buildings again.

"See anything sir?"

"Nothing Roth, nothing. You?"

"No sir, not for the last five minutes. I think they may have pulled out."

"Position your additional troop to cover the farm, then join me at the HQ, we have a change of plan."

Paul jumped up and skirting the hill to the right, hastened along the edge of the trees, swapping remarks with the troopers covering their eastern flank, then back up to the HQ building.

"Enough exercise for you Bergmann?" said Paul grinning at his panting radio operator.

"Plenty sir, I'm sure they put lead weights in these radios."

Once inside the building he sent a runner for Leutnant Leeb. Max came over to him.

"Decision made sir?"

"Yes, we're moving out Max, I just need to go through the route with the Platoon Commanders."

They were joined moments later by Roth, Nadel was already in the building and Leeb joined them minutes later. A paratrooper dished out coffee to them all as they waited.

"Luxury," said Leeb as he joined the group and was also handed a coffee by the paratrooper fulfilling the role of waiter.

"Anyone can be uncomfortable if they so wish sir," added Max.

"To true, to true Feldwebel," he responded clapping Max's shoulder.

"Right listen in," called Paul to the group bringing them back to the purpose of the briefing. "We've got our marching orders, we're extracting from this position. We pull out in ten minutes, but will leave a platoon here to cover our withdrawal. You have the short straw I'm afraid Viktor," he said turning to Leutnant Roth. "You're men are familiar with this position so you can watch our back for us."

"Yes sir," replied Roth nodding his head gently, already thinking through the consequences of being the last platoon to pull out.

"Leeb."

"Yes sir?"

"Your platoon will take the lead. Move your men down to the tree line where we originally approached the town."

"We're going through the town again sir? Isn't there a chance they could be waiting for us?"

"We're going through the town but entering at a different point."

Paul pulled out the map and held it up against the wall and they all gathered around as he tracked their route.

"We're going to skirt the town to the west Ernst. Halfway along, further north than previously, we'll turn east going through the centre until we hit the main road then we'll turn north towards the canal."

"Is it all over then sir?" asked Nadel.

"Just about, but there could still be isolated pockets of enemy troops about, so keep your eyes peeled and your men alert. This is not the time to switch off, understood?" He looked at each of them in turn as they nodded their understanding. "Leutnant Nadel, your men will trail Leeb's platoon."

"Understood sir."

"Right, get your men ready, we move out shortly."

They left to carry out their instructions, but Paul pulled Max aside before he could exit the building.

"Sorry Max, but I want you to stay with Roth's platoon. They are the most inexperienced, so I want you there to bolster them up."

"That's ok sir, but the first ouzo is on you when we get to Corinth."

"You drive a hard bargain Max, but you win," he replied grasping the solid arm, which felt like steel beneath his grip, of his company sergeant and friend.

"Keep sharp sir and I'll see you in a couple of hours."

Paul turned on his heel and headed out to catch up with his two officers, checking all was well with Roth before he left. He took one last look at his temporary HQ. Looking down the slope he could see Nadel's platoon filing along the edge of the trees, getting in position behind Leeb's men so they were ready to pull out on his command. He shielded his eyes, looking at the glaring sun beating down on his men.

"I'll be glad to get this helmet off sir and swill down an ice cold beer," said Max who had come alongside.

"I think we all will Max, I think we all will. See you in Corinth."

He headed off, catching up with the lead platoon, passing two thirds of his company spaced out along the edge of the grove as he went.

Shortly he was alongside his lead platoon commander.

"Ready Ernst?"

"Yes sir," he replied adjusting his kit, tightening his helmet and balancing his MP 40 in the crook of his arm, "Unterfeld Eichel is checking the platoon now."

Paul turned to Nadel, "Dietrich?"

"Likewise sir, we're ready, Fischer has pulled the platoon into position."

"Good."

He turned to Leeb again. "Who is your lead troop?"

"Forster."

"And Fessman will lead the troop?"

"He's the best sniffer dog we've got sir."

"Agreed, but don't lean on him too much Ernst, the others need to learn the skills and share the risk of being on point."

"Understood sir."

"Right, let's head out, the sooner we get into Corinth the sooner we can finish this."

Leeb called softly to Fessman and Forster. "Move out."

Their equipment jangled as the platoon rose up from their crouching position, adjusted their weapons and concertinaed forwards. Leeb tucked himself in about a third of the way along from the head of the platoon, Paul slotting in at the head of Nadel's platoon.

They soon arrived at the tree line position where it all began and after Fessman had scouted forwards, giving the all clear, they crossed the road and started to move into the town, but heading further west to skirt the western edge, avoiding their original route and the church tower.

Halfway along the western edge, and on the instructions of their company commander, they turned east through the central thoroughfare passing through the urban sprawl. A patchwork of whitewashed houses either side of the street, some with whitewashed steps on the outside leading to the roof, others with potted plants outside their front doors. The units split, one file either side of the street, looking across at opposites sides, covering each other, checking the doors, windows and roofs for any sign of movement. Their fellow paratroopers doing the same for them.

Apart from the odd rifle shot and the occasional short burst of fire from an MP40, it was quiet. The streets were also quiet, the occupants choosing to stay indoors until whatever conflict was in progress outside of their homes petered out. Whoever the victor was, they could then continue their daily routines.

After about seven hundred metres, checking every junction carefully before they crossed over, they reached the main road and could look out onto the bay at the southern end of the canal. The sea looked blue, cool and inviting and more than one paratrooper licked his lips at the thought of a cold drink and a dip in the ocean.

Paul instigated a five minute break, sending out three scouting patrols, consisting of a pair of paratroopers in each. All came back with a negative report bar one, they had met up with elements of the battalion involved in the initial assault on the bridge. Paul was relieved, it meant they would have a relatively safe passage through to the bridge.

It was two pm, they had been patrolling for an hour. Roth's platoon and Max would be leaving their position now, tracing the route Paul and his men had just come. All being well, they would have an equally secure passage through the town.

He signalled that they were to move out, ordering Nadel to leave a half section to await Roth's men, warning them that there were friendlies in the area. They advanced north down the road, half the men on each side as they entered the thinly populated urban area again, meeting up with the platoon his scouts had come across earlier.

He conversed with the Platoon Commander.

"There may be the odd enemy soldier about sir," informed the Leutnant, "but they'll either be lost or wounded."

"The rest?"

"It's likely they've moved west sir, but we've still captured over a thousand prisoners."

"The bridge?"

"We took it ok sir, but it was later destroyed. We're not sure how. Could have been explosives missed by the engineers or a stray shell, we just don't know."

"So, were stranded for the moment?"

"The engineers are already on it sir, they'll have a bridge across in no time. Most of the infrastructure was intact."

"What's your role now?"

"We're just protecting this sector and were told to watch out for your men. I've already sent a runner to tell HQ that you are on your way in."

"Well, good luck Leutnant, we'll move back to the bridge then. I have a half section back there," said Paul pointing back the way they had just come, "waiting for my last platoon to come in, they should be with you in about an hour."

"We'll keep watch sir, and send them on their way."

Paul signalled for his men to move out and they continued northwest along the road, turning north and heading directly for the bridge.

They arrived some thirty minutes later. They found more Fallschirmjager and were directed to a makeshift regimental HQ, where they found Oberst Egger.

"Job well done Brand," he said shaking Paul's hand.

"What now sir?"

"You and your men take a breather, find a tavern somewhere and requisition some ice cold beers. Once the bridge is complete I'll have you moved out."

Paul thanked him, reassembled his company, or at least the two platoons with him, and moved towards Corinth, seeking a tavern as instructed. Not a difficult order to follow, thought Paul. They discovered the perfect location situated in a small square where they could easily be seen by his third platoon. The company was sprawled around the small tavern they had commandeered being served by a short, fat Greek waiter who was fussing around them as if they were long lost relatives, when Max's booming voice announced the missing platoon's arrival.

"If I remember rightly sir, you promised me a beer with an ouzo chaser," Max reminded him.

"Pull up a seat Feldwebel Grun and you will be served."

"Does that go for me too sir?" asked Roth.

"Of course Viktor, and I'm paying."

Both Roth and Max pulled up a seat and three beers were placed on the bistro table in front of the three grimy paratroopers, sweat marks streaking their blackened faces, hair dirty and wild now they had removed their helmets, and caked boots up on the table. They clinked glasses, took a gulp of the frothy beer and looked at each other and burst into laughter. They all had the same thought, surreal.

CHAPTER TEN

"Is there a problem with the mail Paul?"

"No Mama, the mail is fine."

"Then why haven't we heard from you?" said his mother rubbing his shoulder gently as he sat at the large kitchen breakfast table.

He had arrived late the previous evening. Once Corinth and the surrounding areas had been secured, his men were given an opportunity to rest, they were exhausted and welcomed the respite. Hauptman Volkman, his Battalion Commander, had joined the unit in Corinth and met with Paul and his officers to congratulate them on a successful mission. He also informed them of another much larger impending operation, Operation Merkur (Mercury) which would be the largest airborne operation ever conducted to date. They would be joined by the rest of the battalion shortly. He also informed them that the battalion was officially being given a special status and would be classed as a Divisional asset.

The one excellent piece of news though, was that Paul and his men had been allowed four days leave. Initially reluctant, Volkman had granted Paul leave to go to his home town, Brandenburg. He had managed to stow away on one of the regular flights to and from Germany, including Berlin. Although two days would be taken up in travel time at least he would have a day in which to go to Charlottenburg and see Christa. Usually your leave didn't start until you got to your home town, or leave destination, but with the upcoming operation it would not be possible.

"Paul?"

"Sorry Mama, what were you saying?"

"We've had no letters from you."

"I have been moving around Mama. I've written to you, but you probably won't get them until I've gone."

"That's not fair on the people left behind at home Paul."

"We're are at war, leave the boy alone," interjected his father, "it's not his fault. Anyway everything is in a state of change at the moment."

"What's changing Papa?"

"Rationing is getting worse Paul," interrupted his mother. "I've had real difficulty in getting your favourite ham."

"It tastes great Mama," responded Paul as he took a bite from a slice of the dark, rye bread inlaid with sunflower seeds, covered in a layer of Westphalian ham.

"We have ration cards now son," added his father. "I told you we're taking on too much, trying to fight with everybody."

"What's rationed Papa?"

"Foodstuffs mainly, but also clothing, leather goods, like shoes. Oh and soap would you believe?"

"It won't last," defended Paul.

"We're only allowed about two kilograms of flour and bread per person per week," his mother said placing a red ration coupon on the table for Paul to see.

"But we still have coffee thank god," exclaimed Paul, as he lifted his cup to take a sip of his morning coffee.

"But not for long, coffee is becoming increasingly difficult to get and we only get fifty grams of substitute coffee a week."

"Look at these," said his father as he threw some coins onto the wooden table.

Paul picked up one of the still spinning coins, tossing it gently in his open hand. "It's light, what is it made of?"

"Zinc, all coins are now made of Zinc."

"Why?"

"You missed the campaign while you were away, there has been a big drive to collect all scrap metal. We've even had to give them our iron railings."

"You're kidding papa, couldn't you have at least kept those back?" responded Paul, taking another bite into his now cheese covered rye bread. "Mmmm, this is good Mama."

His father leant towards him and almost whispered, "The penalty for holding anything back is death son, they announced it at the beginning of March when the campaign kicked off."

"I didn't realise we were so short of metals."

"That's why they're introducing these new coins, they're withdrawing all copper and aluminium coins from circulation."

"Your factory must use a lot of aluminium."

"It does and it's getting increasingly difficult to get hold of. At least the Fuhrer is bringing us out of the economic crisis we were in, I suppose, let's hope these wars don't push us back in to it."

"Enough of this despondency," chided his mother. "Leave the boy to eat, he's supposed to be on leave, resting. You've lost weight Paul, are they not feeding you in the Luftwaffe?"

"Of course they are Mama, but I don't get your cooking while I'm away."

She beamed at the compliment. "Well I shall feed you up while your here. Why can't you stay longer?"

"They have work for me, I must go back."

"When do you have to leave son?"

"Tomorrow night Papa. There is a Junkers going back to Greece and I have to be on it."

"It's not fair," said his mother, fussing around the table placing two boiled eggs in front of him. He cracked open the top of one, the white hard and the yolk soft, just how he liked them.

"So what are your plans son?"

"I'm going to try and see Christa today."

"A lift to the station then?"

"Please, that would be great. What's the city like?"

"Pretty much running along as normal, but the bombing raids have damaged parts of it."

"Have you had any attacks here?"

"No, but there is a public blackout in force and we have to have light proof curtains over the windows and door frames," he said pointing to the additional black curtain pulled back to the side.

"I noticed your car headlights were covered up."

"Yes, they have to be hooded and taped over. We're allowed a small strip of light, but you can't see anything with it."

"It's dangerous Paul," added his mother. "There are no street lights either."

"Your mother's right, you have to drive extremely careful out there. It's not easy for pedestrians either and there have been a few fatalities."

"What else do you want to eat?" asked his mother clearing away the now empty egg shells.

"I'm full Mama," he said rubbing his bloated stomach. "I can't eat another thing honestly."

"We need to go anyway," said his father, pushing his chair back and standing up.

Paul took the last bite of the open sandwich on his plate, not wanting to disappoint his mother, then he to stood up, hugging his mother and thanking her for breakfast. His father would drop him off at the station on his way to the factory where he worked.

After a brief journey, sharing a smoke filled coach with other soldiers and workers on their way into the city, Paul stepped off the train at Bahnhof Zoo, the main railway station in Berlin. On approaching the barrier a conductress, her black, uniform tunic, over a pale sweater, and her black trousers and side hat making her look almost military, checked his ticket, giving him a flirting smile as he passed. He walked out into the cool morning air, the temperature much lower than what he become accustomed to in Greece. He turned right onto the main thoroughfare, but quickly took another left down one of the smaller, less busy streets. People seemed to be going about their business as usual, but his uniform attracted regular glances.

He walked passed an anti-aircraft gun emplacement, seeming alien and out of place in a city such as Berlin. The coal scuttle helmeted soldiers practicing loading the 8.8cm gun, laughing and joking as they did, seeming not to have a care in the world. The NCO in charge brought them to attention and saluted Paul in deference to his rank, his medals also showing that he was very much a real soldier. Here he was teaching children, the Feldwebel thought as he looked at the young soldiers in his flock.

Next to the anti-aircraft gun was a Hitler Youth fire fighting squad, their child like faces donned with police helmets. They were dressed in Khaki uniforms, their triangular district badge showing they belong to the Charlottenburg district. One of the young fire-fighters sported the diamond shaped HJ-Feuerwehrabzeichen, showing he had qualified for the fire service.

The more Paul looked around him, the more he noticed how different things were from the norm. The kerbstones painted white, bands of white around the lampposts at the base and at head height, to guide both pedestrians and cars he surmised. He continued down Goethestrasse, turning right on Leibnizstrasse and left on to Schillerstrasse, his pace quickening as he got closer to his destination. He saw a street sign on the side wall of a building opposite, Krumme strasse, the street Christa lived in with her parents in a top floor apartment. Turning right, he headed for Bismarck strasse where he would cross over continuing on to the next section of Krumme strasse before arriving at Christa's home. Bismarck strasse was busy and while waiting to cross he looked over to his left and could see the Stadtische Oper, the Municipal Opera. The block shaped building with its pillared frontage, tall windows and pyramid shaped roof was impressive to look at and he noticed Elizabeth Grummer, a Soprano, was appearing there.

Paul crossed over, keeping to the left hand side, to the central reservation, a taxi tooting his horn, not in annoyance but in recognition of one of the Fatherland's soldiers. He took his eyes off the Opera house and crossed over to the far side turning right and heading for the crossroads where he would take a left into Krumme strasse again.

He sensed something was wrong almost immediately. The apartments and office buildings on either side seemed customary, but further down the street towards Christa's apartment it looked to have been taped off. He quickened his pace as he saw all was not well, mild panic setting in and a lump rising to his throat. The road ahead seemed blocked by debris and a number of uniformed personnel seemed to be milling around, sifting through the rubble strewn across the road.

It was then that he started to look up from the street ahead and at the apartment buildings on the right and what he saw shocked him. The five storey building that had initially looked normal on the outside, could now be clearly seen to be nothing more than a shell, a skeleton of bricks and glassless window frames, but it had no heart to it, no internal walls or floors, just a barely standing ghostly frame. He recognised Christa's parent's apartment, the balcony still in place where they had last sat together over a glass of wine watching the activity below, laughing and joking about the scurrying ants beneath them.

He looked back down as he neared the tape, and could see more clearly the civilian workers striving to clear some of the rubble to make way for vehicles. He bent down, lifting the tape as he made his way under it to the other side and approached one of the firemen who was picking his way through the remains dispersed across the road.

To Paul's right a uniformed man approached him calling, "Sorry sir, but you can't come over here, its not safe." Paul remained where he was on the unsafe side of the plastic tape.

"What happened?" he demanded.

"It was a bomb sir," replied the man, his uniform showing him to be in the Sicherheit u.Hilfsdienst, where he had been conscripted into one of the civil defence squads. "It was dropped by the English bombers last week, but the building is still unsafe and we haven't been unable to clear the road. So you must go back to the other side of the barrier sir."

"What happened to the occupants?" urged Paul

"They were killed sir, unfortunately no one survived."

"But the building is still standing," exclaimed Paul.

"But the inside of the building is gutted sir. It has completely collapsed, the roof caved in and along with the bomb took all the floors with it," he replied, wary of the hardened soldier in front of him.

"Did you know the occupants sir?" The civil defence conscript ran his fingers around his collar, the green insignia with Gothic 'SHD' collar patches bordered in green and white.

"Sir?" the conscript asked again, looking up at the young officer.

"All were killed you say?"

"Yes sir, we pulled all the bodies out, I mean...." His voice tapered off under the intense stare emanating from the troubled officer.

"Where were they taken?"

"To a local funeral home, but there will be a record of the deaths held at the Town Hall," he replied his nervousness dissipating as he observed the obvious pain in the young man's eyes.

"Where is the Town Hall please?" asked Paul softly, tears starting to well up in his eyes. He needed to get away, he didn't want all to see his pain. Deep down there was still hope.

"It's in Wilmersdorf."

"How far?"

"About ten minutes walk, or you could get a taxi."

"How do I get there?"

"That way sir," he said pointing to the north. "It's off Otto-Suhr-Allee."

Paul thanked him and stepped back under the tape and headed in the direction he had been given, but circumventing the blocked road. He walked blindly and apart from occasionally asking for directions he was oblivious to all around him, his tears running freely. His heart aching like nothing he had ever felt before. He got past the blocked street and headed west towards the Charlottenburg Town Hall. The Town Hall was un-mistakable, built in early nineteen hundred, its impressive three storey frontage towered overhead with its majestic central tower dominating the building.

He entered the Town Hall, seeking out the relevant register of deaths. The short, bespectacled official returned to the counter.

"I'm sorry Oberleutnant, but we can't seem to find anything under that name."

"Are you sure?" Demanded Paul

"Well… we're having one last check."

Paul's hopes soared. Maybe they hadn't been home at the time, or had been taken to hospital and since recovered.

A middle aged woman whispered into the officials ear and handed him a slip of paper, casting a look of sadness over Paul as she left. The deaths of Christa and her parents were confirmed. He stumbled out of the door and collapsed onto the edge of the kerb, his legs in the road, his head in his hands on his knees and he sobbed. He didn't notice the strange looks he was attracting from passers-by, had he seen them he wouldn't have cared. He didn't see the policeman who walked over to him but at the last minute veered off, changing his mind about disturbing the clearly upset soldier, deducing that he had discovered an unwelcome death in the family. He was also sure there was very little he could do to alleviate the pain the young man was obviously experiencing.

CHAPTER ELEVEN

Paul turned over on his wooden framed camp bed, his hands placed behind his head resting on the makeshift pillow of a rolled up tunic, staring up at the peaked roof of the tepee shaped, two man tent. His position as a Company Commander giving him the privilege of having the luxury abode to himself. At the moment it was more than a luxury, it gave him the solitude he desperately needed to mourn his loss.

His return home to collect his kitbag, the frantic fussing of his mother as she recognised that there was something seriously amiss with her son, the journey to the airport and the full day's flight to the airport at Corinth, were just like a dream, intertwined with the nightmare of losing Christa to the English bombers. To twist the knife in further and add to his pain, there had been mail waiting for him on his return, two of them from Christa, reinforcing her feelings for him and telling him of her joy at seeing him very soon. He had taken the letters from Max, who could see that his commanding officer, his friend, was distraught, and fled to his tent racked with grief as he tortured himself by reading the letters over and over again, written by someone who was no longer.

He knew he had to get up soon, although he felt drained from the long journey and a fitful sleep, probably not dropping of for more than a few minutes at any one time, the memory of what had happened shocking him every time he came around. If he didn't get up soon, Max would come looking for him as they needed to prepare the company for the upcoming mission, and as usual, Paul's unit would have a specific task to perform. Before he had left to go on leave, Volkman had informed him of the battalion's special status and independence from the Regiment going forward.

He had met with his Battalion Commander, now Major Volkman, having finally attained the rank that usually went with a battalion command, on his return. He remembered little of the conversation, experiencing a numbness that seemed to freeze his mind and fix his thoughts to nothing other than his loss. He knew he needed to shake himself out of this inattentiveness, he had men to command, he had a company to get ready for battle and he had Platoon Commanders looking to him for leadership, but the enthusiasm, the fire that normally lit up inside of him at the prospect of action just wasn't there.

He flung back the grey, thin, army blanket that was draped over his still dressed form and threw his legs over the edge, placing his head immediately between his knees as the nausea hit. Partly driven by his grief, but also because he hadn't eaten since the small meal his mother had pressed him to eat over thirty six hours ago.

It was now the thirtieth of April, only twenty days until the mammoth assault on Crete. Ten thousand troops, Fallschirmjager and Gebirgsjager mountain troops were destined to attack this long, thin Island, and although Paul's one hundred men were such a small part of the overall force, they would no doubt have a very important role to play.

"Coming in sir," called a voice from outside the tent, a voice Paul instantly recognised as belonging to Max.

The tent flap was thrust aside and Max's thickset form promptly filled what little room remained in the tent. A two man tent it may be, but it would be unenviable for anyone sharing such a small space with this huge NCO.

Paul looked up, his shoulders still slumped forwards and Max could see that he was still wearing his going out uniform and not his combats.

"We need to start getting ready for this operation sir, the platoon commanders are outside."

"Yes Max, I'll be there."

"Do you want a hand getting ready sir?"

"If I was a cripple, I might accept your help Feldwebel Grun," Paul snapped at his NCO. "But as I'm not I am more than capable of getting myself ready."

On seeing the hurt in his eyes as a result of the rebuke, he immediately regretted his retort. "Sorry Max, that was undeserved," he said softly, his voice barely audible. "I'll be along shortly, please leave me now."

"Ok sir." Max pushed the tent flap aside to leave the tent, but turned at the last second, just before he stepped outside. "I'm sorry for your loss sir, she was a wonderful lady. Whenever you need me sir, I'll be there for you." With that he quickly exited the tent.

Paul dressed clumsily on his own, no pattern to it, not the normal efficiency he applied to everything he did, but eventually managing to don his uniform for the day.

He pushed his way through the flap, it was seven am and the sun was above the horizon, already giving a taste of what the heat of the day held out for them all.

His men had remained stationed in Corinth after the battle for the bridge and were billeted at the airfield along with hundreds of other Fallschirmjager, their accommodation again tented and basic. The rest of the battalion were catching up with them, along with badly needed supplies. It would be good to see Helmut again, he thought, but not necessarily his exuberance. He wished he could see Erich, an even closer friend. He could talk to Max a little, Helmut at a push, but Erich, currently attached to the Regimental HQ, his location unknown at the moment, would be the person he could open up to, someone who would listen and understand.

He looked over to his right where there was a jumble of recently erected tents, the congestion making it difficult for the units to put them into the straight military lines that was their preference. Beyond them he could see his three platoon commanders gathered around Max. He presumed they would bombard him with questions about the operation, he also imagined they would have other questions about him, but knowing they would remain unasked and unanswered.

He headed over to them, threading his way in between the staggered rows of tents, some clothes draped on the guide ropes to dry in the steadily rising heat. Beyond he could see the busy airfield, a steady build up of Junkers transports.

It was a small airport, with a few small, scattered hangars, the odd single story terminal building and the two storey whitewashed control tower with a windowed second floor, now manned by Luftwaffe controllers. The rest of the space was swamped by military tents of all shapes and sizes. He needed to get this moment out of the way, but deep down he wanted to run away and hide, internalising his grief, shutting the rest of the world out.

They all came to attention and saluted as he approached.

"Good to have you back sir," said Roth.

"Thank you, an update please gentlemen."

"We're... sorry about your loss sir," informed Leeb his confidence as an officer having grown since the last battle.

"Thank you, Leutnant Leeb, you too," he said to Roth and Nadel, giving Max a knowing look that said I know you broke the news to them.

"But back to work, what's the status of your platoons?"

Nadel shifted his MP40 to the other shoulder freeing his right arm to point. "My platoon is accommodated just to the left of the temporary canteen sir. All are fit and Unterfeldwebel Fischer is going through a full kit check with them, tomorrow we plan to pack chutes, assuming we're jumping onto the target sir?"

"We'll know after tomorrow Dietrich, but assume we will until then, Ernst?"

"We're going through a kit inspection too sir, and parachute packing, but I'm one man down, Oberjager Halm."

"Yes, yes of course." Paul was silent for a moment before saying, "I've written to his family, not much of a consolation I know, when you have just lost a son."

"He wasn't married with children sir, that's the only consolation I suppose," interjected Max. "He was a good soldier and a good comrade."

They all nodded their assent.

"Roth?"

"My platoon have completed their checks sir and are in the process of packing chutes. There was a slot available in the hangars, so we jumped in so to speak."

Paul looked at them all, each in turn. "Don't work your men too hard, they need some time to wind down after the fight. They'll be

107

going into battle again in just over two weeks. I want them fresh and ready, understood?"

"Jawohl, Herr Oberleutnant," they all responded.

"Once we've had the briefing tomorrow, I want to pull in the troop Uffz's and platoon sergeants and go through our objective and run through the tactics."

"Do we know anything about the size of the operation or even the target sir?" asked Leeb, impatient as usual.

"Our Battalion Commander will reveal all tomorrow I'm sure. In the meantime, continue with what you're doing. Any replacement for Halm?" he asked turning to Leeb.

"No sir, and I doubt there'll be one before the big one."

Paul was suddenly silent, not thinking about the operation, not thinking of Christa, his mind vacant.

"Sir?" prompted Max.

He snapped out of his reverie, looking to see the expression of his officers watching him, concern on their faces.

"Carry on, we don't need to meet again until tomorrow's briefing, dismissed."

They saluted and went about their business leaving Paul and Max alone. The hum of vehicles in the distance and the regular drone of Junkers transport aircraft coming in to land filling in the silence.

"Keep me informed Max, but only if there is something significant, an issue that requires my attention. They're officers, they need to start thinking for themselves."

Max looked on concerned.

"Where will you be sir?"

"In my tent Max, I feel tired."

He looked at his commander's face, his usually tanned skin now pale, drawn, his shoulders clearly burdened with the strain of his grief.

"You had a bit of a journey yesterday, a few more hours kip will do you good sir," he saluted and marched off to join the rest of one company.

Paul was just about to head for his bunk, sleep being a luxury that wouldn't come, but at least he would be alone to mourn his loss, when he felt a hand placed gently on his shoulder.

"Here you are Paul."

He recognised the voice instantly as his comrade, Helmut. He turned to face his stocky friend, another friendly face that helped link him to the real world, the world that still existed outside of his grief. They shook hands, Helmut placing a hand either side of Paul's.

"It's good to see you Helmut, when did you get in?" he asked a smile flickering to his lips.

"My company flew in last night, the rest of the battalion will be joining us throughout the day. We're here for the big fight," he said grinning. But behind the grin there was a sadness. He too had met Christa and had seen the effect she'd had on his friend and the effect her loss was having now.

"Feldwebel Grun told me what happened, I'm sorry Paul, really, really sorry." They let go of each other's grasp and Paul looked down, the slump of his shoulders manifesting his grief. He felt like Atlas, the primordial Titan who supported the world on his shoulders.

"Thank you, but I'm still in denial Helmut. She can't be dead, look." He pulled out the recent letters that he received from her, written while she was still alive. "It's us who should have been killed, we're the soldiers, we're the ones that go into battle, not civilians, not women and children." The distress in his voice was obvious.

"I'm going to the canteen, come and have a coffee with me?"

"Thanks Helmut, but no. I'd like to be on my own for a while."

"Just one," he pleaded. "It would be good for us to talk and catch up on events. I want a rundown on proceedings here, an insight into the enemy we'll be up against. You've fought with them, it would help me and my men if we had an idea of their strengths and weaknesses. It would be good for you to talk."

Helmut clasped his arm, propelling him gently toward the canteen.

"Ok Helmut, just one, I know how greatly in need of food you are, so I'll play along with you for now," he said, a thin smile parting his lips, but the gesture failing to register on the rest of his face. Helmut laughed at the attempt by his friend to rib him over his eating habits and they continued in silence towards the canteen.

★★★

The hangar was not the usual size the Fallschirmjager were used to. It had not been built to hold military transport or fighter aircraft, but smaller civilian planes. There was a larger hangar elsewhere on the airfield, but that was occupied by other units that were steadily being flown in as part of a big military build-up.

A third of the hangar was set aside for the packing of parachutes and temporary makeshift tables had been set up for that purpose. Half of what was left was being used to store small arms ammunition and other essential supplies the unit would need if it was going to war yet again, the remaining area was being used for the battalion briefing that was soon to start.

The battalion staff had prepared the area for the briefing as best they could. They had appropriated the ubiquitous six foot wooden table and maps positioned against the hangar wall as a backdrop. Chairs and stools had been dragged in from various parts of the airfield and looking at some of the chairs, Paul suspected they had been commandeered from local houses. In fact he, along with Helmut, Commander of Fourth Company, Hoch of Third Company and Bauer of Headquarters Company, were sat in various styles of armchair. Alongside these were wooden seats, benches possibly from a church or chapel and behind an assortment of seating arrangements, including wooden pallets, empty ammunition cases and an assortment of other objects that could support a perched paratrooper.

In front of the assembly of cobbled together seating, shuffling bits of paper and aerial photographs, constantly cross checking with the maps behind him, was Hauptman Kurt Bach. Once the Raven had received his Majority, Bach's appointment as captain and second-in-command of the battalion was assured. The hangar echoed with the buzz of conversation. It was astonishing how talkative a collection of officers could be when placed in one room prior to a briefing, each one having an opinion of what was to happen and how they would personally recommend it was conducted. Assembled in the hangar were the twelve platoon officers from the four bayonet companies, the four company NCO's, Max being one of them, and the battalion clerks and other staff making last minute preparations.

Meinhard, who was sat at Paul's left, turned to him and whispered, "Sorry about your loss Paul. I'm speaking on behalf of the battalion as a whole. Everyone wanted to pass on their condolences, but we felt it would be better if it came from just one of us, then we'd leave you in peace. But we needed you to know that all our thoughts are with you."

"Thank you. I do appreciate everyone's understanding. It doesn't change what has happened, but your collective concern does help give me the strength to get through the day."

A burst of laughter came from the direction of the senior NCO's, Oberfeldwebel Schmidt, the battalion's most senior NCO, was at the centre of the group obviously giving the men around him a reason to laugh.

Helmut, sat on the other side of Paul, tapping the armchair he was sat in. "This is a bit of all right, I'll confiscate this after the briefing and have it moved to my tent," he said with a chuckle that caused those around him to look on.

"You'll be wanting a Harem next," hissed Meinhard leaning over Paul.

"We'll get one strapped in a tante June for you," added Manfred, sat on Helmut's right.

Paul couldn't help but smile and suspected that the ribbing of Helmut, although a regular event, was on this occasion partially for his benefit, an attempt to bring him back into the fold. The frivolity was interrupted by the loud snap of Oberfeldwebel Schmidt's clicking heels and his bellow.

"Shun!"

The assembled men rose up from their seated positions as one, stood to attention, their arms by their sides as Major Volkman made his way through the menagerie of furniture, his stick tapping his leg in time with his movement forward.

He kept them stood at attention longer than usual. When he arrived at the front of the assembled group, his hooded eyes surveyed the leaders of his Fallschirmjager battalion, the men he was dependant on to do his bidding in a time of war, picking out faces, holding eye contact for a brief second before moving his gaze on. He caught Paul's eye and for a fraction of a second his eyebrows knitted together as he could see the pain etched on the young officer's face.

"Stand easy," he said moving behind the table to join his Adjutant.

The paratroopers sat back down in their comfortable armchairs and the less comfortable stools and crates. The stick was placed on the table, everyone knowing that it would be back in the Raven's hand within seconds, probably without him realising he had ever put it down. It was said amongst the battalion, and even espoused by some senior officers in the Division, that he would rather lose an arm than his swagger stick.

"Gentlemen." He waited until he had their full attention before he continued. "It has been many weeks since the battalion has been together in one place." He moved around to the front of the table and perched on the edge. "We are here for a specific purpose, to support the capture of the Island of Crete."

There was a murmur amongst the group.

"Our special status given because we have proven our capabilities, our skills as soldiers, not just in training, but on the battlefield. Oberleutnant Brand and his men," all eyes turned towards Paul and his officers sat behind him, "in particular have recently distinguished themselves in battle for this very town. Captured enemy soldiers spoke of the terror they provoked amongst their army, operating behind their lines. It is through actions like that and men like you in this room, that we have been favoured by the powers to be selected for special tasks."

Paul's face reddened with the embarrassment of the compliment thrown his way and the back slapping of his comrades, the occasional good humoured jeer at them being selected for this unsought after praise from a man who rarely let slip acclaim. Volkman stood up and started to pace up and down the small space available to him, the assembled men tracking his movement.

"But... to the reason we are here today. Crete gentlemen, Crete is our target."

He paused and slowly turn to face them.

"Operation Merkur is the assault and complete domination of the island, the last Allied and Greek Army bastion in this immediate area. To expedite this assault we'll be bringing the largest airborne force ever, together to complete this task. Flieger Corps XI will be committed to this task, consisting of 7th Flieger Division, made up of FFR 1, 2 and 3, the Luftlande Sturmregiment and ourselves as an independent asset. The Division will also have an artillery, anti-tank, machine gun and combat engineer battalion in support."

He was off on his pacing again, placing his stick on the table and walking away with his hands clasped behind his back only to pick it up on his return leg.

"We will also have our mountain climbing comrades," he said with a smile. "But rather than climbing mountains they will be shipped in a Tante June." This brought a laugh from the group. "The 5th Gebirgs Division brings with them three infantry regiments and an artillery regiment, so you see, a significant force to carry out the task in hand."

He turned to Bach and nodded, moving away from the table, allowing his number two to come to the front. Bach, who had been resting his hands on the table, leaning forward listening intently to his commander's briefing, even though he knew the events that were to unfold, stood up and came round.

"We mustn't forget our fly boys of course. We have at our disposal from Flieger Corps VIII, three Sturzkampfgeschwader with Stuka dive bombers, Kampfgeschwader 2, with Dornier twin engined bombers, Lehrgeschwader 1, with Heinkel twin engined bombers, Zerstorergeschwader 26, with twin engined, Messerschmitt fighter bombers, Jagdeschwader 77, with Messerschmitt fighters and four Geschwader of transports, three of Junkers and one of Gliders."

"Thank you Kurt," Volkman picked up the reins again. "The Fallschirmjager will spearhead the attack." He walked to the map behind the table tapping the western end of the island with his stick. "We only have five hundred transports, so a drop of six thousand is all we can manage in one hit. So, we will initiate four drops on Day 1, Maleme and Hania in the morning and in the afternoon the airfields around Rethymnon and Heraklion."

He stopped to drink a glass of water that had been placed on the table for him by his orderly before continuing. "Group West, consisting of the Luftlandesturmregiment will be in the first wave, their target to secure Maleme airfield. They have all of the glider force gentlemen, so there will be none for us on this occasion," he said looking round the room.

"Group Centre, consisting of FFR3, along with two glider companies detached from the sturmregiment, will land in Prison Valley, here," he said pointing to the map again, "between signal hill and Varipetro. I know you are all keen to know about our task and I will get to it soon. It is important you get a feel for the bigger picture first."

"Group East will be landing on Day 2, with FFR1 along with a battalion from FFR2, their target will be Heraklion. Also on Day 2, Group West will be reinforced by the two battalions from FFR2. A large proportion of our reinforcements on Day 2 will be from our mountain climbing comrades, from the 5th Gebirgs Division who will be flown in to Maleme. They won't have any mountains to conquer, just air sickness," he added gaining a ripple of laughter from his audience.

"Now to the detail and our role in this great expedition," he said tapping the map again. "It all kicks off at 0800, on the morning of the 20th May, gentlemen. The Luftlandesturmregiment, LLSR, landings will begin by seizing the bridge over the Tavronitis River and establish a bridgehead in what we believe to be an RAF camp," he pointed to the bridge on a larger scale map just pinned up by the Adjutant. "2/LLSR and 4/LLSR battalions will land just west of the Tavronitis to make a follow up attack towards the airport. A Company from 16/4/LLSR will land near a small town, Polemarhi," he dragged his stick across the map to a position south of the airfield. "Two companies will be dispatched to take Hill 107 from the south."

He stopped and turned suddenly to face the room, picking out Paul.

"Now to our task," he said, sensing the entire room leaning in towards him to catch every word. "I have nominated your company for this task Brand." Paul sat up and took serious notice of what was being said, peering at the map to where his battalion commander had been pointing moments ago. His grief pushed aside, for the moment.

"You and your men," he continued now looking directly at Paul, "are to land southeast of that hill and provide a blocking force to prevent the enemy reinforcing any troops on that hill, attacking our units from behind and acting as a flank guard for the LLSR in general. Your unit will be isolated Brand, maybe for some time, understood?" Paul nodded in acknowledgement.

"Yes sir." Christa completely to the back of his mind, as his thoughts switched into those of the tactician he was. Rapidly thinking through the complexities, the supplies he would need.

The Raven continued. "3/LLSR will land to the south east of the airfield. This is where the rest of the battalion comes in, just in case you thought you were being were left out Janke."

"I knew you would have a place for us sir," responded Helmut, nudging Paul as he said it.

"But there are no cafe's in that area," added Bach. This brought howls of laughter from the group at Helmut's expense, even Paul struggled to hold back a glimmer of a smile.

"We will be acting as a screen, in company groups," continued Volkman, "shielding the assault on the airfield. They will have enough to contend with once they leave their gliders, so it is down to us to baby sit them while they punch into the enemy. We must take that airfield if we are to fly in reinforcements, our mountain climbers. Brands men will be landing here," he said indicating the small village of Pagantha, on the larger scale map pinned up by the Adjutant. "The rest of the battalion will land here, here and here, he indicated, sweeping a line running north to south, east of the airfield.

"We will need to be in a position to repel any counter attacks that the Allied forces are likely to throw at us. Company groups will be too small to hold them back for long, but we need to hold them back long enough so we can take that airfield," he said banging the table, making some of the assembled men jump.

The Raven returned to the other side of the table and sat down in a vacant seat facing the assembled men and nodded to Bach to continue.

"Order of battle. As a result of our 'special status', we will not have the same establishment as the rest of the Division. But, we will have some additional troopers at Company HQ level but not the mortar troop that our brethren have. But we will have a medic attached to Company Headquarters going forwards and for this operation only we'll have a mortar detachment joining each company, except the Headquarters Company. They will receive two additional MG 34 sections of five men each."

There was a murmur amongst the group. Although they accepted that as a result of their new status they needed to be light on their feet if they were to carry out these independent roles, the lack of mortars did weaken their firepower when compared to standard battalions. Paul thought back to the enemy troops in the farm buildings preparing to assault them on the hillock. A few rounds from a Granatwerfer 36, would have soon smoked them out.

"It will give you some well needed additional firepower," added Volkman, still remaining seated.

"They will be joining you tomorrow," added Bach. "So make them welcome and integrate them into your units. That's all for now, there will be more detailed briefings, by Company, tomorrow, to enable you to prepare your men for what is expected of them. Any questions?"

"What will the mortar troop consist off sir?" asked Helmut.

"Normally it would consist of four tubes and twenty men, but we will be allocated three tubes and ten men."

"How many rounds will we carry sir?" asked Nadel

"Twenty four bombs per tube, so that means additional container drops I'm afraid. You must allow for more time collecting your equipment and supplies in your calculations when planning your movement timings."

Paul started to speak, it came out as almost a croak to start with. "What's our role once we've completed the blocking manoeuvre sir?"

"I'll take that question Hauptman," interrupted Volkman holding his hand up to the Adjutant. "The attacks on Maleme, Heraklion and Hania are just the start. The Division will have to sweep through the entire northern coast of Crete from Maleme to Sitia. Our role will be to shadow the main force on its most southern flank, warning the main body of counterattacks and disrupting those attacks until the main force can respond. So, prepare your men for a prolonged fight."

"Thank you sir," responded Paul.

They spent another hour questioning their two senior officers about the various aspects of the mission, probing their individual areas of concern, Paul's being the difficulty of resupply. Once all had been extracted, the meeting was adjourned, with the entire battalion staff repeating one of the Fallschirmjager's ten commandments.

"You are the elite of the Wehrmacht. For you, combat shall be fulfilment. You shall seek it out and train yourself to stand any test."

CHAPTER TWELVE

"The men are ready sir," said Max, having thrust his head through the tent opening.

"Thank you Max, I'll be with you in two."

Feldwebel Grun left to re-join the assembled men, waiting the attendance of their company commander.

Paul was sat on his bunk, reading a letter, from his mother, he had received the previous day. They both sent their love and wished him safe during whatever it was he was involved in. It had been nearly three weeks since he had been home and the shock of discovering the loss of someone he had grown close to. The ache was still there, eating away at him. Restless, sleepless nights of tossing and turning, his mind running through the events leading up to his first discovery of the bombed out apartment building.

He quickly snapped out of his preoccupation with Christa's death and refocused his attention on this morning's event. A pep talk to his men prior to going into battle tomorrow. They expected it, not so much due to tradition, but more about seeking reassurance from their commander that the strategy was right and the tactics sound. Although all knew, particularly Fallschirmjager, that jumping into the jaws of a hostile force there would be casualties and loss of life, it was still good to know that it was for a purpose and well thought out. Paul was not sure what to say to alleviate their concerns. This was the largest airborne assault ever, and had no precedence, so the consequences of such an action were unknown. He thought about it with some concern. Heavy anti-aircraft fire. That moment suspended in space when they would be exposed to small arms fire from the ground, potentially surrounded by the enemy when they were on the ground and ammunition running short before they had barely started.

He tucked the letter into the pocket of his tunic and eased himself up off the bed. Looking around his confined space, checking off his equipment that was placed ready for when needed, he grabbed his MP40 and peaked cap off the hook suspended from the side of the tent. Ducking under his four pocketed Tuchrock suspended from the centre of his billet, not needed now as he was dressed in his no. 2 pattern jump smock, the new camouflaged version, he headed towards the exit of his palatial abode. He pushed through the tent flap and stepped out into a sunlit dawn, the sun low in the sky. At least the meeting with his troopers would be relatively cool at this time of day. He walked away from the tent, making his way through the bivouacked lines to one of the few grassed areas of the airfield.

His men immediately rose from the burnt grass as he approached, commanded by Max, and stood to attention, the officers and Max throwing him a smart salute.

"At ease, make yourselves comfortable. As comfortable as you can in these salubrious surroundings."

The men sat or crouched back down on the soft grass, smiling at Paul's early attempt at humour.

Paul squatted down in the semi-circle of his assembled men, already feeling more positive being amongst them, another family.

"I just want to get a status check, go through a few minor details before the operation tomorrow and then get what rest or sleep you can. Reveille will be at 0400, and on board the aircraft for six."

He took off his hat, the rest of the unit taking it as a signal to follow suit, the officers removing their caps, the men their Fallschirm, wiping his brow with the back of his left hand.

"Report please Leeb."

Leeb stood up, his face dead pan as he delivered his report on his units readiness for battle. "Platoon present and correct bar one, sir. We've managed to scrounge some extra water bottles, but not enough for two per man."

"Feldwebel Grun, could you use your persuasive powers to lighten the Quartermasters stocks?" Asked Paul.

"Jawohl, Herr Oberleutnant."

"Anything else Leeb?"

"No sir, we're ready."

Leutnant Roth?"

The young officer stood up, although short in stature he made up for it with his eagerness to complete any task given to him. "A full platoon sir. We've also struggled to get water bottles and have been waiting some time for the extra grenades we requested."

"I know sir, use my persuasive skills," interjected Max, drawing a laugh from the Company.

He's coming back into the fold slowly thought Max, who had been worried about his Commander's lacklustre attitude these past few weeks. But there was just the occasional spark, like today, playing their tit-for-tat word games for the benefit of the men, in an effort to help relax them on the eve of battle.

Nadel was the last Platoon Commander to report, raising similar issues to the others.

"Unterfeldwebel Richter, your troop fit and ready?"

The slim, dark haired Commander of the Mortar Troop, jumped up from his sitting position, his narrow face fixed with the confidence in himself, his men and the contribution they would make to the success of the mission.

"Yes sir."

"Any problems?"

"There seems to be a shortage of weapons canisters sir. The sudden demand for canisters for mortar bombs means our battalion allocation is insufficient."

This was always a worry during times of large operations, his company alone would require in excess of one hundred of them. "How many are you short of?"

"Four sir."

The entire company turned to look at the Company Feld, who nodded his head in supplication, Richter looking on in bewilderment at the chuckling paratroopers around him. He was not yet fully indoctrinated in to the tight knit unit and the bond that existed between the Company Commander and his tough Company Sergeant. He was slowly comprehending the high esteem both these soldiers were held in inside the unit and even within the battalion.

"What are the consequences of not having them?"

"We would either have to leave some of our bombs behind or

reduce our reserves of personal ammunition. I suggest we take all of our bombs and depend on the Company's stocks for the rest."

"That could eat into a platoons reserve sir," added Nadel.

"I agree Leutnant, but having mortars will significantly enhance our long range firepower," responded Paul. "Hopefully it won't come to that. I will press for additional containers as it will be much harder for us to be resupplied on the flanks of the main body. Thank you Unterfeld Richter."

The NCO sat back down and Paul surveyed the semi-circle of men in front of him. They looked fit, healthy and all had varying degrees of a tan, which they had acquired from their time in Greece. Although they had been training hard, particularly in incorporating the new addition to their Company strength, the mortar troop, practicing fire request procedures, learning how to get the best effect from a mortar barrage and the consequences of getting the coordinates wrong and hitting their own men with a bombardment, they looked fresh and rested. They emanated confidence. Although he didn't want to dent that confidence, he needed them to go into combat with their eyes open and ready for an enemy that wasn't going to give up the island without a fight.

"Tomorrow we yet again fly into battle. Many of you have fought with me before, some since the start of hostilities in Poland. You know that I will take the fight to the enemy." He looked across and could see Max and many of the others nodding.

"Yes, we are the best, yes we are the elite of the German Army, but do not underestimate what is ahead of us gentlemen. We, in particular, will be fighting on the fringes of the main force. Saying that we'll be thin on the ground would be an understatement. Vigilance is the watchword. Don't take anything for granted and be prepared to react and move quickly as the situation demands."

He looked specifically at the officers directly in front of him. "We must keep the enemy on their toes, so that means aggressive patrolling. If you find yourselves stationery for any period of time, whether for a break, awaiting further orders, or just holding up for a resupply, ensure that scouts are sent out immediately. Don't put them at too much risk, we don't want the entire Company scattered around our sector, but you need to have a good perspective of your area of responsibility."

He waited, letting his officers, NCOs and men digest what he had just imparted. He could see Helmut and the other two Company Commanders waiting for him on the periphery of his briefing. He asked for questions. There was a fifteen minute two-way dialogue before he finally dismissed his men to carry on with their respective duties. He then spent a few minutes with Max, discussing the readiness of the Company as a whole, a brief exchange of views on the shortage of drop canisters and a brief consultation on his views of the integration of the new Mortar troop, but all seemed well.

"They're a good bunch of lads sir and have kept a low profile until fully accepted by all," said Max.

"That's good to hear, the last thing we want is a splinter group in the unit. What about you Max?"

"Rested and ready sir, starting to get a bit restless anyway."

"The trips to the Taverna been successful?" asked Paul with a wry smile.

Max looked at him with a puzzled look on his face. "Someone been talking sir?" responded Max with his arms folded across his stuck out chest.

"Just rumours of Greek women and debauchery Feldwebel Grun." Paul couldn't help but grin.

"God sir, I thought it might have been something serious."

"There must have been tears last night Max, being your last night for a while."

Max leant in to his Company Commander, stretching to reach Paul's ear and whispered, "To tell the truth sir, It was starting to get a bit complicated."

"Ah, so you've two on the go then?"

Max responded with a look of astonishment. "You know me too well sir."

"Well enough to be thankful that you will be with me and the rest of the Company Max, this operation isn't going to be the walkover everyone expects it to be."

Max came to attention, saluted and said, "We'll be fine sir, you'll see us through whatever is thrown at us."

Paul returned the salute. "On your way Feldwebel and get about your business."

Max strode away, the bond between them as strong as ever, and he was joined by Helmut and the other two Company Commanders, Meinhard and Manfred.

"Mr Brand, we are heading out to a little Taverna in the town and insist that you join us."

"What about the Raven?"

"He gave us permission to grab a last drink before the op tomorrow, providing we're back by midday."

Paul's first internal reaction was one of panic. He wasn't sure he was ready for the banter that went hand-in-hand with time spent with his comrades. Once Max had gone he was more than ready to run and hide until his attendance was required again. His heart advocated darkness and solitude, his head counselled him not to spend more time stewing in self pity, but to spend some time with these men, who may well die in tomorrow's battle.

"Sounds like a good idea Helmut," said Paul.

"Great," added Meinhard.

"What are we waiting for then?" said Manfred clutching Paul's arm and steering him towards the town. Helmut did the same on the other side and Paul recognised that they were in no way going to let him change his mind now.

The four men headed away from the aerodrome until they hit the outskirts of the town, picking their way through the restricted, flat cobbled streets, some so narrow that the balconies above them on either side of the thoroughfare almost touched. As they walked, their studded boots clattered on the flat cobbled streets. Three storey dwellings towered above them, a patchwork of colours, many with paint flaking off the walls and in some cases the rendering itself. Although badly in need of upkeep, most houses had a potted plant outside their very narrow doors, Helmut nearly knocking over a potted fig tree.

They arrived at the end of the street coming face to face with a small church, its square white walls topped with an orange, inverted u-shaped roof. Meinhard led them down another side street, equally as narrow, the towns' occupants darting back into their houses on seeing the German soldiers heading their way. Eventually they found a Taverna towards the centre of the town, the streets quiet at that time of day.

The paratroopers sat themselves down on the wicker chairs, around the simple wooden table draped with a plain white table cloth placed diagonally across it, inverted triangular shapes dropping to the four sides. The seats were also a simple affair, wooden backed with woven, wicker seats covered with thin embroidered cushions. Above them an arbour adorned with vines, shading them from the sun that was already starting to glare with its fierce heat.

Paul looked up at the canopy above them, the size of the leaves indicating the type of grape. Gewürztraminer he knew since the leaves were small, but those above were much larger and a mystery to him. The grapevines were bare, the harvesting season was now over. The Taverna proprietor approached them anxiously. He didn't speak German and none of the four comrades spoke Greek, but it didn't take long for International sign language to conjure up a bottle of red wine and some menus.

"Kotsfali," said Meinhard holding the bottle up in front of him.

"Guess what, it's indigenous to Crete, do you think he knows something?" They all chuckled at the irony.

He sipped from his glass. "Tastes a bit like a Bordeaux," he added.

"Never mind the wine, what the bloody hell does the menu say?" Helmut thrust the tatty menu in front of Meinhard, who had, so it seemed, assumed the mantle of a Greek food and wine expert. Before Meinhard could respond, the Taverna keeper, a mop of wavy black hair crowning his tanned leathery face, dark eyes and dark moustache, returned and placed a board with sliced bread on it, a bowl of olives and a bottle with a narrow spout topping it, which turned out to be olive oil, in front of them. He said something they didn't understand and went to another table on the other side of the outside area where four locals were sat drinking black coffee, smoking and jabbering away in their local tongue. As they spoke they occasionally stole wary glances at the German soldiers opposite.

Manfred grabbed the menu from Meinhard and tossing it over to Paul said, "It's in English on the other side. You speak some English Paul, what does it say?"

Paul held the menu up in front of him, scanning the lines of unfamiliar text. Helmut topped up their wine glasses, pulling a face as he sipped his way through his second glass of the day.

123

"A bit rough this."

"You just lack an acquired taste," teased Meinhard

"You can't beat a good Keller bier."

"That says it all."

"Well, what you're eating now Helmut is flatbread," said Paul as he dipped a piece of it into the olive oil, soaking it up and taking a bite.

"What about some appetisers? They have tzatziki, tirokafteri or soup."

"What the bloody hell is that?" responded Helmut, frustrated that he couldn't read the menu and expedite the ordering process.

"Tzatziki is a yogurt, garlic and cucumber dip and Tirokafteri is whipped feta cheese with hot peppers and olive oil dip."

"Yes, but what about the meat?"

Paul scanned further down the menu, struggling with some of the English words.

"There are some baked and grilled dishes, but I'm not sure whether it's meat or fish."

"If it's grilled it will do."

"It will probably be fish as we're so close to the coast," added Meinhard.

But Helmut was too busy breaking up bits of bread and tentatively dipping it into the oil to pay too much attention.

"What's wrong with good old fashioned Bratwurst and Brotchen," he moaned.

The waiter came over and after a few minutes of he and Paul pointing at the menu and using various gestures the order was placed. The Taverna proprietor, who was probably the only one who new what food they were going to end up with, slipped passed the four of them to fulfil their order.

Within ten minutes they were re-joined by the waiter, this time he was carrying a small table which he proceeded to unfold next to them. He placed onto this a large tray overlaid with a further selection of delicacies. They were then joined by a second waiter, sweat marks already starting to show on the armpits of his grey white shirt, his black trousers having never seen an iron. The second waiter placed china plates and cutlery on the table in front of each one of them, adding a white, triangular serviette later. The first waiter, the typical straight nose and strong chin, focused on his task, transferred the dishes from the tray to their table. There was an eclectic mix of food, from steaming, baked fish to a large bowl of Greek salad, covered with feta cheese, tomatoes and swamped with olive oil.

Helmut immediately pounced on something he recognised and scooped large slices of beef tomato, lettuce and tuna onto his plate, already eyeing up what he would sample next. His comrades looked at each other and burst into laughter. He looked up, a mouth full of food. "What?"

Before he continued eating, he did notice Paul laughing along with the others. The first time he had seen his friend do that since his return from Berlin.

"Well Paul, what were the enemy like to fight in Greece?" asked Manfred, his thin face peering at the food in front of him deciding what to put on his plate.

"How were they compared to the Poles?" added Meinhard, holding his glass of wine up in the air, examining its colour through the well used wine glass.

"Nobody can fight as badly as they did," stated Helmut, much happier now he had some grilled fish on his plate.

"The Belgians and the French were no better," suggested Meinhard. "They didn't last much more than six weeks. Let's face it, the Third Reich has the best soldiers, the best armed forces and the best attributes than any where else in the world."

"You've been listening to too much propaganda," rebutted Manfred.

Paul, recognising Meinhard's and Manfred's differing views and sensing a disagreement in the offing answered their question. "Yes, but they hadn't trained for war and their tactics were based on fighting World War One all over again."

"Come on then, tell us," urged Helmut, washing down his food with yet more wine.

"I don't know if they were brave or not, but the Allied soldiers we came up against were certainly aggressive."

"But you beat them."

"Yes we beat them Helmut, but we've fought in Poland, Belgium,

France and Greece. This is probably the first time they've come face to face with experienced professional soldiers."

"Exactly, and Crete will be the same. They will be completely enveloped and destroyed."

"Don't underestimate the enemy Meinhard, they are putting up a pretty stiff resistance in the desert and Rommel will be the first one to admit that they're no walk over. I've heard that they've taken back Halfaya Pass."

"Rommel will kick them back out again Paul, don't you worry about that."

Helmut stabbed at a piece of what looked liked chicken and munched like he had not eaten for weeks, his confidence in Rommel and the Afrika Corps beyond question.

"The Luftwaffe have already started bombing Crete, so they must know we're coming," noted Manfred.

"But they won't know it's a silk drop will they?" suggested Manfred, at the same time adding some baked fish to his salad.

"They will when they see over five hundred Tante Junes flying over them," spluttered Helmut with a mouth full of food.

"The drop in Norway went ok."

"But that was only a couple of hundred men, Manfred, nothing close to the scale of the drop tomorrow," warned Paul.

"The Luftwaffe will soften them up," boasted Meinhard

"They're causing havoc with the British," informed Helmut.

"But they're giving us some stick too. Feldwebel Grun was telling me they've bombed Hamburg again," reminded Manfred.

There was a sudden hush as it dawned on the three officers that they were talking about a subject that lived close to home and Paul's loss was still very fresh. Paul looked up and could see the consternation in their faces.

"It's ok guys, you don't have to tread lightly on my account, she's still here inside." He tapped his chest.

"Anyway, the food's getting cold and if we leave Helmut to it on his own there'll be none left."

This brought a chuckle from the group. They continued with their meal, the conversation focused more on lighter subjects concerning family and friends.

After finishing their early lunch, they paid the bill in Deutschmarks, much to the consternation of the Taverna owner. But that was the way it would be from now on and he was already doing the exchange rate calculation in his head.

They headed back to the airfield and the tented camp to complete any last minute checks with their units. They went back by a different route, not from choice, but as a result of Helmut insisting he knew the way and getting them lost. They made their way through streets that all seemed to look the same, eventually collaring a local who, understanding Helmut's aircraft impressions, pointed them in the right direction.

On arrival at the airfield Paul found his entire company occupying a small section of the taxiway close to the gravelled runway. Groundsheets were laid out to protect the personal equipment that was on display for final checking and inspection.

Max and the three platoon commanders approached him and saluted. Nadel's face still pale compared with his fellow officers, Roth's blond wiry hair bleached almost white from the burning sun. The slim, wiry, Leeb, his confidence as a Fallschirmjager officer growing daily.

"Would you like to inspect the lines Herr Oberleutnant?"

"I'll take a walk around Feldwebel Grun, but not an inspection. I'm sure you gentlemen have everything in hand," he said smiling, looking at the keen faces of his three young platoon commanders.

"Lead on Feldwebel Grun."

The group walked down the neat lines, the troopers running through a final scrutiny check of their kit, wiping a way the dust that was their constant enemy, pervading their weapons, their clothing and even their rations. Secreting away the little extras, such as a bar of chocolate or an orange snaffled from the canteen, which would make life just that little bit more comfortable. The three Leutnant's and Max wandered off to mix with the paratroopers leaving Paul stood above Oberjager Fessman.

The paratrooper looked up at his Company Commander, his hand continuing to polish the wooden stock of his Kar 98K, the metal cup-type butt plate and the enclosed funnel fore sight showing it to be a 98k/42. This was a weapon rarely seen and Fessman must have had good contacts to secure one. He stood up, and even at five feet eleven his wiry frame fell short of his tall commander. His laughing brown eyes looked out from beneath his slightly arched eyebrows. The habit of always having a joke on the tip of his tongue had gained him the reputation as the company comedian.

"Ready for tomorrow Fessman?"

"As I'll ever be sir. If I check my kit again I'll wear it out."

"Nice Mauser you have there."

"Not many were made sir, I was lucky that the armorer owed me a big, big favour."

Fessman shuffled his feet and a sombre looked clouded his face. "Are you scared about tomorrow sir?"

"Probably all of us experience some sense of anxiety about tomorrow, only a fool wouldn't. It's controlling that fear that counts."

"Easier said than done sir."

"Are you afraid then Fessman?"

"Not so much of getting killed sir, more afraid of letting myself and my comrades down."

"That's not something you'll do Fessman," said Paul gripping the trooper's shoulder.

"The men look to your skills and strengths, you'll not let them or me down."

Fessman nodded in acceptance of what he was being told. "Thank you sir."

Paul left him to continue polishing his rifle and made his way further into the lines, chatting to his men who seemed to be in excellent spirits. All were taking pride in their equipment, making sure it was in tip-top shape for the forthcoming battle. Cracking jokes with their commander, asking if it was too late to book some leave.

He came across Unterfeldwebel Richter and his Mortar Troop.

"You have more than most to check today Unterfeld."

Richter stood up, along with the rest of his nine man troop.

"Carry on." Indicated Paul with a hand gesture and, except for the troop commander, they continued checking over their equipment, the mortar numbers bumped up to three.

The eighteen inch barrels of the three Granatwerfer 36, were laid on their sides on a separate ground sheet, alongside their respective baseplate. Each had the key elements to the mortars laid carefully next to the barrels for checking and cleaning, the barrel handle, sliding collar with traversing hand wheel and levelling handle, the traversing bracket and the delicate range finder.

"Did you get the drop canisters you needed?"

"Yes sir, Feldwebel Grun came up trumps. We can now take a full load of forty bombs per tube."

"You're not taking practice bombs with you I hope," said Paul smiling, noticing the blue practice round.

"No sir, just taking the lads through some last minute practice. When you need our punch, we'll be ready sir."

Paul liked this NCO. He was confident but without the bluster and clearly took pride in his equipment and his small unit.

"We'll be operating on undulating ground at times, lobbing some of your bombs will hopefully help to smoke them out."

"We'll be ready for your call sir."

Paul thanked him, spent a few minutes passing the time with the rest of the Mortar troop and then continued threading his way through the display of various weapons being checked, from MP 40s, Kar 98Ks, MG 34s and grenades, firepower that would give the enemy something to think about when they landed. He also noticed there were many water purification kits amongst the trooper's equipment. Drinking could be a real problem on the island, particularly as it was moving into the hot season.

He looked across the taxiway to the other hard gravelled area and could see a Gebirgsjager unit carrying out similar checks of their hardware and trappings. These mountain soldiers were light infantry, well trained and would be a reliable and effective force to have fighting alongside the Fallschirmjager. They would be particularly useful if the battle moved into the higher ground, towards the more mountainous central area where their inherent skills would come to the fore.

Paul studied their uniforms, very different from his and his men's. They wore the typical standard service uniform, the M36, but consisting of special, field grey, heavy-weight and spacious trousers, allowing other clothing to be worn beneath should it be needed. All were wearing their Bergmutze, mountain field cap and on their right sleeve they proudly displayed the famous badge, the Edelweiss. The Company Commander in charge saw Paul watching and raised his arm in acknowledgement. Two men of a similar age, preparing their units for a battle, shared a fleeting connection before being dragged back to the matters in hand.

"We're more than ready sir." Max, contrary to his size always seemed to manage to approach unheard.

"You'll be the death of me Max, unless you make some noise before creeping up on me."

"Just helping you to hone your senses sir."

"Honing is what they obviously need Feldwebel Grun. Unterfeld Richter seems to be a competent soldier Max."

"That he does sir, he fought in the initial assault on Greece. If it all goes to rat shit we may well need him and his boys."

"They will give us an edge in making headway if we get bogged down."

"It's good just to have the extra manpower sir, they make up an additional troop."

"That they do. Are you ready Max?"

"As ready as I'll ever be sir," he replied, taking off his helmet and wiping his forehead with his tunic sleeve.

"Fighting in this bloody heat won't help much."

"I know, but it could get cold during the night hours, so make sure you take some warm clothing with you."

"Already done sir."

"I suppose you've suggested that to the Platoon Commanders as well?"

"I assumed you'd want me to sir," he said smiling.

"Right, well dismiss the men when they're done Max, let them have some space to prepare for tomorrow in their own way."

Paul gripped Max's arm. "I'm glad you're with us tomorrow Max, I will need you at my side for this one."

"I'll be there sir."

The mobile kitchen turned up at that moment, breaking the spell. The two-wheeled trailer was unhitched from its transport, a steady stream of white smoke leaving the chimney of the coal-fired burner, the internal cauldrons awash with soup and hot water for coffee.

"Let's go and get some coffee and grub, eh sir?"

The tall rangy officer and the burly NCO made their way over to the mobile kitchen, a queue already forming. Their bond was intact, their mutual need for each others strength reinforced, they were both ready to confront whatever came their way.

CHAPTER THIRTEEN

It was four in the morning on the 20 May, 1941. The air was cool and although the dawn was some hours away the aerodrome was a hive of activity. Paul's Company were assembled close to one of the hangars, completing last minute checks, taking it in turns to examine each other's gear. Junker 52's could be heard manoeuvring on the taxiways and the single runway, flights of Heinkel bombers from Athens could be heard overhead, escorted by Me 109 fighters from MoaaoI. Although none could be seen clearly, they were just shadows in the darkened sky, their droning engines gave away their positions. A flight of Dornier bombers, their pilots hunched over their control sticks in their distinctive glazed cockpits, chaperoned by Me 110 fighters, were close behind them. They were heading for Crete, each one carrying in the region of 2,000 Kg of bombs to soften up the enemy defences prior to the assault going in.

The Invasion of Crete by the German Army was a milestone in the use of airborne forces. Up until that point the German High Command, the OKW, had used the Fallschirmjager for mainly tactical operations. Battalion sized actions in Poland, where Paul's old platoon had been particularly successful, and later, playing a key role in the seizing of the Eben Emael fortress and facilitating the crossing of the Albert Canal to ensure the successful Invasion of Belgium and ultimately France. They had also been used successfully in Norway, but this was different, this was a full Divisional airborne operation.

Paul thought back to his conversation with the Raven the previous evening. He had informed Paul that advance parties were already being parachuted into the area, radioing feedback on the enemy's activities. He was to be met by one of these small four man groups, who would first guide the Junker's pilots of Paul's company drop, to the drop zone. This one was led by his friend Erich. He smiled at the thought of his friend. His and Helmut's assumption was that Erich had landed on his feet and was, as Helmut put it, ponsing around Regimental Headquarters, shuffling paper.

"Something tickled you sir?"

"Just thinking about Oberleutnant Fleck Max."

"Yeah, that's a turn up for the books. Just when we think he is pandering to his betters he goes and spoils it by doing something useful."

"How are preparations going?"

"Nearly there sir. Drop canisters have been loaded and the men are just sorting out their chute packs."

"Transport?"

"Raring to go sir."

Paul was about to respond when a swathe of dust, kicked up by a departing aircraft, blowing across their faces. The dry, un-metaled taxi-ways and runway created clouds of dust. Not whipped up by the wind, but by the taxiing planes and those flat out on take off. The dust had proven to be the bane of the paratrooper's lives. Grit got into their clothing, their food and more importantly the working parts of their weapons.

"Time for you to get your equipment sorted sir, if you don't mind me saying. I have your chute here."

Max handed him the chute and Paul placed it at his feet, Max then leaving him to organise himself. Paul was wearing, as were the rest of his battalion, his second pattern front-laced jump boots, bloused over with his standard issue trousers. He had already donned his second-pattern, splinter jump smock, an improvement on the first-pattern, which was found to be too restrictive. He had buttoned the shorter section around his upper legs, ready for the jump ahead. It would be warm fighting in this gear in Crete, but there had not been time to change the uniform, which was originally adapted for Central European climate, to tropical gear.

His leather map case and Zeiss binoculars were also laid at his booted feet along with his canvass MP40 magazine pouches. He ran his steady hand through his recently cropped fair hair and touched the scar above and to the side of his left eye. It felt pronounced and swollen and he could feel it pulsing beneath his fingers. His foot caught his battered Fallschirmjager helmet as he moved. No longer the chipped and scarred Luftwaffe blue grey Fallschirm, but now painted a matt beige colour to aid camouflage. But still a deep pitted line could be seen beneath its new coat of paint, a vivid reminder of the day he was downed by a Belgian artillery salvo. Max, he noticed, had covered his with a square of hessian, secured with a length of twine.

He unbuttoned the upper portion of his smock and shrugged it off his shoulders allowing it to drop to his waist, enabling him to then slip on his assault pack, with his bread bag, water bottle and gas respirator attached. The gas respirator case, against orders, was defunct as a gas mask carrier and now contained his personal effects, such as washing kit, rather than the gas mask it was intended for. Most, like Paul, believed that the use of gas was unlikely. He then slung his ammunition pouches over his head and shoulders before pulling the smock back over, wrapping it around his pistol holder and re-buttoning it. He tapped his pockets, his torch in the lower left, along with his first, first aid bandage, compass and in his right a box of Benzedrine and his gravity knife.

Max re-joined him, a lighter and chunk of cork in his hands which he then preceded to burn, applying the black substance to his face, smearing it over his forehead, cheeks, chin and neck. Shine was one of the soldier's key vulnerabilities and one that they needed to counter. A white face could stand out vividly giving the enemy a clear target. There were others, like shape, silhouette, shadow and movement, equally as important in ensuring concealment. Max handed him the now blackened cork and Paul proceeded to darken his tanned, but still white in comparison, features.

"We load in twenty minutes sir."

"Platoon Commanders ready?"

"With their platoons, they'll be over shortly. I said you might want a quick word."

"Thank you Max, but I'll join them with their platoons. Get them to form up in the aircraft groups will you?"

"I'm on it now sir."

Max left and Paul finished plastering his face with the burnt cork, then applying it with equal relish to his exposed arms, his sleeves rolled up above the elbow in an effort to keep cool when the heat hit them. He stuffed the remains of the cork in his pocket, picked up his chute, eased his way into it and buckled it up. It felt strange not having his MP40 at his side, he thought, but that had been secured in one of the many drop containers and was now loaded on his particular aircraft.

He waddled over to join the rest of his men and was greeted with various pronouncements.

"Well this is it sir."

"Has my leave request been approved?"

"Is it too late to put in for a transfer?"

The joviality hid the seriousness of the event they were about to embark on, and helped to steady the nerves, whilst adding to the camaraderie that would see them through what they were about to face.

The men were grouped into their respective sticks which had been assigned to a specific aircraft. Some talked to fortify the link with their comrades or friends, others as a way help master the fear that was building up inside of them. Each trooper prepared himself mentally to board the plane, to make the jump when the time came, to be ready to fight and kill on landing.

Paul joined his stick, in the main it was men from second troop of first platoon, men he had commanded as a Leutnant. Now though he had a headquarters group attached to him; his radio operator, a medic and three troopers, a mini–command within his larger one.

"Radio up to scratch Bergmann?"

"Working like a dream sir, just hope to God it stays in one piece when it lands."

They marched to the waiting aircraft and climbed on board via the four-rung ladder hooked on to the floor of the doorway to the right of the wing. Once on the plane the men settled as best they could in the confined space.

It was relatively silent, the aircrafts engines not yet started. Some men smoked a cigarette, the smoke mingling with the vaporised aviation fuel that pervaded the nostrils. Some checked their equipment over and over again, some men just sat in silence, in their own world, their thoughts kept to themselves. One man, Sommer, was holding a silver cross, stroking it gently with his fingers.

The aircraft juddered as the engines turned over one at a time. Coughing and spitting, as if reluctant to be woken so early in the morning. Once they caught, the pilot slowly increased their revs, listening for the sounds that told him all was well or a problem was in the offing. The Absetzer gave the signal to Paul that they were ready to move and set about securing the door of the plane for take off. The aircraft shook and rattled with the vibration from the engines as the power slowly increased ready to pull the aircraft into position for take off. The force and the noise increased even further as the pilot geared up the plane to move it into position, one of the ground crew dragging away the chocks allowing them to rattle their way into formation, a staggered line, on to the runway.

Once on the runway and given the go ahead by their superiors the engines screamed like banshees and the shuddering planes surged forwards as one after another they built up speed and raced down the hard packed runway, a swirl of dust spewing behind them showering the aerodrome with a light film of grit. They took to the air in sequence, circling to gain height, waiting for the rest of their flight before heading south to their destination, the island of Crete. A host of aircraft blotted out the slowly lightening sky, like a swarm of locusts.

The men were generally silent now, apprehension on some of their faces. In the main they were veterans and had not only parachuted into battle, but had even attacked a target after landing by glider. Bravado wasn't necessary, they didn't need to hide their fear through inane comments now, they just accepted they were going into combat and their best lifeline was to focus on the battle ahead, put the training and the skills they had learnt in to practice.

After nearly two hours of flying, the paratroopers, crammed inside the aircraft, along the canvas seats either side of the plane, were relieved when the Absetzer signalled that they were ten minutes out. Each man did a final check of his equipment and also the man next to him. Five minutes out from the target and the Jump Master gave them another signal. This time they discarded their life jackets, given to them in case they went down over the Mediterranean Sea. The last thing they wanted was this extra bulk as they exited the plane.

Then the two minute warning, the silence was palpable. Even the sound of the plane's thrusting engines was mere background noise, the paratrooper's ears now sensitised to the din, each man lost in his own thoughts, their eyes focused on the still closed door near the wing of the aircraft. Flashes of light erupted in front of the cockpit, flickering inside the cabin, the pilot's eyes squinting, his head pulling back as if to get away from the hostile event occurring in front of him. He sent back a message, warning the passengers to hold on tight as they were coming under fire from the ground.

Paul gripped the plane's infrastructure with both hands, the static line held between his teeth. The Absetzer tapped Paul on the shoulder, it was time. The signal was given to stand and hook up. Each man stood, clipped their static lines onto the cable that ran centrally down the cabin roof and waited the order.

The door was pulled clear and Paul made his way to the opening, the wind whipping through the open space. He got to the doorway, gripped the handles either side and saw the Junkers opposite and slightly back and lower suddenly judder as it was hit two thirds of the way along the fuselage, just behind the wing and in front of the tail. A bright flash, that diminished almost as quickly as it appeared, and the tail section tore itself away from the main body and plummeted to the ground. The front section of the aircraft lost control, banking to the left, fortunately away from Paul's plane, and went into a slow spin towards the ground, leaving a trail of paratroopers and their chutes exiting the door. He counted eight before he was distracted by the Jump Master hailing him.

Suddenly rounds from a British anti-aircraft gun punched through the floor, the forty millimetre rounds tearing jagged holes through the delicate fuselage, the Bofors crew below loading as quickly as possible to attain a rate of fire of over one hundred rounds a minute. Scherer, one of the new men who had recently joined as part of the company HQ strength, took a round through the torso, ripping through his smock and tearing a fist sized hole in his chest. He was slammed into the man behind him before slumping to the floor, leaving a trail of blood and fragments of uniform and flesh spattered on the smock of his newly found comrade, he was dead before he hit the deck of the transporter.

The rounds continued to punch into the stricken aircraft. The pilot rocked the plane from side to side in an attempt to shake them off, but to no avail. Two heavy calibre rounds slammed into the starboard engine, the pilot violently banked left, nearly throwing the unprepared Paul through the doorway. The Junkers seesawed, shaking excessively, the now unstable engine and damaged controls, making it impossible for the pilot to keep the craft steady. The starboard engine caught fire, the prop stopped turning as parts melted and seized, fuel and oil suddenly splaying across the cockpit and along the fuselage, the flames from the burning engine igniting it immediately.

"Aus. Aus. Aus. Out. Out. Out," screamed the Absetzer. "You must get out now. Geh. Geh. Geh."

Paul looked back along the oscillating aircraft, flames already melting through the fuselage, his men cowering away from the flames licking around their shoulders. All were standing, hooked up and ready, each man willing their commander to jump so they could follow and escape the rapidly increasing heat.

"How far are we from our LZ?" Paul yelled at the slowly panicking Jump Master.

"You're due to jump in seconds sir, go now for God's sake. The pilot won't be able to keep the plane level for much longer."

Paul nodded, there was no decision that needed to be made. He looked at his men, motioned they were going and leapt forwards.

At this same time, in the succeeding kette, Max was also stood at the doorway of a Tante June, waiting for the order to jump when one of his kette was hit in the main, central engine. The flames blossomed, the engine exploded, flaming oil and aviation gasoline funnelled back through the body of the aircraft, killing the pilot, his co-pilot and many of the paratroopers sat near the cockpit. The plane banked, out of control, the paratrooper at the doorway was thrown back inside against his comrades, trapping them, submitting them to a horrible death as the aircraft went down on its side, spinning out of control, preventing the troopers inside the opportunity to escape death.

Max swallowed, a troop of men that he knew, would never again fight at his side or laugh at his humour or drink with him ever again. He was tapped on the shoulder, bringing him back to his own circumstances and he leapt from the plane.

The shock of the prop blast tore at Paul's helmet, catching him unawares. Rounds still zipped passed him, the gunners below not satisfied they had decimated their target, they also wanted the deaths of the men falling from the plane above. Paul could see a carpet of chutes below him, drifting south, one of the other companies of his battalion; it crossed his mind that it may be Helmut. If this was bad, he dreaded to think what it would have been like for the units attacking the Maleme airport directly.

As he dropped below the cacophony above and the gunners switched to better targets as more and more Junkers headed their way, it became almost peaceful. Paul looked down and about in attempt to get his bearings. It was light enough now that he could see the mountains to his south, or were they hills. The Gebirgsjager would no doubt class them as mole hills. He couldn't see the coast to the north, behind him, the rest a pale patchwork of rocky undulating ground, covered with various forms of flora and fauna. It would make for a hard landing and be a test for ankles and knees.

He scanned the ground to the east frantically trying to pick out some sign of Erich and his scouts. He thought he picked out a weak flash of light off to his left, possibly from a torch. He didn't see it again, but it did home him on to the red and black swastika flag pinned to the ground by small rocks. They were going to miss it by at least half a kilometre, but he had registered the direction and he felt sure Erich would already be making his way to their likely landing spot. They would be a difficult target to miss, over one hundred men, not forgetting the tens of weapons containers following them down.

Before he knew it the ground came rushing towards him. He struck the ground hard, fell forwards, his cricket like knee pads absorbing most of the force, propelling him forwards on to his gauntlet covered hands and then rolling him on to his side. He jumped up, grabbing the lines of his chute, the breeze slightly stronger at this higher level tugging at the canopy in a vain attempt at jerking the interloper across the rough ground. He wrenched the shrouds towards him and quickly ran round to the end of the chute as fast as he could, collapsing the chute and unbuckling his harness. He looked about him seeing more of his men had landed and were getting rid of their chutes as fast as possible.

Two weapons canisters caught his eye and he sprinted towards the first until he saw the markings were not correct and switched direction to the second one ten metres further on where he hit gold, the markings indicated it is where he would find his MP40, along with weapons for other members of his stick.

CHAPTER FOURTEEN

Paul ripped open the canister, unsecured his machine pistol, unbuttoned his smock and extracted a magazine which he slapped into the automatic weapon. He did another quick scan, there were still no signs of any enemy forces. He slipped his smock off his shoulders, moved his equipment on to the outside and then re-buttoned his tunic.

Paul felt ready now for whatever was thrown at him, up until then he and his unit were very exposed and vulnerable, with only their pistols as defence. Against a determined enemy, with heavier firepower, they would be at their mercy. He completed another three hundred and sixty degree scan of the area, looking for signs of enemy troops, orientating himself with his surroundings and thinking through his next moves. He pocketed his gauntlets, crouched down, one hand on the ground, rapidly withdrawn when it came into contact with a green spaghetti like shrub that proved to be spiky and painful. Two figures joined him, his radio operator, Bergmann and the new medic, Fink.

"The radio ok Bergmann?"

"Seems intact sir. I'll need to do a comms check though."

"See if you can get Regiment, let them know we are half a klick west of our LZ."

Paul scanned the immediate area. To his north and west the ground crested before dropping away. To the east, somewhere beyond the line of trees, the village of Pagantha, his first objective. The backdrop to the south, mountains, with their snow capped tops. He was quickly joined by the key elements of his Company. Max first, followed by Roth, Nadel and finally Leeb. Max's news was not good. He turned towards Nadel.

"Sorry sir, but I think you will be shy a troop. I saw a Junkers break up and go down, I'm pretty sure no one got out. I certainly didn't see anyone jump, it happened too fast for anyone to react."

"What a waste of good men," exclaimed Nadel. "It must be second troop. I've seen most of one and three assembling."

Paul reflected on what he had heard. They had lost nearly ten percent of their company and the battle hadn't even started. He kicked into action, there wasn't time to dwell on it now, that would have to wait until later.

"Leeb, secure the flanks to our west and north. Roth, secure the containers and bring any with supplies or ammo left in them to the northern ridge. Nadel, put out a screen, one hundred metres out, east and south, but watch out for Oberleutnant Fleck and his scouts. We missed the LZ, but he would have seen us and will no doubt be making his way to join us. Unterfeld Richter, assemble your men by the northern edge and check over your equipment. That's all gentlemen; report back when complete, I'll be at the northern edge with Leutnant Leeb."

The officers scattered to carry out their orders and check on the assembly of their platoons.

"Max, I want a full status report on the company. I need to know our current strength and confirmation that the missing troop hasn't suddenly appeared."

"On my way sir."

Max left to gather the information requested and Paul was joined by Bergmann again.

"Any joy?"

"Not yet sir, the radio seems ok, I just can't make contact. Might be a better signal if I join Leutnant Leeb."

"Let's go then."

Paul shot off the two hundred metres to get to the edge of the flat piece of ground, followed by his HQ element, two Fallschirmjager, Mauer, Ostermann and the medic. Scherer was missing, killed by the anti-aircraft shell on their inbound approach. He threw himself down next to Leeb who had positioned one troop along each drop, the third held back close to him in reserve.

"Look down there sir."

Paul surveyed the ground in front of him that fell away beyond the crest as an undulating slope. Directly to his front the terrain was a mix of crumbling, light coloured rocks on reddish brown earth, interspersed with green grasses and scrub, splattered with the occasional flower. Low lying herbs filling in some of the gaps. One lone Olive tree acting as sentry. Looking to the far right, at the top of the perpendicular slope was a stepped terrace of what looked like olive trees in symmetrical lines marching down the hillside, directly beneath them a section of gully joining that slope to the one directly beneath Paul.

The gully probably started somewhere beneath the village, a kilometre to their east. A good place to descend, thought Paul. Beyond, towards the coast, he could see the glistening town of Hania, the steadily rising sun reflecting off the numerous windows. Above could be seen flights of Junkers still depositing their loads and Stuka dive bombers hovering like vultures waiting to swoop down and deliver death and destruction on demand.

The air felt fresh and tasted sweet, clearing his throat and lungs of the taste and smell of burning aviation fuel and oil, his face now blackened with more than just burnt cork. He looked at Leeb to his left, his keen eyes scanning the foreground, seeking out any potential threats. Paul pulled out his binoculars and scanned the mid-ground intently, it was quiet, no signs of movement. In the distance he could hear the crack of rifles and the faster chatter of machine guns, anti-aircraft fire adding to the discord as Junkers continued to fly over the island disgorging their loads.

He turned round to look behind him, the flat, level ground, also strewn with various rocks and scrub, slowly rising in the distance, beyond the mountains with their snow capped peaks. West of him was the start of a shallow escarpment, currently protected by Leeb's men. To the east, the direction of their target, the small village of Pagantha.

In the centre, the rest of his company were going about their business, checking drop canisters for weapons, ammunition or supplies, stragglers joining their platoons, Nadel still wishing hopefully for the arrival of his missing men. Once the contents were either consolidated or dispersed amongst the company, the wheels and handles would be attached and those would be used as transports and dragged to Paul's current location. He could see Unterfeld Richter loading some of his mortar bombs on to his men, the rest would remain in the containers and dragged wherever they went.

He saw a bulky figure running towards him in a low crouch, who he immediately recognised as Max returning to report to him on the status of the company. Max lay prone, next to Paul, peering over the crest, JU 87s in the distance, their inverted, gull shaped wings distinctive. The pilots locating their targets through the bomb sight windows in the floor of the cockpit. Three in a line, they rolled one hundred and eighty degrees, one after the other, the aircraft nosing into a dive.

Paul turned to see what had transfixed Max's attention. The three Stuka's nose dived, close to sixty degrees, hitting a speed of over five hundred kilometres an hour, the Jericho Trumpet, the wailing siren, heard even this far away from the scene of its target somewhere between Hania and Rethymnon. At fifteen hundred metres the bombs were released, the four, fifty kilogram bombs under the wings and the two hundred and fifty kilogram bomb held centrally, hurtled towards the target, engulfing it in a hot blast of shrapnel as the pilot pulled up from the dive, fighting the effects of nearly five g's of force, his vision fogging as he finally levelled the plane and headed for home, a base on the mainland of Greece.

"Christ I'm glad I'm not on the receiving end of that lot," exclaimed Max

"If we don't get our marker flags out we may well be," said Paul turning to Leeb giving him instructions to do just that.

"Well Max?"

Max pulled a small pocket book from his tunic and read the scribbled lines on it.

"It looks like we've lost two troop from Leutnant Nadel's platoon sir."

"Damn, what a waste," cursed Paul. "I knew them all. They fought well in Corinth. To be killed before you have even left the plane."

"The company newsletter says that you and your stick were also lucky to get out sir," said Max looking at his commander's blackened face.

"Very lucky Max. The rest of the company?"

"The rest of the company are present, except for Scherer, who was

144

killed on your flight sir and Forster, who has broken his leg on this God forsaken surface."

"Yes, Scherer was his by an AA round, straight through the chest. I don't think he even knew he'd been hit. Who to replace Forster?" mused Paul. He turned to Leeb.

"Fessman?"

"That would be my choice sir."

"Max?"

"He's more than ready for the opportunity sir."

"Do you want to give him the news Ernst?"

"It would be better coming from you."

"Ok, send him over will you Max?"

Max got up from the ground, reddish soil clinging to his smock, and went in search of Fessman who was on the western edge of the piece of ground they currently held.

Paul heard rustling behind him and turned to see five figures running towards him. The first he recognised as Leutnant Roth, the second, his six foot athletic frame and short blonde hair, helmet strapped to his belt, could only be his friend Erich, his close friend, followed by his three scouts.

Paul stood up and they came to a halt in front of him.

"Sir, this is..." Roth started to say, but Erich strode passed him and gave him a friendly punch on the shoulder.

"I lay marker flags out for you and you still can't bloody well hit the target," he said laughing.

They forgot all those around them as they wrapped their arms around each other, slapping each other's back, like two long lost brothers who had found each other again through such adversity. Realising they had an audience, they parted, but were still laughing, their joy at seeing each other again was clear for all to see.

"God it's good to see you Erich. We thought we'd lost you to the high and mighty life of Regimental HQ."

"I needed to be where the real work's done," he responded.

At that moment Max joined the group, bringing Fessman with him.

"Feldwebel Grun, you don't look any different from when I last saw you, apart from the makeup."

"You seem to have put on a bit of weight since you've been with the hierarchy sir."

They both looked at each other, not a flicker on their faces, Erich's scouts looked on in amazement. Then Erich thrust out his hand, shaking Max's, their grip firm, their faces breaking out into a grin.

"You've not tamed our ex-Hamburg Docker yet then Paul?"

"Did you ever think I could? Erich, I need a couple of minutes, then we can get an update from you, ok?"

"Sure, Feldwebel Grun can update me."

Paul turned towards Fessman, his brown, hawk like eyes looking out from his slightly pinched face, the arched eyebrows questioning his sudden appearance in front of his Company Commander.

"You've heard about Unteroffizier Forster I assume?"

"Yes sir, an unlucky break, if you pardon the pun." Fessman, ever the company comedian.

"Could you caretake the troop in his absence?"

"What, you mean run the troop sir?"

"That's exactly what I mean, command it."

"But..."

"There are no buts Fessman, can you do it or not?"

"Yes sir," he responded bringing his feet together sharply and his arms straight by his sides."

"Good. Well then Uffz Fessman, you had better get your troop sorted, we'll be moving out soon. And your first challenge is to rig a stretcher for Uffz Forster."

"Will do sir. And sir, thank you for the opportunity, you'll not be disappointed."

"I know, now off with you."

Fessman left to join his troop and Paul returned to Erich. The reunion over, they needed to get down to business.

"Max, can you pull in the platoon commanders and platoon NCO's in?"

"Considerate done sir."

"Erich, will you run through what you know about the area?"

Multiple explosions could be heard to the north west towards the coast and Maleme airfield.

"Maleme is getting hit pretty hard, have you put marker flags out

Paul? The Luftwaffe boys will soon be hunting further afield for tasty targets like this. Sorry about Christa," he added, needing to say something to his friend about it.

"I only met her twice, but it was enough to know what a special person she was."

Paul looked down, the pain racing through his body, like an electric current twisting his nerve endings, gripping his heart like a vice, his stomach churning, nausea threatening to overwhelm him. Erich gripped his shoulder.

"Are you ok Paul? I'm sorry, I know it's still fresh, but I had to share with you my condolences, you're my friend."

Paul straightened up.

"It's ok Erich," he said placing his hand on top of his friend's hand.

"Sometimes it's so fresh, even out here, that the pain can be unbearable. There was so much hope for the two of us."

Before they could continue their personal exchange, they were interrupted by the three platoon commanders, three platoon NCO's, Unterfeld Richter, the radio operator and Max.

"Any joy on contacting HQ?"

"No sir, still no response," replied Bergmann.

"Keep trying." The frustration in Paul's voice obvious.

"We've had problems as well Paul," added Erich. "But you will get through eventually."

"Right gather round. For those of you who haven't met him, this is Oberleutnant Fleck. He landed earlier in the morning because he thought we might get lost."

They all laughed, dissipating some of the tension.

"All yours Erich."

Erich cleared a patch of ground, kicking away some of the low lying herbs and small stones until he had a reasonable half square metre of cleared space to play with. He drew a square in the dirt with a stick he had picked up earlier, for this sole purpose.

"To the north, we have the crest next to us here, which drops away in stages to the coast and eventually Hania. To the south, it is similar ground to what we are on now, but slowly climbs up into the mountains you can see behind me. The western edge drops away as

147

well, similar terrain to what we're on now until it hits the coast, some seventy five kilometres away. The important part, the region we'll be heading into, east, about a klick from here is the village of Pagantha, where at least a platoon of British soldiers are held up. It is a route they could use to ferry soldiers to outflank our main attack below. I will leave the rest of that to your Oberleutnant to cover. But back to the village, I'll hand you over to Unterfeld Gerste, he can give you the low down on the village."

A grizzled veteran, who should have been a full sergeant by now, but had been up and down the ranks many times for various misdemeanours, stepped forward and in a gravelly voice explained the layout to the assembled men.

"The village is about four hundred metres long."

He scraped a deep rut running from south to north from one end of the square to the other, with a small bend in the middle.

"This road runs right through the centre of the village with a raised embankment, about fifty metres wide, running alongside it, east, for its full length. Starting from the south. The road leaving the village slopes gradually away to the south, then east, with an escarpment on its left and the embankment to its right. The top of the escarpment has a very thin line of trees and opposite on the embankment is a cream coloured, two storey building with a terracotta roof. Beyond that the ground gradually slopes away, where there is a second two storey building of a similar style."

He placed some herbs he'd picked up and sprinkled them west of the road to represent the trees and two small white stones or rocks to represent the two buildings.

"To the north, the road coming out of the village also slopes away. The road through the village is fairly flat with a slight curve in the middle. Above the road, on the embankment again, is a similar house to the other two. Opposite, on the other side of the road there is a flat stretch for about fifty metres, before the ground gradually climbs upwards, not as steep as the escarpment at the other end, and interspersed with trees until you hit the flat of the plain were on now."

He again sprinkled some herbs to support his description and placed another one of the small white rocks. But he then placed two small sticks just below the house, pointing northwest, getting wider apart the further away they were.

"This is the start of a gully, running pretty much down to the lower land below. That describes the two ends of the village. As you move south along the road, about one hundred and fifty metres in, you have a curve in the road, about fifty metres long, which straightens out almost immediately. Just before this bend on the right of the road." He placed a rock in position. "You have a one storey building, this one is white in colour. Immediately just before the bend." He traced the route with his stick. "On the left, on the raised piece of ground that runs parallel with the road you have another building. This one is more of a pale tangerine colour with a terracotta roof, but this one is quite long, maybe twenty or more metres, possibly two houses back to back. We've nicknamed this the Mandarin."

He placed two rocks to emphasis its length.

"Behind it, there is what appears to be an outhouse of sorts. Again on the other side this piece of land slopes away. The road then continues for about one hundred and fifty metres to the southern point which I covered earlier in the brief."

"Thank you Unterfeld Gerste, any questions?" He looked around the faces of the assembled officers and NCOs.

Leeb was there immediately with a question.

"What's the ground like to the east of the road, other than sloping away?"

"Good question sir. It's not cultivated and underfoot is pretty much like this." He pointed to the ground they were on. "Scrub and all sorts of plant life. There are the occasional trees, the odd olive tree. But the further east you go, the slope starts to drop to the north and becomes one of the sides of the gully."

"Unterfeld Gerste spent most of the early hours of this morning scouting the village, so has a pretty good feel for its disposition," added Erich.

"Do we know anything about the troop dispositions?"

"Roughly Paul. We reckon they're in platoon strength. It looks like they have a half section of five men at each end of the village, the rest of the platoon seem to be occupying the building near the centre. It looks to be the HQ building."

"Where are the two half sections?"

"They're occupying the buildings at the extreme ends of the village."

"What about LPs?" Asked Max

"Surprisingly no, but I would do another recce before you move the Company across there."

"Thanks Erich. Right gentlemen, listen up."

They all moved in closer, stretching their necks to get a good view of the sandbox outline of the village, their ears straining to ensure they caught all of their commander's instructions.

"Orders. Force the enemy out of the village and destroy them."

He looked around at the assembled group, seeing the single mindedness on their faces.

"This is how we're going to tackle it. I want to distract the enemy, blocking them off on three sides, leaving one exit available to them, that's where we will hit them hard. Dispositions. I want Uffz Fessman to take two men and scout the western tree line, check to ensure they haven't placed any Listening Posts since Unterfeldwebel Gerste's last recce. He can do that as we group and then move up to the village."

He looked at Leeb. "Clear?"

"Yes sir."

"Where will he pick us up sir?" asked Leeb.

"If he starts at the southern end and makes his way north, we can pick him up on our way in."

"Understood sir."

"We have three objectives. A blocking force at the northern end of the village. Leutnant Nadel, your platoon have that task. "

"Jawohl, Herr Oberleutnant."

"Make as much noise as you can. I want them to know you're there. I don't want them to even contemplate withdrawing from the village in that direction."

He used the stick he had taken from Erich earlier and pointed to the southern end of the village.

"This will be the killing zone. Leutnant Roth, this will be your objective. Place your platoon along the western edge of the escarpment overlooking the road as it slopes away from the village, but hold your fire until they are well and truly in the zone. If need be let the first couple escape. I want them to think they can get away, I don't want them doubling back."

"Jawohl, Herr Oberleutnant."

"Leutnant Leeb. Once you have Fessman and his men back into the fold, you're platoon will assault the village."

He tapped the ground with his stick again, next to the one storey building on their side of the road, just before the bend.

"This will be our entry and exit point, so leave a half troop here to cover our withdrawal and the other half of the troop, with the MG34, to remain on the high ground on the other side of the bend, covering the main building at the centre of the village. Understood?"

"Yes sir."

"Position one of your troops on the other side of the road and keep one on the west and advance south. Don't advance further than the last house in the village, that will be the kill zone and I don't want any home runs. Leutnant Nadel, you will need to make sure you keep your arcs of fire sharp and Leutnant Roth, no firing north of your target building. We have to be sharp and on the ball gentlemen, there's going to be a lot of activity on and around that road."

They both acknowledged Paul's point.

"And my troop sir?" Unterfeld Richter spoke up.

"We have plenty for your troop to do Unterfeld, don't you worry about that," said Paul with a grin. "You'll be more than busy. I want two tubes dropping rounds all along the eastern edge of the village. I want the enemy to discount going east as an option, forcing them into our kill zone. I don't want any rounds dropping into the village. I'm sure you wouldn't be too happy about that Ernst."

The group laughed.

"What's the risk Unterfeld?"

"We can put them within fifty metres of the road sir, over shooting rather than under shooting. The third tube?"

"That's for the killing ground. Once Leutnant Roth opens fire, drop as many rounds on that road as you can. Once the village has been cleared you will hear Feldwebel Grun's whistle. Ceasefire as soon as you are able. You're actions then are as follows. Nadel, secure the northern end of the village, Roth, the entire western edge of the

151

village and Leeb, the village itself. Then all platoon commanders to me and we can plan our next move. Any questions?"

"Uffz Forster sir?" asked Max

"My scouts will stay with him Paul, unless you have a task for us?"

"You've done your bit Erich, it's our turn now. Keeping an eye on Forster would be appreciated. Right, we move out in twenty minutes. Ernst, send Uffz Fessman to me straight away."

The Platoon Commanders dispersed to seek out their platoons and brief their troop commanders in turn. Moments later Uffz Fessman made his presence known to his Company Commander.

"Leutnant Leeb says you have a job for me sir."

"I do Fessman, and it's right up your street. Take a couple of men with you, the fewer the better."

He took Fessman over to the sandbox and briefed him on the outline of the village.

"Beyond the tree line there, it dips down to a road where there is at least a platoon of British soldiers. I want you to recce the entire length of the western edge of the village, but stay out of sight and stay on the high ground. Start at the southern end and work your way north. We need to ensure that there are no LPs on that side of the road or a potential ambush. We move out in less than twenty minutes to assault the village and will meet you at about fifty to a hundred metres from the northern end. When you get there just go to ground until we pick you up. Ok?"

"Yes sir. Action on contact?"

"Apart from getting your bloody head down, stay where you are and we'll come for you. We will still assault, we will have just lost the element of surprise. So, it's imperative you're not seen."

"You can depend on us sir."

"The us being you and Stumme, who else?"

"Willy Geister sir, he's so short no one will see him."

"Off you go then."

Just before he could leave, Paul tapped him on the shoulder.
"Sir?"

"Congratulations on your promotion, how have the men taken it?"

"They think they're in for an easy ride now Uffz Forster's gone sir. Oh the naivety of the young."

They both laughed and with that Fessman shot off to carry out his task.

"Sir, sir," called Bergmann. "I've got Regiment on for you."

Paul ran over to where the radio set was positioned and grabbed the handset off him.

"It's the Raven... sorry sir, I mean Major Volkman."

"Sir, Brand over."

"Brand, at last. Where the bloody hell have you been?"

"We're one kilometre west of Pagantha sir, over."

"Excellent Brand, what next, over?"

"We're about to launch an attack on a British unit in the village sir, over."

"Once that's completed Brand, I want you to move your company further north, then east to support the units around Rethymnon, over."

"Jawohl, Herr Major. How is the battle progressing, over?"

"Early days Brand, but they've taken a mauling around Maleme airfield, it's not in our possession yet. One more thing, Oberleutnant Hoch has been killed, it has been agreed that Oberleutnant Fleck will assume command of the company. Is he with you? Over."

"Yes sir, over."

"I'll give the coordinates to your radio operator where Fleck can meet up with his company. He should be with them by this afternoon. What's your status. Over?"

"We've lost a troop due to a downed aircraft, one KIA and one broken leg over."

"You've got off lightly Brand, casualties have been much higher elsewhere. Put me on to your radio operator and move your men out, we need to keep the enemy guessing, not knowing where the next attack is coming from. We must take the pressure off the units lower down, over."

"Understood sir, here's Bergmann, over."

Paul passed the handset back to Bergmann and set about getting his company on the move.

The company was formed up in its platoon formations, crouched down, the platoon commanders and Max waiting for the order to move out. Erich and his men on the periphery. He beckoned Erich over.

"Problem Paul?"

"You could say that Erich, Meinhard Hoch has been killed."

"Shit, I knew him quite well. He was a bit too nationalistic for me at times, but on the whole he was ok."

Paul thought back to the lunch they shared together in Corinth, Meinhard explaining the particulars of wine tasting to them. He snapped back to the present.

"He's a sad loss Erich, but Major Volkman has received approval for you to take over command of the company. Bergmann's getting you the coordinates of their location now."

Paul held out his hand to shake Erich's. "Welcome to Raven's Battalion."

Their handshake was firm and sincere. Erich was back in the unit with a command of his own, albeit at the loss of a comrade's life and Paul was getting his friend back in the fold.

CHAPTER FIFTEEN

Max sauntered over to his commander who was stood close to the top of the slope scanning towards the coast as he talked with his friend Erich.

"We need to move soon sir."

"Ok Max. For your info, Oberleutnant Fleck is taking over the command of Third Company, so will be leaving us. I'm afraid we've lost Oberleutnant Hoch. So, we'll need to take Uffz Forster with us to the top of the tree line."

"Scheiße, let's hope he's the last sir, but I've a feeling he won't be."

Max turned towards Erich.

"Congratulations sir, do you by the way need a new company NCO?"

"Feldwebel Grun. Oberleutnant Brand would shoot me for poaching, heaven knows why. And anyway I couldn't cope with your insubordination." They shook hands, Max genuinely pleased that the young officer was back with the unit.

Erich summoned his scouts and after some debate as to the best route to get to the coordinates provided by Major Volkman, they headed north to seek out Erich's new command. Paul and Max brought the command group together again.

"We're moving out in column, but with reasonable spacing. Roth your platoon will lead. Break off when you're about two hundred metres away from the trees. Nadel, you will follow and break off at the same time. Leeb, you'll be next. Unterfeld Richter, you will tail Leutnant Leeb's platoon but you will also break off at the same time as Leutnant's Roth and Nadel. Then set up where you see fit. Scout the road from the tree line if you need to, but for God sake keep your head down."

"Yes sir. Apart from not dropping rounds onto the road, how far out do you want our eastern rounds to be?"

"They're just to scare the enemy into avoiding that route of escape, so allow plenty of safety margin. Try and be within fifty metres if you can. But the kill zone, they need to be spot on."

"Jawohl Herr Oberleutnant, Leutnant Roth and I have worked out some simple signals so they can spot for us."

"Excellent."

Paul checked his watch.

"Let's get this procession moving."

Roth's platoon raised themselves up from their crouched position, weapons at the ready and moved out in column formation, at least a metre or more between each man. As the last of the platoon left the assembly area, Nadel's men tagged on the end, but only two troops, the missing troop failing to manifest itself. Although they knew it unlikely that the missing unit had survived the stricken plane and would never show up, deep down some had the vain hope that one of their missing comrades would suddenly appear surprising them all.

Leeb called his men up and forward, less Fessman and his two scouts who were already traversing the tree line, quietly creeping through the trees and undergrowth, checking for enemy soldiers who could raise the alarm about the advancing company. Paul, Max and the HQ element tacked on behind Leeb.

Unterfeld Richter's men were the last to move as he signalled his men to join the column, bringing with them additional mortar bombs carried in the wheeled drop canisters. He was already running through the mathematics of likely range settings, who would target what and the number of bombs they would use. His men had a critical role to play. Should the enemy manage to escape to the east and miss the trap set for them, the venture would have been for nothing. He was determined that he and his men would fulfil their role and contribute to the success of the mission.

The column moved across the undulating ground, the rustle of scrub and crunch of limestone and phyllite rocks beneath their boots, the only sound to be heard other than the occasional clash of a weapon or the subdued tones of the distant firefight towards the coast. After eight hundred metres, Paul, who had moved to the head of the column, held up his right arm, bent at the elbow, the signal for Roth and Richter to break off to the right. Moments later he repeated the signal with his left arm, Nadel extracting his platoon to move them off to the northwest. As they got closer Paul surveyed the tree line, it looked quiet and undisturbed. He felt optimistic they hadn't been seen and felt confident that Fessman would have found a way to let them know if there was a problem. Had there been an LP, Fessman would have taken them out, silently, or a firefight would have ensued.

Nadel was the first to reach his objective, positioning his two troops to act as a blocking force, denying the enemy the road as an escape route. He scrutinised the area below him, peering through the trees. In front, lower than they were, but higher than the road, set on the embankment, the cream, two storey building, the terracotta roof standing out like a beacon. The road was about fifty metres away, the building some ten metres the other side of that, perhaps two to three metres above it. To his right, he could just make out the one storey building, the starting point for Ernst's assault on the village.

Movement. His binoculars were up to his eyes as he saw an enemy soldier come from the building in front of him, from a door around the back he assumed. He focused in on him. He moved to the edge of the embankment, mentioned earlier by one of Oberleutnant Fleck's scouts, and stared out to sea. The soldier looked over his shoulder and beckoned to someone out of sight. Another soldier joined him. This one had a single chevron on his right sleeve, probably the section's second in command thought Nadel. Both wore Khaki uniforms, with short sleeved tunics with matching knee length shorts, socks pulled to their knees and wrapped over just below.

The Lance Corporal was gesticulating towards the coast. He said something to the other soldier then returned to the house. The sentry sat down on a rock, placed his rifle across his knees and proceeded to roll himself a cigarette, oblivious to the paratroopers watching his every move. Nadel instructed one troop to move to the left, filter down through the trees out of sight of the enemy post and then cross the road. Four men and an MG 34 would cover the road, the other six men would cover the occupied building. Number three troop were spread out along the tree line, the MG 34 on the right, to pick off the enemy once the firing started.

"They will not want to come this way," he whispered to Fischer.

Paul and Leeb met up with Fessman.

"Well?" asked Leeb impatiently. Not nervous or annoyed, just apprehensive. This was the most dangerous period. If they were jumped by the enemy now, they would lose the initiative, they would be at their least prepared.

"Fairly quiet sir. The main building seems to hold the bulk of the force in the centre, although we've only seen half a dozen men. But they're just brewing up, don't seem to have a care in the world."

"What about the southern sector?"

"We've seen five men, we think that's all there is. They too seem pretty relaxed. They were constantly in and out checking out the coastline in the direction of Hania, but apart from that appear pretty much settled."

"They're perhaps not aware of the scale of the attack," suggested Max. "Did you see any sign of comms?"

"We haven't seen any Feldwebel, there aren't any trailing antenna visible in the trees."

"The north?" asked Paul, keen to get the assault moving.

"We saw one sentry, but heard other movement inside the building. I would suggest a half section same as the south sir."

"Ok, thank you Uffz Fessman, re-join your troop."

That simple statement, about re-joining his troop, filled Fessman with a deep sense of pride.

"Deploy your men Ernst, let's get this moving."

Leeb's platoon infiltrated deeper into the tree line, to the edge of the higher ground. Konrad's troop went first, minus four men and the MG 34, who were to stay above and move along further south to cover the central building, the Mandarin.

They dropped down through the trees, coming in directly behind the single storey building, which provided them sufficient cover from the raised ground across the road. They slipped in through the door on the left hand side and quickly covered the two windows facing the road. There was no door or glass in the windows, although it didn't appear to have been abandoned for long. He looked left and could see the house that was being covered by Leutnant Nadel. He couldn't see anybody from this angle, but did occasionally hear the clank of equipment, perhaps a soldier washing mess tins or maybe cleaning his rifle. Then he saw movement, briefly, what looked like a soldier moving away from the building towards the embankment. There were no longer any parachutes to be seen, but there were Stuka's circling, like vultures seeking out their next prey.

Konrad sent a runner back to his platoon commander, giving the all clear for the rest of the unit to move down, and continued to check the positioning of his men, discussing arcs of fire, key points and confirming actions on contact with the enemy.

Leeb instructed Fessman to move his troop down next. He turned to Straube, who would be commanding the MG 34 section that would remain at the top.

"For God's sake keep a good look out for Fessman and Jordan, they will be moving right into your line of fire. Once you see them, just hold your position and cover, understood?"

"Jawohl, Herr Leutnant."

Leeb left them to it and went down to join the rest of his platoon. He was in his element. The skills of a soldier and a leader came naturally to him, reinforced by his Fallschirmjager training and being in combat on three separate occasions.

He moved carefully between the trees, constantly checking the higher ground opposite and joined the rest of his platoon, some twenty seven men crouching in and around the white building. Paul, Max, the medic and the Company HQ joined them. The HQ group would stay with Konrad and his men.

Roth reached the top of the escarpment and studied the target area below him. He handed Kienitz the binoculars. "You can see two soldiers to the right of the house, it looks like they're burning diesel to make a brew."

"See them. They look pretty indifferent sir."

"To the left, one hundred and fifty metres you can make out the Mandarin, probably their main force and platoon HQ."

"Got it. Looks like some movement, may be five or six soldiers getting ready to move."

"Quick, let me see." Roth grabbed the binoculars and swept the area of the building.

"You're right. I bet they're going to reinforce the men at the other end."

"Shall I send a runner to warn the company commander sir?"

"No, it's too late now. I've lost sight of them, they must be around the bend in the road. Wait, there's another group coming out. They're moving this way. They must be reinforcing each end of the village. Let's get in to position quickly."

He arranged his men. Two troops along the escarpment directly opposite the end building and one troop further along the road as it sloped down from the village. The killing zone was set up.

Keller took the baseplate, the traversing and cross-levelling gear off his back pack placing them on the reddish, dusty ground where he had cleared off the scrub earlier. In the meantime, Trommler had removed the barrel and elevating screw pillar allowing them to assemble the 50mm mortar ready for action. Sommer extracted the black stencilled, dull red, one kilogram mortar bombs from their case and laid them down ready for use. Richter ran passed the three mortar positions giving the paratroopers their targets and ranges, two would be targeting the other side of the village road, the third would bombard the enemy as they tried to evacuate the village.

Keller, on the mortar position furthest to the left and one of the tubes used to keep the enemy from escaping the village east, pressed the quick release lever, unlocking the catch of the sliding collar, freeing it to slide in its glide, elevating the barrel. He locked the sliding collar in its glide, then using the elevating screw he finely adjusted it until it was set for two hundred and sixty metres. Trommler, the layer, threw himself down by the left side of the tube, wriggling forwards on his belly until he was able to hold the levelling handles, pressing on the baseplate with his forearms, ready to add his weight for stability. Keller got into position on the other side of the tube ready to load the TNT filled, high explosive bombs. Richter checked each tube, confirming they were ready and verifying the range settings.

Paul instructed his company HQ, including the radio operator and medic, to stay with Konrad's men, reinforcing his reduced troop, there to cover any speedy withdrawal.

He turned to Max. "We'll go with Fessman, Leeb can manage a troop on his own."

"Ok, sir."

He looked at his watch, it was 0830. Running through the timings for Nadel, Roth and Richter to set up in their positions, he concluded they would be ready.

"Let's do it then Max."

He gripped Max's hand.

"And keep that big mug of yours out of sight, it's a target no one could miss."

The confident brown eyes set above the slightly bent nose, broken more than once, looked back at him.

"And you remember to stoop a little sir, or you'll get that head of yours blown off," he said, his face breaking in to a grin.

Paul indicated for Fessman to lead the way and signalled to Leeb that they were moving out. They manoeuvred from around the back of the building where they had been hidden from the road and quickly scurried across, eyes looking left and right and up towards the ground above them, praying they wouldn't be seen crossing the hard packed surface to reach the other side.

They reached the embankment edge undisturbed and moved up the forty degree slope, using the scrub, the odd boulder and small olive tree to keep out of sight. Paul signalled to Leeb, who was still across the other side of the road, to start the advance. They would have to keep checking each others position to ensure one didn't get in front of the other. Fessman took the lead, shadowed by Herzog and Gieb, Paul behind them, then Max and the rest of Fessman's troop.

Leeb and Jordan's troop also set off, making their way south, ten metres from the edge of the road, again using the scattered trees, tall patches of grass and scrub to hide their existence as best they could.

The six Allied soldiers approaching in the opposite direction, to re-join their comrades at the northern end of the village, currently overlooked by Nadel and his men, happily smoking cigarettes and chatting, guns slung over their shoulders, bumped into the darkened Fallschirmjager coming their way.

Fessman was the first to react, his beloved Kar 98K/42, held at waste level, spat out a round that took the Corporal, leading the party, full in the chest. Herzog and Gieb reacting seconds later also fired their Kar 98Ks, Gieb hitting the soldier immediately behind the Corporal in the shoulder, Herzog's round whistling through the air and over the head of a very lucky serviceman. All three, once they had fired, threw themselves to the ground, Fessman already working the bolt like lever of his Carbine, ejecting the empty case and feeding another 7.92mm round into the chamber.

Paul saw the three men dive to the ground and swept the area in front, firing above the troopers' heads, striking the Corporal again as he fell to his knees, his mouth open, but no cry issuing forth, falling backwards from the impact of the round. This was the signal for the rest of the company to react.

Nadel's platoon opened up on their target. The sentry, still sat on the rock, who seconds earlier was happily rubbing fine shag into his cigarette paper, was hit three times, his colleague next to him twice. The two who charged out of the house to take on this sudden appearance of the enemy ran into a hail of fire, one struck down immediately, the other managing to get down the side of the building, sprinting as fast as he could to re-join the main bulk of the force. His luck ran out as in his panic, he collided with Rammelt and Petzel, the troop's tail end charley, who cut him down.

Straube, situated on the high ground opposite the command building, the Mandarin, ordered the MG34 to open up, adding to the dissonance of sound steadily building. A torrent of 7.92 rounds smashed into the HQ building, some punching through the thin walls, some shattering the glass in the windows, others piercing the terracotta roof, fracturing the delicate tiles, broken glass and splinters of tile cascading on the defenders beneath.

★★★

Roth looked at Kienitz, nodded and they continued to wait patiently for their turn to get to grips with the enemy.

★★★

Richter also took his cue and ordered tubes one and two to open fire. Trommler, holding the bomb above the tube, dropped it and immediately went for the trigger, both of them burying their faces in the ground.

Thunk, thunk, the two mortars lobbed their bombs over the tree line, over the heads of the units near the road, landing the other side of the HQ building, left and right. They didn't fire a second round, waiting for confirmation that the rounds had landed where they were meant to.

"There," shouted Keller, seeing a trooper with his rifle held in both hands above his head, the signal that they were on target.

"Now we have work to do," added Richter, giving the order to recommence firing.

They fired the rounds slowly and deliberately, working them along the far side of the road, not the rapid six rounds in eight seconds they were capable of. Instead they created a wall of high explosives and splinters discouraging the enemy from even considering moving in that direction.

★★★

A Bren gun, it's distinctive curved, thirty round magazine clearly visible, had been set up in the upper window at the end of the tangerine house, the paratroopers nicknaming it, the 'Mandarin'. Now it was spitting .303 rounds towards Paul and his men. In the window below it, two men were firing rounds as fast as they could cock their rifles, emptying their ten round magazines, thrusting new five round chargers in as rapidly as they could. Three men who had got out of the door further back had thrown themselves down by the side wall on the side of the road, were also firing back, the rest of the men remaining inside covering other sectors should an attack from another direction emerge.

Jordan, across the other side of the road, could see the firefight taking place and hear the clamour of sound, splintering trees and chipped walls, but dare not fire for fear of hitting his own men.

Bullets whistled passed Paul's head as he too went to ground. He was anxious, he knew they had to do something, or they would lose the initiative and get bogged down. The approaching six men had prevented them from getting close to the house unseen. Richter's mortar rounds were not limitless and a counter attack was inevitable. His tactics were based on keeping the enemy on the move, forcing them out of the village where Roth and his men, supported by Richter's mortars, were waiting to spring the trap. Without another

163

thought, he pulled a grenade from his belt, unscrewed the cap, pulled the string, counted two seconds, and then threw it as far as he could towards the enemy lines, some forty metres away. Before it had exploded he was up on his feet, his MP 40 clutched at waist height, a fresh magazine loaded, was spitting fire at the entrenched enemy.

Rounds zipped past him as he sprinted towards his foes, his boots pounding on the ground, his heart pumping in sync, hammering in his ears. The grenade exploded in front of the soldiers at the side of the house, stunning them temporarily, the Bren gunner ceasing fire as he endeavoured to reposition the light machine gun to fire down on the interloper getting dangerously close.

The two in the doorway both aimed at Paul as he ran through the dissipated explosion, the gleam in their eyes indicating their confidence in being able to kill this German soldier with ease. Their faith quickly evaporating as a 9mm round from Paul's machine pistol struck the soldier on the left and a 7.92mm round struck the one on the right, Fessman's Kar98/42 still smoking as he chambered another round.

Petzel and Stumme with the MG 34, now had their turn, spraying the upper window with a lethal rain, Max's grenade following through, flying through the window finishing the Bren Gun's dominance for good.

The enemy had had enough, evacuating through the rear door of the house, leaving the dead and wounded in their haste to escape the onslaught of these devils, particularly the officer at the front, the manic grin on his blackened face, he was the devil incarnate.

"Cease fire, cease fire," yelled Leeb. "Secure the house, check weapons and ammo, get ready to move forward."

He waved his arm above his head towards Jordan's position across the road letting him know the area was secured and they would be moving on again soon.

Paul stood in front of the doorway, bent at the waist, hands on hips, his body heaving with exertion as he struggled to drag air into his depleted lungs. A shadow loomed over him, its size signifying it could only be Max.

"A word sir."

"In a minute Max, let me catch my breath."

"Now sir."

Paul looked up, could see anger in Max's eyes, his nose, slightly askew caused from a previous injury during one of his many fights on the docks, inches away from his face. He raised himself up to his full height.

"Not now Feldwebel Grun."

"We can have this out here sir, or we can move over to those trees. Either way, I'll say my piece."

A confrontation in front of the men was not good and Paul could already see sideways glances from some of the troopers. He looked at Max's heavy, square jaw, the suppressed anger still hovering beneath the surface. They moved away to the side of some olive trees, gaining some privacy from the rest of the unit.

"What the fuck was all that about sir?" hissed Max.

"We had to break the deadlock Max, we couldn't afford to get bogged down."

"Your suicide charge certainly broke the deadlock sir, but it also nearly got you bloody killed."

"It had to be done Max," Paul responded.

"We're a team sir, we work together. We've survived this far by working together."

"Life just seems so cheap Max."

"Killing yourself won't bring her back," said Max, more softly. "But it could kill these men here, the ones you're responsible for. They need, we need, you to lead us through this mess and bring us all back in one piece."

Paul hung his head, his energy sapped, his truculence evaporating away. He looked up, gripped his NCO, his friends shoulder.

"You're right, as ever. Let's get this business over with, the Company needs its Commander and senior NCO."

There was a moment of silence between them, only interrupted by the continuing exploding mortar bombs throwing up sprays of earth and shattered rocks and splintering trees. Leeb ran towards them breaking the moment.

"The house is clear sir, Fessman is sweeping forwards, we're ready to move out."

"Let's go then Ernst."

★★★

Nadel sent four men towards the house to check and clear the building, disarm any soldiers that may still be alive and secure it. Two soldiers were found dead and two injured, one mortally, the other a minor leg wound. They signalled to Nadel that the house was in safe hands and then patched up their prisoners as best they could.

★★★

Richter, continued to adjust the range and fall of his mortars, allowing for the additional distance as he shifted their fire to the right, tracking the fire fight in progress, updated by the troopers in the tree line.

★★★

Fessman's troop moved forward again carefully. Although the ground wasn't completely open, it lacked the depth of cover they had earlier, the number of trees and scrub severely diminished.

"Petzel, Stumme, I want the MG on the left flank. Watch out for a counterattack, they may risk using the mortar fire to cover an assault."

Crump, crump. Two rounds landed within fifty metres of them, the eruption showering them with debris, a piece of shrapnel glancing off Stumme's helmet.

"Bloody hell, I hope Richter's boys don't get any closer," commented Stumme, ducking his head low."

"The rounds are no where near you Friedrich. Anyway, we need them to keep the British away."

"Just keep a watch for a counter attack along there, mortars or no mortars," ordered Fessman, concerned that the British troops may brave the mortar fire to slip through and fire and attack their flank, or even worse, from behind.

★★★

Jordan's troop, now beneath Straube's MG position, continued to move south, keeping parallel with their comrades across the road. Still no contact with the enemy.

"Aaagh!" screamed Amsel as a round struck him in the shoulder, spinning him round and forcing to fall sideways to the ground. "I'm

166

hit."

"Keep low and quiet," barked Jordan.

More .303 rounds zipped through the undergrowth from the hastily set up Bren Gun, the thirty round magazine emptied in not much more than five seconds, the gunner's assistant slamming a second curved magazine on top of the weapon. Fessman had been right to expect a counter attack.

Once the British had recovered from their initial shock, they had crossed the road with some fifteen men in order to outflank the Germans, not yet aware of the scale of the force they were up against.

Jordan's thoughts raced, but his notion to order the MG to put down suppressing fire, his need to get grenades thrown so they could pull back under cover, were never uttered, were never followed through as he was hit twice as the second Bren Gun magazine was put to use. A .303 round striking his chest, his heart ruptured, both lungs perforated, pink froth at his mouth as he tried to rally and command his men, his last thoughts of thirst and the cold beer with his comrades in Corinth as his spirit left him and he lay sleepily on the ground.

Braemer, a veteran of Poland, Eben Emael and Corinth, didn't need orders to figure out what to do next, it was second nature to him. He plucked three, Model 34, stick grenades from his grenade bag and quickly unscrewed each cap. Keeping his head low, bullets still whistling passed above him. His comrades were now returning fire, the pruurrrrr of the MG versus the heavier, slower sounding thud of the Bren, fighting their own almost intimate clash for supremacy of the battle ground.

But he knew the stalemate wouldn't last for long as a second Bren joined the uproar. He lined his grenades on the dusty ground in front, keeping low behind the scrub in front of him, so far unseen by the enemy, he pulled the cord on the first one. He counted to two, got up on one knee and threw the grenade as far as he could towards the enemy, it landing some thirty metres away. Before it had chance to explode, a second one had been fused and was in the air landing to the right of the first one which suddenly exploded. The third one he threw from a standing position, its flight making some forty metres. The second grenade exploded short of the British lines, but the third landed close to the second Bren Gun team, giving Braemer and his colleagues an opportunity to move to a more advantageous position and extract themselves from the onslaught in front of them. Return fire could now be ramped up in preparation to repulse the attack that was inevitable.

★★★

Fessman ran at a crouch to Paul and Max's position.

"Jordan's in big trouble sir."

"I know, but we daren't fire across the road until we know his and his men's true position."

The MG34, across the road; finally opened up, giving them some indication of the unit's position, but not enough to risk enfilade fire support.

"Uffz, stay here with three men, just in case there is a second counter attack along this stretch, the rest with me. Max, you stay... "

"I'm going nowhere but with you sir."

Paul could see the determination in Max's face and nodded.

"Assemble the men Max, then with me."

The selected men quickly gathered around their leader, heeding his warning to watch out for their own men in the heat of the impending firefight, as the demarcation line was uncertain. Paul saw that a couple had attached their bayonets, clearly expecting to get close in with the enemy.

"Let's go."

Paul dashed off, taking long strides across the uneven ground, shortening them as he continued down the slope hitting the edge of the hard packed road with a thump, his machine pistol flicking from side to side, seeking out the hidden enemy.

Petzel tightened his hand around the pistol grip of the MG 34, settling the butt beneath his arm, his left hand gripping the bipod to control its tendency to rear up when being fired. Next to him was his number two, Stumme, two belts of ammunition criss crossed over his shoulders and chest, looking as much like a Mexican comanchero as a paratrooper, his Kar 98K ready should he need it.

A soldier lying on the ground on the other side of the road, close to the edge, suddenly jumped up, surprised by the sudden appearance of a

168

German paratrooper adjacent to his position. He lunged at Rammelt with his bayoneted rifle. Rammelt, equally surprised at the appearance of the Tommy, leant to his right raising his left arm as the bayonet was thrust upwards towards his face. The muzzle and bayonet of the Lee Enfield, now parried, skimmed passed his left shoulder, just scoring the side of his neck, allowing him to counteract with a butt strike to the soldier's head. His cheek bone smashed, he stumbled and fell at Rammelt's feet, who quickly drew back his weapon from the swing firing a round into his chest, cocking the rifle and firing a second shot.

Braemer suddenly reared up from the undergrowth in front of them to their right, shouting.

"This is the furthest point of our position."

That was all they needed to know. Petzel put twenty to thirty rounds into the undergrowth to their left, before hitting the deck and putting up sustained fire. The rest of Paul's group joined them. Grenades were tossed, the enemy no more than twenty metres opposite them.

Just as the British soldiers thought they had caught the impudent invaders on the hop, the tables had in fact been turned on them and they broke, running back the way they had come, fleeing the grenade shrapnel and heavy gunfire, their only thoughts now, one of escape.

"Cease fire, cease fire," commanded Paul

"Petzel, Stumme, stay where you are. The rest check for any survivors. Jordan to me," he shouted, wanting an update from the troop commander.

Braemer sprinted towards his company commander, never more glad to see him and the rest of his comrades who had come to their rescue.

"Where's Uffz Jordan?"

"Gone sir. He was killed in the first attack and Amsel has a shoulder wound, we need to get to him soon."

"Shit. Right, take temporary command. Secure the British soldiers still alive, see to the wounded and secure this area."

"Jawohl, Herr Oberleutnant."

Braemer left to carry out his orders and was replaced by a panting Max.

"There are five enemy dead sir and two injured."

"Braemer has the troop. They will see to the wounded and secure the area, we need to keep pushing forwards Max. You join Fessman, push forwards again and we will move parallel with you."

"Consider it done sir."

Max sped across the road, up the bank and joined Fessman again and they advanced further along the village embankment, Paul and his force doing the same lower down, across the other side of the road, moving passed the groaning enemy troops, many of them wounded by Petzel's devastating fire and the onslaught of grenades thrown at their flank.

Events then moved quickly, the enemy in a complete rout attempted to extract themselves from the village to regroup and lick their wounds, avoiding the intermittent mortar rounds on their left, constantly stealing a glance over their shoulders for the enemy in hot pursuit behind and looking worriedly at the embankment to their right, they ran into the trap that had been set for them.

Tube 3, tipped off by one of Roth's men, now firing eight rounds in six seconds, helped to decimate the remainder of the platoon, Roth's thirty men finishing them off. One victim blown into tiny pieces, all Roth could see afterwards was a booted leg, a hand still clasping his Lee Enfield and bits of khaki uniform spread across the white, hard packed road.

Max's whistle blew an ear-splitting blast, that even managed to pierce the sounds of gunfire still in progress and the firing slowly ceased and the bombs no longer flew overhead. The air was filled with silence other than the cries and whimpers of the wounded. Even the distant battle near the coast failed to intrude. Some of the injured servicemen clasped their wounds, desperately trying to piece their shattered body together. One soldier's hands skipped over his tortured belly, locating the swelling, lipid mass oozing from his torn abdomen, failing to stop it overwhelming them. His eyes, the wide eyes of an eighteen year old boy, gaping in incredulity at what he was witnessing, knowing deep down that this was the end, but clinging on to life all the same.

Paul approached the scene in front of him and looked about, it was carnage. There was no other way to describe it and he felt sickened by what he had himself instigated. He had wanted this, planned for it. Now it was in front of him he felt nauseous and trembled uncontrollably.

"Max, get Fink up here now. Roth to secure the area, let's see what we can do for them."

Max gripped his arm.

"We had to do it sir, this was what we engaged the enemy for, to beat them. Had we not, then this could have been us."

"I know Max," Paul said. "I know."

CHAPTER SIXTEEN

The Company had merged together at the northern end of the village, just above the gully they would descend shortly. A patch of green, flush with Olive trees, an unexpected idyll before their descent into the more barren gully. The branches so full and low the soldiers could only sit beneath them.

It was an opportunity to grab something quickly to eat from their bread bags, most opening a can of iron ration, meat, and breaking off a piece of dark bread, now dry from the heat of the baking sun, but welcome all the same. Water was next, initially gulping it down to quench their urgent thirst, then sipping it as if wine. They had found a cistern in the village, the water from a spring in the mountains, sweet and cool, allowing them to satisfy their craving and top up their depleted water bottles for later. They were encouraged to gorge themselves with water, to rehydrate their bodies, knowing it could be a scarce resource during their time on the island.

The British soldiers, detached from one of the Australian battalions on the island to secure the village, had been brought together and put in the Mandarin house, over half were dead or wounded and three were missing from the platoon size force. Fink was doing what he could for them with his limited supplies. He informed Paul that at least three would be dead before nightfall and possibly another two not long after, unless they received medical attention in a well equipped medical centre or hospital. The remainder had been patched up as best as the resources and skills available allowed.

A troop of Roth's men were guarding the prisoners, passing round cigarettes, sharing chocolate and swapping stories, Pigeon English and sign language having to suffice. Their weapons had been gathered up and destroyed, their ammunition scattered about the countryside.

Roth's men wouldn't be staying with the prisoners, Paul had made the decision not to leave anyone behind, other than Forster and Amsel. He would need all of his men, the battle for the island was far from over.

He had contacted Major Volkman, a heated argument ensued over the crackling airways. Paul insisting that a German medical team be released as soon as possible to attend to the British prisoners. The Raven's response had been conclusive, stating that medical units would not be free for some time, such was the level of Fallschirmjager casualties. Eventually he agreed, after Paul's persistence, that as soon as a unit was available he would have a British medical team escorted to their location. To reinforce that arrangement, Paul would leave his own wounded men to watch over the prisoners, including Uffz Forster with a broken leg, Amsel with a wound to his right shoulder. Jordan, however, his chest torn apart by .303 rounds from a Bren, had been buried at the top of the gully, a helmet hung on top of an upturned rifle, a mound of reddish earth, now the only visible sign he had existed. They had promised to return when this was over, exhume his body and return him to the Fatherland.

Paul had his officers and senior NCO's gathered around him at the head of the defile. It was one in the afternoon, they had been on the go now for over eight hours. They had taken some shade beneath two fruit trees, laden with oranges, still too bitter to be eaten, much to Max's displeasure.

On the horizon, in the direction of the coast, the air shimmered, the panorama beyond wavering in the rising heat. Close by his men chatted.

"I thought I was going to get killed today," one was heard to say.

"I anticipated a quick death or I would come out without a scrape," said another.

Paul had conversed with his Battalion Commander for as long as the radio signal allowed, talking through what had occurred and what their next movements were to be. He also had an update on the progress of the strategic battle for the occupation of the two hundred and fifty kilometre long island.

At Maleme airfield, second and fourth LLSR had landed west of Tavronitis, with two battalions being sent to secure Hill 107 from the south. Third LLSR, had landed to the south and east of the airfield and suffered considerable casualties.

To the north west of their current position, at Hania, success had also eluded the Fallschirmjager. The Third Fallschirmjager Regiment, 3FJR, supported by an engineer battalion, had landed in Prison Valley, southwest of Hania, again suffering substantial casualties, the third battalion was widely scattered. These isolated units would have to continue hostilities until reinforcements could be flown in. Paul had made sure that the black and yellow recognition strips had been laid out in case a stray Luftwaffe fighter bomber took an interest in them.

He looked around at his men, their blackened, dusty faces, streaks of white where rivulets of sweat had run down their faces during the heat of battle. In spite of being dog tired, the men's spirits were high. He was proud of them, proud of the way they had performed today. Despite the fact that they had outnumbered the enemy force by over three to one and had routed them completely, it was with minimal casualties, Fallschirmjager's skills and professionalism coming to the fore.

The sun was beating down on them and even in the shade of the low olive trees under which they sought respite, the heat was unbearable. Helmet removed, Paul wiped his brow with the sleeve of his smock, catching the slightly extended scar above his left eye.

He turned to the group close by.

"Listen up," warned Max, knowing his commander was ready to brief them.

"The next twelve hours gentlemen. We move out at fourteen hundred, taking a route down through the gully that starts just below us, which will lead us slightly north west. We'll move about two thirds of the way down, then set up a base camp for the night. There will be no fires, so it will be cold food again I'm afraid."

"Jaeger schnitzel not on the menu then sir?"

"No Feldwebel Grun, it will be of the tinned variety," he responded, smiling. All was well again between the two friends, although Max had already resolved to keep a very close eye on his young commander.

"Leutnant Nadel, I want a half troop to explore the upper part of the gully, suss out the lay of the land, but don't go too deep into the defile."

"Shall I send them now sir?"

"Yes, but they need to be back here by thirteen forty five."

"Jawohl, Herr Oberleutnant."

Nadel called over one of his troop commanders and gave them their instructions, Paul waiting until he had finished before continuing.

"For our night stop, I want four Listening Posts out, one either side of the defile exit, one behind and one in front of us."

"How far out do you want the LPs sir?"

"Between fifty and a hundred metres Ernst, but closer to fifty would be better providing they can find cover."

Paul shifted his position to get more shade from the tree, the sun glaring in his eyes, making him squint.

"There will be further landings by our forces, so we need to be in position to watch for any enemy movement and interdict any enemy flanking units attempting a counter attack. Or move further north to support any unit in need."

"After that sir?" asked Max.

"We will move east probably, and depending on the outcome of the battles along the coast, we may need to march some distance and at speed. Hence the break we will have tonight."

"Order of march sir?"

"Glad you asked that Dietrich, your platoon can have the pleasure of taking the lead. You're next Ernst, Unterfeld Richter after you and your platoon can have the tail end position Viktor."

"Headquarters sir?"

"We'll slot in behind Leutnant Leeb. How is Fink doing with the wounded?"

"Amsel is comfortable sir and he has patched up the British soldiers as best he can. Some are in a bad way though," responded Max.

"They should get some help in the next twenty four hours sir," informed Bergmann. "HQ say they've allocated a unit, along with some British medics, who will move up here as soon as they can be released."

"What about the rest of the battalion?" asked Max.

Bergmann looked at Paul for permission to continue, to which Paul nodded his assent.

"The other three companies are in the process of moving lower down from the high ground, just like us and then await further orders. It's all dependent on taking Maleme airfield and landing further reinforcements, Feld."

"So, gentlemen," continued Paul. "We move to lower ground and await further orders. Any questions?"

"What time will we secure for the night sir?"

"As soon as we come out of the defile, probably dusk Ernst. Any more? No? Ok, we move in... " He looked at his watch. "Thirty minutes."

Thirty minutes later, briefed by the recce team that all seemed clear they moved out from their position, dropping into the gully, the initial entrance being quite shallow. The ground in front and around them, strewn with whitish, irregularly shaped rocks, not hard like granite, but not as soft as limestone, somewhere in between, but still able to catch an unwary boot and turn an ankle. The immediate ground in front of them was almost desert like, the trees foliage free, the branches bleached white. The pale pink earth beneath was dispersed with small clumps of scrub and indigenous plants of various types, evidently adapted to the dry terrain. Fifty metres in front, a lone lemon tree stood out, green and yellow in its isolation, its yellow fruit defying the desolate ground.

As they snaked across the terrain, the occasional grunt could be heard from a trooper, his leg jarred by a small hole secreted beneath the scattered plants, catching him unawares. The random chink of weapons and equipment as they continued forwards, their weapons and eyes scanning the ground in front of them, then switching to the sides, feeling exposed now they had left the relative safety of the village. In the distance they could just glimpse the white buildings of Hania, the windows glittering from the reflected rays of the sun. The town framed in a tapestry of colour, ringed by patches of green, red and brown, a streak of blue sea beyond it, the even paler blue sky beyond that.

The unit stopped, Paul and his platoon commanders scanning their frontage and their flanks. Above them to the right, a well worn track snaked down towards them, standing out white against the multiple shades of green, its route lined by the ever present olive trees.

Above this path was a terrace of sorts, with flat green balconies, trees flourishing in lines, clearly cultivated by local farmers or fruit growers. Reddish brown earth sloping down to the next balcony, at least a dozen could be seen. To the left more terracing, but shallower and not man made, weathered and fashioned by heavy rains and tumbling waters that would have rushed down to the ever narrowing gully during the rainy season. They got up from their crouch, Paul satisfied that they were on their own, the men left behind would fire a warning shot if the village was being re-occupied.

A kilometre into the gully and the boundary started to close in, the sides steepening, the terrain rougher as they reached the defile. They moved deeper in to it, claustrophobic after the more open, wider section they had just traversed. Its sides climbing steeply above them, as if swallowing them up. The terraces were now gone, replaced by craggy rock on both sides, lone, dwarf sized trees clinging to its sides, struggling to eke out a living on the dry bare ledges. The occasional clump of yellow gorse was the only true colour to break up the dark grey sides. The ground under foot steadily deteriorated, unremittingly testing their limb articulation and balance, teasing the paratroopers with a sense of firmness, only to give way, jolting a leg. The occasional curse indicating a trap had been sprung, a Fallschirmjager suddenly finding himself on the ground, much to the amusement of his comrades, but who intensified their search for similar traps.

They continued to make their way through the ever narrowing gap until the track they were on was only a couple of metres wide, forcing the column into single file, the company now strung out along a nearly two hundred metre stretch. The narrow gorge continued for half a kilometre before it came to an end, as if slowly opening its jaws, allowing the troopers to stagger their position, the feeling of claustrophobia dispelled. But, they had felt hidden, secure, in the defile, but now, with still a couple of hours of daylight to go, they felt exposed. The land in front of them now levelled out before dropping away again in the distance where they would probably turn east.

Paul called a halt, the view of Hania again in front of him. The sea was bright blue, darker than the pale blue sky that met it. The town sitting in the inverted triangle, between the slopes coming down to border it. The occasional house could be seen dotted on the slopes as they became shallower the closer you got to the town.

He gathered his officers and senior NCOs about him, the rest of the company searching for a comfortable piece of ground to rest, others, under orders, were laying out the recognition signs should one of their Luftwaffe comrades choose to fly over. Some took the opportunity to quench their unremitting thirst, the sun beating down baking their steel helmets. That aside, they were still alert, aware that they were advancing deeper into enemy territory.

Now they were out of the gorge, they could again hear the muffled sound of fighting below them. Although they wished they could be there, supporting their comrades in their struggle to subdue the enemy, they were still recuperating from their own fast moving firefight. Up since three in the morning, they were all experiencing a weariness that was dragging at their limbs, sleep clawing at their tired eyes.

Although Paul couldn't see Rethymnon from their current position, it was some fifty Kilometres east of Hania, they could hear the Luftwaffe attacking targets in and around the town, the Junkers transport aircraft following, dropping their cargo of Fallschirmjager as the second wave of the day was initiated. First battalion of the second Fallschirmjager Regiment landing north of Adele and west of Stavromenos, with the third battalion making a landing between Perivolia and Platinais. A second group was assaulting southwest of Stavromenos.

Paul called his men to order.

"I want five Listening Posts out, we're bivouacking here tonight. Viktor, you're responsible for our route of advance and eastern arc. Put your LPs fifty metres out, no more."

"Jawohl, Herr Oberleutnant."

"Dietrich, cover our left flank and rear. The ground to our left is less steep, so put two out to our left, one at fifty and one at a hundred. And one behind us of course."

"Jawohl, Herr Oberleutnant."

"My platoon sir?" asked Leeb, not wanting his platoon left out of any duties.

"You're to take a patrol further down the gully. I want to know if there are any surprises for us tomorrow."

"A full troop sir?"

"Yes, if you come up against a significant force you may have to fight your way out, although the darkness will give you some cover. Don't take third troop, give Braemer chance to settle into his new command."

"How far down sir?"

"Not much more than half a kilometre Ernst, beyond the level ground it drops down again and we don't know what the route is like, yet. Leave your main kit here, travel light. If we need to bug out, I will leave some men here to cover your withdrawal. Unterfeldwebel Richter, have just one of your tubes set up to cover Leutnant Leeb's withdrawal should he need it. Keep the rest packed in case we need to move quickly."

Richter nodded his acknowledgement.

"Sir."

"Rotate the LPs sir?" asked Nadel.

"I would advise not Leutnant, the ground is too treacherous and they would make too much noise in the dark. I suggest we have three man LPs, allowing them to stay in situ and take it in turns to get some sleep."

"Good point Feldwebel Grun, all LPs to have three men rather than the usual two," ordered Paul.

"What time for the patrol sir?"

"Make it one, so make sure the troop gets some sleep before you go. We'll be losing light soon, so I want everyone fed, in position and ready within the hour."

The officers and NCOs dispersed, orders were given and preparations made.

★★★

The three Fallschirmjager scrambled up the forty degree slope on the fringe of the company's left. It was only fifty metres to the first LP, but the ground beneath them was not allowing for easy movement. They found a spot in the centre of a patch of scrub, where if they lay down they would be invisible to anyone other than someone standing over them.

The occasional tree clinging to the side of the gully were too thinly spaced to hide any advancing infantry, not that they could necessarily be seen in the dark anyway. They felt sure that any approaching troops traversing the side of the slope would be heard by either LP well before they would be seen.

They had agreed a rota and Blau put his head down on a softer piece of gravel and was asleep almost as soon as his head had touched the floor. The LP moving back up the gully over the ground they had recently traversed quickly got into position as did the one covering tomorrow's route of advance. The LP covering the eastern flank found it harder, the ground being much steeper. The rest of the company settled down for the night, the heat of the day swiftly evaporating leaving a blanket of cold over the men, who less than an hour ago were sweltering in the baking sun.

Leeb had his men gathered around him, cicada's chirping in the background, the air cool and fresh. Their faces recently blackened with a concoction of mud and earth. Their packs were secreted with their comrades, stealth being the watchword for this patrol. Each man jumped up and down, checking for loose equipment or anything that could create noise. Satisfied the patrol was ready he led his scouting party quietly north, picking their way through sleeping troopers, the sentries on duty for each platoon watching them go. Leeb was followed by Uffz Konrad and nine other members of second troop.

They made contact with the forward LP who was expecting them, agreed a password for their return, and then headed out into the darkness leaving the safety of the camp perimeter. They advanced slowly, step by step, treading carefully, weapons at the ready, ears alert for any sound that stood out above their carefully placed feet as they progressed across the flat ground.

Fifteen minutes on and the ground started to fall away again, one minute they were enclosed by a few, heavily foliaged trees, the next minute they were in completely open ground, the sides of the gully disappearing above them on both sides, the Cicada's restarting as they left them behind. Having advanced over five hundred metres, Leeb slowed the pace even further as the gully opened up again, occasionally stopping to look and listen, convinced that the small tree or undergrowth ahead was a person. Seconds later the undergrowth seemed to move, staring back. They would blink and it became what it truly was again, a tree or bush and the patrol continued.

Leeb halted the troop, squinting his eyes, looking deep into the darkness, sure he could see a regular shape ahead. He motioned Konrad forward and whispered in his ear.

"I'm sure there's something ahead. Keep the troop here, I'll take Muller and Kempf with me."

"Ok sir." He called the two men forward.

Along with their platoon commander they ghost walked towards the area that had attracted Leeb's attention. They lifted their legs high to avoid any grass or scrub and placed them back down gently, checking for anything that could break or crack, as they put their weight back down, giving their position away. Even though it was cold, the concentration and effort required resulted in sweat trickling down the inside of their uniforms. They peered into the gloom. After a few minutes of walking softly towards their target, their bodies aching from the intensity of the effort required to maintain that posture, they recognised a hut of sorts, built of interlaced stones with a basic thatched roof, no more than two metres wide.

"What was that?" hissed Muller.

"I don't know," responded Leeb. "It sounded like a tin rattling."

"There it is again," informed Muller.

White ghosts leapt out in front of them. Black faces and hooves hidden in the darkness, their shaggy white bodies floating passed them like demented spirits, bells clanging from around some of their necks, wavering cries like deranged souls as they fled into the distance. Something brown shot passed Kempf, horns prominent.

"Hell," hissed Kempf, "it's a bloody goat."

The noise continued unabated as a flock thirty or forty panicking sheep and goats sped past them, bleating fast and furious, bells ringing as they raced down the gully passed the hut.

"Damn. Everyone quiet," called Leeb.

The men hugged the now cold ground, steadying their breathing, listening, watching.

The animals continued to scatter down the draw, the clappers banging out an irregular tune as they went. Leeb focused on the hut ahead of them as a figure emerged, scanning the darkness about him, club held out in front of him. He moved a few feet away from the hut and looked about him listening to the sound of the fleeing animals. The figure walked a full three hundred and sixty degree circuit of the hut, then back to where he started before heading up the gully towards where the Fallschirmjager were hidden.

He was within two metres of Leeb when he stopped, sniffing the air, the club swinging at his side. Leeb froze, his face close to the dusty earth, keeping his breathing slow and shallow, the sound seeming to reverberate in his ears, the sweat cooling and chilling his now still body. The man had no shape, his ragged clothes just draped over his form, the stench of the goat herder, putrid and foul pervaded the air.

After a few moments the herder seemed to relax. His arm holding the club drop loosely to his side and he shuffled back to his hut, hitched up his outer clothes, pulled down his greyish pants and urinated against the wall of the hut, constantly looking about him and back over his shoulder. The occasional muffled explosion, or distant crack of a rifle shot drawing his attention to the coast. He shook himself, re-adjusted his clothing, sniffed the air again and went back inside.

Leeb waited ten minutes before he gave the order to move and led his men quickly back up the gully, checking in with the LP, briefing his commander and settling down, along with his men, for couple of hours sleep.

CHAPTER SEVENTEEN

Although still dark, the sentry could make out one of his comrades cat walking down towards him, placing his hands and knees carefully on the ground so as not to be heard. As he got closer he rose up into a crouch and moved the last five metres until he was next to his fellow trooper.

"There's movement above us, off to the left," he hissed.

"Scheisse. I'll let the Leutnant know. Stay here, don't re-join your LP in case you're heard."

The sentry went swiftly, but quietly, to rouse his platoon commander. Placing his hand gently over Leutnant Nadel's mouth he shook the sleeping form, instantly reassuring him that he was a friendly before Nadel's pistol, close at hand, could be fired.

Nadel was awake in a trice, snatched the sentries hand from his mouth and whispered, "What is it?"

"The LP has just reported in sir, there is movement along the goat track."

Nadel shot up, his mind now fully alert.

"Wake the Company Commander then the platoon commanders." He gripped the sentry's arm. "Quietly though, make sure everyone is quiet."

"Sir."

The trooper left to carry out his orders, but as hard as he tried the ground underfoot crunched as he passed over it. He prayed that the sound wouldn't travel beyond the confines of the gully.

Paul quickly pulled the platoon commanders together and told the trooper from the LP to run through what had been seen.

"The goat track that runs along the slope sir, halfway between the furthest LP and the top, there is movement along it."

Paul reflected, his calculations telling him that they were some two to three hundred metres away.

"How many?"

"I left after about a minute sir, but before that I saw at least a dozen soldiers pass by. But we couldn't see clearly, it was just shadows and the occasional noise of someone stumbling."

"How do you know they were soldiers?" asked Max

"We could tell by the shape of their helmets Feldwebel, they're definitely Tommies. Some had those hats that they pin up at the side."

There was silence as Paul reflected on what he had just heard, tactics and scenarios running through his jaded mind. He felt under pressure. They needed to take action soon, while it was still dark and they had time to react. This force was heading down towards Hania and Rethymnon. The last thing the Fallschirmjager needed was more British troops joining those already there.

"It sounds like they're Australian troops," added Leeb.

"Dietrich, pull in the LP's and get your men ready. I want your two MGs on the eastern flank, get as high as you can but make sure you have plenty of cover. You're going to be exposed up there. That will make your range somewhere in the region of five hundred metres across the gully. Take extra ammo and spare barrels, take them from Leeb's platoon."

He turned to Leeb.

"Ernst, take your platoon back up the defile. We don't know how far back they stretch, so move at least five hundred metres before turning west and come in behind them. It will start getting light in less than an hour so you'll have to be quick."

"Sir."

"Viktor, your platoon is to follow Ernst. Leave a troop at the top of the defile to cover our backs then take the rest behind Ernst's men to cover his back. One on top of the slope and one further west on the flat. I want you to just focus on the enemy to your front."

"What about the rest of my men sir?" asked Nadel.

"They can cover the entrance to the defile and watch over Unterfeld Richter's mortars. I will give you the company HQ as well, except I want Bergmann with me."

They were disturbed by the arrival of the returning Listening Posts.

"Quiet," hissed Max. "Report."

The LP to the rear had seen nothing, the same from the eastern and northern LP's. But, the one furthest west had some information to impart to the assembled group.

"At least one hundred men have gone passed our position sir. They'd slowed down but there weren't any signs of them stopping while we were there."

"Sounds like at least a company sir."

"Yes Feldwebel Grun, so we need to get into position fast. Brief your men, but I want you moving in less than five, time is not on our side. You need to travel light Ernst, leave your kit and MGs here. No, wait, take one MG with you, but move quickly."

"Jawohl Herr Oberleutnant."

His officers scattered and rapidly advised their men of what was to take place.

Within two minutes of Paul's briefing, Leeb recognising how time critical their plan was, a troop from his platoon was already hiking back up the defile they had only descended the previous day. They travelled light, just basic kit, weapons, ammunition and water. They moved quickly, knowing that speed was of the essence, the light of day creeping up on them, the sun ready to pop up above the horizon, sunrise a mere fifty minutes away. Once the enemy could see them, once the enemy knew where they were, the element of surprise would be lost and the enemy soldiers could disperse and even turn the tables on their enemy.

"Max," called Paul in a whisper.

"I want you to control our mortar team. I don't know how effective they will be in this terrain, but we'll need all the help we can get."

"Where will you be sir?"

"I'll go with Leutnant's Roth and Leeb."

He turned round.

"Bergmann, see if you can contact HQ. Let them know what's going on. If the British unit makes a run for it they're likely to head north."

"We're unlikely to get a signal in the gully sir."

"Stick with me then and try when we get to higher ground."

"Yes sir."

"Fink, Mauer, Ostermann, you stay with Feldwebel Grun and cover the mortar team. If we need you Fink, we'll try and get the wounded to you."

"Yes sir," they all responded.

Leeb came alongside.

"We're ready sir, I've sent Konrad's troop ahead."

"Good, let's go."

They moved out. Nadel's two, reinforced, four man MG34 gun groups, laden down with additional fifty round ammunition belts and spare barrels, clawed their way up the steeper eastern side of the gully, their boots slipping on the loose rocks under foot on the sixty degree slope.

Nadel was ahead and looking back he could see his men becoming more distinctive to him as dawn rapidly approached. He looked across the gully to the opposite slope, but could not make out any movement, as yet, the hope being that if he couldn't see them, they wouldn't be able to see him.

Down below him, at the base of the gully, at the narrow exit point before it widened as it continued down towards the coast, the shadows of Feldwebel Grun and Richter's mortar team, like wraiths, could be seen preparing to give the enemy their own surprise. He spotted the small outcrop ahead that he was working towards. It wasn't much, but would furnish them with some concealment and protection. They clambered over the dark green, slightly damp, foliage and swung right to the side of the outcrop, a lone immature olive tree adorning the top. An ideal focal point, thought Nadel, for the enemy to direct fire on to him and his men. He had no option. They needed the height and the angle if they were to bring down sustained suppressing fire to support their comrades, even though the range was excessive.

He studied the facing side of the gully again, this time with his binoculars. But on this occasion he could just make out the lighter line of the goat track and could see darker shadows intermittently spaced along it. Looking down, he could just make out Richter's men crouched next to their mortars, clearly ready to fire. He switched back to the target, noticed the shadows were stationary and then checked his men were in place and ready. All they could do now was wait for dawn to reveal their targets in full.

Leeb crouched breathlessly at the upper entrance of the gorge, the sound of panting Fallschirmjager could be heard all around him. They had dashed up the trap ridden gorge and having been on the go for twenty four hours, with only a couple of hours of uncomfortable and disturbed sleep, the pace was starting to tell.

After exiting the defile, leaving a troop to cover the entrance and Feldwebel Grun's back, Roth's men continued up the more spacious gully, where they had crossed only yesterday, at a faster pace. Now the snaking path and flat green, cultivated terraces were somewhere above to their left, the chalk white path barely discernible in the pale light of the early morning. To their right the shallower, weathered terraces, they would now have to scramble up. Leeb looked at his three troops, two without the familiar MG34. He turned to Paul.

"What do you suggest sir?"

Paul looked up the western slope. "Send first troop with the MG left, scale the slope at an angle, on to the top then advance about one hundred metres beyond. Second troop on the top of the slope and third troop on the goat track."

"Sounds good sir."

Paul looked at his paratroopers, their breathing slowly steadying, a high level of fitness allowing for a fast recovery. It was time to push them again.

"Let's move it."

Paul was up and on his feet and led the way straight up the slope facing them. Fessman took his nine men at a slant, pummelling up the gradient as best and as quickly as they could, driving the toes of their boots into the ground, leaning into the incline as they made steady progress up the punishing slope, noticing the ground was becoming more defined as the light steadily grew.

Reaching the small plateau at the top, he advanced across its surface, placing his troop in a sixty metre line, his MG on the left, a hundred metres beyond the top of the slope and waited. He shifted his body from side to side getting as comfortable as he could on the barren, rock-strewn ground. He could see the shadows of his comrades moving into position on his right, but could see very little to his front. He saw Konrad setting up his men on the top of the ascent and called his men forward until they were in line with Konrad's left flank. He knew Braemer would be lower down covering the goat track. He saw Oberleutnant Brand running along the line, scrunching down, as he moved towards him.

"Ready Uffz?"

"Yes sir. We're going to be up against it this time."

"We are, but Unterfeld Richter's mortars will add some extra weight."

"Leutnant Nadel's lads will give them a headache as well sir."

"As soon as I am back with Konrad, we'll move forward."

"Understood."

Paul left and ran, hunched over, back to the centre of the line. He came alongside Leeb.

"Roth has sent a runner. All is clear back there so he's sent one of his troops here should we need them. More the merrier sir, we need to put them further out, beyond Fessman. It's a big area to cover and it will make it less likely we'll have to contend with a flank assault."

"Agreed. Organise that and position yourself with Fessman. I'll stay here so I can cover the goat track as well."

Leeb left and Paul turned to Bergmann.

"Make contact with HQ. Let them know we're about to bump a company sized force, possibly up to two hundred men."

"Jawohl sir."

Paul looked around him, dawn was drawing near. Soon he would be able to see the enemy, and they him. He needed to close the distance. He looked left, but still couldn't see if Roth's men were in position. If not, they would have to catch up, he thought. He stood up, signalled to move forward.

In a concertina fashion, the entire line of over forty men stood and moved forwards, weapons at the ready. The two MGs on the left flank gripped in front of their gunners, a fifty round belt already in the feed tray.

Keeping in line with their company commander, they slowly gained speed, boots pounding into the ground, scattering small rocks and stones as they advanced in a quick march. Paul picked up speed to a double march, over forty pairs of lungs breathing hard, their limbs jarring against the ground, muscles and tendons still taut from the previous day's events. The line started to stagger, the fitter ones gaining ground, keen to get to grips with the enemy. Those with heavier loads or on rougher ground, found the going harder. But before it became a problem, an Australian unit came into view in front of them.

A group of twenty soldiers were sat close to the edge of the slope, the tail end charlies of the allied unit. Some were lying on the bank staring down into the blackness of the gully below, others quenching their thirst on top of the plateau, or sharing what little food they had left. But now they all sat up from their reclined posture, disturbed by the sudden rush of noise behind them.

Dawn, as if on cue, speedily exposed the contestants of the forthcoming engagement. Paul could now see a long line of allied soldiers sat along the goat path some fifty to a hundred metres below, the line stretching off into the distance, further than his eyes could see. Some were huddled together in groups, others in pairs, threes and fours, whispering to each other or catching some desperately needed sleep, or at least their eyes were closed, others taking dregs of water from their now depleted water bottles. Although he couldn't see to the end of the line, his estimate from what he could see was well over a hundred soldiers, maybe double that including those out of sight.

His mind was now racing. Had he taken on too big a force? Could the lead elements swing round and hit him hard from the side? Maybe even surround him. During the next few minutes, no more, he would have the answers to these questions. He would know if his tactics were sound. He just needed to disrupt the enemy force to such an extent that they would be unable to rally and would have to disperse.

"Hit them hard," screamed Paul.

His advancing force erupted in a paroxysm of fire, Straube to his left pumping rounds into the group of Australian soldiers not more than twenty metres in front of them. The Australians struggled to react quickly enough. Two Bren guns were thrown on to their bipods in an effort to put down some fire, the group tripping over each other in their alarm at the advancing Fallschirmjager. Their battle cries and guns spitting fire, made a terrifying sight. Such was the weight of fire, the Bren's didn't even have a chance to fire a single round as a mixture of machine pistols, karbines and light machine guns devastated their ranks.

Matters were to get worse, Nadel's MG34s were inflicting serious casualties at their rear and on the men strewn along the full length of the goat track, the targets so numerous the gunners were finding it difficult to select.

Richter added to the clamour of sound, rounds targeting the column some two hundred yards ahead. Max recognising the need to keep the head of the column occupied and under intense fire, preventing them from rallying and pulling together a counter attack of any substance against the much smaller German force.

To the far left of the line, the troopers had dropped to their knees, Kar98Ks picking off the scurrying soldiers, many making a dash for the slope to seek cover from the onslaught, only to run into a wall of fire from Braemer's troop covering the goat path.

It turned in to a rout. The Allied troops couldn't advance south towards Paul's men due to the ferocity of fire. To go down the slope would expose them to Nadel's MGs, one already on its second barrel such to the sheer volume of fire being dispensed. To go north along the goat track would eventually get them away from the killing ground, but then they would have to face the mortar rounds that were tearing into the slopes top and sides. One Bren Gun along the line did manage to return fire, but ineffectively, his number two unable to place a fresh magazine into the LMG, his hand frozen to the curved, box like ammunition holder he had been gripping when he had been struck down.

The mortars and Nadel's MGs had split the allied force in to two. One half was extracting itself from the killing ground, heading down the edge of the gully towards the coast, before it too was decimated. The second half, unable to raise their heads, even for a split second, such was the savagery of fire zipping above their heads, the grazing fire picking off other soldiers attempting to flee the scene.

"Cease fire, cease fire," screamed Paul, knowing there was no fight left in the men in front of them.

His ears rang and his voice sounded echoey inside his head as he shouted further instructions to his men. He opened his mouth wide, stretching his jaw trying to clear his blocked ears.

"Leeb, secure the force to the front, but send a runner to Feldwebel Grun and Nadel, I don't want them shooting us up."

The next thirty minutes passed by swiftly. The enemy along the top and the incline had been disarmed and those prisoners in good shape were being used to patch up their own wounded, the company only suffering two casualties. Thirty two soldiers had been killed or wounded, twenty six alive but now imprisoned by their captors, the rest fled down the gully towards the coast. Paul walked through the group of dispirited soldiers, joined by Max.

"They're not in good shape sir."

"Yes, I can see that," he replied looking at one of the injured men lying on his side. There was a hole in the sole of his boot and his uniform, although not ragged, was in a poor state of repair. They came across a Vickers machine gun, lying on its side, not even set up. Max examined it.

"I can't see any ammo belts for it sir, these .303 heavy machine guns usually have belts of two hundred and fifty rounds and can fire four hundred and fifty rounds a minute."

He picked up the cooling water can, still connected to the barrel, just before the muzzle flash excluder, and shook it.

"And this is empty."

"If they'd managed to get that into action Max, Nadel's MGs would have known about it."

"And a reputation for being unstoppable," added Max.

They continued along the top, finding Fink attending to one of the injured Australians. He had performed well, dealing with the wounded in a professional but compassionate manner, showing no signs of panic at seeing the size of the task in front of him, he had moved from one wounded man to the next, assessing their needs and quickly moving on. The young Australian soldier looked up at Paul and Max.

"Mum... Mum..." he cried.

Blood was on his lips and his haunches and legs were daubed and caked in dried blood. He tried to pick his head up, but in vain, Paul gently pushed him back down, finding the soldiers pack close by he pushed it beneath his head, making him as comfortable as he could. He fumbled in his Bread Bag until he found a fresh lemon he had picked earlier. He cut it in half with his gravity knife, and crouching down beside him, he squeezed some of the lemon juice on to his parched lips, the boy licking them gratefully, the juice mixed in with his blood. The soldier murmured something, Paul lowering his head so he could hear. The boy took a deep intake of breath and then sighed, his body limp as it moulded itself to the folds in the ground. Paul looked at Fink who shook his head before speeding off to see to the next patient waiting for his appearance.

Paul looked down at the lifeless body. His mother would not see him again, or hear the sound of her son's voice. His death, although not completely forsaken, his comrades were close by, he could see them looking over, but his family could not take part in it. He and his men had caused so much death in the last twenty four hours.

Paul placed the boy's jacket over his face, his comrades looking on, one grizzled Corporal nodding, acknowledging that although they were enemies, he appreciated Paul's demonstration of compassion. Behind him, tugging him back to the world around him, he could hear Bergmann's radio crackling.

"Venus, Venus, over."

"Venus receiving, strength five, but you are breaking up, over."

The caller could clearly be heard, but the signal was weak and the voice crackling. Bergmann conversed with his fellow operator at the other end.

"Oberleutnant Fleck is moving his company to ambush the rest of the escaping Tommies sir. Wait a minute."

Bergmann listened in to his handset.

"It's Major Volkman sir."

Paul turned to Max.

"Get the prisoners and wounded in to the gully and get the recognition strips out. Visibility is good now and our pilots will be out hunting again. I want the two injured men and two men from Braemer's troop to form a guard. I suspect we'll be moving again soon."

Paul didn't look to see if his orders were being carried out, he knew he could leave it in Max's hands, the Raven was already on the line.

"Outstanding job Brand, what's... condition of... company? Over."

"Still checking sir, but I have a strength of at least two platoons."

"Good. A Junkers... managed to land... Maleme airfield..."

"Does that mean reinforcements sir, over?"

"Yes Brand, so... low lying hills... east, over."

"You're breaking up, head north then east? Over."

"Yes, over."

"We need a resupply, over."

"Liaise with HQ supply, over."

"What about the prisoners sir? Over."

"Leave... small guard. Move quickly... hard time... Rethymnon, over."

"Understood. Rest of the battalion sir? Over."

"Fleck... south Hania... by... company. Janke's company... leap frog them... follow... , over."

"Janke behind us? Over."

"Yes, get going Brand, out."

Paul handed the handset back to Bergmann and sought out Max

"How is it going Max?"

"Most of the wounded are down sir. They're in shit state, even the non-wounded."

"How are they off for water?"

"Not a lot sir."

"Ok, send one of our guys with a couple of prisoners back up the gully to the village to get some water. If they've got a medic send him as well, he can look at their wounded. Then get the officers together Max, we're moving out again."

Paul looked across at the sun, now above the horizon. It was going to be a long, tiring, hot day.

CHAPTER EIGHTEEN

The sun was glaring. Not yet overhead, but already fierce and unrelenting as they picked their way down the gully that was widening the closer they got to the bottom. They passed the goat herder's hut, but of him, or his goats and sheep, there was no sign. A bird circled above them, a 'Bearded Vulture' a knowledgeable paratrooper informed the group, with a wingspan of nearly three metres.

"It's tracking us," one of the men was heard to say.

"Probably a Tommy spy," added another.

Leeb's platoon led the way down the gully, Fessman's troop in the lead as usual. The troop proud of their acting Uffz's reputation and theirs now, as the scouts of the company. Nadel's men followed behind them, then Richter's Mortar troop and Roth's platoon acting as tail end charlie. The headquarters company was ensconced in the middle. The two wounded soldiers from Leeb's platoon and two others from Nadel's already depleted platoon, had been left behind to secure the prisoners. Paul was comfortable they could handle the task, even though wounded. He couldn't leave anyone else, if they met a much stronger force he would need all of his fit men.

The column halted and Paul and Max made their way forward to the front of the line, knowing Fessman would have only stopped the march for a good reason. They arrived at the head of the line, the inverted triangle of Hania much broader now that they were closer, the slopes either side of the gully more shallow, the ground levelling out ahead. Gunfire could be heard coming from the direction of the coast, the 3rd Fallschirmjager Regiment probing the 10th New Zealand Brigades front line.

"We can swing east now sir. It looks like a track about two hundred metres ahead on the right," pointed out Fessman, and handed

Paul his binoculars and shifted his favoured Kar 98K/42 into position to repel any possible attack.

His troop had already fanned out either side of the gully providing cover for the company commander and the head of the column. He takes command well, thought Paul.

Studying the route ahead he could see the ground flattened out further, the drop towards Hania more gradual. There were a number of buildings scattered about before the ground reached the more densely populated town, some two to three kilometres away. To the right, the track Fessman had picked out. He would not normally choose to use it. Everything he had ever been taught about tactical movement, excluded the use of tracks, ideal locations for an ambush. But, he knew he had no choice if he wanted to move east quickly and get to the southern point of Rethymnon and take some of the pressure off the Fallschirmjager there who were battling to clear the landing strip and break out of Stavromenos. He needed the track; to try and move across the rough ground quickly was not an option.

Paul handed the binoculars back to Fessman, looked at his watch, it was showing ten fifteen. He turned to Max.

"We have about three klicks to go until we get to the resupply drop area."

"We'll have time sir, it's not due 'till mid-day. So long as we don't get held up again," replied Max.

They all looked north. The firing south of Hania was escalating, bursts of MG 34s more persistent now as the battle raged.

"Do you think the Tommie's have run into Oberleutnant Janke's boys sir?"

"Quite possibly Max." He turned to Fessman. "Move out Uffz, take the track. I don't need to remind you to keep your eyes peeled."

"Yes sir. Right you lot, move out," he called to his troop, indicating that they angle across to the track ahead.

They moved off. Paul raised his arm in the air signalling the company to move, then, along with Max tagged on the end of Fessman's troop. They turned right along the narrow, gravelled track, almost tinged pink in colour, following its weaving path. To the right, the slope leading back up to the low foothills where they had come from earlier and to the north gently sloping down towards Hania to their northwest.

The first few hundred yards took them passed one of the many olive groves that seemed to dominate the countryside and on their left an orchard of lemon trees. Although the temperature was slowly ramping up to its peak of forty degrees, this early part of the morning was almost pleasant and the steady rhythmic march of boots along the elongated column was therapeutic.

"You wouldn't think we were in a bloody war sir."

"It does seem a bit surreal Max."

"What's that sir?"

"What Max?"

"Listen, it's like a hum, a steady hum, almost a droning sound."

"You're right, I can hear something."

They continued to tramp east, the track taking them left and right as it meandered across the landscape ahead of them. On their right the olive grove had long since been replaced by scattered trees strewn with broken rocks. The humming became louder, clearly heard now above the steady footfall of their boots, the sound almost pulsating.

"There sir," pointed Max to the left. "Beehives."

In a small open patch, there must have been at least thirty beehives, in undeviating rows, alive with drones and worker bees, returning with a stash of nectar appropriated from the nearby plants. Looking more closely at the track side the soldiers could see the purple plants were alive with honeybees darting from flower to flower.

"It's a shame we didn't have time to raid them, fresh honey would be nice," mused Paul.

"You'd be on your own sir, you won't catch me going near them."

The droning sound slowly diminished as they moved down in to a shallow dip in the track, continuing round a long bend, ahead of them row upon row of cultivated trees in yet another grove. The track narrowed even further, overgrown with ankle to knee high grass in places, dropping down to meet the exit point of a small gully, before rising back up again and levelling out. Petzel leading the way, Fessman slightly behind his right shoulder, both scanning left and right, aware of the possibility of an ambush along this particularly narrow stretch of path. Suddenly Fessman reached out with his left hand, grabbed the back of Petzel's 'Y' strap, and yanked him back.

"Down, down, don't move."

At the same time he raised his karbine in his right hand signalling the column to halt.

Paul, Max and Leeb quickly made their way to the front of the file.

"What is it Uffz?" asked Leeb crouching down next to him.

"There sir," he said pointing to the ground about two long strides in front of them, "a trip wire."

"I can't see anything."

"Neither can I," said Paul. "You've got good eyesight Uffz."

He turned to Max. "I want Leutnant Roth watching our back and Leutnant Nadel to put a troop out either side of our line of march. They would have opened up by now had they seen we'd discovered their trap, but I still want the area secured."

Max shot off to carry out his orders and after closer scrutiny Paul and Leeb were able to make out the very small stretch of trip wire that was barely visible passing across a bare patch of grass, its green colour blending in well with the surrounding blades.

"How the hell did you pick that out?" exclaimed Leeb, who even now lost sight of it if he turned away for too long.

"The benefits of being an ex-poacher," informed Max who slid back down beside them. "Troops are moving into position sir."

"If you were going to put down a trip wire sir, it would be the most obvious place, most of the track has been bare up to this point. There's also good cover each side."

"Can you deal with the trip Uffz?"

"I'll do it sir," interrupted Max. "It'll be good to keep my hand in."

"You sure Feld?" asked Leeb

"Yes sir."

"Are sure Max," added Paul

"I'll sort it."

"Right we'll leave you to it. Ernst, move the men back thirty metres."

Max handed Fessman his MP40, helmet and stripped off his Y

straps and any other items he wouldn't need. He took his P38 from his holster.

"I'll hang on to this though," he said, tucking his pistol into his belt.

"Take it easy Max," warned Paul. "We can always go round."

"Oberleutnant's Janke and Fleck wouldn't thank you if they blundered into it."

"Good point Max, but be careful."

"Take it slowly Feld," advised Fessman

Paul and Fessman pulled back to join the rest of the unit leaving Max to study the ground ahead of him. To the right of the trip wire the grasses were much higher, interspersed with small yellow and purple flowers. To his left, a jumble of rocks and a large purple plant, like nothing he had ever seen before. It was the size of a man's head, a velvety, purple, lolling tongue with an even darker protuberance coming from the centre, the flower backed by a ring of large green leaves, the trip wire disappearing behind it.

He lowered himself to the ground, creeping forwards until his face was millimetres from the green trip wire. He looked along the wire, tracking it with his eyes until he could see the end where it was tied off to a thick stalk of a shrub. He could see nothing else around it. He moved gently to the left, even more cautiously now he knew where the device was likely to be. He peered around the purple plant, the sun beating down on him, its rays burning into his exposed skin through his short cropped fair hair, now without a helmet to shield it. Sweat was pooling along his back as he reached out with his left hand and gently pulled aside the plant's leaves, exposing the device.

It was a simple mechanism — a tin can wedged between two rocks, inside a grenade had been lodged. Its pin had been removed, but in the confines of the tin, the lever arm couldn't be released. Had Fessman's lead scout kicked the ankle high trip wire, it would have dislodged the British Mills grenade from the can, allowing the spring loaded arming lever to be released, forcing the firing pin to strike the percussion cap and exploding the grenade. Depending on whether it was a four, four and a half or a seven second fuse would have dictated who in his troop would have been injured or killed. With the longer fuse, Fessman and his lead scout would have been a dozen paces away when it exploded, targeting those in the middle of the patrol.

Max saw a glint in the undergrowth, it was the pin that had been discarded after being taken out of the grenade. He picked up the pin, careful not to dislodge the trip wire and grenade, and placed it down in front of him. Gripping the wire with his right hand, his heart thumping in his chest, his left hand hovering above the tin, he gently eased the Mills bomb out grasping it tightly before the lever arm could be released. He held the grenade tightly, his lungs sucking in air as he had been involuntarily holding his breath for the whole time he was making the trap safe. He buried his face in to the ground waiting for his breathing to slow down and his heart beat to settle before he re-inserted the pin and made the Mills bomb safe.

He got up, wiping the sweat pouring off his brow and running into his eyes, placed the grenade in his pocket, thinking it may come in handy, and turned towards his comrades showing a thumbs up. He was joined by his company commander who slapped him on his back.

"Well done Max, what was it?"

He pulled the grenade from his pocket. "An English egg sir, hard boiled and still intact," he said with a grin.

"Just something left to hold us up, not part of any larger scheme."

Paul looked at his watch, they had less than an hour to get to the resupply point which was still a Kilometre away. He turned round and signalled the company to continue its advance, the two troops on the flanks collapsing back in on the line of march. Max donned his equipment, congratulations and compliments winging their way in his direction and the unit resumed its fast pace east.

They arrived at the chosen location thirty minutes before the scheduled drop time. Recognition markers were laid out and the company set up in an all-round defence. The site chosen was to the north of the track, a flat piece of ground covered in a short layer of grass and a scattering of shrubs. A pillar of smoke was spewing upwards somewhere between Hania and Rethymnon, the battle for the island continuing. All they had to do now was wait.

Bergmann had been in communication with Regimental Headquarters and they verified the drop was still on, albeit running late by up to ten minutes. After a twenty minute wait, they heard a steady drone to their west, parallel to them, the change in the tone indicating they were swinging east to fly over the drop zone. Shielding their eyes they searched for the first signs of the aircraft, the forty plus degree heat causing the horizon to shimmer, distorting all they could see.

"There," pointed out Leeb, "three of them, they're starting to drop down."

The three Junkers were in an arrow formation, slowly descending to the correct height for dropping their loads, on a heading that would take them on a route directly in front of Paul's unit, on target for a perfect drop. The droning grew more forceful the nearer the planes got, eventually thundering by Paul's small force, two Mischlast Abwurfbehälter, wooden drop containers, with seven hundred kilogram payloads, dropped from the two outer aircraft and four steel drop canisters fell from the lead plane.

The aircraft flew so low, the paratroopers could see the pilot's heads silhouetted against their cockpits and waved to them, a link with other German combatants, a much needed reminder that they were not on their own. The chutes deployed and the containers swayed as they were gently lowered towards the ground to land a few hundred metres away from the paratroopers waiting expectantly.

Even before the Junkers had started their climb in preparation to bank towards the north and return back to base, the designated Fallschirmjager were up on their feet, racing across the open ground to recover the containers and their contents. Although fairly confident that the enemy were not in the immediate vicinity, they still didn't want to take any chances. The low flying aircraft may have attracted unwanted attention. With wheels attached to the canisters and the wooden containers unloaded, the supplies were dragged quickly back to the track and the contents checked. Ammunition belts for the MG34s, rounds for the MP 40s and Kar 98Ks were found, along with rations and supplies of water. No mortar bombs had been dropped, they would have to suffice with the ten rounds per tube left.

They distributed the ammunition and rations between the troops, any residual items were left in the wheeled canisters and taken along with them. There was surplus machine gun ammunition and water, although the water wouldn't last long, each man was consuming at least four litres of water a day.

Paul looked around his command. Max directing the men, allocating the supplies fairly across the unit, ensuring all had an equal amount of ammunition to carry, cracking jokes with the troopers.

"How long do you need Max?"

"Ten minutes tops sir. I've dished out the water but it isn't going to last us long."

"We'll keep our eyes peeled for a suitable village or water source on route."

"Right sir, heat exhaustion won't take long to appear in this heat if we don't."

Max then drove the company even harder to ensure they met the target time, he knew his commander was anxious to move on.

CHAPTER NINETEEN

The unit reassembled in line of march and continued along the snaking track, picking up speed as they settled back in to a rhythm. After two hours they came to a small village and took a break, taking the opportunity to scout for water. The occupants appeared to have evacuated the village. There were no enemy soldiers to be seen, but evidence left, like empty ration tins, the odd .303 cartridge, showed they had been there at some point during the last couple of days. A check was made for booby traps, the memory of the one they had nearly stumbled into earlier still fresh in their minds.

Paul allowed his men a fifteen minute break, the company straddling the track that continued east, staking its claim across the base of the low foothills. His men were clustered together in small groups, seeking what shade they could from the burning sun, the temperature soaring well above forty degrees, the soldiers baking in their European theatre uniforms, soaked from the forced march they had just completed. Helmets had been removed, relieving them of their weight for a few precious minutes, but many replacing them as the searing heat burnt into their exposed skin. Some of the olive skinned members of the unit were so dark now, they could have easily passed for one of the locals. Until they spoke that is.

The pale faced Roth on the other hand, had suffered badly, the top of his nose refused to go brown, but stayed bright red as it burnt that little bit more each day. Once he and Max had overheard some of the troopers humming 'Rudolf mit der roten nase'. Roth had turned round sharply, but the troopers quickly stopped and the Leutnant scanned the assembled men trying to establish the culprit or culprits. Both of them had turned away, desperately trying to hide their grins at the discomfort of the red nosed officer. It was not meant maliciously, he was a popular officer with the men and the fact that they had gone out of their way to bait him, was proof of that. He was probably the only paratrooper to have kept his tunic sleeves rolled down, to protect the delicate skin of his very white arms. Max on the other hand, olive skinned, looked like a piece of burnished oak.

The first round struck the trunk of the spindly olive tree that Max and the three platoon NCOs were sheltering under, shattering the silence and splintering the wood causing a sliver of trunk to peel away engulfing the men in its foliage. The rest of the bullets stitched eight rows across the open ground as the browning machine guns hammered the rounds out, ripping furrows into the earth, smashing any rocks they encountered, ripping into a paratrooper, killing him instantly.

The Hurricane roared as it shot passed them at a little above tree top height, shaking the ground beneath them, filling their senses with a its thundering roar. The shadow swept over them and the pilot, who had overshot his target, pulled back on his stick, throttle fully forward, his aircraft oscillating as it screamed in to a climb, its Merlin engine at full power.

"Take cover," screamed Max, not that anyone needed any encouragement to get out of sight of the fighter plane that was already banking round for a second go at the Fallschirmjager scattering below it, two ominous bombs slung beneath its wings.

The pilot finished his turn and pushed the aircraft into a dive again, the wooden, two bladed, fixed pitch propeller, spun by the one thousand horsepower merlin engine, quickly brought the Hawker Hurricane to a speed of over two hundred miles an hour.

The paratroopers scurried around below, seeking what cover they could, some hiding behind trees with more robust trunks, others finding dips in the ground. The sound of an MG34 could be heard, the barrel resting on a low hanging branch as the gunner pumped as many rounds as he could in the direction of the enemy aircraft.

The pilot peered down, searching for targets before he hit the firing button on his control stick, knowing his two and a half thousand rounds of ammunition, with a rate of fire of over a thousand rounds a minute, gave him a little over two seconds of continuous fire. Keeping his bursts short and on target was essential. But, it was all incidental. His concentration was such that the first he knew of the Messerschmitt bf 109, were the 7.92mm rounds from the German's wing guns and engine mounted cannon, ripping through his fabric covered wings and finding their way to his engine. Oil splayed across his canopy blinding him as he frantically threw the plane from side-to-side to escape the murderous fire. The German fighter peeled off to escape the spray of oil that was threatening to also smother his canopy, banking round to get into position for a second attack.

"Recognition flags," yelled Paul. "Get anything you can out on the ground, we don't want him turning on us."

The Hurricane was losing power as the engine spluttered and coughed, flames starting to engulf the cowling, the pilot pulling the aircraft into a climb, desperate to gain some height to enable him to eject and parachute to safety. Just before the merlin engine hacked it's last breath, he pulled back the oil splattered canopy, flipped the plane over onto its back and fell into the open sky, his aircraft spiralling out of control crashing a mere two hundred metres from Paul and his men.

The Messerschmitt dropped low, the pilot checking out the recognition flags and waggling the plane's wings to indicate that he'd IDd them as friendlies, giving his comrades below the thumbs up, but unable to hear the cheering through his canopy.

The engine purred, then whined as he pulled it in to a climb, his ammunition low and fuel almost out he needed to get back to base before he joined the British pilot who was floating down to earth. The Fallschirmjager's attention was now drawn to the white parachute descending to the ground, the RAF pilot dangling below. Apart from a large tear in his uniform, caught on the aircraft as he left the cockpit, a few splashes of oil and feeling the shock, he was unharmed.

Paul dispatched four men to grab the pilot who was about to land, only a hundred metres north of their position. Secured and disarmed, his parachute left behind, he was quickly brought in front of the company commander. The troopers pushed him to the floor. He looked to be about twenty five to thirty years old, his khaki battledress was dishevelled, probably from being on duty almost constantly these last forty eight hours, rather than through lack of care. Although he seemed anxious, he didn't display any signs of fear. His rank showed him to be a Flight Lieutenant and he was still wearing his brown flying helmet, oxygen mask dangling at the side, goggles pushed back on top of his head. Paul ordered them removed.

Ackerman, from Jordan's troop, now under the command of Braemer, who could speak almost perfect English, reached down and yanked the helmet off, revealing a brightly coloured mop of red hair. He smiled up at his captors, his eyes bright blue, his wide mouth showing a set of perfect white teeth. His skin was pale, intimating he hadn't been in this theatre of war for long.

"Ask him what unit he's from," demanded Paul.

Ackerman asked the question, but the pilot did not respond, just looked about him at the pairs of staring eyes.

"Ask him his name."

Ackerman translating on each occasion.

"Flight Lieutenant Brewster," he offered, still smiling.

"Where's his base?" continued Paul.

"Brewster, Flight Lieutenant, 615431," he replied.

"What was your mission today?" The frustration clear in Paul's voice. Ackerman translated.

"Brewster, Flight Lieutenant, 615431," he replied again.

"He's not going to give us anything sir, just his name, rank and number," suggested Max.

"Why does the British air force bomb civilians?"

Ackerman looked at his company commander, who indicated that he ask the pilot the question.

This time the pilot hesitated, clearly thrown by the question, before repeating his name, rank and number.

"Why do your pilots bomb innocent civilians, women and children?" Paul asked, his voice now raised.

The pilot looked up at the faces that surrounded the officer asking the questions, confused. He tried to make eye contact with them, but all he received back were blank stares.

"I don't think he was a bomber pilot sir," suggested Max.

Paul turned and looked at Max and said, "His plane was carrying bombs, wasn't it."

He turned back to the pilot, pulled his Walther P38 from its hard, black holster, pulled back on the slide cocking the weapon and pointed it directly at the head of the pilot, who was now showing signs of fear, franticly looking from one paratrooper to another searching for a friendly face. He started to shake.

"Why do you bomb women and children?" Paul hissed through gritted teeth, stretching out his right arm, his hand visibly shaking, looking down on the prisoner, his pistol less than a third of a metre from the pilot's face.

The pilot's panic stricken eyes now darted from face to face, his anguish evident as he scoured each face hoping to discover that it was all some cruel joke.

There was complete silence. Sweat running in rivulets down Paul's features, matched by those running down the face of his prisoner, the connection only between them, all others on the periphery, were excluded. His finger, squeezing the trigger of his pistol, a hair's breadth away from firing a round.

"Sir," said Max gently, placing a hand on Paul's right arm, slowly easing the gun down.

"He wasn't responsible, he was just doing his job like the rest of us."

Paul's gun arm was now parallel with his leg, the pistol pointing to the ground.

"Our Stuka boys have been meeting out just as much punishment around Maleme and Hania."

He eased the pistol from his commander's hand, took out the magazine and ejected the chambered round, reloaded it, replaced the magazine and return the pistol to its holster.

Paul turned to Max. "Thank you Max," then turned on his heel and walked away.

Max turned to Ackerman. "Explain to him about the Oberleutnant's loss and assure him he will not be harmed."

He then shouted, so all could hear, "Let's get this bloody show on the road. I want the company ready to move out in ten minutes, and God help anybody who isn't ready."

The group that had congregated around the prisoner quickly dispersed, even the platoon commanders not wanting to challenge the tough Feldwebel's authority. Max looked about him, saw Paul collecting his gear, the pain of the memory of her plainly etched on his face.

The company got in to formation and continued their march east, pushed on relentlessly by Max, extolling them to move quickly before Oberleutnant Janke's company caught up and overtook them. The company maintained a steady five kilometres an hour, climbing higher occasionally before dropping back down to lower ground. They soon found themselves south of Rethymnon, the men fatigued by the incessant heat, where they took a break.

The men were even too exhausted to eat, all they wanted was water, their bottles only half full, the supplies dropped to them earlier nearly all gone. The RAF pilot was secreted amongst one of the troops towards the rear of the column, Paul ensuring he had the water he needed.

The battle for Crete continued around them, as they settled down to catch their breath and rehydrate their hot, dry bodies. Two companies of Fallschirmjager had dropped just west of Maleme airfield and although the 100th Gebirgsjager Regiment had started to land by transport plane at the airfield, the area was far from secure. In Paul's area of operation, Rethymnon, the Fallschirmjager were having less success, being slowly pushed north towards the coast. Further east an additional force of paratroopers were being dropped close to Heraklion, his companies eventual destination. 1st and 2nd battalion of FJR1, had linked up east of the runway and a further drop of one hundred and fifty men was expected.

The company picked themselves up again and continued their march, the pressure to be in position to support their beleaguered comrades preying on their minds. As they tramped along the never-ending track, dust coating their hot, dry bodies, adding to their misery, they caught the occasional glimpse of civilisation as the approached the vicinity of Rethymnon. Stopping a few hours later, next to a Church on the outskirts of a small village called Skullfera, an opportunity to rest up and prepare for their descent towards the town the next morning.

A quick recce of the village showed it to be clear of enemy soldiers, the locals choosing to stay hidden, perhaps not even in the village, but hiding out in the hills above them. Tomorrow they would pass through the village, dropping down again until they were just southeast of the town, where they would conduct patrols further into the suburbs, seeking out the enemy, distracting them while their comrades withdrew to better cover or pursued the objectives they had been given.

They mounted security for their stopover, LPs positioned fifty metres out at all points of the compass. The ground around them was fairly open and flat, climbing slightly towards the village, above the village the ground rose steadily towards the upper foothills. Across from them, towards the northeast, Rethymnon. Earlier they could just make out the sea, but now they were not high enough to see the coast or the town, now it was too dark to see either. Only the odd red tracer shooting skywards to then tail down to ground level as it got close to its target, indicated the likely position of the town. The occasional flare, perhaps launched by a nervous soldier certain that an enemy trooper was creeping up on his position.

Paul had set up his company HQ in the church, a whitewashed building, with four, terracotta topped, arched extensions leading away from the central, two storey, octagonal dome. It made an ideal spot to gather his platoon commanders and NCO's together for a briefing. If he was still troubled by the earlier incident with the RAF pilot, he gave no indication of it. Above, in the dome, a terracotta window at each face, now punched out, were three troopers. Although they could only see a few metres beyond the realms of the Church, as dawn approached they would have the best view of any approaching enemy, an MG34 close by ensuring they would give a good account of themselves should they be attacked.

Paul's command group had pulled the benches into a semi-circle, Bergmann and Fink making the assembled men a hot drink. Even though only a dozen men were in attendance, with all of their equipment, the church seemed crowded, but it was cooler inside than out.

"We're going to rest up here until four," said Paul. "So make sure the men get some food eaten, have full water bottles and get a couple of hours sleep. It will be an even longer day tomorrow."

"Uffz Fessman's boys have been into the village sir, and brought back plenty of water. I've got a shuttle system on the go to make sure everyone gets a good drenching before topping up," informed Max.

"Good, ammo status?"

"We used up a few rounds firing at the British fighter plane," responded Leeb, "but my platoon has about five thousand rounds for the MGs and each man in the region of one hundred and forty rounds for their personal weapons."

The remaining two platoon commanders reported roughly the same, they would be able to give a good account of themselves in battle.

"I've got ten rounds per tube sir," added Richter. "So we can still put some fire down if needed. We also have about one hundred and forty rounds per man."

"Food?"

Max adjusted his position on the hard wooden bench, the seat too narrow for him to get his large frame on it comfortably.

"Two days rations, all have been dispensed throughout the company so we can leave the drop canisters here."

"LPs?"

"All out sir," answered Roth. "My platoon is doing the first stag."

"Right gentlemen, I suggest you get your heads down, we'll be moving out first thing. Nadel to lead, followed by Roth, Richter and Leeb."

The group dispersed and the company HQ moved the benches back, scraping the tiles as they did, making room to bed down for the night on the cool tiled floor.

"Lift the bloody things up," bellowed Max, "it's doing my ears in."

They picked the benches up, not wanting to incur the wrath of the Company Feldwebel and found a suitable space. Some were asleep before they even gave any thought to food.

Max sat on the bench alongside Paul, handing him a now lukewarm mug of coffee. He sipped it, the taste bitter and even though only lukewarm it brought out beads of sweat onto his brow.

"How's the pilot Max?"

"He's fine sir, Ackerman told him that he was safe."

"I'm not sure what happened Max," he said, his head drooping with both shame and weariness.

"Something gets to us all at some point in our lives sir, I wouldn't worry about it. The lads respect you no less, why don't you get your head down, things will look totally different in the morning."

"I need to check the lines first."

"With respect sir, you have three Leutnants and a Company Feld to do that, are you trying to put me out of a job?" he said smiling.

Paul's head was nodding, his chin dropping down to his chest, his eyes closed, oblivion close. Max helped him slide on to the floor of the Church, the benches too short for his six foot two frame, and he was asleep before his face had touched the cold tiles. He left him to carry out his inspection of the lines, leaving the young officer to recuperate, they would need him tomorrow.

CHAPTER TWENTY

The paratroopers were roused at four in the morning, the skies still dark, the coolness pleasant after the blazing heat of the previous day. Most had managed to bag three or four hours sleep, even though they had LP and sentry duty during the night. But once released from duty, sleep overwhelmed them. However, faces were drawn with exhaustion, limbs strained and aching, blisters punctured and taped, ready for another days marching or fighting. Some had even attempted to scrape off their two days of stubble, wash some of the grime off their faces, to then re-apply their camouflage. During the six hour break, weapons had been cleaned, dust and grit not only invaded the working parts of their weapons, potentially causing a stoppage, but their eyes, nose and ears, a constant layer of dust grinding its way into their uniforms, rasping their skin raw.

The unit formed up, led by Nadel and his men, and trooped through the blackened village, the whitewashed houses like white ghosts, the occasional dog barking at their departure, seeing them off their territory. Fessman and his band had already scouted the empty buildings again, ensuring they were free of enemy soldiers, tagging on to the procession as it passed through. Their boots clattered on the metalled road, the first one they had encountered since landing on the island, but they weren't to remain on it for long.

Leaving the village, they dropped down again, re-joining the track that continued to take them north east. They could see very little of the countryside either side of them. But as they got closer to Rethymnon and the darkness slowly gave way to the dawn, what they saw differed little from the dry, barren land they had travelled across the previous day.

The occasional dwelling broke up the monotonous scenery as

they got closer to the outskirts of the town, prompting an upsurge in their alertness as they got closer to the concentration of enemy troops ensconced there. The track switched east again, passing Adele to the south, a metalled road running through the village and continuing east parallel to their route of march. After about a kilometre they came across a Wadi and Paul checked his map and conferred with officers and Max.

"This has to be Wadi Piggi," said Paul pointing to the line running south to north on the map, "and back there we've just passed Adele, agreed?"

They all nodded.

"We're getting close now sir, should we fan out a bit?" asked Leeb.

Paul pondered the question. "Not yet Ernst, it will slow us down, we've to keep moving fast. I want us south east of the town by midday and ready to start probing the outskirts, we need to start taking some pressure off our units there. Saying that, make sure your platoons are ready to switch to extended order at a moments notice. Understood?" He looked at each man in turn, checking their understanding.

"How's the prisoner Feldwebel Grun?"

"Apart from being a bit footsore, he's fine sir. Those flying boots aren't made for marching in this terrain."

The group all laughed.

"Have Fink check him over, I don't want him holding us up. We move out in five, Wadi Bardia is about two klicks away."

They moved off after their five-minute stopover and after two kilometres they crossed the Wadi Bardia, continuing east. The baking sun burning their arms and faces as the column hurried east, conscious of their commander's urgency. They pushed forward for a further five hundred metres before running straight into the jaws of an Allied counterattack. Their reaction was instinctive.

Nadel, who was the lead platoon took to the ground, his two troops fanning out, two MG 34s spraying suppressive fire to their front, although they were still unable to catch sight of their enemy. Roth took his platoon to the left and Leeb to the right, wary of a potential attack to their flanks. Paul called his commanders together, crouching low as the firefight built up to a crescendo, the Fallschirmjager putting down a two hundred and seventy degree arc of continuous fire. Their troop commanders reining them back, conserving their limited ammunition.

"What's the situation to your fronts?"

"There are troops to our northeast sir, putting down some pretty heavy firepower," responded Nadel.

"How many?"

"I don't know sir."

"Guess, dammit."

"Could be a platoon or more sir."

"Roth."

"No contact at the moment sir. I have my lads spread out along a hundred metre front, west to east."

"Leeb."

"Nothing yet sir. I've sent a half troop with an MG to cover the road on our right, the rest are covering Dietrich's right."

"Hold position for now, except I want a full troop on the road and I want a troop moved closer to Nadel's position, covering his left. Leave the rest of your platoon where they are; Ernst, but move back about one hundred metres, hold a line across our rear in case Dietrich needs to pull back, he can filter through your position while you cover him."

"And me sir?" asked Richter.

"Place your mortars behind Leeb's line, but keep them silent. We'll keep your boys as a surprise should we need them."

Paul pictured the layout in his mind, Nadel to the front, Leeb covering the road, their right flank and a troop backing up Nadel, Roth covering their left.

"Let's move, Max with me."

The platoon commanders quickly dispersed, Paul and Max running, hunched over, towards Nadel's position, rounds zipped passed them, the relatively flat ground offering little protection. Nadel had shifted his men back about ten metres, finding a shallow dip in the ground to give them some modicum of cover.

"What's happening?"

"There's definitely a build-up sir, there has to be at least two platoons in front of us, but they seem to be bedding down to our northeast."

"Any probing?"

"Nothing sir, just harassing fire, they don't seem to be making any effort to move."

"The buggers are up to something sir," advised Max.

"We could pincer them sir. I could keep them pinned down while Ernst and Viktor attack their flanks."

"Shush," hissed Max, raising his hand for silence. "What's that?"

"All I can hear is gunfire Feldwebel," responded Nadel.

"No, listen sir. Can you hear that clanking sound?"

"Look, smoke," called Nadel, pointing east towards a cloud of blue smoke.

Paul grabbed his binoculars from their case, rounds zipping passed him. One so close, he felt the wind from it against his cheek.

Max pulled him lower. "Best keep low sir, there's no cover here."

"Get their heads down sir," Max called to Leutnant Nadel.

He then turned to Fischer, lying next to him. "Don't forget your training, keep the men changing positions, don't let them home in on you."

Max turned back to his commander. "Can you see anything?"

"Yes, look," he said and handed Max his binoculars.

Max scanned the area in front of him and about three hundred metres away, on a road that ran across their front, he could see the blue smoke spewing in to the air as the two twenty five ton tanks revved their engines, ramping up their speed to a faster than walking pace of twelve kilometres an hour.

"Scheisse, tanks. We've nothing to stop them sir."

"We could use Richter's mortars to try and shed their tracks," suggested Nadel.

"Not a chance sir, the armour is so bloody thick, even the 88s struggle to stop them. They look like Matilda's, Infantry support tanks, and they're designed to take punishment."

The clanking of the two tanks got louder the closer they got, the three man turret of the lead tank whining as it turned towards them.

Boomf.

A 40mm round shot out of the barrel, passing Paul's group some distance away, but they still felt the shockwave as it whipped passed them, smashing into a rock, but there was no explosion.

"It's an armoured piercing round," said Max with some glee.

"They mustn't have any HE shells."

"Max, get Richter to put a few rounds down on top of the tanks."

"They won't do much good sir. The armour must be at least sixty millimetres thick."

"It will keep the heads of their infantry down, give us some time to figure out what's going on. Oh, and get Leeb to move further back towards the Wadi we crossed, anchor a line on that building next to the road. He can cover us if we need to pull back. Take Bergmann and the HQ with you. Get Bergmann to let Regiment know what's happening."

The lead Matilda's engine screamed as it swivelled round on the spot to face them, before moving off the road in their direction, the turret moving to keep it in line with the enemy, its barrel sniffing out new targets. The engine revs remained high as the one hundred and ninety break horsepower of the two diesel engines, pushed the tracks of the tank over the rough ground, its speed now reduced. The second tank continued along the road until it had passed beyond its partner, then after stalling and crashing through the gears, it too turned west to head towards the German paratroopers.

Boomf.

Boomf.

Both fired, now joined by the staccato fire of their Besa, 7.92mm turret machine guns. They were three hundred metres away, slowly crawling towards Paul's immediate front line. He quickly calculated how long they had before they were on top of them. Seven kilometres an hour, he estimated, that would see them amongst his men in less than three minutes.

"Infantry sir," pointed out Nadel.

Paul could see the helmeted, khaki uniforms, some in full battledress, others in shorts with rolled over socks, dashing behind the tanks, seeking cover behind their steel charges, amongst the dust and fumes that was surging around them. Paul's tactical mind ran through what he knew about the situation, the scenario's the enemy could enact and how his men could counter them.

To his right, a metalled road, one of few at this level, ran adjacent to them, west to east, running west back to the small town or village of Adele. Behind him, the Wadi Bardia, that ran down to the coast.

They had crossed it earlier, a good fall-back position surmised Paul. In front of him he had two tanks, at the moment, and about a platoon of infantry. To his left, approximately two platoons probing Roth's position. Was it just a company counter attack, or was their more, he asked himself? What if it was a full battalion out there.

"Scheisse." They could come up the Wadi and attack them from the side and behind, his mind raced.

"Sir?" asked Nadel, trying to ascertain what was wrong.

"One tank has stopped," called a trooper down the line. "Look the crew are climbing out."

"Nadel, as soon as the mortars open up, I want you to pull back. Go through Leeb's line and head straight for the Wadi, got it?"

"Yes sir."

"And make sure you cover it to the north."

"Yes sir." He turned to get his men ready to bug out as soon as the mortars opened fire.

Although the first tank seemed to have stopped, possibly due to mechanical difficulties, it had certainly not been hit, the second one overtook it and continued to rattle towards the beleaguered Fallschirmjager.

Boomf.

Another armoured piercing round sped passed them in Leeb's direction.

Crump, crump, crump.

Three mortar bombs landed amongst the tanks, an eruption of reddish soil and rocks showering the infantry and their juggernauts in a coating of dust, shrapnel and rock splinters ricocheting off the tank's armour, some hitting the accompanying infantry, slicing through their thin uniforms and tearing into their tender flesh, as if mere rice paper.

Crump, crump, crump.

Three more rounds, Richter had certainly proven his worth, thought Paul.

"Run," screamed Paul

They were up off the ground, sprinting as fast as they could as another three rounds landed amongst the enemy, disrupting their advance. One of Nadel's men went down, picked up by one of his comrades, thrown over a shoulder, as his friends covered him, the trooper staggering under the extra weight to the perceived safety of Leeb's line.

"Leave the injured man here," ordered Paul. "Get to the Wadi now."

Max joined him as Fink bolted passed him to help the injured soldier.

"All hell is breaking loose sir. Roth is up against at least two platoons."

"Is he holding?"

"Yes, but it won't take them long to flank him."

Richter thumped down beside them. "I have fifteen bombs left sir."

"Hold off for now, pack up and get back behind Leutnant Nadel's men. Make sure you can cover the Wadi to the north."

They all turned as they heard the clanking of tank tracks. Having survived the onslaught from Richter's mortar troop, the tank continued its trek towards them, although light half a dozen escorts after the mauling from the mortars that had rained down on them. A shell whistled passed them, hitting the house on the edge of the road, where Leeb had set up an MG34, to act as his anchor point for his new extended line.

"You need to move now Unterfeldwebel, we won't be able to hold this line for much longer," Leeb informed Richter.

He hastened towards his troop, to gather up his men, pack up his Granatwerfer 34s, and reposition them west of the line, Wadi Bardia.

"Ernst, give Dietrich five minutes to get in to position, then pull back."

"What about Viktor sir?"

"Max and I will get him now."

Leeb confirmed his understanding of his orders and Paul and Max ran, hunkered down, towards Roth's location. Rounds zipped passed them, like angry mosquitos, but far more deadly. The grazing fire from the enemy was so intense, they were as likely to get hit by accident as they were an aimed shot.

"What's the situation Viktor?"

"Fifty plus sir, by the quantity of iron that's coming our way."

"How's ammo?" asked Max.

"I've restricted the MGs fire to two Feld, were getting through it fast."

"Have they attempted to assault or flank you?"

"No sir, I don't understand it. They're keeping us well pinned down, but don't seem to be in any hurry to take advantage of it. I'm watching my flanks, but nothing."

Paul rubbed the scar above his left eye, a habit he had formed and was trying to break. The Wadi notion flitted into his deliberation again.

"It is the bloody Wadi they're after Max, we need to get out of here now, before they get in behind us. Get Leutnant Leeb back to the Wadi now, we'll be right behind you."

"What about you sir?"

"I'll be with Leutnant Roth, I'll be right behind you."

Max hesitated for a second, gripped Paul's upper arm, a vice like grip. "Keep your bloody head down sir," then he dashed off to carry out his orders, racing across the broken ground, jinking from side to side like a wild hare. Bullets whistled passed him, although the intensity of the fire had moderated, the quiet before the storm, he thought.

Paul grabbed Roth's shoulder, shouting into his ear as a tank round shot past behind them, smashing into the building where moments before Leeb had an MG34 emplacement set up. The projectile pierced the fragile wall, hitting Primke, who had returned to pick up the remaining ammunition, in the chest, punching a hole the size of a man's fist, death was instant.

"Start pulling back, don't bother to skirmish, just get the hell out of here."

"Smoke?"

"Yes, make it two or three."

Roth called out to his men and they prepped themselves to pull out at a moment's notice. Smoke grenades were hurled in the direction of their adversary, an instantaneous smoke cloud forming in the desert like heat. The cloud billowed forwards towards the enemy and about the paratroopers, they didn't need the order repeating when they were called on to pull back.

They had almost made it to the building unscathed, when a rogue

Vickers round struck a man down, clean through his throat. After a few moments of gurgling panic, pink froth foaming at his mouth as the soldier tried desperately to breathe, a quick attempt by one of his comrades to stem the blood that was spurting out from the torn internal jugular vein, spraying their uniforms and faces as they frantically tried to stop the flow, he succumbed and was left. They would have to find time to mourn for their comrade later, now they needed to ensure their own survival.

Paul called encouragement to his men, although not a rout the initiative was not theirs any more. But they didn't need rousing, even with the loss of their comrade their morale was high, their confidence in themselves and their leader unabated. One half of Paul's brain was planning his next move, the other section questioning his leadership, leading his men into a superior force that was now hitting them back, and hard.

Leeb was pulling back as instructed. He looked about him, the ground strewn with empty shell cases. He must do an ammunition check soon, they had expended an inordinate amount these last few minutes. He hit the floor as another armoured piercing round smacked into the building, now completely devoid of any living Fallschirmjager. He pulled Leeb, who had just joined him and also flung himself to the ground, towards him.

"Go passed Wadi Bardia, head straight for Wadi Piggi."

"What about the rest of the company sir?"

"We'll catch up with you. We've walked straight in to a full battalion counter attack. Dig in along the Wadi, we will need to pull back towards you quickly."

As Leeb started to get up, Paul grabbed him again. "Take Richter and his men with you. Get him to set up behind you. Once he's used up his mortar bombs he can watch your back. Now go."

"Sir."

Leeb was off, gathering the last of his men about him, shouting orders, urging them to move quickly, the enormity of what his commander had just shared with him sinking in. Their small force of fewer than a hundred men, would be no match for a full battalion of Allied troops. His men headed west, the intention to pass through Nadel's position on Wadi Bardia and setting up a covering force along the next Wadi, Piggi.

Paul instructed Roth to follow on behind Leeb, his orders to cover Leeb's right flank and the road. Roth's men clattered about him.

"Viktor, leave a troop to cover you, then run like hell for the Wadi. Go, now."

He looked across to his left, the smoke screen was already dissipating, prompting the enemy to take some action, knowing the smoke probably meant a German withdrawal.

Two of Roth's troops picked themselves up off the ground and headed west, covering ground they had transited across earlier.

"Get some fire down," Paul called over to Unterfeld Kienitz, the platoon NCO who had remained behind with the troop who would provide covering fire for the withdrawing forces.

"Any targets sir?"

"Anywhere in front," responded Paul, frustrated that he was losing control of the battle. "Just let them know were still here, give the others a chance to get away."

The troop opened up, MG34 rounds spat towards the enemy positions, covering an arc east to west, knowing their comrades would be well clear of the local area by now. After a couple of minutes, and just before he was about to order the final evacuation, the clanking of a Matilda tank could be heard approaching their position. Max crashed down beside his company commander, his chest heaving from the exertion of the sprint getting here, the midday sun already starting to sap a man's energy and strength.

"We've got a big problem sir, we have to pull back now, there's no time to wait."

"What is it Max?"

"You were right, they were making their way up Bardia, at least a company, if not more."

"Who's holding them, Leeb?"

"Yes sir, along with Leutnant Nadel. Both have lost two men."

"Has Leeb got any men back to Piggi?"

"Yes sir, but he left a troop to back up Leutnant Nadel."

"If we don't go now we're going to be trapped between two large forces," said Paul to himself, but loud enough that Nadel heard him.

"Sir?"

"Viktor, pull back now, and fast. Head for the house, skirt along the road and come in behind Nadel and he can then pull back through you."

Roth quickly issued commands to his men. No panic, although with a sense of urgency, just firm instructions and a controlled withdrawal. The MG fired off one last burst, the platoon then skirmishing backwards, ensuring an intermittent stream of fire found its way towards the enemy, holding off an enemy attack for as long as possible.

They reached the house, now punched full of holes by the armoured piercing rounds from the Matilda's gun, the terracotta tiled roof smashed and all but collapsed. Roth checked off his men, Abt with a shattered arm but able to continue with the aid of his comrades, the alternative of being left behind was not even contemplated.

"Go, go," urged Paul. He needed to get his men on to the road and then race for Bardia, then on to Piggi. Then at least he would have his command in one place and potentially hold their ground until he could plan his next move.

"Max, with me, we'll head straight for the Wadi."

They both slotted fresh magazines into their machine pistols, and then shot off at a fast pace where they would find Nadel's covering force. The dip loomed up in front of them and they could see Nadel's men, along with a troop from Leeb's platoon, withdrawing under heavy fire, swarms of Australian soldiers pouring through the Wadi from the north, forcing their way over the top to pursue the German soldiers they had on the run. The determination was evident on their faces. Gritted teeth, shouts of encouragement to each other, calls of ridicule following the fleeing enemy, pay back for the pounding they had received from the Luftwaffe Stukas and the repeated attacks by the Green Devils.

"We need to run like hell sir," yelled Max.

As he turned to check his company commander was behind him, two rounds from the turret mounted, besa machine gun, slammed into him. The first striking his shoulder, spinning him around clockwise, the second tore into his abdomen, the impact lifting him off his feet and over the edge of the Wadi. His limp body slid down its shallow walls, dust and rocks cascading after him.

"Max," screamed Paul as he ran to the edge, charging down after him, looking down to see his friend lying on his back where he had finished up, next to a small, low, anaemic looking olive tree ringed by waist high shrubs. He quickly examined Max, nothing could be seen on his upper body, but a dark patch was already starting to proliferate along his side.

CHAPTER TWENTY-ONE

Although all the options careered through Paul's mind, there was only one he could truly consider, treating his friends injuries and getting him to safety. During his first action in Poland, Max had saved his life. He would not be here now had Max not interceded, taking the life of a Polish artilleryman who was about to snuff out his commander's life. But, it meant that he had failed as a commander, he had failed his men when they needed him most.

He flinched as a mortar round exploded on the sides and centre of the Wadi, showering the Allied soldiers in shrapnel and dust. Richter had been ready, his action covering the withdrawal of his company, giving them a short respite from the enemy assault, allowing them to dash to safety. Although Leeb was the most junior of the three platoon commanders, Paul was in no doubt that he was the most capable tactician. He would already be planning his next move and making the appropriate suggestions to Roth, the most senior, that they withdraw the full company to the Wadi Piggi.

He snapped out of his reverie, hearing Max groan below him.

"Go sir," croaked Max. "You have a company to look after, not just one man."

Paul's thoughts raced, the enemy would be on top of them soon. He could already hear the Matilda's engine growling as it spun to the left towards the road, in an effort to bypass the German forces. The driver crashing through the gears, knowing speed was of the essence, sideways on for too long and they would make the perfect target for an anti-tank gun. Paul knew the infantry would be on top of them soon.

"Go sir, bloody go."

Paul ignored his plea, moving round to the top of Max's upper body, blood now clearly oozing from his left shoulder, the lower part of his tunic sodden. He needed to get them both under cover first, then see to Max's wounds.

He grabbed the heavy sergeant by his 'Y' straps and dragged him centimetre by centimetre towards the shrubs that would give them the cover they needed. Max groaned, the pain starting to set in as Paul dragged him to cover.

"Sorry Max, I have to get you out of sight."

"Just leave me sir," Max's voice pleaded.

"Quiet, you dumb Hamburger."

He manoeuvred his heavy weight companion in to the protective shrubs, as close to the trunk of the shrivelled tree as he could. The patch they were hiding in was only a few metres across, if they stayed lying down and quiet they could remain undetected. He placed his hand over Max's mouth.

"Shush," he whispered in his ear, as boots thudded across the eastern side of the Wadi, bodies could be clearly heard sliding down the sloping sides. They thudded across the bottom, then clambered up the other side, the pounding of the boots continuing until at least a platoon had passed by them.

To the south he could now hear the tank clattering along the metalled road, the engine powering the tank close to its top speed of twenty four kilometres an hour, the tank commander only slowing to allow his infantry escort to catch him up. It may be a mobile, steel bunker, but without infantry support an enemy could quickly get close to it, disable the tank and the crew would then face capture or death.

Paul peeked out of his cover and could distinctly see the silhouette of the Matilda, its pointed nose on the end of an oblong main body, turret situated well to the front. The clanking of the tracks slowly receded as the 'Queen of the Desert', as it was known, crept along the road towards the next Wadi, Wadi Piggi. Paul's mind wandered to where Helmut might be, how far away is he likely to be from the Wadi where his men were now forming up for another attempt at consolidating and holding off the superior forces heading towards them. Helmut's one hundred plus men wouldn't help to outnumber the enemy, but it might tip the balance.

Crump, crump, crump.

At least Richter was making his presence felt, probably disrupting the Australian advance as they probed further forwards, taking advantage of the mayhem they had caused by pushing troops up the Wadi and hitting the German invaders hard in the side.

Apart from gunfire in the distance, it was now quiet in the immediate vicinity. He turned to Max, now his priority. Max's lower tunic was soaked, the blood still wet even though the temperature was in the high thirties, indicating to Paul that blood was still flowing freely. He pulled his gravity knife from his trouser pocket and cut away the lower part of the blood soaked uniform, Max's kit getting in the way. He unbuckled the belt, unhooked his MP40 magazine pouches, unbuttoned the tunic and pulled it aside, slicing more away with his knife.

The woollen shirt beneath was also soaked, Paul cut into it swiftly, exposing Max's flesh. The blue, black hole, the size of a man's thumb, stared up at him, seeping a steady flow of blood. He attempted to roll Max over to look at the other side, but the Beefy Feldwebel was too heavy to move easily on his own. He pulled the shirt up higher and ran his hand round to the side of Max's back, it didn't take him long to discover the jagged hole of the exit wound. Max groaned as Paul's fingers explored the wound. He was able to push at least two fingers into it. He withdrew his hand, sticky, covered in blood and particles of tattered flesh.

"Sorry Max, I need to get you sorted so we can get out of here."

"S'alright sir... have you... any water?"

"Hang fire for a few minutes more, let me get these wounds fixed up first."

He scrabbled around in Max's pockets until he found what he was looking for, a couple of first field dressings, wrapped in the distinctive black, rubberised fabric. Each man was supposed to carry a large and small field dressing, but Max insisted that each trooper carried an additional large one on him. Unwrapping it, he eased it under Max's waist, pushing the dressing as far as he could, reaching around the other side and pulling it through the rest of the way. Once done, he gently manoeuvred the thick pad until it was directly beneath the wound and tied it off.

Tearing open a second bandage he repeated the process, this time packing it with pieces of Max's shirt he had cut into squares earlier, for extra absorbency, then winding it round Max's body twice, before finally tying it off. Now some direct pressure had been applied to the wound, Paul hoped it would stop, or at least slow down, the bleeding. He padded and bandaged the front of the wound, wrapping layer after layer of crepe around his body until he was satisfied it was well bound and wouldn't slip off.

He severed Max's 'Y' straps and cut away part of his upper tunic so he could get at the second wound. The hole, again the size of a man's thumb, with a slightly raised edge all round, was a black, blue in colour and oozing blood. After exploring further, he failed to find the exit wound at the back of the shoulder blade. Worried that the bullet may still be inside, he cut away more clothing desperate to find an exit wound.

"Got it."

"Sir... what?"

"It's ok Max, nearly finished patching you up."

Just below Max's pectoral muscle was the exit point he was looking for. It looked similar to the entry wound, only slightly bigger, blood running down his hot, dry, pale skin. The bullet must have struck a bone in his shoulder, thought Paul, and was then deflected, traveling down his chest and exiting out of the front. He felt sure it had missed Max's left lung, his breathing, although slightly laboured, was steady and there was no coughing or blood and froth coming from his mouth. Paul smiled to himself, thanking someone for small mercies.

This time he used his own large dressing and Max's small one to bind his shoulder and chest. Max groaned again. Now Paul was satisfied that he had stopped the bleeding, in the short term at least, he could focus on Max's other needs. He rummaged through his bread bag where he knew Max kept some morphine. Finding it quickly, he administered the injection, pushing into Max's muscled upper thigh, his eyes widening slightly as it went in, licking his dry lips, beads of sweat starting to form on his brow beneath his Fallschirm.

He gently eased off Max's helmet, pushing his bread bag beneath his head to act as a pillow as he lowered his head back down. Next he opened his canteen of water, sloshing it around, gauging how much was left. He checked Max's as well, half a canteen each, about two pints of water between them. He raised the canteen to Max's lips, tilting it slowly, allowing Max to control how much he drank, even so the flow was faster than Max's dry, constricted throat could swallow and he coughed and choked, water running down his cheeks and chin.

Paul suddenly removed the canteen, vigilant, listening for any indication that Max's coughing had alerted anyone close by. It was relatively quiet in the dip of the Wadi, although distant gunfire could be heard along with the occasional louder crash of a tank round being fired, then a lone mortar bomb exploding. Richter, although rationing his ammunition, was still dishing out punishment to the enemy.

He turned back to Max and whispered, "Has the morphine helped Max?"

He glazed eyes wrinkled as he smiled, though slightly sunken in his blackened, but paled face. His voice crackled, "Just the job... sir... you need... to go, come... back later."

"I'm getting you out of here Feldwebel Grun," he whispered back with a grin. "Or I'll put you on a report for being absent without permission."

He gave Max another sip of water and gulped a mouthful himself, concerned how little they had, wishing he had replenished his bottle from the company stocks earlier. They would have to be careful. He checked the dressings again, the shoulder and upper chest one still dry, but blood was already showing through on the lower wound.

"Max, I'm going to have a scout around, so stay quiet and I'll be back as quick as I can."

Paul crawled backwards out of the undergrowth, quickly turning round on himself and scanning the base of the Wadi, it was clear. The wadi was only some twenty metres across at its widest point and the sides quite shallow, just above head height. He scooted across the floor of the Wadi and scrambled up the western side, MP40 at the ready, and peered over the top, rivulets of red soil and stones filtering passed him, back into the Wadi.

Pulling his binoculars from their case, shielding the lenses, preventing any reflections giving his position away, he studied the

227

horizon in front of him. He could see a group of Allied troops about three to four hundred meters away, at least a company in size advancing towards Wadi Piggi, where he hoped his men were holding up. He felt a pang in his chest, wishing to be with them now, leading them in the battle and to eventual safety. For a split second he had the ridiculous thought of attacking the enemy from behind, distracting them from their task, but knowing how absurd the idea was, leaving himself dead and Max to die out here alone.

He viewed their hideaway. It was good cover, but wouldn't stand up to close scrutiny. He couldn't see Max, his splinter pattern tunic, Paul had pulled back over him before he left, camouflaged him well, but he did see a glint of metal. It could be Max's MP40, magazines or water bottle. He would hide them on his return, but he had already decided they needed to move from this location if they were to avoid capture. He looked east, but no sign of anyone or thing.

He returned to the bottom of the dry channel and scurried south until he arrived at the metalled road, some two hundred metres away from their hideout. It was a single lane road, wide enough for one vehicle to transit. If it met another vehicle coming the other way, one of them would have to pull on to the roadside to let the other pass. A concrete culvert supported the road across the Wadi, a possible hiding place he considered, but it was too obvious.

He heard a crunching sound on the road to his left and observed a least a dozen soldiers making their way towards him, their tanned legs showing they'd been in this theatre for a while. Their slouch hats and confident stance as Australians marched towards the culvert, more reinforcements to take on his beleaguered troops. He ducked down as they got closer, the hobnailed boots tramping over the culvert, a hollow thump beneath where Paul was hidden, pointing out their progress as they crossed over. Once the sound faded, he peered over the top of the culvert again, watching the sway of their backs as they doubled away to support their fellow soldiers.

Half crouching, he ran back down the Wadi, searching for the props he would need to get Max back to friendly territory and safety. By the time he returned to their temporary camp he had acquired two lengths of wood, one a branch lying on the ground from a broken tree and a second he had torn down himself.

Arriving back, he crawled through the undergrowth and immediately checked on Max, whose skin was hot, his body not having enough liquid to give up as sweat to cool him down. His eyes fluttered open and Paul prised is mouth open gently, squeezing a piece of water soaked shirt above him, the drops of water moistening his lips, most of it making its way into his mouth. Max licked his lips, glad of the refreshing, if not cool, water on his mouth and tongue, that until then had felt furry and too large for his mouth.

"You ok to take a few sips from the bottle Max?"

"Yes... I'll... give it a try."

He placed his hand behind Max's head, lifting it slightly, a white line across his forehead where his helmet had protected him from the burning sun, and placed the neck of the bottle to his lips, the metal top clinking against his teeth. He reached up to take a drink, crying out in pain as he disturbed his wounded shoulder.

"Stay still Max, I'll tip the bottle, you just sip it slowly."

After a few drops, Paul lowered his head back down and made him as comfortable as he could.

"I need to use your tunic Max. I'll cut what I need off you, but I will need to move you. You'll have to grit your teeth I'm afraid."

Although the morphine was easing the pain, putting Max into a relaxed state, any sudden movement caused Max to cry out. His side just throbbed at the moment, but Paul felt there was the greater risk of blood loss if the wound opened up again. He sliced the sleeves off Max's tunic, then cut them down their length, allowing him to remove them with as little discomfort to Max as possible. He would use them later. He also cut into the top of the tunic, freeing his arms completely, nothing holding the tunic to Max's body other than his weight on top of it. Paul flattened it out completely and placed the two lengths of wood on top of the tunic, either side of Max's body, wrapping the edges around them. Using strips he had cut from the sleeves and punching holes in the material with his knife, he bound the tunic to the two poles.

Max spoke through gritted teeth. "You're time... in the RDD... wasn't entirely wasted... sir."

Paul looked sideways and smiled. "This is what makes the difference between and officer and an ex-docker Max"

His eyes closed, just that small effort exhausting him. He dozed quietly. Paul checked his pulse, it was slow but regular, and the steady rise and fall of his chest indicating that his breathing wasn't impaired. He continued binding the poles, the full length of the tunic, a travois slowly forming. He discarded what kit they wouldn't need, cut a square of material from his own shirt to drape over Max's exposed head and face, then he strapped Max to the improvised stretcher as best he could, using the leather 'Y' straps that Max no longer needed.

He leant over his friend. "Right Max, I'm going to try and get us both to the other side of the road, this stretch of the Wadi could get too busy."

Max opened his glazed eyes, but said nothing, thirst and delirium making him oblivious to events. Paul stood up, slowly, in the centre of their cover, ducking his head slightly due to the low branches and resting his hand on the trunk to steady him, listening for any sounds of movement about them. Apart from the distant fire fight and Max's laboured breathing, all was quiet. He wasted no more time, and striding through the cover, he picked up the two extended poles above and either side of Max's head, grunting at the dead weight as he did so.

The shout was sudden and clear and not a moment too soon, Paul dived back into the undergrowth crashing down by the side of Max as he heard other voices. They were English, not German. He heard the owners of the voices slither down the side of the Wadi, egging each other on to join in the fight, running centimetres away from their hiding place. Paul froze, quickly slipping his hand over Max's mouth as he moaned. A soldier stopped, stared at the spindly olive tree, but suddenly knocked aside by one of his fellow soldiers as he rushed passed, what had stopped him forgotten as he shot off after them.

Waiting five minutes until all was quiet again, Paul picked up his burden and walking backwards, centimetre by centimetre, Paul heaved Max's body from the undergrowth, flattening the plants as he did so. Once they were clear of the covered patch, Paul adjusted his position so he was facing forwards, grasped the poles again and step-by-step dragged the travois and ninety kilogram load towards the culvert that supported the road across the Wadi.

He reached it twenty minutes later, his arms aching, almost pulled out of their sockets, tendons stretched and painful, but they had made it. But, it would get harder. The culvert was only just above chest height. He dithered. Should he try and haul his charge up the sides of the Wadi and cross the road, or manoeuvre him under the culvert? He decided on the latter, they would be less exposed.

Paul lowered Max down gently, next to one of the arches of the culvert and lay down under the overhang facing him. Then, bit-by-bit, he steadily dragged the Travois through the opening, shade and coolness beneath a welcome relief after the fiery sun they had left behind. After ten minutes of strenuous exertion, they were through to the other side. After a few more minutes of exploration, Paul had found a shallow depression on the western side of the Wadi, where he could haul Max to the top to continue their journey.

Having arrived at the right place, he ran to the top, checked all was clear, slid back down, hoisted up the two poles and step-by-step, heaved his hefty load to the top, feeling utterly drained when he finally made it.

He rested for a few moments, checked Max's condition was stable, then turned at an angle, south west, where he was sure the ground dipped down, hiding them, before climbing again back up into the upper foothills. He crouched down, gripped the poles, hoisted them up and heaved the travois forwards. He slowly gained momentum, leaning forwards, with his head and shoulders bent, gradually gaining speed as the lower end of the poles scraped two lines across the uneven ground. He estimated he would be at the dip within the hour, but he was far too optimistic. Snaking around the larger ruts and rocks, passing mini craters, the distance had been doubled. Looking back, he could see the twin lines criss crossing the uneven ground. It had taken him nearly three hours.

He would need an overnight stop for them soon, he concluded. He didn't want to move at night, the grinding noise of the travois over the rough ground, would travel far during the silence of the night. An unnatural sound that a sentry may want to investigate further. There was also the risk of tripping over unseen objects or holes, any fall exacerbating Max's injuries.

Paul rubbed his hands together ready to pick up his load again, wincing as his blistered and blooded hands touched. He put on his paratrooper gloves, which, although making his hands hot, would save his palms from being lacerated further. He gave Max a few sips of water, the casualty now delirious and mumbling, the shoulder dressings still dry, but the lower one dark and wet. He would need to change the dressing soon. He continued his journey, a rhythm setting in, forty steps, lower the poles, count to five, raise them, forty steps.

By the time dusk was upon them, Paul had found a small grove, mainly lemon trees, and in the corner a farmer's weather hut, with a thin thatched roof. Barely big enough for the two of them lying side by side, but it would have to do. Paul couldn't take another step. Max had started to shiver as the daytime temperature dropped from the high thirties, the darkness replacing it with what felt like a numbing cold. Not like the cold they had experienced in the Harz mountains, but relative to the days temperature, and their lack of food and water, they both felt its effects.

Once safe in the darkness Paul used his torch, his hand covering the lens, a reddish glow providing the light needed to apply a new dressing to Max's lower injury, the exit wound looking black and ugly. He wrapped his tunic around Max's body to help keep him warm. He was cold too, but his was the greater need. He gave Max a last sip of water, took some himself, then lay by Max's side, getting as close as he was able, sharing his warmth and gaining what warmth he could in return. It is going to be a long night and an even longer day tomorrow, were his last thoughts as he fell in to a deep and fatigued sleep.

CHAPTER TWENTY-TWO

Paul woke with a start as the first bright rays of the sun beamed through the small opening of the hut. He looked at his watch, it was six forty, and calculated that he had slept for over seven hours. He had succumbed to the exhaustion of three days of marching and fighting, and hauling his weighty companion across the rough ground and through the unforgiving heat. He still felt weary, but refreshed at the same time. His body was fatigued, but his mind felt more alert. He had a terrible thirst, his mouth was dry and his tongue felt large and puffy in his mouth. He found a canteen and took a few sips, far from slaking his thirst, it made him want more, but at least it alleviated the furriness of his mouth and teeth. He listened, the occasional pop of a firearm in the distance, but locally it seemed quiet.

He turned towards Max who had been woken by his rummaging, his eyes fluttering open. He went to speak, his lips moving but no sound coming forth.

"Hang on a sec Max, I'll get you some water."

Max's cracked lips broke into a pained smile. Paul pushed some kit beneath his head, raising him up slightly, making him more comfortable, before placing the neck of the water bottle against his lips. Max sipped at the contents for some time, his body's acute need for the lifesaving liquid commanding his brain to take on board as much as possible. Once Paul was satisfied that his immediate need had been satiated, he removed it, replaced the top and attached it back onto his belt. By his reckoning, there was less than a pint left between them, enough to keep an active paratrooper, in this part of the world, going for a couple of hours, but not much more.

Max grimaced with pain and Paul administered another morphine injection, the relief on Max's face palpable as its effects dulled the pain perception centre in his brain. This left just one for later, but only as a last resort.

"Don't get used to this Feldwebel Grun, you're back on beer the minute we get back."

Max smiled, in between grimaces.

"A beer would be good... right now," he replied, his voice husky, dry and pained.

Paul checked over Max's wounds, a few dabs of dried blood on his chest and shoulder, but his waist dressing was dry at the moment. Although concerned that the minute they moved from here there was a possibility that the wounds would reopen again, he knew that to stay here they would both die. To leave Max here on his own, would leave him to his inevitable death, they had to move.

Paul packed up their gear and grabbing the ends of the two poles, he dragged Max out of the doorway, feet first, far enough so that he could move round to the front and continue their journey west along the dip that he had found.

The shallow dip, although paralleling the roadway, it offered them some protection if any traffic, vehicle or people, moved along it. He estimated it was two kilometres to Wadi Piggi, then a further kilometre to the village, or town, of Adele. Once he got close to the outskirts of the village, he would have to move further south unless he saw any signs of his own men, or any other Fallschirmjager unit. He picked up the poles and trudged forwards, quickly settling in to his accustomed rhythm — forty paces forward, lower, count to five, pick up, forty paces forwards.

At around midday, they had reached the Wadi. Paul lowered Max to the ground and ran along the Wadi and across the road. After a quick exploration, all he could find were empty ammunition boxes, empty cartridge cases, both Allied and German, and a discarded water bottle.

He held up the flask, empty, the bullet holes either side testament to how tough the fight must have been. Soiled and blooded dressings were the only other objects he could find. Blood of his men or the enemy, it did not matter for the moment, nothing could be done, Max was his priority now. There were no signs of life, either Fallschirmjager or enemy soldiers, but he could still hear the odd firefight in the distance. He did one last scan of the area and ran back to Max.

Paul looked about him, searching the distant foothills that stretched away from him to the south. To the west, the direction he needed to head for, he could just make out the occasional building on the outskirts of Adele, he was starting to doubt he could continue. In a state of nervous exhaustion, he collapsed in despair, sliding down the side of the Wadi next to Max, who was sleeping again, the drug giving him some peace from the pain and intolerable thirst. He tentatively stood up again, to get a better view of their route ahead, but swaying uncontrollably, he sat back down, totally devoid of strength.

Sat in the dry earth of the Wadi, just scrub and dust for company, the sun overhead beating down on him, burning in to his already reddened skin, lips cracked and sore, an overpowering thirst that was threatening to drive him to despair. Head in his hands, he couldn't go on. His despondency was about to overwhelm him, when he heard Max's cracked voice speak.

"We'll be ok... sir, the bars... will be... open soon."

There was almost a hint of feverishness in Max's voice along with his humour. Paul slid across to him, not sure he was able to stand just yet.

"You'll get your cold drink Max, but for now you'll have to settle for this."

He gave Max a few sips of water, before placing the bottle back on his belt.

Max's one eye opened slightly, "What about... you... sir?"

"I've already had some," he lied.

Paul sloshed the liquid in the canteen, estimating by the sound that they had less than quarter of a pint left, Max would need all of it if he was to survive the day. He rubbed the hot, dry scar above his left eye, then wiped the back of his hand across his parched, cracked lips.

Whump, an explosion was heard somewhere near the coast, a retort of a rifle closer, but still beyond the village.

Paul pulled two lemons from his bag, he'd picked them up from their overnight stop. Cutting them open with his knife, he squeezed the sharp, acidic juice onto his tongue, his lips smarting, but it refreshed his mouth. He knew the relief would be short lived, but he would savour the moment.

He cut into the second fruit and removing the piece of shirt that covered Max's head and face, protecting him from the sun, he squeezed the extract into his mouth, his lips smacking as he attempted to capture every last drop of the liquid, his body thankful for any sustenance it could obtain. Max didn't open his eyes.

Paul shielded his face from the glaring sun, "Are you ok Max?"

His eyelids parted, but he didn't speak. He replaced the cover over Max's face, then checked his dressings, all were crusted dry, the bleeding seemingly under control, for the present.

Paul felt a little refreshed and he finished off his lemon, stripping the moist flesh from the peel. He hoisted the poles one more time and continued to haul his friend, to what he hoped was safety, water and better medical treatment than he was capable of providing. They followed the Wadi south, so he could skirt the village.

Forty paces forward, lower, count to five, pick up, forty paces forward.

Paul switched off. He knew he was leaving them exposed to discovery, but the lack of water, the intense heat, the strain on his arms and legs tottering beneath him, he needed to turn his mind off. He drifted, on autopilot, and had the notion he was looking down upon himself, watching a stranger trudging across this hostile land, the pain his and not Paul's.

After about five hundred metres and forty five minutes of hauling, he turned west, heaving the travois up the sides of the Wadi, grunting with effort, his legs staggering beneath him as he manhandled Max's weight up the crumbling sides of the channel. Although the sides were not much higher than the average man, to Paul they seemed a mountain that needed to be climbed. Once at the top, he lowered the handles with a jolt and collapsed to the ground, Max groaned at the stabbing pain as he was jarred by the rapidly lowered Travois.

"Sorry... Max," was all Paul could muster.

Paul lay down on his back, his right arm raised over his eyes, shielding them and his face from the sun beating down on him, his skin already red and burnt in places, his helmet hanging from his belt, too hot and heavy to wear. He felt tired, needed just a little sleep and he would be ok. If only he could sleep, a nice long, cool drink and then sleep. He thought of the cool waters of the River Havel back home, where he and his school friends used to go skinny dipping.

He awoke with a start, quickly sat up and looked about him, then checked his watch. He had slept for nearly an hour. Although he chastised himself, and felt foolish to allow it to happen, he was mildly reinvigorated, thirsty still, but was ready to pick up his burden again and keep moving.

Paul checked Max over, he was hot and dry. Paul was more and more anxious each time he checked his charge. The wounds seemed to be holding up, but he hadn't been able to check them properly, he wasn't a doctor. He wished Fink was with them, he would know more about what to do. But what he could do, was get Max food and water, primarily water. He made a decision. He would take them west now, skirting the village until directly south and close enough that he could do a recce and scavenge for food and water. With an almost demonic like release of energy, he elevated his charge, forty paces forward, lower, count to five, lift, forty paces forward.

He talked to Max as he walked, not sure if he heard him, he doubted it. The ground swam in front of him and when he lowered the travois as part of his routine, he brushed insects or perhaps just shadows from in front of his eyes.

"We'll make it Max, I'll get us out of this mess. I should have listened to Ernst, maybe he was right, maybe we should have put out a screen well before we were hit."

Lower, count to five, lift, forty paces forward.

"We had to move quickly Max, it was our task to get to Rethymnon as fast as possible. We had no option. But a screen would have picked up the enemy moving along the gully, wouldn't it? But they could have come up behind us way back, even before Adele. We weren't to know."

Lower, count to five, pick up, forty paces forward.

"I'll never forgive myself if I've lost my company through my incompetence. Maybe I'm not cut out to be an officer, eh Max? After this is over, if we get through this alive, I'm going to ask for a transfer, I'm not fit to lead men."

Max remained silent.

Lower, count to five, pick up, forty paces forward.

After three hours, with the light starting to fade, he found himself and Max south of a village, opposite a small rocky outcrop, beneath an overhang overgrown with shrubs of all kinds. But it was somewhere they could both shelter for the night.

He gave Max a small piece of very dry German sausage, getting a mumbled response as Max automatically chewed on the dry meat. Once finished, he gave him the last of the water, using the wet shirt method again, but it didn't seem to bring him round. Although Max was extremely hot, his skin seeming to be on fire, he wrapped his tunic around him knowing the temperature would drop in a matter of hours. He stripped off Max's equipment, just keeping his MP40, two spare magazines and his killing knife. Secreting Max and the remains of his kit in the undergrowth beneath the overhang, he headed north towards the village, less than a kilometre away.

It was now eleven. He had contemplated waiting until the early hours of the morning, but felt that any unusual noise at that time would attract the attention of any sentries on stag, or even a dog. He was sure dogs would be around somewhere. At least at this time of night there may be some activity that he could use as cover, to disguise his own noise and movement.

Three hundred metres out, he came to the first building, just a small hut adjacent to an olive grove. Beyond the grove he could make out a row of buildings, the start of the village, the odd light peaking from behind a blind or curtain. He knew the other side was the road that ran through it.

He crept up to the hut close by and peered through the open doorway, it was empty. He inched his way from the building, then ghost walked his way towards the edge of the village, which straddled the road that ran through it, east to west. He crept between two of the houses that lined the road. He ran his right hand along the whitewashed wall of the single story building, avoiding the woodpile, winter fuel or perhaps for cooking, as he made his way along the ten metre gap between them. Stepping carefully over the remnants of the chopped branches and sticks scattered about, he got to the front and peered up and down the road.

The house he was leaning against had two tall, narrow windows to the front, along with a single doorway facing the street. The door to the house was shut, the nearest window either curtained or covered with wooden blinds. He had ducked under a small window at the side, it was high and small, and it was unlikely he would be seen. There was nothing at the back and a corrugated roof sloped towards the road.

On the other side of the gap, a bigger house, two floors, better quality with a terracotta roof and pale tangerine walls. Directly opposite, a church, slightly set back from the road, shaped like an upside down letter U, two doors facing the cobble stoned street. On top of the orange tiled roof, at the front, a structure supported two bells on the outside, probably ropes leading down inside the church so they could be rung, calling the locals to prayer. In the darkness, he couldn't see much more than that.

He heard laughing to his left, further down the road, it sounded like men, or soldiers, sharing a joke. He turned back to the church and straining his eyes in the dark, looking down the side, he could make out what appeared to be a square, with an ornate structure in the middle. It looked familiar somehow. After his befuddled brain subconsciously went through all of the options, pictures of familiar shapes flashing through his memories, one stood out. A well. It couldn't be he thought, but it was too good an opportunity not to be investigated.

He looked left and right, a dog barked way off in the distance, too far away to concern him, and scooted across the street, the extra socks he had placed over his jump boots muffling the sound his studded souls would have normally made, and down the side of the church, keeping close to the flaking wall.

He stopped, listened for any sign he had been seen or discovered, his MP40 held at chest height and ready. It remained quiet. He looked about him and couldn't believe his eyes, it was a well in the middle of the square. He could slake his thirst, fill up the water bottles and be back with Max in a couple of hours at the most.

There was a grove behind the small square, which he aimed for, darting along the church wall and quickly across until he was at the edge of the orchard. He eased in between the trees and watched and listened. From this position, he could nip across to the well, drink all he wanted, fill the bottles, return to the dead ground and he would be in the clear.

He crouched down and moved forwards, directly in front of him, in the ornate square, was the well. It looked functional.

A burst of sudden laughter grabbed his attention, then voices and Paul spotted a group of soldiers walking alongside the church towards the well. He edged back, further into the grove, catching his MP40 against a tree, freezing immediately as he did, quickly checking the approaching soldiers for any sign that they had heard. They continued with their chatter and laughter. Paul moved deeper in, nudging an object with his foot as he did. He felt down and around him and could feel a man's boot, a soldier's boot, a jump boot, a Fallschirmjager's boot. It startled him. He looked around behind him and could see three darkened shadows, three German soldiers, three Green Devils.

He spun round as he heard a clinking sound by the well, followed by bellowing laughter. He moved forwards so he could see better. There were about half a dozen men, two of them carrying oil lamps, the flames flickering as they were moved about. Although the officer, the two stars on his shoulder boards denoting him to be a Lieutenant, dressed in a British Officers, No.1, style tunic, his ball shaped helmet, with its short visor and flared sides showed him to be a Greek officer. The Sam Browne Belt with the unusually crossed straps, confirmed it. The flying bombs on what seemed to be purple tabs, denoted him to be from an engineer unit. The other five or six men were dressed in khaki No.2 uniforms with British style puttees and French style boots. At least one of them was an NCO, a Sergeant, showing two yellow chevrons.

One of them hoisted a bucket from deep down in the well, plonked it on the side of the wall around it and used a ladle to drink. They each took it in turns to satisfy their thirst and then, still talking and laughing, headed back from whence they had come, going passed the church and turning right down the street.

Once again it was quiet.

Paul went and re-examined the three soldiers. He couldn't make out any faces or much detail, but he had an uncomfortable feeling they were from his company or battalion. Black stains covered their bodies and uniforms, and using his torch, shielded by his clenched fist, he could see they were covered in multiple stab wounds. Bile rose in his throat and he gagged on it, burning his throat as he swallowed the acidic contents back down.

He looked at their faces, but with the darkness, the dim light of the torch and their faces blackened, he couldn't make any one of them out. He checked them over one by one, searching their pockets for anything that could identify them, letters, photos, tags. Nothing. He stayed silent for a brief period of time, sharing a moment with his comrades. Whether or not they were from his unit, they were Fallschirmjager — family. He vowed to return to give them a proper burial, a soldier's burial.

Paul sidled up to the edge of the grove again, it was quiet by the well and the local area and he slipped quickly across, ducking down behind the wall. The bucket was still half full of water. He lowered it down to the ground and gulped water from it with the ladle, letting the warm liquid run down his face and over his shirt. Despite the fact it was slightly brackish, it tasted like honey. He gulped down as much as he could, until he felt like he was going to burst, then he gulped down some more.

Paul settled himself, checking that no one was approaching and then he filled the three bottles, the fourth holed by a bullet, another bullet meant for Max, showing just how close to death he had been. He may yet die, thought Paul, now eager to get back to his companion and share this luxury with him. He took one last drink from the ladle, his stomach now gorged with water, sloshing about inside of him as he scuttled passed the church, across the cobbled street, and in between the two houses, where he stopped to remove the socks from his jump boots. He would need the boot's grip on the way back.

He suddenly heard voices coming down the street, it sounded like two or three men. He quickly moved to the middle, grassy patch, in between the two houses, his dark form would be spotted easily up against the white backdrop of the house wall. He lay down, just in time as they passed the gap. He was just about to get up and return to Max, when he heard loud voices, although unintelligible to Paul he did recognise it as mockery as one of them broke away from the trio, turned the corner of the house wall, at the same time undoing his flies. He swayed about four steps down the edge, then turned towards the wall and started to urinate up against it. From the back, Paul could see it was a Greek soldier.

The soldier leaned forwards, head against the wall, clearly the worst for drink, soaking his boots as he did so. He stood up cursing, redoing his flies at the same time as flicking the urine off his boots, swishing them through the grass, staggering as he did towards Paul's location. If he didn't see him soon, he would certainly trip over him, then he would be discovered and on the run.

Paul made a snap decision. The soldier's friends had continued walking on, so before he could turn round again, or stagger in the direction of Paul's position, he picked up the half metre long piece of wood lying next to him and rose up from the ground. He could smell the alcohol in the air, he was that close to his quarry.

With one end of the branch gripped in his right hand, he flung his arm around the front of the soldier, grabbing the other end of the branch with his left hand, and before the Greek engineer could react and cry out, he snapped both arms back. Pulling the piece of wood tight under the man's chin, embracing him close to his own body, crushing his oesophagus with the wood, preventing him from calling out, he threw himself back onto the ground, taking his adversary with him, wrapping his legs around the soldier's legs, pulling back on the wooden branch for all he was worth. The man started to strike backwards with his head, attempting to butt his attacker, but all Paul did was stretch his own head further back, pulling even harder on the piece of wood, wrenching the soldier's neck rearwards. His legs now thrashed about in desperation, but they were gripped too tightly by Paul's own long, sinewy legs. He pulled at Paul's arms, but deprived of oxygen, his strength was leaving him and in his wretchedness he started to pound the sides of the ground, quickly fading to a tremble as life left him.

Paul held him in that position for a full minute, his entire body locked in place until he came to his senses and released his victim. Concerned that eventually his friends would come searching for him, he dragged the lifeless body around to the back of the house, laying him down before making his way quickly away from the village before any alarm could be sounded.

He moved quickly, heading south, using the hut he saw earlier as a landmark. Suddenly it was their, in front of him, he had been moving faster than he thought. He checked it quickly and once he confirmed it was still empty he made his way across the rough ground towards their hideout. At first, he failed to find the outcrop, a good indication that they would be well hidden, during the hours of darkness at least. Eventually it loomed above him and he pushed his way through the undergrowth.

"It's just me Max, I've got water," he hissed, fearing Max may open fire on him if he was conscious.

But there was no response. In fact, as he explored the ground around and in front of him with his hands, he found nothing, the hideout was empty. He searched around again, calling out Max's name quietly, but found nothing.

Paul wondered if Max had, in his delirium, got up and walked off, but the travois had gone as well, someone must have taken him. Paul quickly scrambled outside, doing a metre-by-metre search of the local area, looking for the travois or Max's body, or both. He covered an arc twenty metres out, if they intended to kill him they wouldn't have bothered to drag him any further, but he found nothing.

Paul sat down on a rock close by, weary from lack of sleep, anxious about his friend, the anxiety turning into fear. His head bowed, bolstered between his hands, a deep melancholy looming.

CHAPTER TWENTY-THREE

Paul snapped his head up. The dog's bark couldn't have been more than a kilometre away, in the direction they had initially been travelling, west. He jumped up. It was a long shot, but his options were not countless. He checked his MP40, made sure his two remaining stick grenades were secure, then headed as quickly, but as quietly, as possible west towards the location of the dog's bark.

To his left the shadow of the foothills, to his right he was leaving the village behind, the thin covering of stars above him the only light source available to show him the way. The dog barked again and Paul quickened his pace. He loped across the open, spongy ground, his long legs giving him the necessary speed, though he often tripped and stumbled over unseen obstacles in the gloom. On one occasion falling to all fours as his boot caught a hole in the ground.

As Paul approached the source of the sound he slowed down, to avoid alerting anyone to his presence. He was sure he had seen the flicker of a flame, possibly from a fire. As he got closer, he was sure he heard the yelping of the dog and even the whinny of a horse. He slowed further and crouched down, selecting his footsteps carefully.

As he got nearer, he could see it was a fire. Feeling exposed on the flat, open ground he moved across to what looked like a copse, a dark shadow along side of it, possibly a wall. He crept closer still. The gentle breeze shifted slightly in his direction, the aroma of roasting meat wafted towards him, his senses going into overdrive as his stomach contracted with pangs of hunger. He pushed the cravings of hunger aside, quickly crouching down again when he heard a single high pitched laugh.

Creeping to within a stone's throw away, nudging up to a wall on his left, he could make out a group congregated around a wood burning fire, half a dozen of them leaning against the stone wall, an extension of the one Paul had sidled along. They were sat close to what looked like a one room, single storey, low building, a bit like the Herder's hut they had seen the previous day, or was it the day before that, he thought. He racked his brains and couldn't even conjure up what day it was today.

The wall they were sat against followed the edge of a vineyard, a slight curve on it allowing Paul to move carefully along it, hugging it closely, allowing him sight of the group, but keeping him hidden from their prying eyes. He got to within twenty metres before he had to stop.

He felt the gentle breeze again against his cheek and could see the dog sniffing the air. He felt sure the dog's nose would be overpowered by the scent of the roasting goat or lamb, which was slowly being turned on a makeshift wooden skewer above the red flames of the fire. He was down wind, and so long as the orientation of the air currents did not shift, he felt safe from the dog's innate sense of smell.

He studied the band in front of him, flames from the fire flickering eerily over their faces and clothing. From what he could see, there seemed to be eight of them. A young boy, aged anywhere between the age of fourteen and seventeen, was turning the skewer, hot fat dripping onto the flames, causing the fire to flare and the boy to flick his head back in case he got splattered by the hot oil. He was deep in concentration on this clearly important task. The rest, bar one, who was acting as sentry, were sat with their backs to the wall, talking and sharing a bottle of wine that was passed up and down the line. There was another young boy, nearest him, three men in their twenties, an older man, heavily bearded, wearing a sleeveless sheep or goatskin jacket to keep out the cold. He wasn't sure about the sixth, but was certain it was a woman, perhaps the instigator of the high pitched laugh he'd heard earlier. She was the furthest away, close to the wall of the hut. Standing opposite, but apart from them, stood a man in his forties, a Lee Enfield Rifle resting in the crook of his two arms.

He heard a groan coming from the other side of the sentry, it was then Paul could make out a small pony, next to a bundle on the ground. The sentry strolled over to the pony, stroked its flanks, then strode over to the bundle on the ground and kicked it, cursing something in his native tongue, something Paul didn't understand. Paul cursed beneath his breath, it had to be Max. For a fraction of a second, he considered jumping up, opening fire and killing them all. But came to his senses and sidled along the wall until he was certain they wouldn't be able to see him, and considered what his next action would be.

Max's rescue was imperative, Paul had no idea what state he was in, or what they may have done to him. Max would be dangerously dehydrated by now, his wounds making matters worse, his lack of water complicating matters still further, a vicious cycle. He thought back to the three Fallschirmjager bodies he had seen in the grove, in the village. Suppressing his anger, he thought through his options. He needed a clear head, needed to think rationally, his and Max's life depended on it.

He edged back along the wall. If he stood up, the top of the wall would be level with his upper arms, so it provided him with good cover. He checked nothing had changed and apart from the sentry now sitting with the main group, replaced by the young boy, someone else, the woman, now tending to the sizzling meat, all was the same. They seemed completely relaxed and the bottle was still being passed from one to another, so he returned to his original position. Paul shook his weary head, desperate to clear it of any clutter.

He tried to make out Max's form again, if it was him, but it was too dark to see anything other than the outline of the pony. Then moving east along the wall, built up of randomly shaped rocks and stones, layered to form a barrier that protected the vineyard, he got to a position that was suitable for what he had in mind. He was now well away from the group and more importantly, out of earshot. As a result of the fire being directly in front of them, the glimmering flames would not only inhibit their night vision, but its reddish glow would prevent them seeing much beyond the position of the pony.

He discarded his water bottles and any other unnecessary items. They wouldn't be needed and would potentially restrict his movement, or make a noise catching against something. He lowered himself onto his hands and knees and slowly moved in an arc across the rough ground, gritting his teeth as he jarred his knee on a sharp rock, the pain lancing up his thigh. He waited until the pain rescinded to a mere throb and continued forwards, constantly glancing left, tracking his position and progress against the light of the fire and keeping a watchful eye out for movement amongst the group.

Paul stopped to catch his breath, water still sloshing around inside his stomach from when he had gorged himself. Now he had been partially rehydrated, sweat poured down his face and back. He didn't stop for long, the chilled air quickly gripping his body in its embrace, cooling his wiry frame rapidly now he was stationary.

He pushed on with his ungainly cat walk towards his target, on reaching it he was directly opposite the fire. He lay down and surveyed the ground in front of him, wishing he had brought his binoculars now. All he had was one grenade, his MP40, fully loaded, two spare magazines and his killing knife. They would have to do him.

He was about thirty metres away from the wall and the fire, but only twenty metres away from Max, the pony just beyond him to the right. A plan was forming in his head, but he would need to get a little closer to implement it.

He started to leopard crawled closer towards Max, his MP40 resting in the crook of his arms. He pushed off with his right leg, his left leg bent forwards and close to his chest. He then repeated the manoeuvre, pushing off with his left leg, his bent right leg moving forwards, his elbows alternating as he slid across the ground, stopping after each movement, scrutinising the group for any signs that he had been discovered.

He edged his way closer, using Max's form and the pony to hide behind. He daren't go too far to the right in case the pony caught his scent and reacted, warning his owners that someone or something was close. He was ten metres away from Max. He was loath to move any closer, should the sentry catch his movement out of the corner of his eye. He had considered moving along the back of the wall, approaching them from the building, but he had seen the dog lying there, chewing on a stick or a bone. Not only could the dog have been alerted by the noise of his approach, but the route would have taken him upwind. Although the dog may have been distracted by the smell of roasting meat, he could well have picked up Paul's human scent.

He waited, watched and waited, watched and waited.

Then the golden opportunity he had been waiting for, as he

anticipated it would, arrived. The sizzling feast, slowly turning on the spit, was ready.

The group, along with the woman and the sentry, hungrily gathered round the fire to tuck in to the food that had been tantalising them for the last twenty minutes. A small confrontation ensued between the old man and the boy who had been on sentry duty. The young boy returned to his post, grumbling, the old hunting rifle, perhaps his father's, barrel down in protest, resting on the toe cap of his shabby boots, which seemed two sizes too big for him. He stared hungrily as the meat was torn off in strips and passed around. The woman, her thick dark hair covering her face and eyes, obviously feeling sorry for him, brought him a bone, slithers of meat still attached. Paul froze, pressing his body in to the ground, wanting it to swallow him up. The boy took it, leaning the butt of the rifle against his chest as he attacked the feast in his hands. The woman, her guilt assuaged, re-joined the others.

This was Paul's moment, the moment to take the initiative, while they were all distracted. He picked up the stick grenade he had placed in front of him earlier, the end cap already unscrewed and ready. He rose up from the ground, an apparition, a manifestation of death. His MP40 held firmly in his left hand, his right arm twisted back behind his shoulder, he threw the grenade the twenty metres necessary to be on target.

The grenade landed exactly where Paul had aimed for, the junction of the wall and the stone built side of the hut, less than two metres from the group. He threw himself to the ground, the noise of his throwing and the subsequent crashing to the ground alerting both the group and the young boy, whose rifle crashed to the ground alongside his half eaten bone, as he fumbled with the butt attempting to bring it to a position where he could fire at the intruder.

Some of the others realised something was wrong as the grenade bounced off the wall of the hut, landing at the base of the wall, directly in front of the older man. Who, still chewing on a piece of lamb, fat dribbling down his chin, discarded the piece of meat he was holding and grabbed for his Sten Gun, a gift from a British Soldier. He didn't make it.

The grenade exploded.

Although partially absorbed by the two walls, as intended by Paul, to reduce the likelihood of the blast hitting Max, the eruption hit the group from the side, the explosion bursting the ear drums of the leader, the woman and the second eldest man, lacerating their exposed skin, slithers of shrapnel ripping through their clothing and digging deep into their flesh. The force of the shock wave shoved them aside, the grey haired partisan sprawling across the fire, unconscious as flames licked around him, his beard shrivelling to nothing in a fraction of a second.

Paul leapt up, machine pistol in his hand and opened fire on the group, aiming left at the three young men and teenager, who were recovering from the shock and their minor injuries, since the three elders having taken the bigger percentage of the blast. Grabbing for their weapons, a mixed assortment, one an antique, single barrelled shotgun. But they were too late as Paul's machine gun's fire scythed through them, cutting them down before they could aim a shot in return. He continued to fire until his magazine was empty, dropping it to the ground and slamming a fresh one back in.

He heard a shout. The young boy had recovered the sports rifle and aimed it directly at him, jabbering in his foreign tongue. The rifle was shaking as he gestured with it, the gesticulation obvious, he wanted Paul to drop his gun. Paul knew that the explosion and subsequent gunfire would have already alerted the village.

Not only was the boy's rifle shaking, but the boy was also visibly trembling. Paul heard a groan coming from the direction of the fire. One of the partisans, although badly wounded, was able to move and was shouting something to the boy, the same word, three times. Paul didn't understand what was being called, but he suspected it was, 'kill, kill, kill'.

The boy raised the rifle higher, it was now pointing directly at Paul's chest, his shaking arms been brought under control, everything in his face's expression told Paul he was getting ready to fire. The boy's fingers squeezed the trigger of the rifle more tightly. The wounded partisan rose up on his knees, his Lee Enfield also now aiming at Paul, he had left it too late, he had lost.

Crack!

The boy jerked as the bullet smacked into his side, the ensuing crack from the P38 pistol slamming a second round in to the boy's chest. He toppled backwards, sprawled on the ground, blood trickling from his mouth. Paul reacted immediately, shooting the other partisan before turning to identify the location from where the shot had originated. He saw nothing. He made sure the young boy's rifle was clear. But he was slowly dying, unable to take advantage even had the weapon been close. He would never fire a rifle again, or savour his favourite food, roast lamb, his spirit left him, his heart punctured and failing.

Paul ran across to where the rest of the group was situated, the old man now a blackened corpse, the smell of burning flesh making him gag. Some were dead, all were injured in some way, most would die soon without immediate medical aid. He ensured they were all disarmed, smashing any weapons he found to destruction against the wall.

He ran back across to check on Max, his next worry, knowing they needed to move quickly, the noise of the action was bound to have got the attention of the village. He crouched down by the still form, the pony nickering and whinnying close by. His eyes were closed, but a P 38 loose in his hand, Max had been his saviour.

"Max."

His eyes fluttered open. He croaked an unintelligible response. Water, thought Paul, he must be in desperate need of water. He sprinted back to the wall, scouting along it until he found the items he had left there, including the water bottles. He hurried back to Max and quickly pressed the bottle to his dry, cracked lips, the water still cool as it slopped across his face, some of it making its way into his mouth. The effect was immediate. Like a wilting flower, perking up after receiving a sudden down pour of rain.

The dehydrated sergeant opened his eyes, as he attempted to guzzle the water, but choking on the attempt.

"Steady Max, there's plenty, there's no rush." As he said it, he knew they would have to go soon, but Max's need was great. He managed a quarter of a pint before Paul stopped him.

"Enough for now, eh Max? We don't want to overdo it. We need to move now, ok?"

Max's pained face cracked into a flimsy grin, "Sir."

Paul trotted over to the pony, who was shuffling nervously on his fetlocks, tugging at the reigns secured to a rock close by. Paul stroked and patted the pony's neck and flanks, talking to it, soothing him as best he could. Although the pony's eyes remained wild and staring, he seemed to react to Paul's foreign voice and settled, although still a little skitty. He turned the travois round, dragged it across to the rear of the pony, and hoisted it up on to the rope loops either side, placed there by the partisans to bring Max to this place. He tied it off, checked it was secure, then made sure Max was still on-board and hadn't slid off. He was ok, the 'Y' straps Paul had used to bind Max to the stretcher were holding out and his construction was keeping its integrity.

Paul took one last look around him, before hoisting his MP40 onto his shoulder. Some of the bodies near the fire were moving, the fire eerily flickering around them, beyond its radius of light, just darkness and shadows. He loosened the reigns of the pony, encouraging him forwards, pulling Max behind them.

CHAPTER TWENTY-FOUR

They kept to the wall for some time; it then disappeared off to the south continuing to box in the large vineyard, now just the dark shape of the foothills his constant shadow. With the wall gone, Paul felt exposed and hurried the pony along, but slowing down again after realising that Max was getting a rough ride. The pony picked its way across the broken ground, the travois jumping as it caught on a rock or a hardy shrub. Paul looked back over his shoulder, the fire was no longer visible, and the lights of the village had long gone. He had no idea how far he was from the road or what lay in front of him, but decided that if he kept the foothills in sight it would keep him from straying too far north.

Although concerned about the effects of the journey on Max's condition, Paul pressed on. He was torn between stopping and checking Max's dressings and even putting on a fresh one, the last one, on the wound to his abdomen, or putting as much distance as possible between them and the village. Paul was certain that if he kept moving west, kept out of sight, he could avoid the enemy and hopefully bump into his comrades, perhaps even his own company.

A few hours on, dawn now getting to grips with the nights shadows, he scanned the area in front and around him. Not only keeping a watchful eye for enemy forces, but somewhere to stop and rest, he was desperate to close his eyes, if only for a short time. His legs were ponderous, his eyes heavy, head bowed. Paul gripped on to the mane of the pony who at times was pulling them both along.

An hour later and he spied the ideal place, a small copse above them and to their left. Perfect for hiding not only him and Max, but also the pony who had served them well. As a result of his new found, four legged friend, they had made good progress, far more than if Paul was to haul the stretcher himself.

He steered the pony towards the copse of olive and lemon trees and others he didn't recognise, dispersed amongst a thicket, which provided ideal cover. The pony changed direction, dragging its load now up the gentle slope. Paul tethered the pony, unhooked the travois and dragged it into the centre of the cluster of trees and bushes. He then moved the pony to the northern edge, further out of sight, leaving it to pick at what little grass there was about him.

The copse was composed of a dozen trees clustered tightly together, their branches low and sweeping close to the ground, touching the dusty soil where it sloped upwards away from them towards the hills, Paul having to duck constantly. The sun was now peeking above the horizon, giving him some light to check over his charge, before the blistering heat of the day made any form of movement unbearable.

"Are you with us Max?"

His eyes fluttered open, his grimy, bristled face eased into a smile and he croaked back, "Where are... we?"

"Were back south of Rethymnon. We'll stay here for a bit. Give me a chance to get some sleep and then scout around later."

Max winced.

"Are you in much pain Max? I have one syringe left if you want it now."

"Save it... maybe later."

"Not addicted to it yet then eh? More than we can say for German beer."

"Water?"

"Hang on Max, I'll grab some."

Paul rummaged around his bread bag, secured to his belt at the back, and produced a water bottle.

"Here you go. Take your time."

Max sipped the water, slowly, still cool and refreshing.

"I owe you my life Max, again. If you hadn't shot that boy..."

He pulled the water bottle away from Max.

"You owe me... a beer... not getting away... without paying your debts."

"I need to look at your dressings, ok?" Max nodded his head slightly.

Paul pulled back Max's shirt. The shoulder and chest dressing were encrusted in blood, but were both dry. He decided to leave them for now. The abdomen dressing was black with blood, although not soaking, just damp. Max had noticed Paul's pained expression.

"I'll be ok... sir."

"I'm not going to move you unnecessarily Max, I'll just lift the bottom bandage and pack a fresh one underneath."

Max smiled. "Just... do it."

He packed bits of kit beneath Max's buttocks and torso, raising his body on the one side, pulling the older bandage, which had loosened these past couple of days, away from the wound. He sniffed the wound for any signs of infection, and finding none, he placed the fresh one underneath, binding the old one on top of it. Paul felt sure the rear part of the wound was the worst, but at least there was a clean bandage against it now and the old bandages would act as packing to control any bleeding. Once completed, he gave Max some more water and left him to recover from the treatment he had just doled out.

Moving to the northern edge of the copse, he looked out and scanned the terrain. They had dropped much lower than he had anticipated and he could see the coast and the sea clearly, already heavy with its blue tint as the sun's power increased. Although he had heard the occasional gunshot during the night, there seemed to be a steady build up in the last hour or so, a fire fight was in progress somewhere to his west, not that far from here he surmised. Paul moved back slightly, positioning his back against a tree and dozed for a few hours until the intense heat of midday woke him up.

Paul was groggy with sleep and licked his dry lips, but resisted the temptation to partake in a drink of water, instead he split open a lemon he had picked earlier, sucking its bitter juice and eating the pulp, temporarily slaking his raging thirst. He felt hot, dry and drained.

Paul went back into the cover of the thicket to check on Max's health. He looked ghastly pale, his skin almost translucent beneath the veneer of his tanned face. Rather than disturb him to give him water, he let him sleep, where at least the discomfort and pain of his wounds were put aside for the moment. Shaking the water bottles, he estimated they had two pints left between them, Max needing all of it if he was to survive the day. He would have to go out and scavenge again.

He made his way back to the edge of the copse and studied the ground in front of him. Gently sloping down, an undulating mish mash of scrub, rocks and trees and reddish earth spread out until it hit the southern outskirts of the eastern part of Rethymnon, some four kilometres away. There were a number of houses dotted about between his position and the town. Paul imprinted their positions on his internal map.

He reflected on the fact that he hadn't take any of the roasted lamb, but the smell of burning flesh had been too much, the thought of it even now making him gag. He slumped against a tree trunk. Nervous anxiety, a constant state of alertness, lack of food and water along with the ceaseless heat was taking its toll, both on his body and his mind. He constantly worried about his men, angry with himself for deserting them, but equally glad that he was able to aid his sergeant, and friend, who would have died long ago had he not done so.

Looking west, he was sure he could see another gully and studying it with his binoculars he could make out the steepness of its sides. He would never get the pony and travois across that, and made the decision to move lower, further north, although this would take him dangerously close to civilisation, before picking up the trail west again. It was risky, but he had no choice.

He closed his eyes, feeling sleepy and dozed, the sun's rays quite pleasant at the moment, its full force filtered by the canopies of the trees. He must have cat napped for half an hour before being woken with a jolt as a military vehicle screamed by on the road below. Only the top half of the truck was visible, canvas covered so he couldn't see inside, but got a view of the khaki clad soldiers over spilling the tailgate, the inside packed to capacity, as it sped away. The truck disappeared leaving a trail of dust and blue smoke, the engine rattling, struggling with the full load and on its last legs.

Paul slipped further back into the copse ensuring he wouldn't be seen. He saw something move. There it was again, a flash of khaki passed between the gaps in the trees that lined the road. He pulled out his binoculars and looked more closely. Allied soldiers. Bedraggled, heads bowed, weapons slung, an army in retreat. He couldn't help the smile that cracked the firm lines of his dust encrusted face. Behind those soldiers, he knew, would be his army, the Fallschirmjager, his unit.

He watched them pass for the best part of the day, at least five hundred men, including a mixture of Greek soldiers and the occasional armed civilian. At one point they scattered into the undergrowth as a gaggle of German planes flew high overhead, bypassing the tasty target below. Paul looked up, surmising that they had already hit their target and were returning to base, or were on route to a second objective. He moved back in to the centre of the copse.

"Max, Max," he hissed, touching his good shoulder. "It looks like the enemy is pulling back."

Max croaked an unintelligible reply, his condition clearly worsening.

"Take some water, then I'm going to scout the road and suss out what is happening. Keep an eye open for our boys eh Max? They will be coming for us soon."

Although Max didn't verbally respond, he did instinctively drink from the water bottle that Paul offered to him.

Leaving Max, he went to the edge of the copse, scanning the road with his binoculars searching for signs of the enemy, or even friendly forces. There was nothing, it seemed still. Paul exited his hiding place and skirmished down to the road, less than half a kilometre away, his Fallschirm heavy on his head again, his MP40 at the ready.

Paul found a small ditch close to the road and collapsed in to it, exhausted. The half pint of water he had allowed himself had long since evaporated, his body craving for the life sustaining liquid that he had previously taken for granted. He crawled to the edge of the road, his splinter pattern tunic helping him blend in with the undergrowth. He was now too low to see far and could no longer see Rethymnon to the north, but some six hundred metres away a large house stood in isolation and he logged it away in his mind as a possible target for later that night.

To his immediate front a small hut, but he saw no signs of life. He looked along the road that seemed to skirt the steep gully he would need to avoid on his journey west. It was a dilemma, cross it close to the road and he risked being seen by passing vehicles, move further north and he would be too close to the approaching outskirts of the town.

He pulled the undergrowth about him, confident that anyone

walking passed, unless they deliberately studied his position and looked at him directly, would walk by without seeing him. His camouflage was tested only minutes later as an enemy unit approached from the west, at least a platoon in size. They looked like they were the tail end of the larger unit that had passed throughout the day, constantly looking over their shoulders at the invisible enemy tracking them.

Paul gripped his MP40 tightly, in case he was discovered, pushing his face into the ground, the earthy smell of the undergrowth filling his nostrils. He need not have worried, the soldiers were too occupied with looking to their rear to worry about looking for a dishevelled Fallschirmjager in the undergrowth. They passed him by, their ammo boots clattering on the road as they shambled passed, the sound diminishing as they faded into the distance, leaving Paul alone again.

It was four in the afternoon, light would be fading soon and he questioned whether he should stay where he was and wait for friendly forces, or head back to the copse. He was loathed to leave Max alone for long, reminiscing on what had occurred last time he had been away. But his decision was made for him as he saw movement down the road, soldiers in file either side, close to the verge, their weapons sweeping from side to side as they patrolled towards him in good order. The distinctive rimless helmet, the profile of the tunics, their confident bearing, all indicating they were Fallschirmjager.

Paul waited until they moved closer, not wanting to startle them into thinking it was an ambush. As they got nearer, their studded jump boots scraping across the surface of the road, their eyes flicking left and right, the furthest forward scanning the undergrowth at the roadside, the scouts of the unit, searching for signs of the enemy.

"Venus," Paul called out. "Venus."

The advance party's reaction was instantaneous, scattering to each side of the road, throwing themselves to the ground. It was only the voice that had spoken in German that held them back from spraying the ground in front of them with gunfire. One trooper was already clutching a hand grenade, ready to inflict death on any potential attackers.

"Comet," called the leading soldier, an Unteroffizier.

"Show yourself, but keep your bloody arms at your side. If you have a weapon sling it."

Paul rose slowly from his hiding place in the undergrowth, his MP40 slung over his shoulder, his hands low and spread wide either side of his body.

"Unteroffizier Spiegler."

"Gott im Himmel, Oberleutnant Brand. Where the bloody hell have you been sir? Sorry Oberleutnant, but we've been looking for you."

Paul moved closer, he had recognised the Unteroffizier as being a troop commander from Helmut's unit.

"Watching your back for you Uffz."

The Uffz grinned back. "Pardon me for saying so sir, but you look a bloody mess, are you wounded?"

Paul looked puzzled, then looking down at his tunic and trousers realised he was not only covered in dust and grime, but Max's blood as well.

"No, but Feldwebel Grun is, he's back up at that copse."

Spiegler turned to the paratrooper behind him. "Get Oberleutnant Janke now and Keufer."

He turned back to Paul. "We'll get him out of there sir, I'll have a medic up there sharpish."

His friend came striding in to view, the stocky Oberleutnant, although grimy like the rest, his square jaw was clean shaven and his arched eyebrows rose and his brown eyes twinkled as he caught sight of Paul. He clasped Paul's shoulders with his shovel sized hands, rocking his taller comrade on his feet.

"You look like hell Oberleutnant Brand, but it's bloody good to see you. Don't they have razors where you've been swanning? Are you hurt?"

Paul placed his hands on Helmut's shoulders, almost leaning on them for support. The relief of not being on his own, of Max being safe, being amongst his own again, sapped what little strength he had left.

His friend gripped him firmer, holding him up, knowing that he may even collapse in front of them.

"Max is wounded Helmut."

"How bad, where is he?"

"Quite bad I think."

"Keufer is already on his way with some of the boys to fetch him down sir," informed Spiegler.

"Thank you Uffz. Find Feldwebel Jung and have the company in a defensive position here, I'll talk to the platoon commanders in a minute."

The Uffz sped off to carry out his commander's orders.

"What happened Paul?

"What about my company? Are they safe? How many got away?"

Helmut stepped back, his friend having clearly regained some of his strength.

"They're in good shape. A bit shot up, like us all, but they've reformed."

"Where are they now?"

"Following behind us," Helmut said, pointing back down the road towards the west. "About a kilometre away. They should be here within the hour. Erich's somewhere behind them."

"Practically the entire battalion."

"Yes, apart from HQ company and the Raven, they're still in the middle of the fighting around Hania."

"How's the battle going, I've sort of been out of touch?" announced Paul with a smile, his whole persona relaxing in the company of his fellow soldiers and friend.

"Got off to a sticky start, but we've got five Regimental Groups pushing them back. More of that later, let's get you sorted out, you look like shit. Have you eaten recently?"

"Some water would be good."

"Let's go and get you some, we have some fresh from a cistern, should still be cool."

They moved deeper into the company's position, a platoon had been positioned either side of the road, some crouching down behind the bank either side, the rest spreading out to cover their flanks, the third watching their rear. The platoon Leutnant's acknowledged Paul with a nod. He was already a legend within the battalion having seen more action than most, but the fact he had made it back through enemy lines, carrying the company sergeant, was already adding to it, giving him the mystique of the archetypal Fallschirmjager officer.

"I want to see my men again Helmut."

"I know, I understand. I've already sent a runner back to let them know you are alive, that should quicken their pace."

Just then a panting pony trotted along the roadway, its hooves clip clopping, the paratroopers accompanying it pulling it to the side where Helmut had set up a temporary company HQ for himself.

Keufer acted immediately, instructing the troopers close by to lift the unconscious sergeant off the travois and on to the hard packed ground on the side of the road. The soldiers worked quickly, but carefully, not wanting to jolt their wounded comrade.

Under instruction from Keufer, the soldiers got busy. Some went to fetch water, others erected a make shift shelter, made of branches and ground sheets, to protect him from the rays of the sun, which although slowly descending into dusk, still had enough glare and heat to make the patient uncomfortable.

Keufer hacked away at Max's tattered and blooded clothing exposing the badly stained dressings. He stabbed him with a syringe and started to pat his face gently.

"Feldwebel, Feldwebel."

Max's eyes cracked open slightly and Paul made to go over and talk to him, but was held back by his friend.

"Leave Keufer to work on him, Max is in good hands."

Max groaned and the medic beckoned one of the soldiers forward with water, who proceeded to administer sips whilst the medic tended to his wounds. The medic cut away the dressings with a pair of scissors, exposing their blue-black hue, the lower one at the back looking angry and inflamed, puss oozing from it.

Keufer produced some clean rags from his bag, soaked them in a bowl of water containing an antiseptic solution and proceeded to wash the wounds. His approached seemed rough after Paul's more gentle approach, but Keufer obviously felt it necessary to clean the wounds well, even if it meant rubbing hard. He seemed confident in what he was doing and worked fast. He picked out bits of debris and lint's of uniform from the depths of the wounds, cutting away any flesh he was sure was now dead, then wiping the wounds again thoroughly. Max groaned, but a smile filtered across his face in his delirium.

Having cleaned the wounds meticulously, and with the help of the soldiers nearby, the medic rolled him on to his side and put a few stitches in the larger wound. After smearing it with an anti-inflammatory and antiseptic ointment, he bandaged him carefully, packing the wounds tightly and binding them with layers of gauze, particularly the wound to his side, wrapping it round and round his stomach. Once finished, he did the same with the upper wounds and rubbed his hands in satisfaction at his work. Paul walked over now Keufer had clearly finished.

"Well, how is he?"

"His shoulder and chest should be ok sir, providing he isn't moved too much, and will heal eventually and apart from a few scars will be ok," he answered washing his hands in the small bowl of water. "But the lower wound is a bit of a mess, it looks like the bullet may have shattered on entry and has torn a hole in his side. I don't know if there is any more debris left inside, he needs to be in a hospital for anything else to be done. I've put some stitches in, but too much movement and they could tear."

"I'm ok... sir... feeling better... already."

Paul crouched down.

"You're in good hands Feldwebel Grun, Max, so no lip to the staff right?"

Max's right arm rose steadily and he gripped Paul's arm with it. Even in his dehydrated, weakened state, he could still feel the power in Max's grip.

"Thank you... sir. Without you... I would have been... in dockyard heaven."

"It's no more than you would have done for me my friend. I'll leave you in Keufer's capable hands, the company is on its way in and I dread to think what state they'll be in without the company sergeant keeping them in line."

Max made to lift his head, Paul gently held him down.

"I'll sort them Max, you rest for now. You can make sure they're all ship shape when you return, ok."

Paul stood up and turned to Keufer. "What now?"

"We'll keep him as comfortable as we can sir, and pump him full of fluids and wait."

"Wait for what?" asked Paul impatiently, not happy with Keufer's laid back response.

"Until Rethymnon is taken and we can get them all in to a hospital there."

Helmut pulled Paul back, recognising the signs of his impatience getting the better of him.

"We're going to set up a joint base camp here, if you're in agreement, collect all our wounded together centrally and wait for further orders."

"What are your orders so far?"

Soldiers milled around them, setting up defence positions. A troop had dug shell scrapes either side of the road, their arcs of fire to the east, the other two troops from each platoon had spread out across the flat ground for at least two hundred metres either side. MG34s were being set up on the extreme flanks, their muzzles sniffing out for any sign of the enemy, ready to meet them with a hail of fire. Helmut's third platoon were covering the rear, with one troop scouting further east looking for signs of the enemy returning, in the centre his mortar troop, ready to fire in a three hundred and sixty degree arc if necessary. Away to their north the eastern outskirts of Rethymnon, to their south the copse Paul and Max had used to hide in overlooked them.

The walking wounded were being led to the new casualty collecting station a hundred metres off the road and positioning recognition flags about the area and on the building's roof, warning the Luftwaffe of their presence.

"Our orders, yours included, are to sit tight and wait for the big push to come to us. We're pretty low on ammunition and other supplies. In fact, we only have enough ammunition to put up a token defence.

"What happened to my company after we'd been hit?"

"They were pulling back in good order. You chose the right moment to get them out of there. You were in the middle of a full scale British counter attack."

"Go on, go on."

"Well, they were rattling through the ammunition. Even using it sparingly, they gave a good account of themselves."

"Where did you catch up with them?"

"We heard the fire fight first and were pretty sure it was you, so headed east as fast as we could to come and assist. They had pulled back as far as the north of Adele, in good order, a platoon at a time. They had practically a full battalion on their heels."

"Excuse me sir, we've got a platoon covering the road and one protecting the casualty station, where do you want mine?" asked the handsome, oval faced young Leutnant, helmet off showing his, short, dark stubbly hair. A deep brown like Helmut's, so dark it could be mistaken for black. He looked at his commander and Paul with unhidden admiration.

"I also want your men close to the medical centre Aldrec, but put one of your troops back along the road, say about one hundred metres and one at the other end. Make sure they keep a look out for Oberleutnant Brand's men, they'll be along within the hour. Understood?"

"Yes sir," and turning to Paul said, "and glad to see you and the Feld back with us sir." With that he left to carry out his duties.

"You and Max are getting quite a reputation for yourselves Paul."

"I'd prefer to get that reputation some other way, things could have gone smoother," he responded with a wry grin.

"What are you on about? As far as HQ are concerned, particularly after they interrogated some prisoners, you guys have caused the enemy mayhem. The Allied command thought there was a full battalion poking around in the foothills and diverted troops to dig you out."

"What happened to the unit we ambushed on... not sure when now. When was it? What day is it today?"

"It's the 24th today," chided Helmut slapping his friend on the back. "You mean the one you caught napping on top of the gully?"

"Yes, they headed north."

"We got there just as they did, so we didn't have time to set up an ambush, but we still hit them hard and they headed north east as fast as they could."

"What about my company, you hadn't finished?"

"Yes, as I was saying. They pulled back north of Adele holding off the Allied attack and one from the Greeks that had poured out of the town, so we hit the Greek Army and both company's pulled back in good order."

"I saw some of our men in the town."

"Your men? Who?"

"I meant Fallschirmjager, I couldn't see who they were, it was too dark. But it looked like they had been stabbed repeatedly."

"Scheisse," exclaimed Helmut. "We have three men missing. Bastards, wait till I get my hands on those Greek scum. There have been a few reported instances of soldiers being mutilated by civilians, or partisans as they like to call themselves. What were you doing in the town anyway?"

"Getting some water, we were craving for water, so I had no choice. How many losses in my company?"

Helmut turned round, hearing the stomp of boots behind him.

"They'll be able to tell you themselves, here they are."

Paul turned and followed his gaze and could see Leeb's troop out in front, Fessman, his wiry frame, leading the way. Compared to the rest he looked fresh and fit, he had a knack for always being clean shaven, his uniform always well turned out, even in battle. The others looked hot, dusty and sweat stained. Fessman walked up to him, his normally laid back, seemingly unemotional approach pushed to one side as his face beamed at seeing his company commander. His hawk like eyes examined Paul, his face seeming even more pinched through days of combat and restricted rations and water.

"Wondered when you would turn up sir," he said shaking Paul's hand, "but it's bloody good to see you."

He turned to his grinning troop who had gathered round them, Helmut slipping back from the group, leaving Paul alone to reunite with his men, who were unquestionably pleased to see him. He ordered one of his men to run and fetch the platoon commanders and within a matter of minutes, Paul had his three platoon commanders stood in front of him along with the rest of the company, all patting his back, cracking jokes about he and the Feldwebel being on Urlaub, holiday, nipping down to the coast for a bit of swimming. It slowly dawned on the group that the giant Feldwebel was not there and the joy turned to questions regarding the whereabouts of their company sergeant.

Leeb disbanded the group, claiming they would make the perfect target for the Tommy air force, ordering them to set up where Oberleutnant Janke had instructed, his chiselled angular features breaking into a smile as he approached Paul.

"Report Leutnant Leeb," said Paul, smiling, equally pleased to be back with his men.

"First things first sir, is Feldwebel Grun with you?" asked the slim officer, his brow furrowed as he looked around, expecting to see the stocky Feldwebel not far from Paul's side.

"Yes Ernst, but he's badly shot up. Keufer, Oberleutnant Janke's medic is looking after him at the company first aid post."

"I'll get Fink over there sir, to check on him."

"So what happened?" cross examined Paul.

"Once you gave us the order to pull back and we got detached from you and the Feld, we regrouped on Wadi Piggi to try and hold them back, so we could counter attack and come to yours and Feldwebel Grun's aid."

"If you hadn't pulled us back when you did sir," added Nadel, his normally pale face flushed with the heat, "they would have got right in behind us, then we'd have been hit from all sides."

"But there were too many of them," interjected Roth, the tip of his nose still red and burnt from the sun, "and when the tank turned up we had nothing to throw at it."

The dark haired commander of the mortar troop joined them, his helmet hanging from his belt, sweat running down the sides of his rectangular face, his piercing eyes taking in his bedraggled company commander.

"Even Richter's boys couldn't dent it," chipped in Nadel.

"But we had a secret weapon sir," claimed Leeb, excited now at the retelling of their story, but reliving an event that could have been the death toll for all of them. "Fessman."

"He, and one of his men, Stumme, ran like hell along a fold in the ground," said Roth picking up the story.

"After throwing smoke," threw in Nadel.

Roth turned towards him, his cherubic face nodding excitedly. "They ran right in amongst the enemy infantry protecting the tank and chucked three grenades into the tracks."

"They must have shattered a pin or one of the treads, because the track came off and it slewed to the right and that was the end of it," said Leeb bringing the story to a conclusion. "They still manned the guns, but they couldn't advance any further forward and threaten to overrun us, all they could do was use it as a pillbox. But more reinforcements piled in and we had to pull back, there were just too many of them sir."

"Then you bumped in to Oberleutnant Janke?"

"Not a moment too soon sir, we had a Greek unit come at us from the town of Adele, but his boys soon showed them off and we pulled further back. We didn't want to leave you and the Feld behind sir, but we had no choice, they would have overwhelmed us if we'd have stayed."

Paul nodded, picturing the scene, the bedlam, the pressure his platoon commanders and their troopers would have been under. Over five hundred men assaulting them from the front and side, a tank to contend with, the Greeks throwing another few hundred troops at them from their other flank. They did well in the circumstances.

"What about casualties Feldwebel?"

Paul stopped in his tracks, about to ask Max for the status of his company. He would have known how his unit had fared. But he wasn't here, he was fighting for his life in a stone built hut, in the middle of a hostile country. They said nothing.

"We've lost twenty killed and six wounded sir, including Feldwebel Grun."

Paul reflected on the numbers, he had lost nearly a quarter of his company. He turned to Richter. "How many bombs do you have left?"

"None sir. We'd hoped for a resupply, but the last drop was just ammo, food and water."

"It seems the mortar stocks are being held back to support the main push along the coast sir," contributed Leeb.

Paul rubbed the scar with his left hand, analysing what he had just been told and thinking through the options facing him. He still had a company to lead and no doubt they would be given a task to support the main thrust.

"Right Unterfeld, you are now the acting Company Feldwebel. You will take up your duties immediately and assume Feldwebel Grun's responsibilities until further notice, at least until the Feldwebel is back with us."

"My troop sir?"

Paul turned to one of his officers. "Dietrich, take the Feldwebel's men under your command, appoint an Uffz and incorporate them as a third troop."

"Jawohl Herr Oberleutnant."

The three officers all shook Richter's hand vigorously, in complete agreement with Paul's choice. He had proven his worth many times and with his leadership of the mortar troop had help them win some of their fire fights.

"Your first task is to provide me with a complete rundown on ammunition stocks, food and water supplies. Find Bergmann and send him to me immediately." He turned to the three platoon commanders.

"The copse back up the slope," said Paul, pointing back up towards the copse he and Max had been hiding in before the arrival of the Fallschirmjager troops. "Make that the Company Command Post and deploy your platoons around it and await further orders. I need to consult with battalion HQ."

They all dismissed and went about their duties. Richter still coming to terms with his appointment, wondering how it would be received by the rest of the unit, him being a new comer.

Paul walked amongst his men, chatting to them, re-establishing the link that existed between them. Most had fought with him before, some since the start of the war, back in Poland. He searched their faces, looking for anger or distrust as result of him leaving them to fend for themselves. But most of the talk was their inquisitiveness in how he had made it back through enemy lines, most joking about the added complexity of having to haul the Herculean Feldwebel on his back. Paul, with a twinkle in his eye, reminded them all, that when the Feldwebel returned to duty, he may want to question them about their comments. To which they all laughed.

They were all relieved to hear of his return and throughout the day they took it in turns to slip away and give him their good wishes. They were equally pleased to have their company commander back. Although the three platoon commanders had led them well, it was Oberleutnant Paul Brand who had their complete trust and confidence.

CHAPTER TWENTY-FIVE

Paul's company spent the night securing their positions, sending out night patrols, keeping the enemy on their toes, not knowing where the invaders were or what they were up to. During the day the two companies split. Paul's group covered the southern outer limits of Rethymnon, sending probes into the outer limits of the town. One led by Paul, met allied troops pulling back from Hania. His platoon sized force exchanged a few shots, but they retired quickly, ammunition stocks being too low for an extended fire fight. But their objective had been achieved, to put doubt in to the enemies mind as to where their attackers were. In their minds the Fallschirmjager seemed to be at their front, side and rear, making it difficult to decide where best to place their defences.

All along the stretch from Hania to Rethymnon, the Raven's battalion of four companies, one now commanded by his friend Erich after the loss of their comrade, Oberleutnant Meinhard, provided a screen to the flanks of the army that was now aggressively pushing east. At this moment in time, the Ramke Group was pushing in to Hania, supported by the 100th Gebirgsjager Regiment and the 3rd Fallschirmjager Regiment, with the 141st and 85th, Gebirgsjager Regiment's thrusting south of Hania in the direction of Souda and Rethymnon.

During the hours of darkness, Paul pulled all of his forces back to their prepared positions, having insisted that his men dig shell scrapes for added protection. He would have gone for deeper trenches, but in their weakened state through lack of food and water, and being in almost constant battle since they landed on the 20th May, he resisted it. He wouldn't send out any night time patrols close to the town, but he would still put out Listening Posts around their perimeter and a small security patrol should the enemy head their way. The sky frequently lit up with flashes from explosions, testament to the battle still raging down below them and to their west.

He stood with his three officers and the new Company Sergeant, Acting Feldwebel Richter, on the northern edge of the copse. Paul's company now covered a full one hundred metres either side, running north to south, securing Helmut's right flank. He turned to Roth.

"I want four LPs out tonight, all points of the compass. And keep a watch out for Oberleutnant Janke, they may well return tonight," he said pointing back to the west.

"Jawohl, Herr Oberleutnant."

"Dietrich, I want a troop sized patrol out, early hours, say three. It's just a security patrol, don't go beyond three hundred metres, but do a full circle of the perimeter. They're not to get in to contact; they are purely out there to ensure the enemy isn't sat in the undergrowth waiting to ambush us at first light. Understood?"

"Yes sir."

"Ernst, your boys get the night off, but we'll take out your full platoon in the morning and patrol close to the town again. We leave at five."

"Yes sir."

"Ammunition status Feldwebel Gru... sorry Feldwebel Richter?"

"MGs have two belts each and about sixty rounds per man sir."

"One heavy action would see that off," mused Paul, it's worrying that we're so low on 34 ammo. Make sure Leutnant Leeb's platoon have at least three belts per MG. You'll have to make do with one hundred and fifty rounds per troop Ernst, so if we so come in contact with the enemy, make sure they use them sparingly, and only to cover our withdrawal."

"I'll tell them sir."

"To make up for it I want your MP40s to have at least eight magazines."

"That will reduce the ammunition for the other platoons sir," informed Richter.

"That's as may be, but if Leutnant Leeb's men bump into the enemy, they will need all of it if they are to extract."

"Jawohl sir."

"The wounded?"

"We lost one during the day, Kohler, from Oberleutnant Janke's company. The rest will hold out I think sir."

Paul's thoughts drifted to his units losses. Scherer, newly attached to the company HQ, didn't even leave the Junkers transport plane, shot through the chest by a 40mm, Bofors round, a hole the size of a man's fist punched through his chest. Nadel had lost his entire 2nd troop, trapped in a flaming Tante June as it plummeted to the earth, a death Paul could not even contemplate. Forster got off lightly with a broken leg, still probably guarding the prisoners near the top of the gully they had descended only a few days ago. He hoped that a team had reached them by now to provide medical aid and bring them down. His fellow company commander, Meinhard, killed in action early on in the invasion of the Island, his company now commanded by his close friend Erich. Amsel, from Jordan's troop, with a shoulder wound, his shoulder blade shattered. He would not fight again, but if he remained in the Fallschirmjager he would be destined for the training depot, passing on his experience to raw recruits. Jordan had been less lucky, killed during the same fire fight, Braemer assuming command of the troop. Two men lost in the gully itself, when they ambushed the Allied unit, a soldier killed on their way to Rethymnon, brought down by a burst of fire from a British Hurricane fighter. Then they had hit a wall of enemy fire as they walked in to a British counter attack. Nadel lost another man, Primke from Leeb's platoon hit by a tank round, a Vickers machine gun dispatching one of Roth's men as they withdrew. Both lost a further two men at the Wadi Bardia. The next, Abt with a shattered arm, Roth losing two more as they pulled back north of Adele. Then there was Max. He must go and see Max now.

"Sir... sir, are you ok?"

"Ok, to your duties, Feldwebel Richter please remain behind."

The three platoon commanders drifted off to prepare their units for the duties allocated. The LPs, perimeter patrol should ensure they didn't get caught unawares, thought Paul.

"How have the men been?"

"Seem to have accepted it sir. I'm no replacement for Feldwebel Grun. For all his tough discipline, the men seem very loyal towards him."

"Most have fought with him since 1939, and for some this would have been the fourth fight. They will try to test you Feld, but I've no doubts that you'll be able to handle their moods and mischief."

"They are some of the best soldiers I have fought with sir. I will try and live up to yours and their expectations."

"Don't give them an easy ride," said Paul smiling.

"I have no intention of that sir, if you would excuse me I need to sort out the ammunition."

"Dismissed."

With that the slim, dark haired ex-commander of the mortar troop went to carry out his tasks for the night. Paul followed him as he moved amongst the men, giving orders regarding ammunition with confidence. Paul had no doubt he would be as good, although not quite as good, but close, as Max. He turned to go and check up on Max and saw Bergmann stood close by.

"Sir."

"Bergmann, still hugging that box around with you I see,' he said smiling, the radio tucked inside a wheeled weapons canister. He looked across at the rest of the HQ element, Mauer, Ostermann, heading towards the copse.

"I thought it might come in useful sir. Major Volkman will no doubt be expecting you to make contact."

"Set up the HQ element by the copse back up the hill, find Leutnant Leeb and he'll show you where to bed in. Once I've seen Feldwebel Grun I'll join you."

"Sounds like it's been a rough few days sir."

"We're back in the fold now Bergmann, have comms ready for when I get back."

"Jawohl sir."

Paul stepped off, crossed the road and headed towards the temporary medical post, picking his way across the rough ground, the light already fading into dusk. Sesson, who he recognised from 1st Platoon, acknowledged him as he walked passed. He pushed the groundsheet, suspended across the entrance, aside and ducked his head under the low doorway, the inside hot and stuffy. A flickering oil lamp, snaffled from a local's house, cast shadowy shapes on the inside of the stone walls. He recognised the shape of Fink, his company medic, as he got up from crouching over one of his patients.

"Evening sir."

"It's bloody warm in here Fink."

"We've had them outside most of the day sir, round the back, in the shade. The heat in here was even worse during the day, but we've brought the worst of the cases back inside before the temperature drops."

"Where's Feldwebel Grun?"

"Over there sir," he said pointing to a large shape lying close to the far wall.

The hut could only accommodate five people lying down, with just enough space between them for the medics to get access to them to take care of their wounds.

"Here sir," said Fink, handing Paul a second oil lamp he'd been using to examine his charges. "I think it's sheep or goat fat with a wick dipped in to it. It's pretty basic, but it gives us some light to work with."

Paul grabbed the cylindrical container, an old tin can with a crude handle stuck on the side, a cap on the top with a protruding, yellow, flaming wick. He stepped carefully over the other bodies, shining the light over their faces, giving them an encouraging smile, not wanting to touch them in case he caught their wound. He didn't recognise them, they would be from Helmut's unit. He crouched down next to the form he was told was Max.

"You look like a ghoul sir."

"I could charge you with being offensive to a senior officer Feldwebel Grun."

"It was a compliment sir," his voice croaky. "You always look better in the dark."

"Is Fink taking good care of you then Max?"

"They're both doing great."

Max caught his breath as a shaft of pain stabbed through his side.

"Anything I can do to make you more comfortable?"

"A feather mattress... would be good... I feel like... the princess and the pea."

"I think you would be the frog Max. Have you had any pain relief?"

"None left... sir. But Keufer's done a great job... patching me up."

"You'll be as good as new in no time Max, and back with the company."

"Richter will do a good job in my absence sir."

"You know?"

"Nothing... gets by me," he said with a cracked smile. "He's only standing in for me. I'm still the company Feldwebel."

They locked eyes.

"We'll get you out of here Max, back on form, back with the unit, that's my promise."

"I know sir. If you don't mind... I feel tired... you have a company to lead."

They gripped hands. A little more strength back in Max's.

Paul headed for the exit, handing the lamp to Fink on his way out.

"A quick word outside Fink."

They moved a few metres away from the hut.

"How is he?"

"His shoulder and chest wounds are painful, but clean. I think they will both heal well. But the wound in his side, his abdomen, is chewed up inside. Until we have some decent light and a good surgeon to work on it, we won't be able to tell how bad it is or repair it."

"Have you stopped the bleeding?"

"Yes sir, for the moment. Its infection setting in that worries me. It smells clean at the moment, but we need to get him out of here as soon as possible."

"All in good time Fink, all in good time. We'll get them all out of here soon. Let me know immediately if there is any change in his condition."

"Understood sir."

"How are the rest holding up?"

"Oberleutnant Janke has a few badly wounded, but the rest of our boys are holding up."

"Are they outside?"

"Yes sir."

"I'll see them before I go."

Paul started off, then turned round, "You're doing a good job for our men Fink, I'll leave you to it."

He chatted briefly with the wounded Fallschirmjager from his company and those from Helmut's, and then made his way back to company HQ. After a brief communication with his battalion commander, the Raven, instructing him to sit tight, hold the flank and await the main advance, he checked the lines and grabbed a few hours of much needed sleep.

★★★

Over the next two days the battle intensified around Hania, Souda and Rethymnon, the five regimental combat groups hitting the Allied forces hard. The 5th New Zealand and the 19th Australian Brigades counter attacked the lead elements of the 1st battalion of the 141st Gebirgsjager Regiment forcing them to retreat. But, by twenty two hundred hours, on the 27th May, the two Allied brigades started to withdraw. By the 28th May, the defenders were slowly pushed back and during the 29th May, elements of the 141st Gebirgsjager Regiment passed through Paul's and Helmut's lines on their way, supported by the 85th Gebirgsjager Regiment, to relieve the beleaguered Fallschirmjager in Rethymnon and Heraklion. Paul, Helmut and their men were stood down and ordered to move to Rethymnon to link up with the rest of the battalion, where they regrouped and the Raven's unit was stood down.

The rest of the German force pushed the remnants of the allied troops south, towards Sphakion, forcing the evacuation of the town, the Royal Navy using Destroyers to evacuate the troops trapped there. By the evening of the 30th, the German forces were less than three miles from the town, the rest of the Island now in German hands. On the morning of 1 June, 1941, at nine am, Lieutenant Colonel Walker delivered the surrender to the 100th Gebirgsjager Regiment, leaving the Germans in complete control of the island.

CHAPTER TWENTY-SIX

Paul stood to attention in front of the Raven as the battalion commander rifled through the papers on his desk in front of him. His dark, deep set eyes scanning the documents searching for the one he needed. He had requisitioned one of the municipality buildings in the town of Rethymnon, a three story structure once used by the local officials. Through the tall window behind the battalion commander, Paul could just make out part of the sweeping bay that bordered the town, the sea calm, the odd palm tree with, their thick, bulbous, spiky trunks, brown tipped green fronds extending upwards, moving slightly in the gentle breeze.

The room wasn't large, but the Raven had made it his own, choosing a sea front view on the second level, a large balcony behind him, framed by black railings, the open window allowing some fresh air in to the stifling room. No doubt a room next door had been turned into his sleeping quarters by his orderly, Bachmeier. The dominating piece of furniture in the room was the large, ornate desk Volkman was stood behind. Possibly teak, or maybe a local wood unknown to Paul. It had a leather chair with curved arms, the same colour as the desk, supported by four feet on a central pillar. There were two smaller matching chairs in front of the desk, where Paul was now stood in between them and slightly behind.

Sweat was running down his neck and back, his Fallschirm pressing down on his skull making his temples throb and his head ache. The scar above his left eye pulsated in time with the beat of his heart, the desire to touch it growing ever stronger. But he resisted, remaining at attention.

Looking out of the corner of his left eye, Paul could see his reflection in the large mirror, its ornate frame pinned to the wall above an unused open fireplace, there to keep the occupants warm during the bitter cold winter nights. Even though he had been rested for three days and had been given the chance to clean up, shave and eat some decent rations, he was surprised at how his image looked back at him. His face was drawn and pinched, his uniform loose on his wiry frame, eyes sunken.

Although the battle for Crete had been over for a few days now, his duties as a company commander were not. Ensuring the wounded were cared for, billets and rations organised, his unit rearmed ready for battle if called upon and taking their turn to guard the many prisoners that had befallen as a result of the Allies surrender. The pilot, who they had captured earlier and who had been released during the battle north of Adele, was amongst them. Paul had spoken to him, and with the assistance of Ackermann, their company interpreter, had asked after his wellbeing and apologised for his earlier behaviour. The pilot had thanked him and offered Paul his condolences at his loss and even intimated that, but for the war, he would have liked to have talked more about their individual backgrounds.

The Raven suddenly grunted, pig like, and picked up three sheets of paper. He peered down his slightly hooked, Roman like nose, the reason for his nick name, his dark hooded eyes scanning Paul's face.

"Your report Brand," he said brandishing the document in front of Paul.

He turned away, stepped towards the open French window of the balcony and breathed in the fresh air deeply.

"I'll not be sorry to see the back of this place Brand," he said tapping his swagger stick against the side of his left leg, Paul's report in his right hand thrust behind his back.

"Remove your helmet, you must be sweating like a pig," he ordered without turning around.

Paul took off his helmet, placing it by his feet and returned to his position of attention.

"The operations conducted by you and your men have been exemplary Brand. The routing of the enemy at the village of Pagantha, the ambush of the British company in the gully, forcing them into another trap. A truly remarkable achievement."

He walked completely on to the balcony, both hands behind his back as he peered over the black, iron railing. Turning on the spot, he walked back in to the room and looked at Paul.

"Even when you encountered a battalion sized counter attack, supported by tanks, you gave them a bloody nose. I have put Uffz Fessman forward for the Iron Cross first class, as you recommended, and have confirmed his new rank."

He tapped the report. Paul remained quiet, still stood at attention. He knew it was not the moment to interrupt his commander.

"Leutnant Leeb has also been put forward for an award. From what I can gather, although he was not the senior officer when you were detached from your unit," Paul swallowed, his adams apple bobbing up and down, "he was the one who got to grips with the enemy, coordinating the actions of not only his platoon, but the others as well. He seems to be a good tactician like yourself."

He locked eyes with Paul.

"It's a pity you got separated from your unit at such a crucial time Brand, and if I thought," the intensity of his voice rising, "for one minute, that you chose to go to the rescue of your Company Feldwebel rather than re-join your unit, I would have you court marshalled."

He slammed the report down on the desk in front of him and Paul made to speak.

"I suggest you remain quiet for the moment Brand. Your duty is to your company, not an individual soldier. If I thought you a coward or a shirker, I would have you thrown out of the Fallschirmjager."

There was a moment of silence, before Volkman added, "Stand at ease and be seated."

Paul sat down on the seat to his left, MP40 across his lap, helmet on the floor between his feet. The Raven sat on his chair, the seat creaking as he swivelled it towards Paul.

"How is Feldwebel Grun?"

Paul's voice cracked as he tried to speak, his throat dry.

"Wait." Volkman held up his left hand and with the other pulled two glasses and a bottle from his desk drawer. "We have a victory to celebrate Paul," he said as he poured them both a drink of schnapps.

"We have secured the island, a successful airborne invasion."

He clinked his glass with Paul's then threw the drink down his throat, immediately pouring another, the bottle hovering, waiting to top Paul's up when he had finished. The gesture implicit. Paul held back the cough that was welling up in his windpipe as the raw alcohol bit in to his throat. Volkman topped up his glass and asked Paul the question again, "How is Feldwebel Grun?"

"He's improving sir. Not out of his bed yet, but I'm sure it won't be long."

"The doctor tells me his fighting days are over."

"I'm not sure the Feldwebel would agree with you sir, he's already making noises about returning to the company."

"He can't even stand yet," said Volkman as he sniffed at his drink, the aroma strong and pervasive, and sipped it more sedately this time. He held up his glass. "Need to go easy on this Brand, supplies are low until I can secure some more. You need to be ready to accept that the Feldwebel will not be returning to his unit, your unit. How is Richter settling in?"

"He is a good replacement sir, proven himself in battle, a good organiser and respected by the men. He has proven to be a good leader."

"Yes, his mortar troop did some damage I believe. Sorry I couldn't get you any more ammunition for his tubes, but all supplies were being diverted for the big push."

"How is your injury sir?"

The Raven touched the taped dressing above his right eye. "A piece of shrapnel Brand, lucky it wasn't lower. Only a small scar they tell me," he said smiling for the first time.

"Richter's rank of Feldwebel has been confirmed and I suggest you accept that his role is permanent."

Paul contemplated the enormity of what he was being told, of what he had already accepted in his own mind. Max would not be at his side for his next fight.

"What plans for the battalion now sir?" asked Paul, changing the subject.

"We need to refit as quickly as possible, then we're being shipped back home."

"Have they something planned for us?"

The Raven stood up and beckoned Paul to follow him out on to the balcony, the sea stretched out in front of them, blue and welcoming in the heat of the day, the heat omnipresent as soon as they stepped out of the room. The Raven, swagger stick tucked under his left arm, rested both hands on the black, ornate rail.

"They always have plans for us. Something is brewing Brand, I can feel it."

"Surely we need time to recuperate sir, rest, reinforcements."

"Reinforcements will be waiting for us on our return, the Stendal machine hasn't been idle in our absence."

He pushed himself up off the railings and turned to face Paul.

"Our battalion, my battalion has excelled during the invasion. We have caused mayhem for the enemy. A battalion sized force has effectively kept Brigade sized units on their toes, causing them to shift reserves away from the main points of contact and from where they would have been most useful. We have been recognised by our masters for our efforts, be assured they will want us ready for action again as soon as possible. Are you up to it Oberleutnant Brand?"

Paul clicked his heels together and thrust his arms down by his sides. "I am a Fallschirmjager Herr Major, I will do my duty."

There was a moment of silence as the Major searched the young man's face, looking for weakness or doubt. But, all he saw was strength and an officer who was resolute.

"You are my best officer Brand. The most skilled, the most imaginative, my strongest leader. Your men seem to hero worship you. But, you are also the one I worry about the most. Prepare your men, kit sorted, weapons canisters ready. We move out within the week, dismissed."

Paul saluted, picked up his helmet on the way out and headed out of the door, down the stairs and out of the central doorway at the bottom.

He walked forward until he was stood next to the wall overlooking the sea and the rocks below, exposed now the tide was out. The sea was already on its way back in to reclaim its territory and they would again soon be hidden from view. To his right his eye line was dominated by the fortress on the edge of the town, positioned strategically on the peninsula, overlooking the coast, its sturdy walls with its earthworks sloping down towards the coastal road. The

Fortezza of Rethymnon, dominated the tip of the peninsular. Although various stages of the fortification began as far back as the third Century, the current structure had been completed between 1573 and 1580.

Looking to his left, Paul could see a peninsula of lesser importance, which jutted out on the other side of the sweeping coastline. He moved up to the wall, resting his knees against it, he breathed in the salty, sea air, listening to the gentle lapping of the water against the rocks below as it moved slowly in. He cocked his ear and listened. Apart from the odd engine revving in the distance, the gentle lapping of the waves and the odd rustle from the fronds of the Palm tree, it was quiet. Suddenly dawning on him, there was no gunfire, no screaming aircraft, no explosions, it was peaceful. It was time to go and see Max.

CHAPTER TWENTY-SEVEN

The main medical centre in the town had been swamped with casualties, whether Fallschirmjager, Gebirgsjager, Allied troops and even some civilians, so an administrative building had been converted in to a temporary hospital.

The double wooden doors of the four story building were open, a stream of soldiers, medical staff and civilians moved in and out of the hospital. It's plastered facade a mottled, dull grey, pink and orange, flaking in places, the odd scoring from a ricocheting bullet. There were four tall, narrow windows at ground level, two either side of the entrance, boarded up with shutters, steps leading up to its entrance.

The building was in the centre of a terrace, at one end the start of another terrace, the other end dominated by an orthodox church, its clean white front supporting a single bell tower on top, had survived the battle that had ended only a few days earlier. Many other buildings were not so lucky, having succumbed to bomb damage, or at least splattered with shrapnel scars or bullet impacts.

Paul stepped up into the building, his breath quickening as he was hit by the distinctive smell that seemed to emanate from all hospitals. It wasn't the smell of sickness or disease, but the smell of disinfectant used to clean the walls and floors and antiseptic used to treat wounds. Images flashed through his mind. Lying on a stretcher, carried in to a Maastricht hospital, doctors and nurses cutting away his uniform, exposing the gaping wounds and the clinical smell that seemed to have imprinted itself on to his senses. Then later, a nurse caring for him and his shattered body, Christa, her auburn hair tucked beneath her white cap. His thoughts were interrupted abruptly.

"Yes Oberleutnant, what can we do for you?"

Sat behind a small wooden table, her uniform crisp and fresh, sat a senior nurse from the German Red Cross, the gate keeper of the premises. Paul snapped out of his reverie and turned to her, a small oil lamp providing some light in the narrow, darkened corridor. She cocked her head at him, the pips on her blue and white striped tunic showing her to be a Vorhilferin. A white cap, with a red cross on the front, tied at the rear, held back her shoulder length, brown hair. An enamelled brooch pinned at the centre of her white collar showing her to be a fully qualified nurse.

"Herr Oberleutnant?"

"Sorry Vorhelferin, I am looking for a Feldwebel Grun, he is badly wounded."

Her serious expression eased in to a gentle smile, the stern look she normally kept for visitors melting away as she saw the strain and weariness on the young officer's face.

"They are all badly wounded here Oberleutnant."

She pulled a leather bound book towards her and scanned through the lines of entries, tapping the one that she had been looking for.

She looked up. "Feldwebel Grun, Fallschirmjager. He is on the second floor. When are you relieving us of him Oberleutnant?"

"Is he causing problems?" replied Paul, his face concerned.

Her smile widened. "Only to the nurses Oberleutnant. His wounds are serious and will take some time to heal, but his flirtatious nature has been far from suppressed. You will find him on the next floor, ward 2/1."

Paul thanked her and walked to the end of the corridor that got darker the further away he was from the entrance. He climbed the steps to the next level and scanned the doors as he walked along the first floor corridor. He found the door he was looking for at the opposite end, the last on the left. He opened the door and entered the room.

The ward was very compact. Two tall windows overlooked the town. Four beds lined each side, the one on the far right surrounded by Fallschirmjager.

"Who have you come to see Oberleutnant? It is not convenient to have so many visitors at one time," said a short, stern faced Sister, hands on hips, round faced jutted towards the top of Paul's chest.

"I've come to see Feldwebel Grun."

"That's impossible Oberleutnant, he is already mobbed with visitors, can't you see?" she complained, her grey haired head bobbing up and down as she pointed to the group of paratroopers congregated around the end bed.

One of them turned to see what the commotion was, it was Leutnant Leeb. When the other two turned round he could see they were his other two platoon commanders, Roth and Nadel, all three made their way over to him. They saluted Paul, then Leeb, his angular features breaking in to a smile, placed his arm around the Sister's shoulder.

"There, there Sister, we're going now so there will be plenty of space."

She allowed Ernst's arm to remain where it was.

"We've been here half an hour now sir, so we were about to go," informed Roth, his skin still peeling from the effects of the burning sun on his pale skin.

"The Feld's looking well sir," added Nadel, his normally pale complexion unusually brown, "but you'll be able to see for yourself."

The Sister extracted herself from Leeb's embrace and patted Paul on the arm.

"If these men are going now, I see no reason for you not to visit him, providing you don't disturb the other patients," she said shooing the three platoon commanders out of the ward.

He walked over to Max's bed and rather than coarse, Luftwaffe blue blankets, they were a mixture of brown, red, orange, some of the beds even had pink covers on.

"Not very military is it sir?" suggested Max, propped up in his bed, four feather pillows supporting him.

Paul scanned his face. The dark tan that had been burnt in to Max's skin during their time in this climate, from Corinth to Crete, had now faded slightly, his heavy set jaw having lost some of its definition, but the brown eyes still exuded strength.

"I would have thought you'd have gone for a pink cover Max."

"I didn't want to leave the others without sir."

"It looks better than some of the places I treated you in."

"You never did have any style sir," he said with a smile, his still cracked lips expressing his pleasure at being able to crack a joke again with his commander, and friend.

"How are the wounds?"

"They hurt like buggery, but I'm told I'm on the mend. They said if it wasn't for you patching me up in the first place and getting me back here, I'd have been a goner."

"Couldn't be doing with all the paperwork if I'd lost you."

"I'll be out of here in no time. How's Feldwebel Richter shaping up?"

"He's doing ok. Hasn't quite mastered your insolent approach to everything, but then who could."

"Make sure he doesn't get too settled sir, I'll be wanting my job back soon."

Paul sat down on the edge of the bed to continue their conversation, when a young, slim, blonde haired nurse slipped passed him and plumped up Max's pillows.

"I don't want him over excited now Oberleutnant, he's not as well as he tells people."

A veil of pain descended across Paul's face, picked up instantly by Max. A flash back of a dark haired nurse, leaning over his hospital bed, doing and saying the very same things.

"No more than ten minutes do you hear?"

Max's muscled arm patted the nurse's arm gently. "It's ok Anneliese, he won't stay long."

She looked from one to the other, now seeing the pain in the young officer's eyes and the concern on her patient's face. She finished adjusting the sheets around Max's waist and left them in peace.

"I'm well looked after here sir."

Paul came out of his reverie, his eyes moist, but no tears came.

"It looks like you have every reason not to come back to the unit in a hurry Max."

"My boys need me sir, so I'll be back soon."

They talked about the battle for Crete, the thousands of their Fallschirmjager comrades killed or wounded in this hellish battle. Some of the glider units landing on or near the airfields were all but decimated. Then they joked and laughed about their journey through enemy lines.

"That pony didn't half stink. Every time I looked up, all I could see was its arse. I prayed every time we stopped that it wouldn't crap on me."

They both laughed out loud, others close by joining in, having heard the banter.

"Did you go back to Adele sir?"

"Yes. We buried the three men. They were Oberleutnant Janke's boys."

"I bet the lads were furious."

"There was a brief moment when I thought they might tear through the village. But they're Fallschirmjager, Helmut soon brought them under control."

"Had they been mutilated?"

"Not as bad as some of the others that were found on the island, but they had been repeatedly stabbed in what could only have been a frenzy."

The nurse stood at Paul's shoulder.

"He really does need some rest Oberleutnant, as do the others. The two of you are entertaining the entire ward."

Paul stood up. "Anything you need Max?"

"It's bed bath time sir, what more could I want?" he whispered.

They both laughed and Paul made his exit. On the way out he had a quick chat with the other occupants on the ward, a Luftwaffe pilot shot down over Rethymnon, four Gebirgsjager and a Fallschirmjager from Erich's company, then left.

The nurse came over to Max, "He looked really sad."

"It's a long story, a long story. But when I get out of here I'll fix him up. Now, bed bath time?" he said with a beaming smile.

CHAPTER TWENTY-EIGHT

Paul stepped out of the hospital entrance to be greeted by his fellow company commanders, Helmut, who immediately punched him playfully in the shoulder, Erich and Manfred.

"Have you heard?" exclaimed Helmut.

"Heard what?" replied Paul trying to calm the excited Helmut down.

"Were shipping out in two days," informed Erich.

"We fly to Athens, then trucks and trains we've been told," added the thin faced Manfred. Although tough and wiry and only just above five foot nine, he was very slim. When stood next to his fellow officers he looked thin, but next to the gargantuan Feldwebel Grun, he looked positively beanpole like.

"Some of the guys came from Germany the same way, it was a bloody nightmare," informed Helmut

"Yeah, the roads are pretty bad," agreed Erich.

"But do you know the best bit?" Helmut whispered.

Their heads automatically moved closer together, four Fallschirmjager officers in a huddle.

"After we refit, we're going to Russia."

★★★